WIDOW'S TEARS

SUSAN WITTIG ALBERT

WIDOW'S TEARS

BERKLEY PRIME CRIME, NEW YORK

THE BERKLEY PUBLISHING GROUP
Published by the Penguin Group
Penguin Group (USA) Inc.
375 Hudson Street, New York, New York 10014, USA

USA / Canada / UK / Ireland / Australia / New Zealand / India / South Africa / China

Penguin Books Ltd., Registered Offices: 80 Strand, London WC2R 0RL, England
For more information about the Penguin Group, visit penguin.com.

This book is an original publication of The Berkley Publishing Group.

WIDOW'S TEARS

Berkley Prime Crime Books are published by The Berkley Publising Group.
BERKLEY® PRIME CRIME and the PRIME CRIME logo are trademarks of Penguin Group (USA) Inc.

Berkley Prime Crime hardcover paperback ISBN: 978-0-425-25572-8

An application to register this book for cataloguing has been submitted to the Library of Congress.

FIRST EDITION: April 2013

PRINTED IN THE UNITED STATES OF AMERICA

10 9 8 7 6 5 4 3 2 1

Cover illustration copyright © by Joe Burleson; *Background* © by Hemera/Thinkstock.
Cover design by Judith Murello.
Interior text design by Tiffany Estreicher.

PUBLISHER'S NOTE: The recipes contained in this book are to be followed exactly as written. The
publisher is not responsible for your specific health or allergy needs that may require medical supervision.
The publisher is not responsible for any adverse reaction to the recipes contained in this book.

This is a work of fiction. Names, characters, places, and incidents either are the product
of the author's imagination or are used fictitiously, and any resemblance to actual persons,
living or dead, business establishments, events, or locales is entirely coincidental.
The publisher does not have any control over and does not assume any responsibility for
author or third-party websites or their content.

For my friends in the Herb Society of America,
who have named me their
honorary president for 2012–2014.
China and I thank you.

Note to the Reader

Flo-rig'-ra-phy (flō-rig'-ra-fē), n. [L. *flos, floris,* flower + -graphy.]
The language or symbolism of flowering plants, as expressed in
historical literature.
Webster's New International Dictionary of the English Language

People often ask me the question "What exactly *is* an herb?"

I've never liked questions that have to be answered "exactly," because I appreciate a little ambiguity and mystery in my life—it makes things much more interesting. That's why I like the Herb Society of America's definition of an herb: "a plant for use and delight." It's an impossibly broad definition, yes. But it's a definition that invites us to explore the widest possible uses of plants to provide taste, scent, medicine, fiber, dye, tools, artifacts, and symbols, from the distant beginnings of human culture to the present time.

Almost all societies have assigned symbolic meanings to plants. In China, for example, bamboo (which provides medicine, food, building materials, paper, and textiles) represents longevity, strength, and grace. In Hindu cultures, jasmine (used as a medicine, a flavoring, and a fragrance) symbolizes love, while once upon a time in the British Isles, green willow symbolized untrue or immature love.

Throughout human history, these symbolic meanings have been elaborated in art, poetry, and literature. During the early Victorian period, for instance, wealthy and leisured ladies and gentlemen frequently exchanged floral gifts in which a fanciful "language of flowers" was encoded. As Kathleen Gips puts it in her introduction to *Flora's Dictionary: The Victorian Language of Herbs and Flowers*, "people expressed flowery thoughts by exchanging bouquets composed of carefully chosen plant words."

The definitions of these encoded "plant words" or floral symbols—collectively, a *florigraphy*—were published in Europe and America in an enduring and highly popular literary tradition made up of dozens of elaborate manuals that appeared in multiple editions. At their best, these were attractive, leather-bound volumes with gilt-edged pages and engraved illuminations, occasionally hand-colored. At the end of this book, you'll find some suggestions for further reading that will lead you deeper into the study of florigraphy and its many historical transformations. It's a subject that many garden and literary study groups might find interesting.

Of course, while herbs and plants are an important thematic and plot element in the books in the series (it's amazing how many mysteries there are in the lives of plants!), you're probably even more interested in the characters. China Bayles, of course, has always been front and center, with her herb shop, her lawyerly logic, and her tendency to be drawn into . . . well, murder. And, of course, Ruby Wilcox has never been far behind, playing the role of an intuitive Dr. Watson to China's logical Sherlock.

But now it's Ruby's turn to play Sherlock. *Widow's Tears* is her story—and it's about time, don't you think? We've already learned about her shop, her family (the daughter she gave up for adoption and who reappeared in *Hangman's Root*; the mom who has Alzheimer's), and her everyday life. We know about her bout with breast cancer (in *Mistletoe Man*) and her adventures with the Ouija board (*Rosemary Remembered* and *Bleeding Hearts*). In *Widow's Tears*, Ruby shows us just how good she is at looking deeply into mysteries that are hidden from everyone else—even from China. To help while Ruby is doing this, Dawn Zudel of Columbia, Tennessee, (the winner of Story Circle's character raffle) has volunteered to tend her shop. Thanks, Dawn!

Widow's Tears is also the story of the Great Galveston Hurricane, which forms the historical backdrop against which Ruby's story unfolds. The hurricane—to this day, the deadliest natural disaster to hit the United States—struck Galveston Island on September 8, 1900. It killed some eight to twelve thousand people (nobody really knows how many), wiped out whole families, and changed the destiny of the city of Galveston, which at the time rivaled Houston for the position of the most important city in Texas, indeed, on the entire Gulf Coast. I have created a fictional character, Rachel Blackwood, through whom to tell the story of the hurricane. But Rachel's story is based on the real stories of hurricane survivors recorded in many documents of the period. I've listed my sources in the resource section at the end of this book.

An important reminder: throughout the China Bayles series, you will read many descriptions of the therapeutic uses of plants, both modern and historic. China and I fervently hope that you will seek informed, reliable advice before you decide to use any of these herbs to treat whatever ails you. Medicinal plants are "natural," yes, but plant chemistry is not always well understood—and the more we understand, the more cautious we are likely to be. Many herbs have potent side effects, especially when combined with over-the-counter and prescription drugs. Do your own careful home-work and use all medicines, plant-based or otherwise, with mindful atten-tion. China and I would not like to lose any of our readers—especially *you*.

Susan Wittig Albert
Bertram, TX

WIDOW'S TEARS

Prologue

Galveston, Texas: The Oleander City
Saturday, September 8, 1900

The coast of Texas is according to the general laws of the motion of the atmosphere exempt from West India hurricanes and the two which have reached it followed an abnormal path which can only be attributed to causes known in meteorology as accidental. . . . It would be impossible for any cyclone to create a storm wave which could materially injure the city [of Galveston].

"West India Hurricanes"
by Isaac M. Cline, Chief Meteorologist
Texas Section, U.S. Weather Bureau
Galveston Daily News, July 16, 1891

Rachel Blackwood got up early that morning. She had not slept well: her youngest daughter, three-year-old Angela, was suffering from a sore throat and had cried often for her mother in the night, needing to be soothed.

But it wasn't just Angela's whimpers that had disturbed her mother. It was the thunder of the waves on the beach that had kept her awake—and the heat, the unspeakable, unbearable heat. According to the daily newspaper, the *Galveston News,* sultry weather had smothered almost the whole of the country that summer, from the Rockies east to Pennsylvania, from the Great Lakes south to the Gulf of Mexico. Thirty people in New York

City had died one awful August Saturday. Dozens of others had succumbed in Chicago and Memphis, and at the St. Louis zoo, two bears and a leopard had been felled by the heat.

On Galveston Island, summers were usually cooled by ocean breezes, and the miles of shining white-sand beaches, groves of palm trees, and extravagant flower gardens made the city seem a paradise. But this year, summer in paradise had been marred by both sultry heat and unusual rains. During July and August, tropical storms had drenched the city—sixteen inches of rain in one downpour, nine inches in another. Boys sailed the flooded downtown streets in wooden tubs, fish flopped across lawns, mothers despaired of ever getting the laundry dried in the damp air. And there were the morning fogs, and the foghorn in the lighthouse on the Bolivar Peninsula, a forlorn ghost calling, calling, calling through the dim gray mist.

The Blackwood household—Rachel; her husband, Augustus (the newly appointed vice president of the Galveston National Bank); the five Blackwood children and their fifteen-year-old nurse, Patsy; and Mrs. O'Reilly, the family's longtime cook-housekeeper—seemed to be moving in a languid and stuporous dream that summer, half-asleep under a sweltering blanket of humidity and heat. The thermometer on the back porch had registered 90 on Thursday and 91 on Friday, and when Rachel had taken the children the four blocks to the beach, they had complained that the Gulf was as warm as bathwater.

The morning air was cooler, though, and for the first time in weeks, Rachel could draw a deep breath as she slipped out of bed and dressed. But she had awakened to the strange, unsettled sense that something was different, something was . . . menacing. She went down to the kitchen to oversee Mrs. O'Reilly's breakfast preparations and review the plans for Matthew's birthday supper that evening. Then out to the garden to pick an armful of dewy white roses and rosemary sprigs and the last few pink oleander blooms for the bowl on the table in the morning room. But all the while, she could not shake the feeling of apprehension. And even as she arranged the flowers in a crystal bowl, wondering once again why white roses were supposed to signify sadness when the rich scent of their silvery petals gave her so much pleasure, she was uneasy. Perhaps it was Angela's worrisome illness, or the rising north wind, unusual for September, that made a peculiar whistling in the eaves. Or the pounding of the surf that seemed much louder now than when she'd gotten up, and the tremors of the wooden floor under her feet.

Rachel had occasionally felt the floor trembling during Gulf storms, although it had never been quite so pronounced as now. The Blackwood house was located on Q Avenue, just off Bath Avenue, only three blocks from the white-sand beach. The highest ground in the island city, on Broadway, rose only 8.7 feet above the Gulf, and some (perhaps remembering that Cabeza de Vaca had named the island *Malhado,* "misfortune") had cautioned that a strong storm would flood the entire city. A seawall had been proposed as early as 1874 and several times since, but was considered to be too expensive and unnecessary. Isaac Cline, a noted meteorologist and chief of the Weather Bureau's Texas Section (and the Blackwoods' neighbor on Q Avenue), had written in the *News* that it was "simply an absurd delusion" to believe that Galveston could be seriously damaged by a tropical storm. The city was protected by "the general laws of the motion of the atmosphere."

Nevertheless, many prudent Galvestonians built their houses on pilings, and Rachel's husband, Augustus, was one of these. He had ordered his house to be constructed atop wooden piers driven deep into the island's sandy soil, ensuring that it would stand well above the highest of storm tides, locally called "overflows." As he explained to Rachel, it was the piers, standing eight feet above the surface, which transmitted the shudder of the waves against the beach to the floors of the house. The trembling, he said with a confident smile, was in fact a token of the strength and security of its anchorage to the earth.

Indeed, it was not just a secure and solid house but a splendid house, as befitted a man of Mr. Blackwood's rank among Galveston's men of finance. It was a large, three-story towered and turreted Victorian, with a drawing room where Rachel served tea to the ladies who called every afternoon and a library filled with Augustus' fine collection of books and a music room fitted out with a Steinway grand piano. There was a magnificent oak staircase, fireplaces with gleaming marble mantels, and glorious stained glass windows in the dining and drawing rooms, commissioned from the Tiffany Glass and Decorating Company. The opulent furnishings and draperies, all in exquisite taste, had been brought from as far away as Paris and New York.

Painted a sober brown with red trim, this fine house was set back from the street behind a wrought iron fence, a border of oleanders and hollies, and a row of date palms, which in the late summer produced an abundance of fruit. The steps up to its wide front gallery were guarded by twin stone lions, each head turned to gaze thoughtfully at the other. The heavy bronze knocker on the oak front door wore the enigmatic face of Neptune, the god of the deep. And the steep slate roof was crowned with a wooden-railed widow's walk that offered a panoramic view of the island paradise and the vast blue-green Gulf stretching to the eastern horizon.

But while Mr. Blackwood prized his house for its solidity, its splendor, the beauty of its furnishings, and the view from its roof, Rachel prized it for far more. It was the home of her heart. It held all that was dear to her— Augustus and her children: stalwart Matthew, ten years old this very day; sweet in-between Ida; the five-year-old mischievous twins, Peter and

Paul; and dear baby Angela. To Rachel's great delight, the children were all very musical. Just the night before, they had all gathered in the music room. Matthew, a gifted young pianist, played the "Maple Leaf Rag" on the Steinway—Scott Joplin's song was wildly popular everywhere. Then Rachel accompanied the children in one of the family's favorite songs, "Sweet and Low," while Matthew played his flute, Ida played her harp, and Peter and Paul sang sweetly. Baby Angela, in her little red-painted rocking chair, laughed and clapped her hands. On the sofa, Augustus read his newspaper, smoking his favorite cherry tobacco. Rachel thought then that she had never been so happy. She could not know that she would never be happy again.

Since the house had been recently built, it made all sorts of interesting new-house noises, murmurs and sighs and groans as the pilings and joists and beams and rafters settled into place. All five of the children insisted that the house talked to them. Rachel often made an amusing little game of it with them, asking what the house was whispering today, what secrets it had to tell, what stories it wanted to hear. With giggles and great delight, they would tell her what the house had to say—oh, such miraculous tales of intrigue and mystery! And then they would run to whisper their stories into the waiting ears of the stone lions that guarded the steps, for the lions were their dear friends and would keep them safe always, just as the house kept them safe.

At the morning breakfast table, Mr. Blackwood always read aloud items of interest from the *Galveston News*, believing that the children should know what kind of world they were going to inherit. The front page story concerned the Boxer Rebellion in China, where an eight-nation alliance was fielding an army of twenty thousand men to take Beijing and release the Americans and others held captive there. On page two, the latest census dominated the local news. Since 1890, Galveston's population had grown by nearly 30 percent, a rate much higher than rival port city Houston. (This news cheered Mr. Blackwood greatly, for he was a Galveston booster.) On page ten, Weather Bureau officials reported that they were monitoring a storm that appeared to be passing the Louisiana and Mississippi coasts, and while they felt it would probably go ashore somewhere in eastern Texas, they did not anticipate a "dangerous disturbance." On the back page, the Galveston forecast was reassuringly routine: "For eastern Texas: Rain Saturday, with high northerly winds; Sunday rain, followed by clearing."

Mr. Blackwood put down the *News* with a smile. They must all be grateful, he remarked genially, for the good north wind, which would push the heat and humidity out into the Gulf and make for a cooler, pleasant weekend. An afternoon picnic at the beach tomorrow would be in order, he suggested with a glance at his wife. Rachel smiled and nodded as the children shouted gleefully. And of course, there was Matthew's birthday to celebrate that afternoon, with the chocolate cake that Mrs. O'Reilly was this minute baking in the kitchen. Rachel had invited two of the neighborhood families—enough to fill all eighteen chairs at the dining room table.

Most Galvestonians worked a six-day week, so when breakfast was over, Mr. Blackwood set off as usual for his downtown bank. Rachel sent the children out to play with their friends—all but little Angela, of course—but she had become increasingly uneasy. She could feel even more strongly now the trembling of the house under her feet and hear its sighings and moanings. If she could only have understood its language, she might have heard the house whispering to her of a powerful storm, even now churning and turning in its unstoppable journey across the Gulf. She might even have heard its insistent whisper, as plain as words, as urgent as a shout: "Run, Rachel! Take your children and go, *now,* while there's still time to leave the island!"

Rachel did not speak the language of the house and could not understand its warning. Still, she felt the tremors and thought apprehensively that the floor was beginning to vibrate in a subtle and unusual way, a drum thrumming in tune with the thudding waves, accompanied by the eerie, high-pitched whistle of the wind in the eaves. She finished consulting with Mrs. O'Reilly about the menus for next week—now written on the menu board in the kitchen—then lifted her skirts and went quickly up the wide, curving stairs.

Three flights and a few moments later, she was opening the door to the widow's walk at the top of the house. As she stepped outside, she pulled in her breath, startled. When she had glanced out the bedroom window at first light, the sky over the Gulf had seemed to be made of iridescent mother-of-pearl, tinted in glorious pinks and lavenders. Now, it was a flat, ominous slate gray, with heavy-bellied clouds, flushed smoky-orange by the sun, sulking along the eastern horizon. To the north and downtown, atop the Levy Building at Twenty-third and Market, the storm flag fluttered, a crimson square with a black square at its center, topped with a white pennant, both hoisted yesterday morning by their neighbor, Isaac Cline, who was in charge of the island's weather bureau. The red-and-black storm flag meant that heavy weather was rolling in; the pennant meant that the winds would come from the northwest. But to anyone who knew his weather, the flags were reassuring, for together they predicted that the storm would come ashore to the east of the city. Galveston was not likely to see much of a blow.

But it was the sight of the Gulf that most startled Rachel, for the normally blue-green waves were a thick, chocolate-pudding brown, laden with sand and laced with ropes of seaweed. And they weren't waves at all, not in the usual dancing way. These were slow-moving swells, heavy, mud-brown hills of water that crashed with a roar higher and higher upon the beach,

7

the sound shuddering through the earth, through the wooden pilings and floors and frame of the house, so that even at the highest point, on the widow's walk, Rachel could feel the whole weight of each wave almost as if it were crashing directly against her feet.

She could not know what was to come. No one in Galveston could know, or even imagine, that by midnight, over eight thousand of their fellow citizens would be swept away by the hurricane and drowned.

But she could feel it coming and was afraid.

Chapter One

Mugwort. *Artemisia vulgaris.* "By-foot," one of the many folk names of *A. vulgaris,* is derived from the belief that a poultice of mugwort leaves bound to the legs and ankles can reduce a walker's weariness. Roman soldiers placed mugwort leaves in their sandals to ease the pain of marching. Mongols massaged mugwort oil on their thighs to lessen the fatigue of riding, and into their horses' legs to promote endurance. In traditional Japanese and Chinese medicine, cones made of powdered mugwort (or "moxa") are burned on the body to stimulate circulation in a practice called "moxibustion" (moxa + combustion). By extension, it was thought that burning moxa in the footprint of a thief would cause him to get a "hot foot" and that his uncontrollable dancing would reveal his criminal activity.

In the language of flowers, mugwort represents the hope that the traveler will enjoy a pleasant, unwearied journey and a safe arrival.

China Bayles
"Herbs and Flowers That Tell a Story"
Pecan Springs Enterprise

"I'm outta here," Ruby said, coming through the connecting door between her shop and Thyme and Seasons. It was warm for early May (the high was forecast to be in the 80s) and she was wearing a full-skirted lemon yellow sundress that bared her freckled arms. Her carroty red hair was snugged into a ponytail and fastened with a hank of yellow yarn, and her yellow sandals displayed red-painted toes. She looked bright and perky, like a retro 1960s sunbeam—a six-foot, red-haired sunbeam, sure to attract attention. But Ruby is magnetic. She attracts attention, whatever she's wearing. She can't help it. She's a sight for sore eyes.

"How long will you be gone?" I asked, looking up from the books I was inventorying. "Is Dawn Zudel coming in this morning?" Dawn is Ruby's current shop helper, and a dynamo, with merry green eyes and copper-brown hair cut into a chin-length bob. She worked in a law office for eight years, then "retired" to several years as a full-time mom. Now, she comes in when we need extra help and takes care of the Crystal Cave whenever Ruby takes a few hours off, which isn't very often. In fact, I couldn't remember the last time Ruby planned to be gone for more than a day.

Ruby hooked her bag over her shoulder. "Yes, Dawn is opening this morning. She'll be working for me in the tearoom, too. You know how good she is with people." She frowned worriedly. "I told Claire I'd stay for a week. But maybe that's too long. Is that too long, China? You're sure you and Cass and Dawn can manage without me?"

"Good, no, and yes, in that order." I patted her bare shoulder reassuringly. "A week is a long time, and we will definitely miss you. It will be next to impossible to manage in your absence, even with Dawn on the job, but we'll do it. Don't worry about us, Ruby. You've been working so hard— you deserve to take some time off." It was true. I'd been worrying about her. She had been burying herself in her work lately, scarcely coming up for air. "It looks like you'll have good weather, too, at least for another day or two," I added.

Ruby looked doubtful. "Didn't I hear that there's a tropical wave or something out there in the Gulf somewhere, heading toward South Texas?"

"Not to worry," I said comfortingly. "It's only a baby—doesn't even have a name. It's way too early in the season for serious hurricanes. And where you're going, you'll be a hundred and twenty miles inland. Think sunshine, and lots of it."

Before Ruby gets out the door, though, maybe we'd better pause for introductions. If you've visited Thyme and Seasons before, we've probably met, and you can skip the next few paragraphs. If not, this might help. Here goes.

My name is China Bayles. I am a former criminal defense attorney who once worked for a big Houston law firm that represented big bad guys with enough *dinero* to pay for a pass out of the justice system. I left my law career and the city in search of a gentler, less sadistic way of life and ended up as the proprietor of an herb shop in Pecan Springs, a friendly Texas town just off I-35, halfway between Austin and San Antonio, at the eastern edge of the Hill Country. I'm married to Mike McQuaid, a former Houston homicide detective, currently a part-time faculty member in the Criminal Justice department at Central Texas State University and a more or less full-time private investigator with his own firm. McQuaid and I are the parents of two great kids: his son Brian, who just graduated high school and is headed for University of Texas at Austin in the fall; and twelve-year-old Caitlin, my niece and our adopted daughter.

Now for that six-foot sunbeam. Ruby Wilcox and I aren't just best friends but longtime business partners. Ruby owns the Crystal Cave, in the same building as Thyme and Seasons. The Cave is the only New Age shop in Pecan Springs—which isn't surprising, I suppose, since most good ol' Texans are brought up to be fidgety about things like astrology, tarot, and the Ouija board. But the shop is a perfect fit for Ruby, who is so perceptive that she sometimes scares me. It scares her, too. She doesn't like to go too deep into otherworldly stuff, but she can tell you things about yourself that you haven't yet discovered, and she can coax the Ouija board (as our friend Sheila Dawson puts it) to tell more tales than the gossips at Bobbi Rae's House of Beauty. The idea that Ruby Wilcox might encourage their womenfolk to tune into something more soul-satisfying than *The Young and the Restless* tends to make male Pecan Springers . . . well, restless.

Wait—there's more. A couple of years ago, Ruby (who has the soul of a psychic but the planning skills of an entrepreneur) proposed that we open Thyme for Tea in the space at the back of our building, a two-story limestone structure a few blocks east of the courthouse square in Pecan Springs. We signed a partnership agreement (a good thing to have when people decide to pool their time, money, and resources on a long-term business project), rolled up our sleeves, and got busy remodeling—a lot of work, especially the kitchen, which had to meet state licensing requirements—but a big payoff. Even when the shop traffic slows down, our tearoom usually shows a profit.

And then two more things happened. Ruby came up with the idea for Party Thyme, our catering service, and Cassandra Wilde came along with a proposal for the Thymely Gourmet. Cass uses the tearoom kitchen not only for tearoom meals, but to prepare both our catering menus and the meals she schleps to well-heeled clients who can afford to pick up the tab for their own personal chef. The business is a natural for her: Cass spent nearly fifteen years in the food service industry and is certified as a personal chef by the American Culinary Federation.

In Cass' words, this menagerie keeps us on our toes and moving fast, like a trio of lady lion tamers with a pride of lions at the tips of our whips. But we're a great team, working well together, in synch like choreographed dancers. And even though we are really too busy, we always remind one another that it's better to be busy than otherwise. *Busy* is what counts when it comes to the bottom line. And the bottom line (black, not red) is what counts when it comes to the bank.

So that's us. Where our businesses are concerned, Ruby, Cass, and I are your basic, no-nonsense, hard-working, go-for-it-now-and-don't-stop girls. Still, every now and then even the most committed capitalist has to stop and smell the daisies. Cass took off for a few days in March to go camping with a friend. McQuaid and the kids and I stayed at my mother's ranch near Kerrville during spring break—maybe the last time Brian will be content to spend spring break with the family.

Now it's Ruby's turn, and yes, she definitely needs some time off. Spring is a difficult time for her, and the last few weeks have been especially hard. Colin Fowler, the love of her life, was killed—murdered—in late April two years ago, so this is an anniversary of sorts. She was madly in love with him, and when Ruby is in love, it is total, no-doubts-no-worries free-fall. She takes a deep breath, opens her heart, and flings herself into the void, doing double somersaults all the way down, with no bungee cord to brake her fall at the bottom, while her friends stand at the precipice, cover their eyes, and cry "Ruby, wait! What are you *thinking*?" With Ruby, love is either a passionate, whole-hearted, hang-onto-your-hat affair, or it isn't. Isn't love, that is.

Their affair was fatally flawed from the very beginning, because Colin wasn't who he said he was. He was Dan Reid, an undercover Dallas narcotics agent who was assigned to get the goods on a Pecan Springs businessman in cahoots with a Mexican drug cartel. Ruby loves mysteries (Agatha Christie, Sue Grafton, and Carolyn Keene are among her favorite authors), but she didn't have a clue about Colin's secret backstory. Her quite remarkable intuitive abilities seem to click into the "off" position when love (and/or lust) switches on.

Ruby was devastated by Colin's murder. She was more devastated when she learned the complicated truth about his life and still more when she discovered that she was the beneficiary of his substantial insurance policy, which she has set aside for Grace's college fund. She's never gotten over him, in spite of the persistent attentions of Hark Hibler, the editor of the *Pecan Springs Enterprise*. Hark is a man of gentle and generous spirit who truly cares for Ruby and can provide the kind of stability she needs and wants. But in every relationship I've known about, Ruby has adored the significant other more than he has cared for her. As long as something inside her continues to believe that love isn't love unless it's a one-way affair, she and Hark are not going to make it. And really—isn't it time she got over Colin? It's been two years, for crying out loud. And they weren't married. She's not a widow.

But there's no room for anyone else in Ruby's heart, which is why April and May are such difficult months. And it's why I've encouraged her to take some time off to visit her friend—although I'm not entirely sure she wants to go.

Ruby began ticking off items on her fingers. "Okay. Mrs. Wauer will come over to the house to water the plants and feed the cats. Ramona will keep tabs on Mom at the nursing home. Dawn will be in every day to manage the shop—she knows a lot about everything that goes on there, but if she can't find something, she'll ask. I'm worried about Grace, though. Amy says she has another nasty sore throat. I really hate to go away when Grace is sick. Could you check on her every so often?"

Mrs. Wauer is Ruby's next-door neighbor, the one with the yappy little poodle. Ramona is Ruby's sister, who recently moved out of Ruby's house and got a place of her own—and a good thing, too, since they're not the most compatible siblings in the world. Dawn Zudel is an indispensable helper in the Crystal Cave, now that she has gotten her kids—

all five of them!—raised and on their own. Amy is Ruby's wild-child daughter, partnered with Kate Rodriguez for over three years now, which is longer than some marriages last. And Grace, nearly three years old, is Ruby's granddaughter—although Ruby definitely does not look like your average granny.

I put down my list of books. "I'll be glad to. But how come you can't call and check on Grace yourself?"

"No phone. The previous owners of Claire's house never had a phone put in."

"You're kidding," I said incredulously.

Ruby shook her head. "Nope. It's the truth. And the phone company wants to charge Claire a fortune for the installation, since hers is the only house on the road."

"Can't you use your cell phone?"

"Maybe, but Claire says not to count on getting a signal. Sometimes it works, sometimes it doesn't." She paused, looking a little apprehensive, I thought. "The house is out in the middle of nowhere, you know, seven or eight miles past Round Top, at the end of a private lane off a county road. It's isolated. I mean, really." She caught her lower lip in her teeth. "To tell the truth, I sort of wish I . . . That is, maybe I shouldn't have agreed to—"

"Agreed to what?" I prodded, watching her closely. "Take some time off, you mean? Or go visit with Claire?"

"Visit with Claire." Ruby gave me a slantwise look. "She's one of my oldest friends, but I haven't seen her in quite a while. I don't really know why she—" She gestured. "Couldn't you maybe . . . you know, like, text her? She said she gets text messages better than voice. You could tell her we got an unexpected catering job and you can't spare me to—"

"Ruby," I said firmly, "I refuse to take you off the hook. If you don't want to go, text Claire yourself."

Claire Conway is a girlhood friend of Ruby's. She worked as an editor of a magazine in San Antonio until she inherited a large old Victorian mansion in the wilds of Fayette County, off Highway 290 between Austin and Houston. She's trying to decide what to do with the house—not an easy decision, I guess. She asked Ruby to come for a week and help her figure it out.

Ruby sighed. After a moment, she shook her head. "I guess it's too late to back out now. Claire's counting on me. I just wish the Blackwood house weren't so remote. I'd like to be able to call if I need help . . . or something," she added lamely.

I frowned. Need help? Why should she need help? "You wouldn't back out just because of a problem with your cell phone, would you?" I pressed. "It sounds like a great adventure. Anyway, surely there's no place so remote these days that it isn't serviced by one carrier or another." I paused, then added teasingly, "Or maybe it's Claire's ghosts that are jamming up the signal. Maybe they don't want anybody messing with their haunted house."

Ruby hadn't told me the whole story, only a few tantalizing bits and pieces. The gist of it seemed to be that her friend Claire would like to get the Blackwood mansion (the place she had just inherited) named to the National Register of Historic Places. Then she would turn it into a bed-and-breakfast and cash in on the tourists who visit the area. Round Top itself may be a tiny town, but it plays host to a large, twice-a-year antique fair; to the Round Top Festival Institute, which provides summer educational programs for young musicians (Caitlin is signed up for a violin clinic in July); and to Shakespeare at Winedale, a performance study program sponsored by the University of Texas at Austin.

But the old Blackwood mansion has something quite different going for it: an odd history and a persistent local reputation for being haunted.

And although Ruby hasn't confided the details—in fact, she has been un-characteristically tight-lipped about it—I've gathered that she has some sort of personal association with the place. She and Claire apparently visited there when they were girls. Ruby hasn't said it in so many words, but I suspect that she might have been invited for a reason: to persuade the spirits to pack up and go somewhere else so Claire can live in the house without fear of . . . whatever it is she's afraid of.

Now, if you're acquainted with Ruby, you're likely thinking that this is a natural mission for her, since she is adept at communicating with the Beyond. You're imagining that she should be looking forward to the visit, like an eager-beaver bargain hunter suiting up for Black Friday. But I know Ruby pretty well, and I could read the signs. Whatever her reasons, she was not thrilled down to the tips of her red-painted toes at the idea of a ghost-busting holiday. Did she think there was something going on in that house that she should be afraid of?

"Jamming up the signal?" Nervously, Ruby fished in her bag for her sunglasses. "Don't make fun, China. It's not a good idea to laugh at things you don't understand. You might antagonize . . . whatever's in that house."

"I'm not laughing," I protested. "I would be the last one to aggravate the spirits." That's not true, of course. I was laughing because I don't believe in ghosts. I don't believe in haunted houses, either. But Ruby does, so I keep my heresies to myself. Still, it sounded to me as if Ruby was looking for a reason not to go. I could help with that.

"You know, you don't have to do this if you don't want to," I remarked judiciously. "Claire is a big girl. Since it's her house, she has a certain responsibility in the matter that you don't have. And didn't you say there was somebody else living there?"

17

Ruby nodded. "On the property, but not in the house. A man and his wife, I think. Caretakers. The woman told Claire they'd be glad to help if—" She broke off.

"Well, there, you see?" I replied brightly. "You don't have to go if you don't want to. Claire and these people who live on the premises ought to be able to arm wrestle any ghosts who get out of line."

Ruby gave me an oblique glance. "It's not as simple as that, China. This thing with the house—it goes back a long way with me. Back to when I first began to understand that I could . . . that I wasn't . . ." She gave me a smidgeon of a smile. "Wasn't like other people. I didn't know how to deal with it then. To be honest, I'm not sure I can handle it now."

"Ah." So that was it. It wasn't just somebody's haunted house, it was *Ruby's* haunted house. And it wasn't just one or two abstract ghosts lurking at the bottom of this, it was her very own personal dragon.

I've known for a long time that Ruby isn't always comfortable with her psychic talents. She prefers to use her intuition to fool around with the easy stuff, like the readings she offers with her Ouija board or the I Ching. She'll tackle the more intense stuff if she has to, but she'd really rather not—unless she feels absolutely compelled. Which she doesn't, very often. In fact, she goes out of her way to avoid it. She deliberately tries not to intrude into people's thoughts. (If she looked into mine, for instance, she'd see that while I sometimes think of her as a flake, I secretly admire her intuitive abilities, especially her skill at reading people's fears and motivations.) And she doesn't like to be pulled into scary events or places. I remembered once, when her intuition—or her gift or her sixth sense or whatever it is—led the two of us to a dead body stashed in the basement of an abandoned school in the little town of Indigo. After that, she swore off psychic stuff for months.

Now, I'm not psychic myself, not by a long shot, and I don't pretend to understand how Ruby's intuition operates. She doesn't talk about it, and I don't like to pry. But I've seen her in action often enough to know that she has an impressive talent. Whenever she uses it in a serious way, to deal with a serious matter, it's a huge drain on her energy resources. It's like she's suddenly powered up by a massive electrical charge, and when it's turned off, she's limp and listless. Nobody wants to go through life like that: pumped up by something you can barely control, debilitated when the energy abandons you.

"Listen, Ruby, maybe you shouldn't go," I said. "If you're at all apprehensive about this—"

She looked as if she were glad for my support. "You're probably right. I think I shouldn't. But Claire needs me. And if I don't go, I'll never know—" She pressed her lips together.

"Never know what?"

Her glance slid away. "Nothing."

Never know what really happened in that house? Never know whether what she saw was actual or imaginary? Never free herself from this particular dragon? Never *what*?

But Ruby wasn't going to tell me. "Just . . . nothing," she said again. Her voice was thin.

I gave her a compassionate hug. "Stay here, Ruby. There's always plenty to do." This is true. If we aren't waiting on customers or working in the tearoom or catering a party, there's the bookkeeping, the inventory, the herb gardens, the classes. Being a small business owner is a full-time job and then some, with no overtime pay for nights and weekends.

She squared her shoulders with her Ruby-the-Brave smile. "I'm going," she said, putting on her sunglasses. The yellow plastic rims added to her retro look.

"Okay, then go," I said agreeably. "Have fun. Bust those ghosts. Purge those poltergeists. Get rid of those ghouls." I was beginning to giggle. "Banish those banshees."

"I'm gone," she said, heading for the door.

"Exterminate those entities," I chuckled. "Spook those specters."

BANG. She slammed the door in my face.

I pulled it open and went after her. "I'm sorry," I said. "Really, Ruby, I apologize." I bent over to pick up a pot of mugwort and plucked a couple of gray-green leaves. "Here," I said contritely, catching up to her and holding out the leaves. "Put these in your sandals. And when you get where you're going, stick them under your pillow."

Ruby pushed up her sunglasses and frowned down at the leaves. "Put them in my sandals? What in the world *for*?"

"Don't you remember what Kathleen said at the workshop? About mugwort, I mean. It was one of the plants she talked about."

The previous Saturday, Kathleen Gips had led a workshop for us on plant symbolism. Kathleen owns the Village Herb Shop on East Orange Street in Chagrin Falls, Ohio—and if you haven't visited there, you really must. She is the leading American authority on florigraphy, the traditional vocabulary of herbs and flowers, and she speaks and lectures all over the country. She has done a couple of workshops here before, and it's always standing room only for her program.

"Mugwort." Ruby thought for a moment, then rolled her eyes. "Okay, China, I give up. Maybe I skipped out to help Cass with the sandwiches when Kathleen was talking about mugwort. What did she say?"

"She said it symbolizes safe travel," I replied. "During the Middle Ages, no traveler would ever start off on a hike without mugwort in both sandals and a poultice of mugwort leaves wrapped around his legs. It protected him from wild animals, sunstroke, and goblins."

"I don't know about wild animals, but where I'm going, goblins might be an issue." Ruby took the leaves, pulled off her sandals, and inserted one leaf in each. She straightened, frowning. "What's the deal with the pillow?"

I raised my eyebrows. "I'm surprised at you, Ruby. With all your witchy research, I thought you'd know about that. It has to do with astral travel, out-of-body experiences, that sort of thing. Mugwort under your pillow is like mugwort in your sandals, except for the psyche instead of the physical body. It's supposed to protect you while it enhances your receptivity. Something like turning up the volume on your dream receiver, with a surge protector in case of lightning strikes."

Chuckling, I held out the pot. "In fact, maybe you should just take the whole plant. If Claire's ghosts are sending signals from the astral plane—"

Ruby snatched the pot. "Good-bye," she said firmly, and started for her car, a yellow Chevy Cobalt parked at the curb. The gangly mugwort nodded over her shoulder.

"Good hunting!" I called, laughing as I waved. "Extinguish that ectoplasm!"

Had I but known, I would not have laughed.

Had I but known . . .

Chapter Two

Oleander. *Nerium oleander.* Oleander is considered to be one of the most toxic of commonly grown garden plants, its cardiac glycosides making it dangerous for both humans and animals. Despite its toxicity, however, ancient Mediterranean and Asian medical texts describe a variety of medicinal uses. It served as a folk remedy for skin diseases, asthma, epilepsy, and malaria, and was employed as an abortifacient, a heart tonic, and a treatment to shrink tumors and hemorrhoids. In China, the same cardiac glycosides that render *N. oleander* toxic also made it an important traditional treatment for congestive heart failure. A non-FDA-approved extract of the plant is currently being used as an experimental cancer treatment, with reported success.

Galveston, Texas, is known as the "Oleander City." The first plants were brought from Jamaica by Joseph Osterman in 1841 as a gift to his wife. They flourished in the subtropical climate, the alkaline soil, and the salt spray of the Gulf of Mexico. The city is home to one of the most extensive collections of *N. oleander* to be found anywhere in the world

In the language of flowers, oleander signifies warning: "Act with caution. Be careful. Beware."

China Bayles
"Herbs and Flowers That Tell a Story"
Pecan Springs Enterprise

Ruby turned up the car's air-conditioning another notch and settled back in her seat. It was nearly eleven, and the morning traffic on Highway 290 had all but disappeared. The drive from Pecan Springs to Round Top took only two hours, and the day was glorious. The grass and trees were warmed by the bright spring sun in a clear, blue sky, with only a few storm clouds piled up along the eastern horizon. The bluebonnets had already bloomed and faded, but the roadsides were decorated with cheerfully variegated blankets of blue widow's tears, purple verbena, burgundy winecups, bright yellow wild mustard, pink phlox, white prickly poppy, yellow-orange coreopsis, and the blossom-cloaked towers of Spanish dagger. Along the grassy median between the eastbound and westbound lanes, clumps of blooming oleander shrubs were shrouded in translucent clouds of pastel pink, red, and white. The radio was playing an old Frank Sinatra song, "Come Rain or Come Shine," and Ruby hummed along.

As she drove, Ruby thought of what China had said—and what she hadn't. Ruby knew, of course, what China had been thinking: that it was time she buckled up and stopped mourning for Colin. They hadn't been married, for crying out loud—she wasn't a widow. She should learn to love Hark the way Hark loved her. She should get on with her life. And all of it made perfect sense. China was right, as usual, her logic perfectly indisputable.

Like nobody's loved you

Ruby sighed. Except that it didn't work that way. Her grief for Colin (it didn't matter that his name was Dan—she would always think of him as Colin) couldn't be turned on and off like a stupid faucet. Most of the time, she managed to keep it hidden from everyone except China, but it was always there, come rain, come sun, a permanent sadness shadowing her

24

heart. She valued Hark's affection, and she appreciated his intelligence and his quiet kindness. She even enjoyed the occasional cowboy who found her attractive and sexy and with whom she had a brief and gratifying fling.

But Colin, dead, was as unrelenting as he had been in life. He haunted her still, just as if they had been married. Cloudy days, sunny days, he was always in her thoughts, a spirit who refused to be exorcised. And until he was gone, there was no room for Hark. Oh, she could pretend, but that's all it was—just an act.

A slat-sided cattle truck passed her, an eighteen-wheeler loaded with a half dozen forlorn steers on their way to market, and Ruby slowed to let it move into the right-hand lane ahead of her. There was something else on her mind, something that China had not managed to guess—not yet, any-way. She was wondering whether it might be time to sell the Crystal Cave and her interest in their partnership. She had rejected the idea when it had first tiptoed into her mind, but it had returned, then hung around, and now seemed to be making an attractive nuisance of itself. Maybe, if she moved on to somewhere else, did something else, she could leave Colin's ghost behind.

The truth was that, while she liked what she was doing, she had painted herself into a corner. There was simply too much administrative stuff, which was satisfying in its own way but was eating her alive. The irony of this, of course, was that she was the one who had proposed the tearoom and the catering service and had been eager to jump on Cass' idea for home deliveries of gourmet meals. But while their three-ring circus (as China liked to call it) was still fun and interesting, it simply consumed too much time. She'd had to cut back on her teaching, for instance, which had always given her so much pleasure. When was the last time she had offered an I Ching class?

And she was neglecting her quilting and yoga and meditation—things that she especially loved to do, that energized her and kept her healthy and focused. She didn't have to be psychic to recognize the signs and symptoms. She was trying to keep too many balls in the air at one time. She was on the slippery slope of too-much-to-do. At the bottom lay an arid desert littered with dried-up dreams. Burnout.

The radio DJ must have been theming his choices around rain songs, Ruby thought, for the next one he played was the old 1960s calypso piece, "Don't Let the Rain Come Down." She slowed, then swung off the four-lane highway and onto the asphalt road that headed south across green meadows and low, wooded hills.

She had been thinking about this problem—the threat of burnout and what to do about it—for several months now, as the feeling became more urgent. But selling the shop was problematic. The economy wasn't all that great, and she didn't know anybody who had the money to buy her out. And it had to be somebody she knew. The Cave was as dear to her as a child. She couldn't bear the thought of handing it to a stranger. And it had to be somebody who understood what the business was all about, and who could teach the classes that brought people into the shop. Who did she know who could teach astrology, for heaven's sake?

And then her sister—three years younger—had come back into her life. As kids, she and Ramona hadn't been especially close, partly because of the age difference but mostly because they were just plain different. Sure, they had the same frizzy red hair and freckles, although Ramona was short and plump as a dumpling and Ruby was tall and pencil-thin. But the most significant difference had to do with something that wasn't visible to the ordinary eye: the share of Gram Gifford's gift that each girl had inherited. Ruby had gotten almost all of it, although, when Ramona paid careful attention, she could sometimes tune in to what other people were thinking.

And she could sometimes make weird things happen, moving things around and turning them upside down.

As they got older, the differences multiplied, Ruby becoming more laid back and easygoing, Ramona more competitive, especially when they were together. They had mostly gone their separate ways—until the previous autumn, when Ramona divorced her philandering husband, left her Dallas career in advertising, and moved to Pecan Springs. She had her own place now and pots of money (the divorce settlement had been a liberal one), and she was looking for a business to invest in. For a while, she had thought she might buy into the Hobbit House, a children's bookstore next door to Thyme and Seasons. But she and Molly McGregor, the owner, hadn't been able to come to terms. So she was still looking. And last evening, over dinner at Beans' Bar and Grill, she had brought up the idea of buying a half interest in Ruby's business.

"Or maybe more than half," Ramona had said, popping a french fry into her mouth. "I have a hunch that you're thinking of getting out of it altogether. Correct?"

Ruby didn't answer directly. "Do you really think you'd like it, Mona? I know you could manage the business side of things—the inventory, the ordering, the bookkeeping. With your skills and experience, I'm sure that part of it would be easy. But you've never seemed very interested in . . . well, the occult."

Ramona was intrigued by the tarot, she showed some promise with the Ouija board, and she knew her rising sign and what it meant. But that was the limit. And she definitely wasn't a teacher. Even if she'd had the knowledge, she didn't have the patience.

"You're right, I'm not super interested in that side of things," Ramona conceded. "But I was thinking that maybe you could stay on to teach classes and read palms and birth charts and all the other goofy, far-out things you like to do, while I took care of the rest of it." She picked up her knife and fork and cast a critical look at the massive mound of gravy-smothered chicken-fried steak on her plate. "This is humongous," she said. "It better be good." She began cutting off a corner. "Oh, and not just the Cave, either, Ruby."

Ruby frowned. "Not . . . just the Cave?"

"Uh-uh." Ramona shook her head emphatically. "If I'm going to invest in this enterprise, I wouldn't want just a little piece of it. I'd want the whole thing. The Cave, the tearoom, Party Thyme, the Thymely Gourmet. The whole enchilada."

Ruby sucked in her breath. Everything? Ramona would set her free of the entire three-ring circus?

"Naturally," Ramona went on in a careless tone, "I'd be willing to pay a very good price for those pieces of the action. In fact, I'll pay almost any price you ask—within reason, of course. Thanks to my ex, I've got more cash than I know what to do with." She forked up the cut-off corner of her chicken-fried steak. "Ain't that a hoot? He had to pay me all that money just for the privilege of marrying that not-so-dumb blonde who got her hooks into him." With a chuckle, she stuck the meat into her mouth. "Getting what he deserves, if you ask me," she added, chewing.

Ruby regarded her sister with near-disbelief. Sell her businesses to Ramona? Get rid of all that administrative stuff? The idea was so tempting that she almost blurted out an immediate and excited "Yes! Oh, Mona, yes!"

But she'd stopped herself in time. There was a catch, and one that she wasn't sure she could explain to her sister without hurting her feelings. If Ramona took over her part of the three-ring circus, she would have to work with Cass and China—especially with China.

And that would not be easy. China was entirely logical, one of the strongest left-brained people Ruby had ever known. From China's über-rational point of view, Ramona was, well, ditzy. She attracted bizarre events, like the time a car passed her on the freeway and flung a hubcap through her windshield. Or the evening the three of them were cooking dinner at Ruby's house and a hanging rack of pots fell down when Ramona came into the kitchen. When she turned around, the blind snapped up, knocking a flowerpot off the windowsill, and two cupboard doors flew open. Ruby had once tried to explain that such events were related to Ramona's piece of Gram Gifford's gift, but she gave it up. China was open-minded about most things, but poltergeists weren't something her left brain was prepared to accept—without more concrete evidence, that is.

But there was something else. China was her own woman. She did not like to be managed. Ramona, on the other hand, was a born manager. She was competitive. She liked to have her way—to be the boss. It would not be a match made in heaven.

As it turned out, however, Ruby didn't have to hurt her sister's feelings. "Of course," Ramona added thoughtfully, "China might not be overjoyed if I dealt myself in." She dug into her taco salad. "Cass and I get along okay, but China isn't my biggest fan."

Ruby almost laughed. Ramona had obviously managed to tune in to China—and had gotten the message, loud and clear. But she only nodded. "That's a tempting offer, and I'm grateful, Mona. Let me think about it for a few days." She hesitated. "The idea is really attractive. If you took over all that management stuff, it would solve so many problems. But of course, I'd have to talk to China."

And at the thought of telling China what she was considering, her insides tightened into a cold, hard fist. They were best friends and close, in many ways closer than sisters, certainly closer than she and Ramona. They

---

had worked together for years and years, and while they'd had the occasional minor spat, they had always ironed things out. Leaving the partnership wouldn't be easy, that was for sure. Even though she would still be in and out of the shop, teaching classes and consulting and the like, it wouldn't be the same.

"I'm not sure I understand." Ramona was scowling. "Why do you have to get permission from China to do what you want with your business? She's not your *boss*, is she?"

"Of course not," Ruby snapped, then softened her tone. "We've been together for a long time. I just . . . I just have to think about it for a little bit, that's all." She would also have to look at the partnership agreement she and China had signed. It seemed to her that she remembered some sort of language about what they would do if one of them wanted to back out.

She was still thinking about it five miles later when she pulled into the village of Round Top (population 77), consulted the clock on the dashboard, and made a quick left on Main Street. Halfway down the block, she pulled into a parking space in front of Royers Round Top Cafe, a funky little place that had once been a filling station. She hadn't been sure what time she'd get away, so she'd told Claire not to expect her for lunch. Anyway, Royers was reputed to serve the best hamburgers in South Texas and the best pie in the whole world.

A hand-painted sign beside the door said, *Oh No, Not You Again!!* And when she opened the door, she saw that the inside was every bit as funky and fun as the filling-station exterior. Oilcloth-covered tables and mismatched chairs were crammed close together. The walls were completely plastered with hand-lettered signs (*For Those in a Hurry, Go to Houston!!!* and *Eat Mo Pie*), slogan T-shirts signed by customers (some of them famous), postcards and clippings and advertisements for Royers' world-famous pie. It was still a little early, so she had the place almost to herself.

Royers' reputation was not exaggerated. The burger was generously topped with bacon and blue cheese, and the coffee was great. Claire had warned that she wasn't much of a cook, so they wouldn't be having any fancy meals, but Ruby thought it wouldn't matter now. After this lunch, she couldn't eat for a week. And the Blackwood house wasn't that far away—if they got really hungry, or if they just wanted to get out for an evening, they could come here.

At the thought of Claire, she frowned. The whole thing had been so extraordinary, so unexpected. It had happened on Sunday evening, when Ruby had been sorting through Gram Gifford's pieced quilt tops (she had inherited those, too), some of them made of marvelous old Depression-era fabrics. She had promised to give one to her quilting club, the Texas Stars, to quilt for the silent auction at the Pecan Springs library in July. Which of course had made her think of Gram and their wonderful summers in Smithville. Which had reminded her, inevitably, of their last summer together and Gram's gift and the Blackwood mansion. And of Claire, who had been her very best friend when she was a girl, and who had been at the Blackwood house with her the day Ruby discovered that she had inherited Gram's gift.

At that very moment the phone had rung, and Ruby had raised her head, knowing with a stabbing conviction that it was Claire on the other end of the line. Over the years, the two of them had gotten out of the habit of staying in touch, although they still exchanged birthday and Christmas greetings and kept up to date on major events in each other's lives. Claire had had her problems when she was in her twenties—drugs and alcohol among them—but she had straightened herself out, married a great guy, and seemed to be doing well. She had a good job at a magazine in San Antonio and did freelance writing and ghostwriting on the side. The last time she had called was when Colin was murdered. The last time Ruby had seen her was at the memorial service for Claire's husband, Brad, two months after Colin's death. Brad had died of pancreatic cancer. Ruby had called a couple of times after that, but Claire hadn't returned her calls.

Ruby put down the quilt top she was holding and stared at the phone as it kept on ringing. She knew it was Claire, and she knew what Claire was going to say—going to ask, rather. She didn't want to hear it.

Well, she didn't have to listen, did she? She could lift the receiver and break the connection. Or she could let the machine pick up, then (accidentally on purpose) erase the message without replying. But that wasn't fair to Claire, who'd had a hard time of it in the past couple of years. And anyway, Ruby knew with a disquieting certainty that this wasn't going to go away. She could listen now or she could listen later. She reached for the phone.

Claire got straight to the point. Someone in her family had died and left her an unexpected inheritance.

The Blackwood house, Ruby thought.

"The Blackwood house," Claire said brightly, too brightly. "Do you remember the place?" She didn't wait for Ruby to answer. "Long story short," she hurried on, "I have to figure out what to do with it. Maybe turn it into a bed-and-breakfast, or try to sell it, or . . . something."

She needs advice.

Claire's voice changed. "Look, Ruby, I need advice. So of course, I thought of you, because you were here with me when we were girls. You know the place, and—"

She broke off. There was a silence, the sound of quick breaths, then a half-despairing whisper: "Come and help me understand what's going on here, Ruby. Please come. I can't do this by myself."

But even before Claire had finished, Ruby was shouting a silent *No, no,*

I can't, I won't, no. Not that house again, please, not that place, no, not even for you, Claire.

But there was a right and a wrong answer here and *No, I can't* was wrong. This was something she couldn't hide from. And even as the goose-flesh crawled across her shoulders and her stomach knotted, she knew she didn't have any choice. She was being directed to go, by whatever force in the universe made these arrangements.

Come and help me understand, Ruby. Please come.

So Ruby had said yes, mostly because she knew that *no* was wrong, but also because Claire sounded so desperate. And also because there was something in her, stubborn and insistent, that wanted to revisit the place and know the truth of what had happened a long time ago. She had been young and inexperienced in handling her gift. She might have misremembered, or been mistaken, or exaggerated, or fabricated. After all, it had been the first time, hadn't it? And it wouldn't be surprising if a first-timer got it wrong. In fact, it might be surprising if she got it *right*.

She might have a gift, but that didn't mean she couldn't screw up.

Ruby picked up her coffee cup, propping both elbows on the table. In the background, the café's music system had been playing an old Texas song by Willie Nelson and Waylon Jennings, "Mammas, Don't Let Your Babies Grow up to be Cowboys." Now, it switched to Connie Francis' recording of "My Wild Irish Rose." An interesting coincidence, Ruby thought. But of course it wasn't a coincidence. This was Gram Gifford's all-time favorite song, and Ruby was just this moment thinking of Gram, and of Claire.

Besides China and Ramona, Claire was the only other person in the world who knew about the gift Ruby had inherited from Gram Gifford. Ruby's other friends and the people who took her classes—they understood that she was psychic (when she wanted to be), and they accepted it as a quirk of her personality. But Claire had been there when it had first happened and they had talked about it later, in whispers, because the idea was so overwhelming that they couldn't say it out loud. Claire knew that Ruby had inherited it from Gram Gifford, who had inherited it from her mother, Colleen, who—

The rest of the story was lost in the mists of time, and Ruby had never traced it further. She had never wanted to know where the gift came from or what it had meant to her ancestors. In fact, it made her so uncomfortable that, early on, she had taught herself how to flick the switch off (as she thought of it to herself) and how to dial it down, and she left it in the off position as much as she could. If she hadn't, she would've been inundated by incoming messages, competing noise, other people's *stuff*. There were some very good reasons, she often thought grimly, not to be entirely grateful to Gram.

Gram's mother had come to America from Dublin when she was a young girl and had bequeathed to her daughter not only her red hair and her gift, but also her sense of Irish fun. Annie (Gram's given name) was soft and round and warm and cheerful, the kind of grandmother any little girl just had to adore. She had lived most of her life in Smithville, a small town about thirty miles west of Round Top, where Ruby and Ramona had spent their summers, wonderful, unforgettable summers, busy with picnics and popcorn and read-alouds at bedtime.

That is, that's where they had spent their summers until the year Ruby was ten, Ramona was seven, and their father and mother divorced. Their father, Gram's only child, had been killed in an automobile accident shortly after that. Gram, too, had died not long after, and from then on, their mother had sent the girls to spend July and August in Lubbock with her sister Dorinda, a strict Bible-believer who had laid down a long list of rules that little girls had to follow. If they didn't, God would send them straight to hell when they died—and hell was a very unpleasant place. Aunt Dorinda was nothing at all like Gram Gifford, who thought that God loved everybody, even when they didn't manage to do everything just right.

Gram had worked at the Smithville library, just a few blocks down the street, and pretended with some success (because she was easy and comfortable with her gift), that she was just as ordinary as her neighbors and friends. But by that last summer, Ruby had begun to understand how it was that Gram could always tell what she and Ramona were thinking, why she knew when company was coming and who it was, and how she could predict the arrival of a particular cat at the bowl of kitty food she kept on the back porch for the neighborhood's feral cats.

"Just you watch, Ruby," she would say softly, as they looked out the window. "That big black tom with the torn ear will be jumping over the fence in a jiffy, he will." And in a jiffy, there he was, as if Gram had conjured him up by naming him.

Years later, after Ruby had more experience with her gift, she wondered whether Gram's gift had been somehow different, and that was why she had been so easy with it. Maybe she'd seen less or *felt* less—or had seen and felt mostly cheerful, comfortable things, like the big black tomcat coming over the fence to get his dinner. Or maybe it was because Gram had been using her gift for such a long time that it had become second nature, and she knew there was nothing to be afraid of.

Claire, who was the same age as Ruby, lived across the street and came over every day. She was cute and energetic and full of ideas for things to do—tomboy ideas, mostly, because that's the kind of girl Claire was—and they became fast friends. They walked over to Burleson Street for ice cream, or climbed trees in the park, or rode bikes out to Shipp Lake to go fishing, although of course Ramona couldn't do that, because she was too little.

And one hot July day, Claire invited her to visit her great-aunt Hazel, who lived all by herself in a large, old Victorian house—the Blackwood house—out in the country, past La Grange. It was the summer of the divorce, the very last of the beautiful summers, when Ruby had learned that she was different, that she was like Gram. That she knew things that other people didn't know, saw and heard—yes, and felt—things that others didn't see or hear or feel. It had been such an awful, overpowering experience that she—

"More coffee, hon? And how about some pie?"

The woman's voice startled Ruby, and she jumped. "Oh," she said, putting down her cup with a clatter. "Yes, just a little more, thanks. But I think I'll take a pie with me." She studied the photos on the menu. "The buttermilk pie with chocolate chips, pecans, and coconut looks really good."

"Tastes good, too." The woman—Monica, according to her name tag—poured hot coffee from a carafe. Her name tag also bore a red sticker with a skull and crossbones and the words *No Frickin' Frackin'!* "You from 'round here?"

"From Pecan Springs," Ruby said. "Halfway between Austin and San Antonio, on I-35."

"Oh, sure. Nice little town. My granddaughter's in college there." Hand on one ample hip, Monica grinned. "Not as little as little ol' Round Top, o'course. But we're big for our size." She paused, and Ruby chuckled appreciatively. "You here for one of the Institute programs?"

"No, actually, I'm visiting a friend." Ruby took a breath. "At the Blackwood house. That's what it used to be called, anyway."

Monica pulled her brows together. "Yeah, that's it. Widow Blackwood's place." Her voice had changed, and Ruby, glancing up at her, knew why. "You say your friend *lives* there?"

"She's recently inherited it," Ruby replied carefully. "I'm not sure whether she's actually living there yet." Claire hadn't said, either, although Ruby wondered whether she was being forced by financial circumstances—the cost of Brad's long illness—to take on the house. She had just said, *Come . . . please come.*

"Your friend's a braver woman than I am." Monica leaned over, lowering her voice. "Not tellin' tales, but ever'body in these parts knows the place is haunted."

"Really?" Ruby shivered. She wasn't surprised that the house had a reputation, just hoping for an explanation or a little more information. "Haunted . . . how? I mean, how do you know?"

Monica's eyes glinted avidly. She was obviously not unwilling to talk. "The place has been sittin' empty while the estate got sorted out, which is takin' a while. Way I heard it, there was some kinda question about the will." She took a breath. "Anyhoo, the lawyer for the estate, Mr. Hoover, over in La Grange, he figgered he'd put the place up for rent while things was still up in the air. Like for summers, y'know, bein' as how the house is still full of furniture and all. He and his wife went out there to stay for a week so he could see what'd be involved if he decided to rent it. They lasted three days."

"Why?" Ruby asked.

Monica leaned over. "Place is *haunted*," she replied, giving the word a spooky quaver. "That's what Mrs. Hoover told my sister-in-law Betty, who cleans at her house. Said she just flat refused to sleep another night out there, and if Mr. Hoover didn't drive her home, she would start walkin'."

"Oh dear," Ruby said.

"You bet yer boots." Monica nodded vigorously. "So Mr. Hoover, he hired some folks from around here—Sam and Kitty Rawlings, Sam used to run a gas station over in Ledbetter—to live in the hired man's house and keep an eye on things. Caretakers, y'know." She paused, eyeing Ruby with a curiosity. "You goin' out there to see yer friend?"

"That's the plan," Ruby said, summoning a cheerful tone. She smiled. "That's who I'm getting the pie for."

"Yeah." Monica picked up the empty dishes. "I'll get it for you, hon. But you wanna be careful, now—d'ya hear? Can't prove it by me if that place is haunted or not, but whatever's goin' on out there, it ain't good." She cocked her head to one side. "And then there's the drilling."

"The drilling?" Ruby frowned.

"I guess you ain't heard. Oil shale, is what it is. The oil companies have been coming in here like a flock of buzzards, gobbling up leases like they was roadkill. BP, ConocoPhillips, Exxon, Shell, you name it, they're here. Two hundred an acre for two years with a two-year option and royalties if there's production. Some folks want to cash in, and I guess you can't blame 'em. But where there's drillin', there'll be frackin'."

"Uh-oh," Ruby said. She had read enough about fracking to know how environmentally damaging it could be.

"Uh-oh is right," Monica said darkly. "The lady from the Railroad Commission says it's all hunky-dory, no problemo. Frackin' is money in the bank for Texas, and it won't hurt the water, neither. But most people 'round here feel like we don't have enough water as it is. They don't want the oil companies suckin' up what little we got and pumpin' it down the gas wells. They figure the bad stuff is goin' to start comin' out of our faucets, too."

"I can see why everybody's upset," Ruby said.

"Yeah. Anyway, there's a piece about it in the *Record*, if you want to know more." She nodded toward the red-painted newspaper rack at the front of the café. "You enjoy your coffee, hon. I'll go'n getcha that pie. Yer friend is gonna *love* it. It'll take her mind off those ghosts, fer sure."

While she waited for the pie, Ruby bought a copy of the *Fayette County Record* and scanned the front page. The lead story was about the robbery of the Schulenburg branch of the Fayetteville Bank, apparently one of an ongoing series of small-town bank robberies—no indication of how much the robbers got, although the sheriff's office said it was a "substantial amount."

But what she was looking for was the next story, below the fold. The four-column headline read, "Fracking, Groundwater Issues Explained." The spokeswoman for the Texas Railroad Commission, which regulates drilling, reported that the Eagle Ford Shale formation in Fayette County could be an "economic supernova." So far, she said, over $3.5 billion in energy investments had been poured into South Texas because of oil companies' interests. There would be increased job opportunities, higher salaries, greater sales tax revenues, higher property tax revenues, and overall increases in local commerce, and all because of the Eagle Ford Shale. "I'm here to assure all of you that fracking is safe for you and your drinking water," she said. "You have nothing to fear."

But a citizens' group affiliated with Food & Water Watch was being formed to organize opposition. "Texas should be looking at wind and solar," the spokesman said. "Fracking wastes water, contaminates our groundwater resources, and fouls the environment."

"Here's your pie, hon," Monica said, handing her the box. "Don't eat it all in one sitting now, y'hear?"

Ruby frowned down at the newspaper. "I thought I heard that there were going to be some rules about fracking," she said.

Monica heaved a heavy sigh. "So did we," she said sadly. "So did we."

Her face darkened. "Folks around here aren't in favor of the frackin', I can tell you that."

"You said that the oil companies are buying up leases," Ruby said. "Do you know where?"

"Not 'xactly," Monica said, fishing in her apron pocket. "But I heard they've been talking to a couple of ranchers south of the Blackwood place." She pulled out the check. "Here ya go, hon. I'll take it at the register."

Ruby tucked the newspaper into her bag and paid the check, giving Monica a nice tip to thank her for the service—and the information. She carried the boxed pie out to her car, noticing that the pickup trucks parked on either side of hers wore *No Frickin' Frackin'!* bumper stickers. Obviously, this was a hot-button issue.

While Ruby was eating lunch, a billowy bank of thunderheads had built to impressive heights in the eastern sky and the sun was veiled by skeins of silvery clouds. It looked like they might get some rain that afternoon. That wouldn't be a bad thing, Ruby thought as she climbed into her car, putting the pie box carefully on the seat beside her. It had been a dry spring across Central and South Texas. A little rain would be welcome. She had to smile when she turned on the ignition, the radio came on, and she caught Judy Garland in the middle of "I'm Always Chasing Rainbows."

A few minutes later, the song lyrics still echoing in her mind, Ruby was driving south and east, past red barns and neat ranch-style houses, past brown-and-white cows with their noses buried in green grass and young foals kicking up their heels in swathes of wildflowers. As she approached a small, white cottage embraced in a glorious border of roses and a tidy patch of garden, and the sun broke out momentarily. She slowed. *My goodness*, she thought, as the awareness blossomed in her mind. *It's for sale!*

And in confirmation, the next thing she saw was the For Sale sign. She pulled over to the shoulder of the road and gazed at it, thinking. If she did sell the shop and her interest in the tearoom and all the rest of it, maybe she could buy a cottage like this one, out in the country. She could put up a discreet sign beside the door—*Tarot and Birth Chart Readings—By Appointment Only*—and spend her days quilting and baking bread and raising vegetables and a few chickens for eggs. Oh, such a lovely way to live.

The sun faded behind a cloud, and Ruby sighed. She was chasing rainbows, of course—and most of her dreams were as elusive and ephemeral as the clouds building against the horizon. She paused a moment longer, gazing at the cottage, reluctant to leave. But then she heard Claire's words in her mind, desperate words. *Come and help me understand . . . Please come.* It was time to move on. Reluctantly, she put the car in gear and pulled back onto the two-lane highway.

A few miles farther on, she came to the county road that Claire had mentioned in the postcard that had followed her phone call, and the sign that read "Cedar Creek Methodist Church Camp." Claire had sent directions because, as she said, it had been a great many years since she and Ruby had visited the house together, and Ruby had likely forgotten the way.

But she hadn't, of course. She would have recognized it even without directions. It was bordered on each side by a lace of tall white prickly poppies, graceful on gray-green stems, their ruffled paper-white blossoms fastened with bright yellow buttons. White poppy, Ruby thought, remembering that Kathleen Gips had mentioned the meaning of the plant in her workshop—it signified forgetting and consolation, Kathleen had said; a sleep of the heart—although if China were here, she would no doubt point out that Kathleen was actually referring to the opium poppy, a powerful narcotic that had long been used to put people to sleep.

But still, this was a white poppy, Ruby told herself, and that's what it meant to *her*. She needed a sleep of the heart, a forgetting, a consolation. If she were living in that pretty little cottage, she would surround it with a

41

whole field of white poppies. She would forget Colin altogether and be consoled and content—not happy, perhaps, but content. Wouldn't she?

The sun hadn't reappeared. The thunderheads off to the left seemed higher and nearer, the clouds overhead lower and darker. She shivered and took her foot off the accelerator, feeling suddenly that she was in no hurry to get where she was going. Silly Claire, to think that her friend might have forgotten the way. It was true that she had been here only once, a very long time ago. But the image of the house was indelibly imprinted in her memory, like the image left on the retina after a powerful flash of lightning. She couldn't have forgotten it.

Another familiar mile went by, and then another, and then on the left she saw the black mailbox on a red-brick pillar, heaped over with wild purple morning glory. The box bore the name Blackwood, hand-lettered, very small, as if it wished not to call attention to itself or perhaps supposed that it would be recognized even if it did not bear a name.

She loosened her hands on the steering wheel—she had been gripping it so tightly that her knuckles were white—then braked and turned carefully between formal-looking red-brick pillars, head high, leaning crookedly like twin Towers of Pisa on both sides of the graveled lane. The pillars looked alien and out of place in this Texas landscape, where most of the ranchers put up cedar poles topped with cows' skulls and signs formed from rusted barbwire: "Bar-B-Q Ranch" or "The Double D." The space between the pillars was so narrow: surely they had been built when cars were smaller, or even before cars came into everyday use. The Blackwood house was at least a century old, Ruby remembered. It wasn't hard to imagine a horse and buggy moving smartly along this old road.

The lane was a rutted two-track with grass growing down the middle, bordered on both sides by a six-foot hedge of untrimmed holly bushes. The branches grew into the road, and their sharp-pointed leaves threatened to scratch the paint off any vehicle brave enough to run the gauntlet. Three hundred yards farther on, the lane took a turn, a sharp one. The holly bushes were left behind, and now there were open meadows on either side, the patchy grass studded with Ashe junipers and wild lantana and prickly pear. The lane was strewn with rocks and the ruts were deeper here. At the end of seven jolting miles, it snaked through a long *S* curve, climbed a slight rise, and headed down again, more steeply down, and down some more. Ruby shifted into a lower gear.

And then she saw the house, and her foot came off the accelerator with a jerk. The car lurched, stalled abruptly, and died. She didn't try to start it again. She lowered the window and just sat there, chewing on her lip. On her childhood visit, she'd been riding in the backseat of Claire's mother's car, and she hadn't seen the house from this angle. The view was . . . disquieting.

Built on the lower slope of a hill and surrounded by several spreading live oaks, the Blackwood mansion overlooked a shallow, spreading stream that looped through a green meadow. Whoever constructed the house must have considered it grand, but to Ruby's eyes it was an out-of-proportion hodgepodge of Victorian towers and turrets that reminded her uneasily of Agatha Christie's *Crooked House*. Or Shirley Jackson's wretched Hill House, with its "maniac" juxtapositions and "badly turned" angles. Or the old English nursery rhyme that began "There was a crooked man" and ended "And they all lived together in a little crooked house."

Except that this crooked house wasn't little. It was huge, a Victorian mansion, and in terrible need of repair and repainting. The somber brown walls had been scoured by the wind and bleached by the sun, and the chipped slates on the precipitous roofs—there were many roofs, all at strange angles—glinted dully, like broken teeth. A widow's walk, bizarre and alien in this land-locked place, extended the length of the central spine of the house, its railings broken and hanging. Oddly, the house was raised above the ground on tall piers, as if to avoid flooding—certainly an unlikely event on this hill. A pair of equally unlikely lions flanked the steps up to the gallery at the front of the house, glaring at each other with stony suspicion. The yard, weedy and badly mowed, was surrounded by an unkempt border of gnarled oleanders and hollies interspersed with straggly date palms.

A rusty iron fence was wrapped around the house and yard, its sections leaning crazily, first one way, then another, some of its posts scattered like a litter of loose iron spears across the ground. From this enclosure, there were only two ways in and out: a double iron gate in front (centered with a large and ornate letter *B*) and a smaller gate in back, half-hidden in an overgrown clump of chaste trees. From the back gate, a graveled path edged with iris meandered haphazardly past a well-tended kitchen garden, then forked. One branch continued on to a small fenced plot at the edge of a wood, the other went to a barn, a double garage, and a small frame house—the caretaker's cottage, probably. Behind that were a kitchen garden, a chicken coop and fenced yard, and several sheds.

Ruby took a deep breath, then another. Nothing much had changed in the years since her first visit, except that the house, still out of place and uncompromising, had grown older and more worn and tired. Seen from this angle, it was even more maimed and misshapen than she had remembered, as though it had been copied from a construction plan but hurriedly and imprecisely, or perhaps not even from a plan but from memory—a faulty memory, flawed. Parts were joined at incongruous and inharmonious angles. Some parts were larger than they should be. Others were smaller, so that the whole thing seemed wretchedly out of alignment. It wasn't evil or malicious or malevolent, like Hill House. It was just . . . just crooked. Crooked and sad and out of place and *wrong*, in exactly the same way it had been wrong all those years ago, when ten-year-old Ruby had seen it for the very first time.

The first time? Ruby closed her eyes, then opened them again, feeling the same prickling sensation of déjà vu that she had felt during that childhood visit, only stronger now—much stronger and more unsettling. She wondered with something close to panic whether that first visit had really been the first, or whether she had known the house from some previous time, some other place, when it had imprinted itself on her imagination so powerfully that it could never be forgotten.

But now, as then, what struck Ruby with the force almost of a blow was not just the wrongness of the physical structure and its outlandish unsuitability to the place where it had been built, or even the unsettling sense of déjà vu. It was its heart-wrenching *sadness* that brought quick tears to her eyes and made her instinctively turn away, as if to escape an embrace. For she felt exactly as she had felt that long-ago July afternoon when she and Claire had come here to visit: that the house, saturated in its own bitter sorrow, was waiting for her. It wanted to snatch her, clutch her, drown her in its devastating grief, as if—

She pulled in a steadying breath and shoved the thought away, but her hand was trembling and her fingers were icy. She turned the key, but the ignition only clicked, and the engine didn't turn over. She was about to try again when she glanced out of the window to see a slender woman emerge from the clump of chaste trees at the back of the house and open the low iron gate. She was wearing a gray shirtwaist blouse with a black ribbon and a darker gray ankle-length skirt, smoothly gored in the late Victorian style. Her dark hair was piled on her head, and over her arm she carried a woven basket filled with white roses. Her figure had the weight and dimension of reality, but there was a certain insubstantiality to it, a wavering quality, as though she were seen through a veil of falling water.

45

And then, as Ruby watched, the woman turned, lifted her hand to shade her eyes, and looked up the hill toward the car. Then waved as if in greeting, as if she had recognized Ruby, as if she had been waiting for her and was glad she had come at last.

Ruby swallowed. The perspiration broke out on her forehead and she shivered, squeezing her eyes shut. She had seen the woman before, during that first visit with Claire. The woman had turned and waved to her then, too. That was the moment that Ruby had realized that she had Gram's gift, that she—

"Hey!"

Ruby gasped and jumped, startled half out of her skin. A man was leaning over to peer in the car window. He was tall, square jawed, with gingery hair and hard gray-green eyes and he smelled of tobacco. It was difficult to tell his age. From the lines on his face, he might have been anywhere between forty and sixty, and he had clearly spent most of those years working outdoors in the wind and sun. He wore an oil-spotted denim shirt, open at the throat to reveal a frayed and dirty T-shirt, and a sweat-stained Dallas Cowboys gimme cap. The phrase *There was a crooked man* elbowed itself into Ruby's mind.

"Who're you?" the man demanded roughly. "This is private property, y'know. It's not a public road. If you're lookin' to buy an oil lease, you can just turn right around. The owner doesn't want drilling on this land."

"I'm not here about oil leases," Ruby said. "My name is Ruby Wilcox. Claire Conway invited me to spend a few days with her. You are . . . ?" She knew who he was, though. He was the caretaker the waitress had mentioned. Sam Rawlings.

and he walked a crooked mile

"Rawlings." The man straightened. "Miz Conway shoulda told me you were comin'. You got a problem with the car?"

46

"I . . . I just stalled it," Ruby said, feeling that she had been reprimanded for bad driving. "I'm sure it's okay." She turned the ignition key and, to her relief, the motor sparked into life.

He found a crooked sixpence

"Well, at least you didn't flood the damn thing." Rawlings slapped the roof of the car with the flat of his hand and stepped back. "I'll let Miz Conway know you're here. Drive on around the back of the house and park beside the garage, then go on to the kitchen door. Leave your bags by the car and I'll bring 'em in for you." He paused, adding pointedly, "When I get around to it."

"I can manage," Ruby said distinctly. "I wouldn't want to trouble you."

"Suit yourself." The man turned abruptly and headed toward a faint path, like a narrow game trail, that led downhill in the direction of the house.

As Ruby put the car in gear and started off, she looked back over her shoulder. To her relief, the woman in the gray dress was gone. But the windows of the crooked house, like sad and empty eyes, seemed to follow her as she drove cautiously down the hill and across the low concrete bridge over the gravel bed of the creek.

Chapter Three

Galveston
Midday, September 8, 1900

Many persons now took receivers off the hooks of the wall telephones, rang the operator, and asked for 214—the number of the Weather Bureau office. The weatherman had only a word of advice for those in the low areas: get to higher ground.

A Weekend in September
John Edward Weems

As far as the Blackwood children were concerned, it was the most wonderful of mornings. After breakfast, the three boys and even Ida, who was usually a perfect little lady, had begged to put on their oldest clothes and go out and play in the warm rain. They were so excited that their mother felt she had to let them go, even though she was increasingly uneasy about the threatening weather.

Rachel had lived in Galveston only since her marriage to Mr. Blackwood some nine years before. She had little experience of tropical storms. But her cook-housekeeper, Mrs. Colleen O'Reilly, was one of the survivors of the hurricane of 1886, which had roared ashore a hundred miles to the south, turning the thriving port of Indianola—a rival of Galveston—into a ghost town. This morning, she was visibly apprehensive, which gave Rachel another reason for concern. Mrs. O'Reilly, who was not yet thirty, red-haired and with a generous sprinkling of freckles across her cheeks, had a touch of the second sight.

Rachel might not have believed this if she hadn't witnessed it for herself. One bright summer afternoon, the two of them had been in the drawing room, laying out tea for the Ladies' Guild. Mrs. O'Reilly had glanced out the drawing room window and seen Mrs. Neville, the Blackwoods' next-door neighbor, crossing Q Avenue in front of the house. And then Mrs. Neville suddenly vanished from view—simply vanished, as if she had never been.

Mrs. O'Reilly had burst into tears and turned to tell this to Rachel, crying out in her rich Irish brogue that she feared for Mrs. Neville's life. Scoffing to herself (she wasn't in the least superstitious), Rachel had soothed her and sent her back to the kitchen. But two days later, Mrs. Neville was struck down in the street by a runaway horse. She died on the very spot where Mrs. O'Reilly had seen her vanish.

When Rachel told Augustus what had happened, he had shrugged, then smiled indulgently. "Another reason to canonize our Colleen," he'd replied mildly. Like Rachel, he had a special fondness for Mrs. O'Reilly, who had become a mainstay in their home. Not only was she an extraordinarily competent cook-housekeeper who could (as Augustus said) work miracles with the loaves and fishes, but she loved the children in the same warmly protective way that she loved her own young daughter, Annie, whom she often brought to play with the Blackwood children.

This morning, visibly anxious, Mrs. O'Reilly had hurried through the preparations for the noon meal: meatloaf and mashed potatoes with green beans and cabbage and carrot slaw. That done, she hurriedly frosted Matthew's birthday cake, added ten candles, and made sandwiches for the afternoon birthday party.

Then—even though it was not yet eleven, with the rest of the day's work yet to be done—she took off her apron and announced that she was going home.

"Sure 'n this storm is goin' to be a bad 'un," she said. "I will be takin' me mother an' Annie to the Ursulines." The convent was a strong building just a few blocks from the small frame house where Mrs. O'Reilly lived with her mother and three-year-old daughter. She tilted her head with an oddly intent and listening look. After a moment, she added urgently, "Ye must come, too, an' the children, Mrs. Blackwood. We'll be safe with the sisters." She paused, fixed her gray-green eyes on Rachel's face, and repeated: "Truly, ye *must*. I know it."

A little frightened by the young woman's intensity, Rachel hesitated. But the rain had stopped, and the wind—that peculiar keening wind that whistled so eerily in the eaves—had abated somewhat. She summoned her courage and smiled. "Thank you for your concern, Mrs. O'Reilly, but Mr. Blackwood will be home for lunch. I shouldn't like him to find an empty house."

Pulling on her waterproof, Mrs. O'Reilly had nodded gravely. "Mayhap ye'll change yer mind. If ye do, come. The sisters will give ye shelter." There was something in her eyes that frightened Rachel. She added, with an emphasis she had never used, "*Please come*."

When she had gone, Rachel's courage began to fade. Mrs. O'Reilly had known of Mrs. Neville's accidental death, which could not have been foreseen. What if she was right about the storm, too? Rachel went to the telephone, rang the operator, and asked for 214, the number of the Weather Bureau. Mr. Cline was the bureau chief and her neighbor—he would be honest with her. There was a lengthy wait, but when at last he came on the line, he assured her that there was no need for worry.

"Your house and mine," he said confidently, "are built well above any possible overflow. People in low-lying areas should go to higher ground, yes. But you need not trouble yourself, Mrs. Blackwood. You'll be fine." She was not quite reassured, but she thanked him before she hung up.

The other mothers in the neighborhood did not seem to share Rachel's concern. The children were out in force, splashing joyfully through the water that was surging up from the beach. The heavy brown waves were laden with fascinating flotsam and jetsam—shells and seaweed, jagged scraps of signboards, a bundle of rags, a broken beach chair. A salvaged wooden pallet made a fine raft for Matthew with a broom handle for a mast and a handkerchief for a pennant. There was even a curiously woven basket that Ida rescued and took to her mother, to be used in the garden.

And the toads, oh those toads! The tiny, brown freshwater creatures were everywhere by the thousands, the millions, hopping frantically for higher ground, away from the salty sea water. Ida and the twins caught a bucketful and then got bored with the effort and let them all go free, turning instead to collect the hermit crabs that were being tossed up by the waves. When the storm was over, they promised their mother, they would return the little creatures to their homes on the beach.

For other observers, there were even more interesting sights to be seen at the Midway, a ten-block stretch of souvenir peddlers, grimy shacks, boardwalk shops, and food stands selling boiled shrimp and beer, all just a few yards from the sandy beach. A large crowd of onlookers had gathered, muttering at the sight of the giant swells as they thundered like great brown dragons, mounting higher and higher on the shore. The watchers had come mostly by the electric streetcar, although the conductor had stopped the car several blocks away. He'd had to, for the street railway trestle that ran along the beach was being battered by the waves. It might have been demolished at any moment.

Some of the watchers had come to be amazed, for word of the mammoth waves, greater than any that had ever been seen, was spreading around the city. Others had come for fun and were dressed in bathing costumes to enjoy the surf. But no one now dared venture into the water, for the waves had become too powerful. The rain was coming harder, like shotgun pellets flung by the wind, and the dragon-breakers were beginning to swallow the Midway shops and splinter the flimsy bathhouses. As the spectators gawked, the waves destroyed even the giant Pagoda Company Bath House with its twin octagonal, pagoda-roofed pavilions, built at the end of a nearly four-hundred-foot boardwalk that rose sixteen feet above the beach. Hastily retreating to safer ground, the spectators found themselves wading through surging water up to their knees.

On Strand Street at Ninth, in the narrow upper part of the island, stood John Sealy Hospital, an imposing stone-and-brick edifice only ten years old, studded with picturesque Victorian towers, turrets, and chimney pots exuberantly rendered in shape, color, texture, and detail. The hospital was the architectural work of Nicholas J. Clayton, who was responsible for many of the grand Victorian flights of fancy that Galvestonians loved so much—so many, in fact, and so grand (or grandiose) that the period was known as the "Clayton Era." He was "excessively fond," one critic later said, of decorative brick and ironwork.

At the hospital that morning, someone—a nurse, an aide—glanced out of a west-facing window toward the bay, a hundred yards away. She described the scene in a letter she was writing at that moment: "It does not require a great stretch of imagination to imagine this structure a shaky old boat out at sea, the whole thing rocking," she wrote in her spidery hand. ". . . Like a reef, surrounded by water . . . water growing closer, ever closer. Have my hands full quieting nervous, hysterical women." An hour later, more anxious now, she added another paragraph: "The scenes about here are distressing. Everything washed away. Poor people, trying to save their bedding and clothing . . . It is a sight. Our beautiful bay a raging torrent."

Galveston Bay—the usually placid harbor where the big ships rode at anchor—was indeed a torrent. The north wind, which seemed to become more violent by the minute, pushed the bay water over the wharves and sent it, thick as molasses with bay mud and debris, sloshing across the Strand. More than a dozen large steamers lay in the harbor that weekend, including the three-year-old, 3,900-ton British vessel *Kendal Castle*. Almost all the ships were working their engines to ease the strain on their anchor lines, their crews tending frantically to the moorings. The tide was extremely high, and the waves lifted the ships ten, fifteen, twenty feet above the warehouses along the piers, stretching the taut hawsers and anchor chains to the breaking point. Onlookers watched from the safety of the Strand, fascinated but fearful that the waves would rip the ships loose and fling them like so many toys onto the shore.

A few blocks away, downtown, it was a different story. Augustus Blackwood, like most of Galveston's businessmen, had more important things to do than worry about a tropical storm. To be sure, there were reports of flooding in the lower-lying areas and some intermittent power outages and news of damage to the Midway and the beach streetcar trestle. It was even said that the streetcars had stopped running at the eastern end of Broadway, where Gulf waters had pushed inland as far as Twelfth Street. But the electricity had stayed on at the bank, there was the usual pressing business to transact, and the morning had been very much like any other stormy Saturday morning. Quite naturally, financial matters took precedence over the weather any day of the week.

By the time Augustus Blackwood prepared to go home for his dinner, however, the rain was much heavier. He looked out of his window, debating whether to stay downtown and have lunch or endure a thorough soaking on his walk home. His mind was made up when a man with whom he had done some personal business—a man from Beaumont, Texas, from whom he had bought some land in Fayette County, as well as some highly speculative mineral rights—dropped in. Augustus suggested that the two of them take a table at Ritter's Café and Saloon, just two blocks from the bank. He telephoned his home and spoke briefly to his wife, informing her that he would be lunching downtown. He was surprised at Rachel's response: she begged him to come home immediately.

"The water is in the yard, Augustus!" she cried frantically. "It's flowing all around the house! And it's not rainwater, either. I tasted it—it's *salt* water!"

He was surprised at this news and somewhat concerned, since he had never seen the Gulf send waves so high as their street. But his client was an important man and he had already made his plans. "Surely you're not afraid of a little water, are you, my dear?" he teased. "I'll tell you what. I'll be at Ritter's for the next hour or so. If the storm doesn't let up by the time I've eaten, I'll come straight home. The bank can manage without me for one afternoon. And tomorrow, when the storm is over, we will all go down to the beach and see what the tide has left for us. The children will enjoy that." His voice softened. "And we'll take a picnic, my dear. What do you say to that?"

It was much more difficult to get to the restaurant than Augustus had thought, for the streets were running full to the gutters, the rain was coming down in sheets, and the gale-force wind turned his umbrella inside out and tore it from his hands before he was fairly out the door. By the time he and his client arrived at the restaurant, they were wet through.

But Ritter's was warm and bright and bustling and the two men arrived just in time to be shown to seats at a table near the front window of the large, high-ceilinged room. The restaurant, which occupied the ground floor of a brick building that housed a second-floor printing shop, was popular with the men who represented the city's increasingly powerful financial interests.

They came to discuss business over drinks and good food in congenial company. Today's storm might have made them a little jumpy, but they enjoyed a lighthearted moment when someone pointed out that there were thirteen diners in the room and wondered if it was bad luck. Stanley Spencer, a steamship agent for the Elder-Dempster and North German Lloyd lines, replied loudly, "You can't frighten me. I'm not superstitious."

Joining the general laughter, Augustus and his companion ordered cocktails from the bar, as well as a large platter of fresh oysters and fried shrimp, to be followed by the house specialty, steaks as big as a dinner plate with sides of fried onions.

"Rare," Augustus said in a jocular tone to the white-jacketed waiter. "I want to hear it moo."

But the men did not get their steaks. Before the waiter could turn in the order, the gusting wind muscled off the building's roof. The brick walls of the second-story print shop gave way. The floor joists, fastened to headers with twenty-penny nails, snapped loose with the gun-shot sounds of cracking wood. Only a few men had time to scramble for safety under the bar before the print shop collapsed and a torrent of bricks, desks, chairs, printing equipment, and two massive printing presses cascaded into the dining room.

Five men died, including the unsuperstitious Stanley Spencer. Five others were badly injured. The café's owner sent one of the waiters for a doctor, whose office was located in the nearby Strand. On his way, the waiter was swept off his feet by a surging wave from the bay. He was drowned.

Augustus Blackwood was among the dead. By the time his body was pulled from the wreckage and someone thought to call his wife with the tragic news, the telephone exchange was flooded. The telephones were no longer working anywhere in the city.

But there was worse to come. Much worse.

Chapter Four

The genus name *Vinca* comes from the Latin *vincire* "to bind, fetter." The plant is a fast-growing perennial groundcover with blue-violet flowers and evergreen or variegated foliage, native to Europe, Africa, and Asia. Interplanting with other plants is not a good idea, for this highly invasive plant produces stems that root along their length, so that the bed quickly becomes a hard-to-manage tangle of binding vines.

In England, vinca is called periwinkle; in Italy, the Flower of Death. In the ancient world, the flowering vines were used to garland human sacrifices. The tradition persisted into the Middle Ages, when criminals were hung wearing crowns of vinca. The association with death was preserved in the tradition of weaving vinca wreaths to decorate the graves of infants. In Europe, the plant was known as the Sorcerer's violet and was believed to have the power of exorcizing evil spirits and demons.

In the language of flowers, vinca or periwinkle is an emblem of affection and friendship, binding even to death.

China Bayles
"Herbs and Flowers That Tell a Story"
Pecan Springs Enterprise

Ruby left her small suitcase in the car and walked up the back path, the potted mugwort in one hand, the pie box in the other, and her purse over her shoulder. The house, gaunt and misshapen, leaned toward her, watching her as if it, too, like the woman with the roses, had been waiting for her and was glad she had come at last. She ducked her head, shivering.

And they all lived together in a little crooked house.

"Ruby!"

It was Claire, apparently alerted by Rawlings, waiting eagerly on the back porch, which wrapped itself like a gallery around the back of the house. "Ruby!" she cried. "Oh Ruby, I'm so glad you've come!" And with that, she held out her arms and burst into a storm of sobs.

Immediately touched, Ruby pushed her apprehensions away, put everything down, and held her friend close. "Well, golly," she murmured against Claire's hair, "if you're so glad, how come you're crying, huh?"

Claire stepped back and wiped the tears away with the back of her hand. She was wearing denim cutoffs, a pink boat-necked shirt with a coffee stain on the front, and sneakers. Her usually neat chestnut hair was disheveled, and the skin around her caramel-colored eyes was swollen and bruised-looking. Ruby was taken aback to see how much weight she had lost since the last time they'd been together, at Brad's memorial service. She looked just plain awful.

"I'm crying because . . . Well, damn it, Ruby, you're one of my oldest friends and I haven't seen you in forever. I can cry if I want to, can't I?" Claire stage-managed a smile, but Ruby, looking closely, thought that she looked exhausted, as if she hadn't been sleeping well.

"Cry as much as you want to, it's okay." Ruby spoke in a comforting tone, although she had the uneasy feeling that it really wasn't okay. There was something very fragile about Claire. "I'm here to rescue you. From whatever." She hoisted the boxed pie. "See? I even brought dessert. Pie to die for, straight from Royers Cafe. Oh, and a plant from China Bayles. Mugwort. Not much to look at, but it has other good qualities."

That brought a real smile. "Ruby, you are a saint." Claire led the way through the back door and into the old-fashioned kitchen.

"What? For a little pie and some mugwort, I've been canonized? What would I get if I—" Ruby put her bag and the mugwort on the table and looked around in wide-eyed dismay. "Wow," she whispered. "Like . . . just, wow."

On her first visit, Ruby had missed the kitchen. It was huge, with one long wall of ceiling-high glass-fronted cupboards filled with china and crystal. A mammoth black iron cookstove stood against one wall with a small four-burner gas stove beside it, and next to that, a pine-topped work-table and a hanging rack of pots and pans, old and well used. Beside the pot rack was a small blackboard with a piece of chalk and an eraser in the chalk tray. *Menus* was printed at the top in old-fashioned script. Below was what looked like Claire's shopping list: bread, milk, yogurt, coffee.

On the opposite wall, beneath a window, was a rust-stained porcelain sink that looked like it belonged in an antique shop. A round-shouldered 1950s Crosley Shelvador refrigerator hunched against another wall under an old-fashioned clock that said it was just a little past one. The floor was dark green linoleum, worn through in front of the sink and table. The walls were a lighter green, dingy and darkened with smoke over the cook stove. A round oak pedestal table and two wooden chairs stood in the middle of the room. In the middle of the table was a crystal vase filled with fragrant sweet peas and iris, with sprigs of parsley and rosemary and trailing stems of vinca.

"That's exactly what I said when I saw it," Claire replied. Her voice was thin and reedy. "Wow. You could cook for an army in here."

There was a long silence while Ruby took it all in. "Well, I hope you're not cooking on *that*," she said at last, pointing to the iron stove.

Claire shook her head. "No, but my great-aunt Hazel cooked on it until she died. Which is maybe *why* she died." She chuckled wryly. "I'm just kidding. Mom talked Aunt Hazel into getting the gas stove installed, and a water heater, too, so there's hot water for laundry and baths. But to tell the truth, I haven't been doing a whole lot of cooking since . . . for a long time," she added in an apologetic tone. "Soup and sandwiches are usually enough for me. I hope you didn't come for the gourmet food."

"Hey," Ruby said lightly, "who needs gourmet? We're having an adventure, aren't we? It's like being away at camp or something. We can live off the land. We can roast weenies over a fire in the backyard and get all sticky with s'mores. Or we can drive into Round Top and pig out to our heart's content, which I highly recommend, come to think of it." Claire needed to get some real meals under her belt, Ruby thought. She had always been slender. Now she was much too thin. Taking a breath, Ruby added, "Aren't you going to show me around?"

"Y . . . es." Claire was hesitant. "But maybe it would be good if we talked a little bit first. You probably have lots of questions."

Questions? Ruby thought of the woman with the basket of white roses and shivered. Yes, lots of questions, although she wasn't sure that Claire would have any answers.

"Sure," Ruby said easily. "If there's something cold to drink in the refrigerator, we could have a piece of the world-famous pie Saint Ruby has brought just for you. As you say, it's been forever since we've been together. We need to catch up."

"Iced tea?" Claire opened the refrigerator door and pulled a dinky metal ice cube tray out of the tiny, frost-crusted freezer, which was just about big enough for the tray and a quart of ice cream. The ice cube tray looked as antique as the fridge.

"Super." Ruby opened the pie box. "Knife? Forks? Plates?"

Getting out a pitcher of tea, Claire nodded toward the cupboards. "Over there. You're bound to find something." Half to herself, she added, "I can't figure out why there are so many dishes. It's like somebody was planning to do some serious entertaining—half the county, maybe. It's the same with the linens. There are two linen closets, stuffed full of old stuff. High quality, but really old, all of it monogrammed with a *B*, for Blackwood, I suppose. A lot of it has never been used."

Ruby pulled open a drawer and found the silver, opened a cupboard and took down two small plates. "When did you get here?"

"Two weeks ago." Claire banged the ice cube tray on the table and the cubes spilled out. "The longest two weeks in my life. To tell the truth, there've been days when I wasn't sure I was going to make it. Nights, too. Nights especially," she added, in a lower voice.

Considering that, Ruby found a knife and began cutting the pie. "You've been staying out here all by your lonesome?"

"Well, yes and no." Claire was putting ice cubes into two glasses. Her voice was flat, hesitant, as if she were measuring her words. "There are the Rawlingses, of course. Sam and Kitty. Mr. Hoover—he's the lawyer for the estate—hired them to look after the place. Sam does the mowing and keeps up the outside work. Kitty helps out in the house and manages the veggie garden. She keeps a few chickens, too, so if we run out of food, we can always raid the henhouse for eggs." Claire nodded toward the flowers. "She brought me those this morning. The sweet peas are blooming all over the garden fence."

Ruby moved her shoulder bag onto the floor and put down their plates of pie. "I met Sam," she remarked. "He was . . ." She stopped, not quite sure how to put it. *There was a crooked man and he walked a crooked mile*

"Abrupt?" Claire prompted, into her hesitation. "Impolite, maybe?"

"Try bad mannered," Ruby said. "As in rude."

Claire made a face. "I'm never sure whether he's doing it on purpose or whether he's so naturally tactless that it just comes out that way." She poured the tea and put the glasses on the round oak table, and they sat down across from each other. "The place has been empty for so long, he's begun to think he owns it. I'm not comfortable with that."

"He thought I might be with one of the oil companies," Ruby said, picking up her fork. "If I were, I could turn the car around and get the hell out of Dodge."

"Those companies have been a serious nuisance," Claire said ruefully. "The big guys send letters or work through the landowners' lawyers. But the little guys just show up at the front door, and they don't want to take no for an answer. Kitty had some trouble with one a few weeks ago, and it pissed Sam off. He doesn't like intruders—which is good, I guess. He's like a watchdog, a Rottweiler, maybe, or a pit bull. And judging from past behavior, it's even possible that his bite might be worse than his bark."

"Kitty is Sam's wife?"

"Uh-huh. She's pleasant enough, but she's shy. It's hard to get more than a couple of words out of her. Sam has her pretty much under his thumb. The two of them take quite a bit of time off—a day or two a week, sometimes. If I stay, I need to find somebody else to live in the cottage and help. But then again . . ." Her face looked drawn and tired. "Mr. Hoover says it's not easy getting people to work out here. And if I'm serious about turning this place into a paying proposition, it's going to need a *ton* of work—plumbing, electrical work, painting. And money, of course. And I have to—"

Claire's voice became indistinct, as if it were drowning in a dim distance, and Ruby lost track of what her friend was saying. She looked across the table and saw a gray shadow, like a fugitive wisp of fog, curling around Claire's head and shoulders. There was a faint metallic odor, and she shivered, feeling suddenly, helplessly cold and shimmery and remote, as if part of her had become detached and moved outside of her, *above* her, and was looking down at two women—herself and Claire—seated across from each other at the table. The image rippled, broke, and reformed, as if she were seeing through water.

The feeling was profoundly disorienting, and Ruby knew that if it went on for more than a moment, she would start to feel the flickerings—quick flashes of thought, images, sensations, emotions. She would know what Claire was feeling, thinking. And she didn't want to. She *never* wanted to know what was going on inside her friends. For one thing, it could be painful. Once, just out of curiosity, she'd let herself go into China's mind. She'd seen that China thought she was a flake, a sweet, silly, lovable flake, but a flake just the same. At the same time, she'd understood that China envied her intuition and her perceptive abilities. China saw her as someone who—

But Ruby had stopped right there. It was one thing to guess what a friend might think of you. It was another to peer into her mind and *know*. It simply wasn't fair. Everybody was entitled to her own private thoughts without other people poking around, turning things over to look inside and underneath, like curious buyers in a shop.

These uninvited, inadvertent glimpses into another person's mind had occurred often when Ruby was younger, when she trying to learn how to manage her gift. But they came less frequently now that she had figured out how to defend herself against them. When the shimmer began and the flickering came, she had trained herself to throw up what she imagined as her deflector shield, a metaphor that she had picked up from *Star Trek* reruns years before. In the beginning, it had taken a great deal of focused, sustained effort to raise the shield and keep the flickering at bay long enough for her to get control of what was happening, to dial it down or flick it off altogether. After a while, it got easier: she would be talking with somebody and start to feel shimmery and up came the shield almost automatically, like an arm flung up to deflect a slap. A moment later, the flicker faded, the shimmery feeling disappeared, and the conversation went on just as if nothing had happened. The other person never noticed a thing.

As time passed, though, Ruby had learned that it was possible to skim across the shimmers and flickers and use them without getting sucked in too deep. When she was doing birth chart readings, for example, or transits. Most of the time, she just stuck to reading the chart, which almost always gave more than enough information. All by itself, an astrological chart was incredibly revealing when you knew how to read it. You didn't have to be psychic to get what was important; you just pointed out what the chart said and let the client do the work of making the connections to her inner and outer life. It usually meant more to the client that way, too, when she made her own personal discoveries.

But sometimes the chart blossomed out like a suddenly significant Rorschach and Ruby caught a flicker she wanted to hang on to for a moment without lowering the shield too far. Or she might be teaching a class in runes or tarot or I Ching, and the shimmer would come, along with a quick flicker of something interesting that she could pass along to her students without getting pulled in very deep.

That kind of thing was harmless, Ruby told herself, it was just fooling around, playing games. She had often wondered how professional intuitives managed. They took money to do readings for people, which meant that they were obligated to go as deep as they could. How in the world did they protect themselves? How did they keep from going too far into someone, too *dangerously* far? How did they avoid getting tangled up in other people's stuff, like a diver getting tangled in a bed of kelp? What kind of defenses did they use? Or maybe they treated it like a game, the way she did. Or were only pretending (which was probably true of at least some of them).

Ruby occasionally worried that she was trivializing Gram's gift by using it in such a superficial way. But the other thing, the *whole* thing, felt much too big and risky, and the few times she had used it seriously, it had terrified her. She was afraid of being overwhelmed or even swallowed up entirely by some power she couldn't even begin to comprehend. It was like standing at the opening of a long tunnel that sloped away beneath her feet into utter blackness, with no light visible at the far end. It was easy to step inside a few feet, because she had the option of jumping back out at any time. Who knew what might happen if she went farther, went all the way? Who would she *be* when she came out at the other end? Would she come out at all or—

Ruby steadied her breath, making a strong effort to pull all of herself back to the chair she was sitting in, and risked another glance. The wisps of gray fog around Claire's head had disappeared and her words were more distinct.

"—I have to get that woman—that ghost or whatever she is—out of this house," she was saying, her words hard and edgy. She leaned forward. "You remember, don't you? The woman you saw on the stairs that time? When we were here together, when we were kids?"

The fragrance of the sweet peas had dispelled the metallic odor, and the shimmery feeling was going away. Ruby began to feel warmer and connected again, all of a piece. She heard herself say, in a light, half-amused tone, "Oh, *that*. I scared you silly, didn't I? I told you I'd seen a ghost. But you know how kids are. Surely you didn't believe—"

"A woman in a long gray skirt and a gray shirtwaist with a black tie." Claire's voice was taut and thin, like a plucked string. "Dark hair, piled up on her head like a Gibson Girl. That was how you described her the day Mom brought us here to visit Aunt Hazel. And then you told me about your grandmother's . . . gift. And we talked about it. Not just then, but later." Her voice went up a notch. "Don't tell me you don't remember, Ruby! I can't bear it if you do."

Ruby met her friend's eyes. "Yes, I remember," she said, after a moment. "That was what I saw. And yes, we talked about it." She paused, wondering if she should tell Claire what she had seen from the car this morning. But something stopped her, at least for now.

"Good. I'm glad I didn't make it up," Claire said, sounding relieved. She put her elbows on the table. "Anyway, after you told me about her, every time Mom and I came here to visit Aunt Hazel, I would go to the foot of those stairs and look up. I wanted to see your ghost."

"*My* ghost?"

"That's how I thought of her," Claire replied. "Ruby's ghost. But I could never see her. I finally decided that you must have been pretending, or maybe I had to have your grandmother's gift to see what you saw. Or that the ghost or whatever she was had gone away. But none of that is true." She had given up all pretense of eating her pie, and now she pushed the plate away and clasped her hands in front of her. "You weren't making it up, and I didn't need your Gram's gift to see her. And she hasn't gone away. She's here, Ruby. Now. Still. After all these years. And I don't mind telling you, I am *scared*."

Ruby put down her fork, her own pie untasted. Outside, there was a distant rumble of thunder. Inside, the air was hot, heavy, almost steamy. "You've . . . seen her?"

"Three different times." Claire wore a vulnerable look, and she was twisting the ring on the fourth finger of her left hand. It was her wedding ring, Ruby noticed with some surprise. She was still wearing it, although Brad had been dead for a couple of years. "The first time was on the back staircase going up to the third floor, late one evening. She was carrying a kerosene lamp in one hand and lifting her skirt with the other as she climbed the stairs. She didn't look back, and I lost sight of her when she reached the third floor hallway." She swallowed. "Another time, she was just going into the cemetery, early in the morning, right after the sun came up. My bedroom faces in that direction. I saw her through the window."

"There's a cemetery here?" Ruby asked. But that wasn't unusual. Many old houses in rural areas had graveyards. They dated back to the days when families lived in the same house, generation after generation. Now, a lot of them were abandoned.

"Uh-huh." Claire flicked her tongue across her lips. "If you go out the back gate and take the path that goes off to the left, you'll come to it. Aunt Hazel took me there once when I was a kid. That's where old Mrs. Blackwood is buried, and Aunt Hazel. But there are other headstones, too, a whole row of them, and a big, white Victorian marble angel. The woman I saw that morning was carrying a basket filled with white roses. I got the idea that she was taking the flowers to put on the graves."

So that was where she was going, Ruby thought to herself, feeling suddenly chilled. *The woman I saw from the car. She was taking flowers to the graveyard. I wonder who's buried there.*

Claire tightened her fingers as if to control the shakiness in her voice. "She looked more or less like . . . like a real person, dressed up in a Victorian blouse and skirt. But she was, well, indistinct somehow, and not quite . . . sort of shimmery, I mean." She cleared her throat. "Wavy. Rippled. Like I was . . . like I was seeing her through water."

Ruby tried to speak calmly, thinking about the kinds of logical questions that China might ask if she were here. "Is it possible that the Rawlingses might have something to do with this? Like, maybe Kitty dressed up to fit the part?"

But how would Kitty Rawlings know what kind of clothes to wear? Unless, of course, Claire had said something to her. "Did you happen to tell her what this woman looked like?"

"Uh-uh." Claire shook her head emphatically. "I haven't spoken to Kitty about it. I thought of asking her if she'd seen anything, but I decided against it." She chuckled ruefully. "For one thing, I thought it might scare her. She'd probably tell Sam, too, and for some reason, I didn't want him to know. Anyway, the woman I saw was tall and elegant and graceful. Kitty is . . . well, kind of dumpy. You'll see when you meet her. You'd never get the two confused."

Ruby asked the second part of the question. "So you don't know if she's seen anything? Or if her husband—"

"Uh-uh." Claire shook her head again. "I suppose I could ask. Only, if they haven't seen anything, it's going to sound a little nutty, don't you think?" Her chuckle sounded forced. "'Excuse me, Mr. and Mrs. Rawlings, but I'm wondering if you've happened to notice a ghost wandering around—maybe out near the graveyard? Carrying a basket of white roses? If you see her, give her my regards, would you?'"

Ruby had to agree. It definitely sounded screwy. "You said there were three times. Once on the back stairs with a lamp, once on the path near the cemetery. When was the third time?"

"Just before I called you the other evening. I was walking beside the creek. We'll have to go down there later, Ruby—it's really beautiful, especially with all the wildflowers in bloom. It felt so good to get away from this house for a little while." Claire took a breath and went on hurriedly. "But that's another story. Anyway, when I was coming back up the hill, I glanced toward the house and saw her—the woman—on the widow's walk, up on the roof."

"On the roof?" Ruby asked in surprise, and then thought to herself, *Why not? Why shouldn't she be on the roof, just as easily as the stairs or the path to the cemetery?* "What was she doing up there?"

"Nothing. Just standing there, looking off toward the east." Claire was twisting her wedding ring again. "The wind was blowing her skirt, and her long hair kept coming loose and getting in her eyes. I got the idea that she was waiting for something, and that she was frightened, or at least apprehensive."

"How? I mean, how did you get that idea?"

"I really don't . . . I don't know." The question seemed to puzzle Claire. "It was—it must have been something in her posture. I think she was worried because something was coming. Something very bad, and there was nothing she could do about it. Anyway, I just kept on watching, for two, maybe three minutes. Then I heard somebody driving down the hill and I glanced in that direction. It was Sam in his old green pickup truck, coming back with the groceries from town. When I looked back at the house, she was gone."

Ruby felt no surprise. "Just . . . gone? No theatrics, no crash-bam-boom?"

Claire nodded. Her brown eyes were very large in her pale, heart-shaped face. "But here's the thing, Ruby. There's no way to get up to the widow's walk now, or to get down. There used to be a ladder and a trapdoor on the third floor, and when I was a kid, my mother would take me up there sometimes. She always held tight to my hand, which was good, because it's high—almost forty feet off the ground—and the slate roof is steep. But after Aunt Hazel died and Mr. Hoover took over the management of the house, he had the ladder taken away and the trapdoor nailed shut. He told me he had been thinking of renting the place to summer visitors, and he didn't want any little kids playing Superman off the roof."

She stopped twisting her ring and flexed her fingers. "I looked, Ruby. That trapdoor is still nailed shut."

Ruby took a breath. "So you went to the phone and called me." She frowned. "No, you couldn't have done that, because there's no phone in the house. Right?"

"Right." She looked uncomfortable. "This is going to sound pretty silly, but the truth is that I was . . . well, the only way I can say it is that I got a message to call you."

"A message?" Ruby asked in surprise. "Who?"

Claire shrugged. "I don't know who. It just . . . it just popped into my head when I was coming downstairs from checking the trapdoor. *Call Ruby.* And then, as if there might be some mistake, *Call Ruby Wilcox.* But when I thought about it, I realized that it was exactly the right thing to do, not just because you're my oldest friend, but because you saw her. You saw her *first.* So I got in the car and drove out to the county road, where I got a signal. I could have texted you, probably, but I thought this was way too complicated for that." Now, Claire's words were tumbling out in a breathless rush. "This whole thing is so wild, Ruby—I mean, really *bizarre.* The house itself is bad enough, the crazy, crooked way it was cobbled together in the first place, as if Mrs. Blackwood was making it up as she went along. And there's the wind and the weird weather that seems to happen here and nowhere else. And on top of that, there's this ghost or poltergeist or whatever she is, and I'm at a loss to—"

"Poltergeist?" Ruby interrupted. "Have there . . . have you seen or heard anything else? Besides the woman, I mean?"

Claire's glance slid away. "Actually, yes. I've heard . . ." Her voice trailed off. "But maybe you won't . . ."

"Try me," Ruby said. "What's going on?"

"I wish I *knew.*" Claire's voice was dry and scratchy. "But since you ask,

70

well, yes, I've heard a few things. There's a harp in the music room, I've heard that—no melody, just a faint jangle, like fingers running across the strings. A foghorn, distinct but far away—and of course, the closest foghorn is over on the Gulf coast. The wind whistling in the eaves, even when there's not a breath of a breeze." She cast an apprehensive glance at the pans hanging from the rack over the worktable. "Those pans rattling. A bell tinkling, a ball bouncing, a window breaking. A woman crying—weeping as if her heart would break. The sound of dripping, like a faucet. I've seen some things, too. Puddles in the downstairs hallway and water stains in the third-floor ceilings that seem to come and go—"

"*Water* stains?"

Claire spoke quickly, as if she'd been saving all this and was glad to get it said. "And sometimes there are odors. Cherry pipe smoke. Violet perfume. The smell of chocolate cake baking."

"Jeepers," Ruby said quietly.

"Yeah. Jeepers. Jeepers creepers." Claire pushed out a ragged breath. "It's like . . . it's like the house is inhabited, Ruby. What I'm hearing is just the daily stuff going on, people moving around, leading their lives, somebody doing things in the kitchen, children out in the yard. Except it's *not*. Not inhabited by anybody else but me. I'm the only one here." She rubbed her hand across her face. "I don't make noises, or smoke cherry tobacco, and I haven't baked a chocolate cake since Brad died."

Since Brad died. Briefly, Ruby wondered whether this might be psychosomatic, whether it had something to do with Claire's grief. "The weeping," she asked. "Does that happen often?"

Claire nodded. "At night, mostly." Her voice was unsteady. "It's . . . heartbreaking."

"And scary, I guess. All of it, I mean," Ruby added. "Not just the crying."

71

Claire considered. "Well, in the beginning, I thought it was my imagi-nation." A wry smile ghosted across her mouth. "After all, I just spent sev-eral months in rehab, drying out. For the first few days, I thought maybe it was something like delirium without the tremens. But then I got involved in trying to chase down the sources of the sounds and the other stuff. That turned out to be pretty unproductive, but at least it kept me busy." She paused and looked down at her hands. "But the crying—that happens at night. And yes, it's scary. It starts off slow, somewhere in the distance, just one voice, a woman's voice. And then it builds, and in the end, it's as if . . . Ruby, it's as if it's coming from everywhere. From the walls, the floors, from the whole house. It's as if the house is weeping."

Ruby covered Claire's hands with her own. They were very cold and the fingers were trembling. "It sounds frightening," she said quietly.

Claire nodded, trying on another smile. "I'm not saying there's any-thing malicious or evil about this," she said earnestly. "It doesn't feel like that, really. The worst is the crying at night, and in the daytime, it's the sound of glass breaking, which is always so real that I have to go around and check all the windows. Oh, and there are the puddles on the floor. When I'm down on my knees wiping up, I go a little crazy trying to figure out how they got there." She reclaimed her hands. "But most of it is just like . . . well, everyday life, like maybe a noisy family living in the duplex next door—except that there's no duplex next door, and no family. And there never was, ever. So far as I know, the only people who have ever lived here are two little old ladies. The woman who built this crazy old house, and my great-aunt."

"Just two old ladies, in this great big house?" Ruby frowned, thinking that Claire had mentioned a row of graves. If only two people had ever lived here, who was buried in the graveyard? *Who?* Her skin prickled and she began to feel shimmery, as if—

"I know how idiotic this sounds," Claire said. "But since you saw her when you were a kid, I figured you would believe me. At least, I *hoped* you'd believe me." She swallowed. "You do, don't you, Ruby?" When Ruby didn't answer right away, she put out her hand with a pleading look. "Please say you don't think I'm nuts. Tell me that this house really is haunted—that there's a ghost here, and that I'm not imagining all this crazy stuff."

Ruby's energy shield came up and the shimmering faded. She took a deep breath. "No, of course I don't. I believe you, Claire. In fact, I saw her myself, just this morning."

"You *did*?" Claire cried. "Oh, Ruby, that's *wonderful!*"

"Well, I don't know about that," Ruby said cautiously, and told Claire about stopping on the hill and looking down at the house and seeing the woman in the shirtwaist and skirt, carrying the basket of white roses.

"And then Sam showed up," she concluded, "and when I looked back, the woman was gone."

There was a crooked man

Ruby frowned. Why couldn't she get that silly nursery rhyme out of her mind? It kept repeating itself like a broken record.

"Good old Sam," Claire's laugh was brittle. "He seems to appear at just the right time, doesn't he? Or the wrong time, depending on how you look at it."

found a crooked sixpence

Claire looked at Ruby, half-tilting her head. "But I'm really glad you saw her—again, I mean. This morning. It means you didn't imagine her the first time. And I didn't imagine her, either."

Ruby tried to laugh. "But maybe we're both imagining it, Claire, then and now. You know—the power of suggestion."

Claire shook her head. "I know what I saw. And what you saw. And what I've heard." She leaned forward, her voice becoming quietly insistent.

"I hope I haven't scared you, Ruby. I don't want to chase you away. I need you. Say you'll stay and help me. Please. *Please*."

Ruby thought of her suitcase, still in the car, her car keys in her purse, little Grace with a sore throat, the shop and the tearoom that Ramona wanted to buy, and her other obligations. She pressed her lips together. She understood Claire's need, and she was sorry that all this was happening. But she was in way over her head here, and she was . . . she was scared. She had no business trying to deal with this situation. She should just go home. She glanced at her watch. If she left now, she'd be back at the shop before closing time.

She was opening her mouth to explain to Claire why she had to leave when the cell phone in her bag began to buzz. Then it swung into the first few bars of the old Buddy Holly song, "Raining in My Heart," Colin's favorite. He had downloaded it to her phone and she'd never changed it.

"Hey," she said, picking up her purse and fishing around for her cell. "I thought you said we couldn't get a signal here."

"Sometimes the magic works," Claire said with a shrug. "If it's a text, you might get it."

Ruby found her phone and flipped it open. That's what it was, all right. A text message. From China.

"Oh no!" she muttered, reading it, then reading it again. "Oh *no*!"

Claire frowned. "What's wrong?"

"Just about everything," Ruby replied distractedly, and read the message for the third time.

Ramona says Doris escaped. Hark says watch for TS Amanda. Amy says Grace needs tonsils out. Tonight. But we can handle. Stay where you are. Don't come home.

Chapter Five

The genus name *Iris* is derived from the Greek word for rainbow, referring to the wide variety of flower colors. In Greek mythology, Iris was the messenger of the gods and is usually depicted as descending from her home in the rainbow.

The rhizomes of three species of iris (*I. germanica, I. florentina,* and *I. pallida*) are known as orris and are prized in perfumery for their violet scent and their ability to fix other scents. The Egyptians and Greeks used orris to treat chest complaints. Pieces of the root were strung and worn around the neck as a protective charm—later, as rosary beads. In aromatherapy, essential oil of iris is used to soothe and calm. And in wetland management, *I. pseudacorus* (yellow iris) is being planted to purify water. The rhizomes are capable of consuming large amounts of *E. coli* and *Salmonella* bacteria, as well as excess nitrate from agricultural runoff.

In the language of flowers, the iris represented "I have a message for you." A blue iris flower symbolized the messenger, a red flower suggested a passionate message, and a yellow flower might be read in one of two ways: as representing cheer and warm feeling or deceit and cowardice.

China Bayles
"Herbs and Flowers That Tell a Story"
Pecan Springs Enterprise

After I saw Ruby off, the day turned into a busy one at Thyme and Seasons. Dawn was on the job, capably handling the Crystal Cave and the largish lunch crowd in the tearoom, where Cass had outdone herself with the food. (It's no wonder that the *Pecan Springs Enterprise* recently gave Cass a full-page feature, which has resulted in more lunch traffic and several more regular customers for the Thymely Gourmet.) Our guests could choose between Tomato Quiche with Basil and Green Onions, served with a cup of Spring Green Bisque; or a bowl of hearty Two-Bean Soup with Herbs, served with chunks of hot Garden-Style Cornbread. Both entrées came with Ruby's Romaine Salad and Orange-Ginger Dressing. And for dessert, there was Rose-Geranium Pound Cake with White Chocolate Glaze. Next time you're in Pecan Springs, stop in and see what's on the menu. Cass is always coming up with something different and delicious.

There's usually plenty of traffic in the early afternoon, when the lunch crowd migrates into the shops and the surrounding gardens. Thyme and Seasons and the Cave are situated in a 120-year-old building I bought when I cashed in my retirement account. It was built of native stone by the German stonemasons who constructed most of the early buildings here in Pecan Springs, as well as in the neighboring towns of San Marcos, New Braunfels, and Fredericksburg. All four were settled some 160 years ago by German immigrants who'd endured the long, miserable ocean voyage to Texas because the Old World was wall-to-wall people and Texas is (or was then, or at least seemed to be) a wide-open new world with room for all, if you could stand the heat. When you visit Pecan Springs, take some time to admire the vernacular German-influenced architecture. It's different from the Spanish hacienda style that's become a cliché in South Texas—and very special.

The Crystal Cave takes up half of the front of the building, the tearoom is in back, and Thyme and Seasons takes up the other front half. The hand-cut limestone walls, well-worn wooden floor, and beamed ceiling are a picture-perfect setting for the antique hutches and wooden shelves that I stock with herbal vinegars, oils, jellies, and teas. The old pine cupboard in the corner displays personal-care products: herbal soaps, shampoos, massage oils, fragrances, bath herbs. In the middle of the room, a wooden rack is filled with gallon jars of dried culinary and medicinal herbs, along with bottles of extracts and tinctures and aromatherapy products. There's a four-tiered bookshelf, as well as stationery and cards and gift baskets. Look around and you'll see that the walls are hung with seasonal wreaths and swags. There are buckets of fragrant potpourri in the corners, as well as tall stalks of dried sunflowers bound with cheerful yellow ribbon and woven baskets of artemisia, larkspur, yarrow, and tansy for dried arrangements.

When you go out the front door, turn left and follow the path around the corner. There you'll find racks of herbs for sale in six-inch and one- and two-gallon pots—all the usual culinary herbs (parsley, sage, rosemary, thyme, bay, chives), plus a good selection of medicinal and native plants. Follow the path, and it will take you through the theme gardens: the kitchen garden, the fragrance garden, the apothecary garden, the zodiac garden, and the dyers garden (the coreopsis is in bloom right now—the flowers yield a yellow, orange, or brown dye, depending on the mordant you use). Keep going and you'll find your way to the cottage where Kathleen Gips led her Language-of-Flowers workshop the week before.

Thyme Cottage began life, back in the horse-and-buggy days, as a stone stable. But the previous owner, an architect, reincarnated the building (by then a garage) as a lovely one-bedroom guesthouse with a fireplace, a built-in kitchen, and a hot tub in its own private patio garden. Ruby and Cass and I schedule workshops there, since the main room—we call it the

Gathering Room—is large enough to accommodate a crowd, and the open-plan kitchen is ideal for cooking and crafting demonstrations. When there's no workshop on the calendar, the cottage is available as a guest-house, which I advertise on the Internet and in the *Pecan Springs Bed-and-Breakfast Guide*. It's a good source of extra income, and only a little extra work.

I had just got the last lunch customer out the door and settled down to a few housekeeping chores when Ruby's sister phoned with a problem—a big one. Ramona was calling from the Castle Oaks Nursing Home, where Doris (Ruby's and Ramona's mother) lives in the Alzheimer's wing. Doris was one of those mothers who like to call the shots in the family. For instance, when Ruby was nineteen, pregnant, and unwed, Doris insisted that she give up the baby for adoption. It was a long time before Ruby could forgive Doris for interfering—and forgive herself for letting her mother bully her into doing something she didn't want to do. But a couple of decades later, the long-lost daughter found her way back into Ruby's life. Things were a little . . . well, tumultuous for a while, but Amy has made Ruby a proud grandmother. Both of them are still busy making up for lost time.

Meanwhile, Doris is no longer calling the shots. Instead, she has lost her marbles. After an agonizing few months trying to cope with distance care (Doris was living an hour's drive away, in Fredericksburg), Ruby and Ramona made the decision to move their mother to Castle Oaks, here in Pecan Springs. The nurses give her good care, and the facility tries to keep its patients under lock and key. But like many dementia patients, Doris has a tendency to wander. What's more, she's a wily old lady. Not long ago, she filched a coat and slipped out the front door with a gaggle of visitors. At the neighborhood supermarket, she liberated a bottle of apple juice and some Hershey bars. When a clerk asked for money, she told him that she had twenty-three million bucks in the bank but she couldn't remember where she'd left her checkbook. The clerk called the cops, and Doris got an armed escort back to Castle Oaks, which pleased her no end.

Doris was on the lam again today. Sightings had been reported from the H-E-B grocery; Walgreens, where Doris made off with a box of Clairol Ultra Light Natural Blonde and a giant-size bag of Cheetos; and Wag-A-Bag, where she dumped her Cheetos down the toilet, causing a flood in the ladies'. The Pecan Springs PD had been alerted and a Silver Alert posted. (The Silver Alert is modeled after the Amber Alert and lets people know that a senior with mental impairment has gone missing.)

Ramona, meanwhile, was about to go cruising, on the lookout for her errant mother. She was phoning to tell me that she hadn't had any luck reaching Ruby via her cell phone. She wanted a phone number for the place where Ruby was visiting so she could call and let her know that Doris had gone AWOL again—but that everything was under control because Ramona was in control. Ramona resembles her mother in that regard. She likes to call the shots.

"I don't have a number because Claire Conway doesn't have a phone," I said. "You could try texting."

"I don't know how," Ramona said. "I just got this phone, and I'm lucky to be able to turn it on. This thing is smarter than I am." She sighed, not bothering to conceal her vexation. "Well, if Ruby calls in, tell her not to worry—I'll find Mother. She doesn't try to conceal her whereabouts. It's just a matter of following the clues."

"Go get 'em, Sherlock," I said.

While I was talking to Ramona, a couple of customers had come in. I put the phone down, rang up *The Herb Society of America's Essential Guide to Growing and Cooking with Herbs* ($29.95, but worth every penny), two bars of home-crafted lavender-oatmeal soap ($1.25 each), and a very nice eighteen-inch-tall bay plant that would more than pay back its cost ($5.95) when the leaves were harvested next fall, and every fall thereafter.

I had just thanked the customer and said good-bye when Cass Wilde, looking warm and sweaty, came in from the tearoom. Cass has a personal style that's every bit as outrageous as Ruby's, and until last autumn, there was quite a bit more of her, so there was quite a lot more outrageousness. Since then, though, Cass has been on a personal weight-loss campaign. She's lost about twenty pounds with another twenty-five to go—for health reasons, she says, not because she thinks skinny looks better. "I believe in curves," she says. "I love soft. Angles and bones just don't do it for me."

She's also doing it for business reasons. Quite a few of Cass' customers are upscale singles who commute for a couple of hours a day, don't have time to cook, but want to improve their eating habits and keep their weight down. So she has developed a line of low-calorie, heart-healthy, home-delivered vegetarian gourmet meals, made with Texas-grown vegetables, many of which come from Mistletoe Creek Farm on Comanche Road, south of Pecan Springs. The farm's owner, Donna Fletcher, delivers Cass' order right to the kitchen, which ensures that the veggies are as fresh as they can be—another selling point. Unless people hang out at the Pecan Springs Farmers' Market on Saturday mornings or subscribe to Donna's weekly CSA baskets, they won't find fresher vegetables.

"I figured I'd better slim down some to advertise the new line," Cass says with a frank grin. Today she was wearing blue denim capris and tennies and a loose, blue cotton tee with pushup sleeves, her long blonde hair hanging loose under a blue denim baseball cap with a button pinned to it: *Eat Healthy or Die Early.* She's a good advertisement. Customers who knew her "before" can see the "after" difference.

"All done," she announced cheerfully, wiping her round face on her sleeve. "The kitchen is clean and tomorrow's lunch is queued up. And Big Red Mama is loaded and ready to rock and roll."

Big Red Mama is the beat-up red van we bought to replace our beat-up blue van a couple of years ago. Cass uses it for deliveries, Ruby uses it for the catering business, and I use it to haul plants. Mama's former owner was a Wimberley artist named Gerald, who got himself arrested for cooking crystal meth, which doesn't belong on anybody's menu. The Hays County sheriff confiscated Mama and put her up for sale in the semiannual sheriff's auction. When Ruby and I saw her, we fell in love with the wild designs that Gerald, perhaps under the influence of a certain mildly hallucinatory herb, had painted all over her squat red body. Cass says that Mama looks like a cross between a Crayola box on wheels and a Sweet Potato Queens' parade float.

"Sounds good," I said absently, making a note to call the nursery. The bay plant I'd just sold had been the last one. I hoped to reorder, but bay isn't the easiest plant to propagate, and the nursery always sells out early. "Safe travels, Cass. Oh, and better check Mama's right front tire. It looked a little low this morning."

I waited on several more people, then helped Dawn locate Ruby's last deck of Motherpeace tarot cards for a customer. I left her explaining the principles of the tarot to the woman, who had a great many questions, and began reshelving the herb and garden books. I try to keep them organized, more or less, to make restocking easier. I was jotting down a list of titles to reorder when the phone rang.

It was Hark Hibler, the editor of the *Pecan Springs Enterprise* and Ruby's current flame. That is, Hark has a flame thing for Ruby. Her feelings for him are considerably less incandescent. He got right to the point.

"If you're in touch with Ruby, please let her know that the little tropical wave out there in the Gulf has blown up into a full-fledged tropical storm. NOAA has just put out a warning."

"Really?" I was surprised. This was a little unusual. "It got promoted from wave to storm without sitting around for three or four days as a depression?"

"She."

I frowned. "She what?"

"*She* got promoted. Her name is Amanda, and she's already made landfall a little north of Corpus Christi. I thought Ruby should know. Just in case, I mean."

"I'm sure Ruby will be thrilled," I said drily. "But really, Hark, this place where she's gone to visit—it's nowhere near the coast."

"Oh." There was a silence. "I thought Ruby said she was going to Houston."

"No." Hark may be in the news business, but he doesn't always listen when you tell him something. "Halfway to Houston. Off 281, south of Round Top."

"Round Top," he said thoughtfully. "That's in Fayette County, isn't it?"

"Yup," I said, moving Jim Long's *Making Herbal Dream Pillows* back to the shelf where it belonged. It's a popular book. On the shelf, it tends to migrate.

"The *San Antonio Express-News* ran a story yesterday," Hark said. "It was about the oil companies buying up leases in Fayette County—all the land they can get their hands on. Looks like there's a fracking boom." Another silence. "Well, tell her anyway. Sometimes a storm like this can be pretty rainy. It can cause a lot of trouble if it happens to stall somewhere. Like Allison. Remember Allison?"

Allison was the first storm of the 2001 hurricane season. She came ashore at Freeport, then stalled over Houston, where she dumped thirty-five inches of rain overnight before she drifted back into the Gulf, then wound herself up and headed for Louisiana. Twenty-three people died in Texas; seventy thousand homes were flooded in Houston. On the Gulf, early-season storms can be nearly as bad as full-blown hurricanes. I had the feeling, though, that Hark wasn't really worried about Amanda. He was missing Ruby, and since he couldn't reach out and touch her, I was the next best thing. But I didn't say that.

"Of course I remember Allison," I replied. "Do you remember Josephine?"

"Do I ever," Hark said with a chuckle. "She was the hurricane that hit the weekend you and Mike got married." Pecan Springs is a couple hundred miles inland, but Central Texas occasionally gets slammed, especially when a hurricane landfalls around Victoria.

"The wedding party was marooned by high water," I said, remembering. For a while, all of us thought we were having fun—until the bridge went out. There was no champagne left at the end of that party. No food, either.

"Yeah," Hark said. "That was one for the record books. Well, tell Ruby anyway," he repeated. "Amanda, landfalling around Corpus, heading inland. She should keep an eye on the weather." He paused, then added a little shyly, "Oh, and give her my love." He hung up.

Twenty minutes later, just at two, the phone rang again. I picked it up quickly, thinking it might be Ramona reporting on the whereabouts of the fugitive Doris. But this time, it was Amy, Ruby's daughter, calling from the pediatrician's office. Grace's sore throat was worse, and the doctor had said that she needed to have her tonsils and adenoids out. Grace would be in the hospital overnight.

"It's not a terribly serious thing," Amy said, sounding like the grown-up she had become since she gave birth to Grace. "I'm sure Kate and I can manage. I don't want Mom to think she needs to come home—she's earned some time away from the shop. But she'll be upset if I don't let her know what's happening. I've tried her cell with no luck. Can you reach her, China?"

"Did you try texting?"

"No," Amy said, "I didn't. I thought she'd like to hear my voice so she could be sure I'm okay with Grace being in the hospital." There was a pause, and I could hear voices in the background. "Could you try, please? Oops, the doctor is looking for me. I have to go. Mega-thanks, China! I'll get back to you when we've got something definite." Click.

Now, my fingers are not as nimble as those of your average nine-year-old (although I probably spell better). I prefer to talk to my kids rather than text, so that I know they've gotten my message and can't ignore me. What's more, the smartphone that McQuaid gave me for my birthday auto corrects my fat-fingered typing, which has resulted in some funny and embarrassing messages. (I'm not the only one that grumbles about this. McQuaid told me he texted Blackie, his partner in the private investigation business, and asked him to "come here for a sec." His smartphone knew better: "Come here for a sex." And a friend of Ruby's once texted her that they had "just bought a large condom." It took a couple more messages to clarify that she meant "condo.")

But I gave it my best shot: *Ramona says Doris escaped. Hark says watch for TS Amanda. Amy says Grace needs tonsils out. Tonight. But we can handle. Stay where you are. Don't come home.*

I checked to make sure that the autocorrect genie hadn't taken the liberty of changing something, and hit send. Then I looked at my message again and wondered if I had been too blunt, too direct. Maybe I should've tried to soften it a little. Or split it up so there wasn't so much to read.

But it was what it was. Surely Ruby would understand.

Chapter Six

Garlic (*Allium sativum*), along with its cousins the onion, shallot, leek, and chive, is a member of the *Allium* family. In human use for more than six thousand years, garlic is native to central Asia. It was well known to the ancient Egyptians and has been used throughout its history for both culinary and medicinal purposes. The Greeks and Romans associated garlic with the planet Mars (the god of war) and used it to enhance stamina and as a blood cleanser and performance-enhancing male aphrodisiac (a kind of ancient Viagra). Garlic continues to be a staple of the Indian Ayurvedic healing system and an essential therapy in Chinese and Korean traditional medicine. In Europe, in plague season, it was worn around the neck and had the virtue of keeping possibly diseased people from getting too close.

Garlic has long been considered a powerful force against evil, the devil, and ghostly spirits. In the Mediterranean region, it was hung over the bed to protect from evil spirits or ghosts while sleeping. In Slavic countries, the magical powers of garlic were believed to guard against witches, vampires, and sorcerers. In India, a string of garlic, lemon, and red peppers was hung over the door to keep out evil influences, thieves, and unpleasant people. And in the familiar tale of Dracula, garlic is an effective vampire repellent.

In the language of flowers, garlic represents protection against evil. It has the additional meaning, "Go away. You're not wanted."

China Bayles
"Herbs and Flowers That Tell a Story"
Pecan Springs Enterprise

"What's wrong?" Claire repeated.

Ruby shut her phone with a snap. "You name it, it's wrong," she replied dispiritedly. "My mother is on the lam from her nursing home—again—and my sister is trying to find her. My sweet baby granddaughter has had a miserable sore throat, and she has to get her tonsils out, right away. And somebody named TS Amanda—whoever *he* is—is on his way to Pecan Springs. But China says they can handle it. They don't want me to come home. I'm supposed to stay where I am." Feeling suddenly sorry for herself, she made a whimpering noise. "I'm not wanted."

"I'm sorry about all that," Claire said sympathetically. "But don't you get it, Ruby? It's not just a message from your friend China, it's a warning from the powers that arrange such things. You're not supposed to go home. You're supposed to stay right here and help me deal with this . . . this whatever-it-is."

Ruby looked up. "You think?" Suddenly China's text message made a different kind of sense, like a message from the Ouija board. Important things were happening at home, yes, but China and Amy and Ramona could handle them. *Stay where you are. Don't come home.* It was as if the universe were giving her an assignment.

"I think," Claire said definitively.

"But I don't know *how* to deal with whatever is happening here," Ruby protested. "And to tell the truth, I've spent years trying to ignore my so-called gift. I can cope with it on a minimal level, as long as I don't take it seriously, but that's about all."

But Claire wasn't paying attention. She held up her hand and tilted her head, listening. Now she leaned forward. "Do you hear that, Ruby?" she whispered intently.

"Hear what?" Frowning, Ruby listened. "It's just the wind." Now that she actually *listened* to it, she realized that she had been hearing it for several minutes—an eerie sound that constantly changed in pitch, sometimes deep and hollow, like somebody blowing across the top of a bottle, sometimes high and whining, like a child crying.

"Right. The wind." Claire nodded knowingly. "But take a look out the window."

Ruby went to the window over the sink and looked out. The sky wore an oddly opaque sheen and the light seemed to be fading as she watched. She could hear the wind even more loudly now, rushing past the window with the sound of a gale. But the trees and grasses stood utterly as still as if they were frozen in the peculiar light. Not a leaf or a blade was stirring.

Ruby felt the goose bumps rise along her arms. "What in the—" She left the word hanging in the air.

"Yes." Claire joined her at the window. "Exactly. What in the world is going on here?"

"The wind—does it sound like this all the time?" Ruby asked.

"Pretty much, although it's intermittent. Sometimes I can barely hear it, other times it rattles the windows. But when I look outside, it's always dead calm. Not a breeze. Not even a breath." She lowered her voice. "This has got to be connected with the ghost, Ruby. Get her to leave and this will stop. As long as she's here, and these noises, I can't turn this place into a bed-and-breakfast. People will stay away in droves." She went back to the table and sat down. "I have no idea what the protocol is—how you talk to ghosts, I mean. But maybe you could find out what she wants."

What she wants? Ruby thought uneasily, following Claire back to the table. *Why would a ghost want anything? Would she* know *what she wants? And assuming that she wants something and knows what it is, how would I go about finding out? And then what?*

But Claire was going on with even more eagerness. "Yes, that's it, Ruby.

Find out what she wants, and let her know she can't keep hanging around. The noises have to stop, too."

"Are you sure about that?" Ruby asked tentatively. "Maybe you could advertise the place as a haunted B and B. You could tell people about this woman—that is, if you could find out who she is and something about her." She grinned, trying to make a joke of it. "You know, like the Lizzie Borden Bed and Breakfast, in Massachusetts. I read that they have a museum and a gift shop. They even serve a breakfast that's supposed to be the same breakfast that the Bordens ate before they were murdered—their last meal."

"Lizzie Borden?" Claire asked, frowning.

"You know. 'Lizzie Borden took an ax and gave her mother forty whacks. And when she saw what she had done, she gave her father forty-one.'"

"Good lord," Claire said faintly. "I'd forgotten about her. But she wasn't convicted, was she?"

"No. They never found out who did it—officially, that is. But all the evidence seemed to point to her."

Claire's eyes widened. "Ruby, you don't suppose our ghost was murdered, do you—*here*, in this house? And that's why she's hanging around here?"

"I don't have the slightest idea." Ruby thought of the headstones in the cemetery. "I don't think there's any law that says that only victims get to be ghosts," she added in a lower voice. "I suppose it's even possible that a ghost could be the murderer."

"I hadn't thought of that." Claire pulled her brows together. "You mean, *she* could have killed somebody? In this *house*?"

Ruby shrugged. "I don't see why not."

"Let's not go there, okay?" Claire said nervously. "And as far as the idea of advertising the haunting— Well, maybe the Borden ghosts aren't real. Maybe they're just a way to attract customers. This one is for *real*, Ruby. I don't think I could keep my guests if one of them happened to catch a glimpse of her up on that widow's walk, staring out into the distance. She is just too creepy." Claire put out a hand. "You will help, won't you?"

"How can I help when I don't have a clue?" Ruby asked matter-of-factly. "I don't do séances. I've never tried to talk to the dead—or the un-dead. I don't know why the ghost would want to communicate with me."

"Undead." Claire shivered. "I wish you wouldn't put it that way."

"What other way is there to put it? Anyway, how would we know if we were successful? Maybe she'd only pretend to go away and then come back later. It's not like we can ask her to punch in and out on a time clock."

"You won't know if you don't try," Claire pointed out. "Anyway, there's no penalty for failure."

How do you know? Ruby wondered, thinking of those headstones. *And what if there's a penalty for* trying? She pressed her lips together. "Honestly, Claire. I . . . I don't think I'm qualified. How about asking a priest? Priests do exorcisms. They say prayers and burn incense and the spirits get scared or something and go away."

"I don't know any priests," Claire replied. "But I know *you*. And you've seen *her*—twice now, years apart. That qualifies you."

Ruby had to admit that it sounded reasonable, especially when she was getting messages telling her not to go home. But maybe there was another way to approach this. She picked up her glass and sipped her tea. "You said you inherited this place. How much land is there?"

"About fifteen hundred acres."

"Fifteen hundred!" Ruby exclaimed. "Wow. That's a lot—even for Texas. Why don't you just sell it and use the money to buy another B and

B, if that's what you want to do? That way, the ghost is somebody else's problem."

"I would if I could." Claire sounded wistful. "But I can't. I have to live here."

Ruby frowned. "I don't—"

"It's complicated," Claire said. "Long story short, my great-aunt Hazel was a companion to Mrs. Blackwood, the woman who built this house. They lived here for decades, just the two of them, never going anywhere. Mrs. Blackwood died in her late nineties and left the house and her money to Hazel. The house was hers to live in and dispose of at her death. But if she went to live somewhere else, the house would be torn down and the acreage and any money would go to the church camp. The camp property adjoins this, on the north side."

"But that was your great-aunt Hazel," Ruby pointed out. "What about—"

Claire raised her hand. "Chapter one was Mrs. Blackwood. Chapter two was Aunt Hazel. She lived here until she died, never married, never had kids. Upon her death, she left the property to her niece, my aunt Ruth. There wasn't much money by that time—bad investments, I guess— although there was enough to repair and modernize the place. But Aunt Hazel imposed the same condition. If Ruth didn't live in this house, the house would be razed and the church camp would get the land."

Ruby felt as if she had missed something. "Your aunt Ruth? But I thought *you* inherited it."

"Be patient. Now we're in Chapter three, Aunt Ruth's chapter. She kept telling the lawyers she was moving out here, although I'm pretty sure she had no idea of doing anything of the sort—she was just trying to figure out a way to get around the requirement. Anyway, things dragged along for several years until the lawyers for the church camp got tired of waiting and threatened to sue, since Aunt Ruth wasn't living up to the terms of Aunt Hazel's will. Then Ruth complicated things still more by getting herself killed in an automobile accident." Claire sighed. "End of Aunt Ruth's chapter."

"Oh dear," Ruby murmured sympathetically.

Claire nodded. "Yeah, really. After Mom died, Aunt Ruth was all the family I had left. But things got complicated—legally, I mean—when it turned out that she didn't have a will. I was her closest kin, but I wasn't in a position to accept the bequest right away, because—" Her glance slid away. "Because I was . . . well, in rehab."

"Oh," Ruby said, and with this second mention of rehab, the pieces clicked into place. The long silence after Brad died. The times she had called but Claire wasn't available and hadn't returned her calls. Rehab. Addiction. It all made sense. "I'm sorry, Claire. I know you've had a difficult time."

Claire straightened her shoulders. "My own fault, I guess. I haven't been able to get over Brad's death. Somehow, I've gotten stuck. I can't break away from the past, from Brad, from losing him. I just keep wallowing in my grief. The sleeping pills and alcohol—they're only another way to dull the pain." She eyed Ruby. "I guess you know about that, after losing Colin. The pain, I mean," she added, "not the rest of it. You're not the wallowing type."

Ruby smiled a little. "Well, there are lots of ways to wallow. I haven't done pills or booze, but that doesn't mean I don't—" She stopped. This wasn't about her and her troubles, it was about Claire.

"I actually thought I was going to make it," Claire said. "I'd been thinking of leaving the magazine anyway. I had been hired to ghostwrite the memoir of a woman entertainer. I won't tell you her name because I signed a nondisclosure agreement, but you'd recognize it. She's a big-name singer in the Texas music business. Plus I had a couple of freelance editing projects on the desk. The trouble was, though, that I'd been taking sleeping pills since Brad's death. And I was drinking again, too. And between the grief and the pain and those god-awful bills, I was a mess. Things finally got so bad, I didn't have any choice but to go for treatment. Then Aunt Ruth got killed, and when I got out of rehab, I discovered that I had inherited this place, together with just enough money to fix it up. My career was in shreds and I didn't have a way to support myself. I'm sure you can guess how I felt."

"That it was a gift from heaven, I suppose," Ruby said. *From heaven? If there was a ghost involved, did heaven have anything to do with it?*

"Exactly. A gift from heaven." Claire nodded emphatically. "I figured I could live here, build up my ghostwriting and editorial work, maybe even write that novel I've been thinking about. But the writing won't bring in enough money. The house itself will have to produce an income. That's why I thought of a B and B."

Ruby thought about what Monica had told her and what she had read in the newspaper. "Do you own the mineral rights as well? You could sell them, couldn't you?"

"Yes, but that's not the answer," Claire replied. "It doesn't matter what the oil companies are paying for a lease. The chemicals they use for fracking can get into the groundwater, not to mention the huge amounts of water they pump out of the aquifer to force up the gas. And there's all the noise and the trucks tearing up and down the roads, and I wouldn't have any control over where they put their wells." She shook her head violently. "No. No lease. Period. End of story."

"I see your point," Ruby said.

Claire was going on. "I've *got* to make this work, Ruby." Her eyes filled with tears, and she reached for a paper napkin on the table. "It's my last chance."

Ruby's heart went out to her. She knew exactly how Claire felt, for she had gone through the same thing after Colin was murdered: the sense of hopeless loss, of despair, of nothing left to look forward to. Grief was a terrible thing. It could drown you. It could flood your soul. It could suck out every bit of hope you had for the future and shriek for more.

After a moment, Claire blew her nose. "I'm sorry," she muttered, balling up the napkin in her fist. "It's just that I'm desperate, Ruby. No family, no income, no home—except for this place." She wiped her eyes with the back of her hand. "But to make it work, I have to get rid of whatever or whoever is in this house."

Ruby was silent, wondering whether a haunted house was the best place for a recovering alcoholic to live. But it sounded as if it might be Claire's last, best hope. They might not have seen each other often in the last few years, but Claire had been a friend for a very long time, and she needed help.

And there was something else, too. Deep down inside, Ruby was scared—not just tense or nervous but truly terrified—at the thought of somehow using her gift to explore the energies that seemed to have collected in this house. But at the same time, she realized that there were questions here she wanted answers to, mysteries that needed solving, things she urgently wanted to *know*. Who was the woman she and Claire had seen? Why was she here? The things that Claire had heard and seen in the house, and those headstones out there in the graveyard—what was all that about? She was surprised by the insistent power of the curiosity that had suddenly seized her.

The silence stretched out. The noise of the wind had disappeared, but the sky outside the kitchen window was darker and in the distance, there was another long, low rumble of thunder.

"Finish your pie," Ruby ordered. "And then you can give me the tour of the house. Assuming we're not frightened off by your ghost, that is." Playfully, she raised her voice. "You hear that, house? Behave yourself! No harp, no bell—"

Behind her, in the rack over the table, pans rattled loudly.

Startled, Ruby turned in her chair. The two pans in the middle of the rack banged together once again, violently. Then the movement subsided and the pans hung innocently, side by side. The wind? But the kitchen door was shut, and so was the window. And outside, the trees were still, the leaves pale in the peculiar light.

"You see?" Claire's smile was crooked. "That's what I'm talking about. Just a few little everyday noises. The wind blowing, pans banging, a ball bouncing. Nothing to be afraid of—right?"

"I think we should find ourselves a priest," Ruby muttered.

There was another rumble of thunder. Ruby thought it almost sounded like a chuckle.

Chapter Seven

Galveston
Afternoon, September 8, 1900

"At 3:30 p.m. [2:30 Galveston time] I took a special observation to be wired to the Chief at Washington. The message indicated that the hurricane's intensity was going to be more severe than was at first anticipated. About this time, my brother [Isaac Cline, chief of the Bureau's Texas Section] paused in his warnings long enough to telephone from the beach the following fact, which I added to the message: 'Gulf rising rapidly; half the city now under water.' Had I known the whole picture, I could have altered the message at the time of its filing to read, 'Entire city under water.'"

> *When the Heavens Frowned*
> Joseph Cline, Assistant Observer
> Galveston Weather Bureau

Hunched over his desk on the third floor of the Levy Building, Joseph Cline spent a few precious moments encrypting his telegraph message to Willis Moore at the Washington Weather Bureau so that it could not be easily read along the route. If it were known (in Houston, for instance) that Galveston could be flooded by a storm, the city's reputation as a port might be damaged. By the time he ventured out to the Western Union office, the surging water along the Strand—the street that ran along the western side of Galveston, beside Galveston Bay—was already knee-deep, filling his rubber boots. The wooden paving blocks had popped up and were bobbing in great flotillas along the street, so that Joseph had to fight his way through them as well as through the water. The wind, gusting at over fifty miles an hour, was ripping slates from the roofs of buildings and sending them hurtling through the air. There was a fateful irony here, for after a great fire had swept through the city in 1885, the city fathers had mandated that the roofs be constructed of slate instead of wooden shingles. Now, the slates designed to protect the city from fire had been turned into deadly missiles by the wind, and Joseph found that he had to duck and whirl to avoid being slashed.

It was only a few blocks, but every step was a battle, and Joseph, still a young man at twenty-nine and strong, was near exhaustion when at last he reached the Western Union office. He was astonished to learn that the wires had been down for two whole hours. What's more, the clerk told him, the railroad bridge across the bay was now underwater and the trains had stopped running. In fact, a relief locomotive had had to be sent out to rescue the passengers on the 9:45 from Houston. They were safe, but the noon train from Beaumont hadn't been heard from and was feared stranded—or worse. Normally, it stopped at the tip of the Bolivar Peninsula to transfer its passengers to the *Charlotte M. Allen* to be ferried across the two-mile-wide ship channel. But today, the wind had prevented the ferry from docking at the Bolivar pier. Later, it would be learned that ten passengers had abandoned the train and made for the Point Bolivar lighthouse, a quarter mile away. It was constructed of brick sheathed with metal plates, and it already housed some two hundred refugees, crammed into the staircase that spiraled a hundred feet to the top, where the kerosene-fueled light still shone out through the storm. Eighty-five passengers stayed with the train, trusting that its massive weight would withstand the winds and surging waters. It was the wrong choice. By Sunday morning, when the survivors emerged from the lighthouse, the train was gone, and with it, all sign of their fellow passengers.

But Joseph was determined to send his telegram. Thinking that the Postal Telegraph might still be operating, he struggled to the nearby post office, where a woman, white-faced and tense, told him that he was too late. Their wires were down as well. There was no telegraph service out of Galveston. He had heard about the second floor of Ritter's Café smashing in on top of the first-floor restaurant, had he? So many dead, even more injured and some couldn't be pulled out because the rescuers were afraid that the rest of the brick building would be blown in at any moment, or the building next door would go down, and even more would be killed. She was closing the office right now, collecting her sister and her children, and seeking refuge in City Hall, where they would be safe.

Joseph was incredulous at the news of the collapse. At first he doubted the woman, but because the restaurant was less than two blocks from the Weather Bureau, he went to see. He was horrified by the sight of the wreckage, and even more by the helplessness of the dazed and rain-soaked onlookers. Wasn't safe to go in to get the dead and injured, they muttered, shaking their heads. Nothing could be done until the wind dropped. Seeing Joseph and recognizing him, they gathered around him eagerly. What did the Weather Bureau say, eh? How bad would it get? When would it be over? *When?*

"It doesn't look good, boys," Joseph replied grimly. "Afraid it's going to get worse before it gets better." And with that, he made his way back to the Weather Bureau offices. Now desperate to get his message to Washington, he took his last shot: he picked up the phone and tried to call the Western

Union office in Houston. The Galveston long-distance operator was ada-
mant: there were thousands of calls ahead of him. Joseph would simply
have to wait his turn.

But after putting his case to the telephone office manager and pleading
that this was a vital Federal government message that had an emergency
priority, Joseph at last got through to Houston. He dictated his telegram,
stressing that it was highly confidential. He didn't want officials in the rival
port city to know about Galveston's dire plight.

A few blocks away, at the John Sealy Hospital, the anonymous letter-
writer added one more paragraph to her letter: "Am beginning to feel a
weakening desire for something to cling to. Should feel more comfortable
in the embrace of your arms. You hold yourself ready to come to us should
the occasion demand?"

Shortly after the writer finished her letter and Joseph completed his
telephone call, the long-distance wires went down. No rail, no telegraph,
no telephone. Galveston was now completely cut off from the rest of the
world. The horrors that were to come that night would be remembered
only by those who witnessed them—and who lived to tell the terrible tale.

AT the Blackwood house on Q Avenue, Rachel was holding the fort as best
she could. Augustus still had not come home, so she had directed Pokey,
the man who did their outside work, to fasten the wooden shutters over the
windows and secure anything that might be blown away. The electricity
had gone out, and while there was still light, she and Patsy, the children's
nurse, gathered the household supply of kerosene lamps and set them out
on the round oak pedestal table in the kitchen. Rachel and Matthew and
the twins made a game of lighting one after another in turn to make sure

that they still worked, while Ida carefully polished the chimneys and Angela looked on from Patsy's arms, clapping her hands—although Patsy herself was white-faced and frightened.

That chore done, Rachel focused all her efforts on behaving in as ordinary a way as possible. But as the wind rose, the rain lashed the windows, and the house trembled more noticeably than ever, she, too, could feel the panic rising inside her. She needed her husband. And Mrs. O'Reilly, who had a way of calmly managing in a crisis. Colleen had gone home several hours ago, but she had left a plate of chicken salad sandwiches—cut into tiny shapes to please the children—and sugar cookies and a pitcher of lemonade.

Now, Rachel laid the dining room table with a pretty cloth and crystal plates and glasses and the morning's bowl of white roses—the last she would likely see this year, for the garden was already inundated by the surging brown water. Then she poured the lemonade and put on a shawl. She would go out on the front gallery to watch for their father, she told the children. He would surely be along any minute now, and when he came, there would be such fun! Matthew could open his presents and blow out his candles and they would all have a piece of birthday cake—two pieces, if they liked, for it was a large cake and the storm would keep the neighborhood families from joining them for the party. And after that, they would have music.

But when she went out onto the gallery, Rachel could see how much higher the waters had risen around the house, and she grew more frightened. The wind had shifted farther to the east and was blowing much harder. Where in the world was Augustus? It had been noon when they'd talked, and his lunches—even his leisurely businessman's lunches at Ritter's—never took more than an hour. He had promised to come straight home if the storm hadn't let up by the time he was finished eating. The bank could do without him for one afternoon, he had said, and Rachel had fervently agreed.

Well, the storm had definitely *not* let up. The water was lapping at the fourth step of the gallery, a good five feet above the ground. Then, with a gasp of sheer terror, she saw the roof—the entire roof, all in one piece!—snatched from the single-story Baxter house, down the block on the Gulf side of the street, and sent tumbling over and over like a giant's open book. A moment later, the Baxter house slumped into the surging water.

Rachel clung to a gallery post, breathing in short, hard gasps. How amazingly lucky it was that the Baxters were not in the house! Mr. Baxter had gone to San Antonio on business earlier in the week. Mrs. Baxter had become so nervous that, two hours ago, when the water on Q Avenue had risen knee-deep, she had gone with her sister to seek refuge in the Tremont Hotel, pausing to knock at the Blackwoods' front door and ask Rachel if she wouldn't go with them.

Rachel had been torn. She had already found herself wishing that she and the children had gone to the Ursulines with Mrs. O'Reilly. But to leave seemed to her a betrayal of her husband's confidence in the storm-worthy house he had built for them. She would stay where they were, she told Mrs. Baxter. Mr. Blackwood would be home shortly. And the storm would surely blow itself out soon.

But that had been two hours ago, and things were much worse. She peered through the sheeting rain and saw with a leap of her heart a man coming down the street, bent over against the wind and struggling to wade through the rushing water. A breathless moment later, she saw that it wasn't her husband but their neighbor, Isaac Cline, on his way home from his work at the Weather Bureau.

She tried to swallow her disappointment. "Mr. Cline!" she called, and waved to attract his attention. "Mr. Cline, is there any news about the storm? Will it let up before dark?"

But the wind was so loud that she had to repeat her question when Mr. Cline had waded through the yard and stood at the foot of the steps up to the front gallery. His face drawn with worry and strain, he spoke gravely. "I wish I could tell you that it will be over before nightfall, my dear Mrs. Blackwood, but I can't. The wind is swinging around to the east. This will raise the level of the tide, so there is likely to be more flooding."

More flooding? More than . . . what? Rachel pushed down a rush of hysteria and asked, "And the wind?"

"Oh, a bit stronger, I should think." He paused. "You're not alone? Your husband is with you?"

"He went to Ritter's for lunch," she said. "I haven't heard from him since—although of course the telephone lines are down," she added, not wanting to sound like an accusing wife. "I'm sure he'll be along any minute. My housekeeper and her family went to the Ursulines, and Mrs. Baxter and her sister went to the Tremont. I was just wondering whether I should perhaps have gone, too."

"Ritter's?" Mr. Cline's tone was jarring and there was something in his eyes that made her suddenly afraid.

"Has there been—" She stopped. No, surely not. Ritter's was in the heart of Galveston's energetic commercial quarter and was patronized by the most prominent businessmen. There could be very little flooding there, and the buildings, all of them well built and three and four stories high, would break the wind.

Mr. Cline seemed to consider her unfinished question for a moment. Then he replied, in a soothingly careless tone, "Oh well, not to worry. I'm sure he's just been detained. In places, the flooding has made it a bit of a challenge to get around. As far as your safety is concerned, I believe that

101

you and the children will be as secure here as you would anywhere in the city. But while you're waiting for Mr. Blackwood, you might move your most valued possessions to the second floor—and perhaps the papers from Mr. Blackwood's desk, as well. That way, they will be safe from any flooding that might occur."

"Move our possessions—" She stared at him, then looked down at the level of the water. In the little while she had been standing on the gallery, the water had risen from the fourth to the fifth step—the fifth of seven. Two more feet and it would come in through the front door.

She picked up her skirt. "Why, yes, of course," she said with a forced cheerfulness. "What an excellent suggestion, Mr. Cline. It's something that the children can help with—while they're waiting for their father."

Mr. Cline smiled cordially. "Very good, Mrs. Blackwood," he said. "I shall wish you a pleasant afternoon, then." He bowed slightly and lifted his hat exactly as if the two of them had been chatting on the beachfront promenade. Then he waded away, stepping aside to avoid a bobbing barrel labeled *Pickled Herring*.

"Mama! Mama!" Behind her, Matthew was shouting excitedly. "Mrs. O'Reilly's come back for the party! And she's all wet!"

Rachel turned. There, in the front doorway, stood strong, capable Colleen O'Reilly, her carroty hair in a tumble of wet curls around her shoulders, her skirt—soaked literally to the waist—clinging wetly to her legs, her Irish freckles standing out like brick crumbs across her nose and cheeks.

"I'll have t' trouble you for somethin' dry to wear, ma'am," she said apologetically. "It's a mite deep out there, and the rain's pourin' down to beat the band."

"But I thought you were going to the Ursulines!" Rachel exclaimed, astonished. "Where you'd be safe."

Little Ida came running with a towel, and Mrs. O'Reilly wrapped it turban-style around her wet hair. "I did that, ma'am. I took Mother and me little Annie and left 'em in the sisters' good hands. And then I thought . . . Well, I thought of you by yourself and that you might be needin' me, so here I am."

Rachel, nearly overcome with relief, thought she had never been so glad to see anyone in all her life. "Thank you," she whispered. "Thank you!"

"No need for thanks," Mrs. O'Reilly said sturdily. "I'm glad to do it."

Matthew was hanging on her arm. "We've only had sandwiches," he said. "We were hoping you'd come back in time to see me blow out my candles."

"Well, I did, didn't I?" Mrs. O'Reilly twinkled at the children. "An' now that I'm here, we can do it up proper." Then she did a very strange thing. She held out her hand to Rachel as if they were friends or even sisters.

And they all went back into the house together.

Chapter Eight

In the language of flowers, several plants might be used to convey the same message, but with subtle differences that were known to the people of the period.

Protection against lightning and storms: Mistletoe (*Viscum album*) was thought to have been planted in trees by bolts of lightning; hence, mistletoe hung in a house would protect against lightning and storms. In the language of flowers: "I overcome all."

Protection against evil: The Greeks offered the smoke of burning juniper branches to the gods of the underworld, and juniper berries were burned at funerals to ward off evil spirits. In the language of flowers: "I protect."

Protection against disease: Feverfew (*Tanacetum parthenium*) was once used as a treatment for fevers, flu, sore throats. Leaves of the plant were bound around the wrists at the first sign of a fever. In the language of flowers: "I remedy."

Protection against violence: The crushed leaves of pennyroyal (*Mentha pulegium*) have been used since ancient times as a flea repellent. A tea made of the leaves was used to induce abortions. (Ingested, the essential oil can be a deadly poison.) Ritually, pennyroyal was used to protect against domestic violence. In the language of flowers: "Flee! Escape!"

China Bayles
"Herbs and Flowers That Tell a Story"
Pecan Springs Enterprise

Ruby kept a wary eye on the pot rack while they finished their pie, but the pans hung motionless and quiet, not a peep out of them.

"I guess that was just the house's way of saying hello and welcome," Claire said with a crooked smile. "We're lucky. It might have been a broken window. Or a puddle in the hall."

"That I would like to have seen," Ruby said. Then she thought better of what she'd said and added, loudly, "On second thought, maybe not so much."

Claire pushed back her chair and stood up. "Come on. I want to show you around the main floor. Leave your stuff here—we'll take it upstairs later."

Ruby followed her out of the kitchen and into a wide, oak-paneled hallway that stretched the length of the house. Oddly, the incongruous *wrongness* of the outside didn't seem to persist inside, and things seemed in decent repair. It wouldn't take much work to make the wood floors gleam. The brass fittings of the old-fashioned wall sconces could use a polishing, although they were clean and unbroken. When the dark Victorian wallpaper above the paneling was replaced with something lighter and a few pictures and potted plants were added, the hallway would be gorgeous.

"Mrs. Blackwood and Aunt Hazel seem to have neglected the exterior," Claire said, "maybe because they didn't like the idea of strange workmen coming around. But indoors, they took care of things. Of course, there's still a lot to be done. Old draperies and rugs that need replacement and furniture that should be reupholstered or gotten rid of—that sort of thing." She opened a French door. "This is the dining room."

Ruby followed her into a large room, the walls richly wainscoted in oak with wine-and-gold wallpaper and a ceiling that featured a crystal chandelier hung above a long table of polished mahogany. On the opposite wall were four French doors that opened out onto what might have once been a rose garden. At one end stood a tall, glass-fronted cabinet filled with fine china; at the other, nearest the kitchen, was a large sideboard. The oriental carpet still glowed with vivid reds and blues.

"Amazing," Ruby muttered, counting. "Sixteen, seventeen, eighteen chairs! Mrs. Blackwood must have intended to throw some big dinner parties. I wonder where she thought she'd find the guests, way out here. Invite them from Houston, maybe?"

Claire chuckled wryly. "Aunt Hazel said there never were any parties. At least, not in her day. She came here to live in 1925 when she was sixteen years old. And she died here at the age of ninety-six."

Ruby did a quick calculation. "Eighty years," she marveled. "Imagine living in one house for that long and never seeing anyone. I'd go crazy."

"I can't begin to imagine it," Claire replied. "But Aunt Hazel always seemed content, at least when I knew her." She grinned crookedly. "And no, I don't think she was crazy. She was in her early sixties when old Mrs. Blackwood died, and my mother invited her to come and live with us in Smithville. But she wouldn't. She said she liked it here. This was her home."

"Did she ever mention the . . . ghost?" Ruby asked warily.

"Not to me," Claire said. "And my mother died a few years ago, so we can't ask her." Then, as if she wanted to get on with the tour, she pointed to the china cabinet. "Mr. Hoover had the good china—it's Haviland and very old—put into storage when he was thinking of renting the place. He sent it back a few days ago, and I unpacked it and put it in the cabinet. There's a box of silver to put away, too. I think I'll put it in that sideboard . . ."

Her voice trailed off. The sideboard was a large, mahogany affair. Over it hung a large, gilt-framed oil painting of what looked like a tropical garden paradise: oleanders, palms, roses, and, in the distance, a white sand beach and a great blue-green ocean. As Ruby and Claire looked at it, the painting tilted slightly.

Ruby cleared her throat. "Did you see *that*?" she said into Claire's ear.

"I guess I forgot to mention that one," Claire said apologetically. "For some reason, that painting simply doesn't want to hang straight. I mean, I could go over there and straighten it, and two minutes later it would be tilted again."

Ruby bit her lip. "You think the ghost . . . ?"

"I don't know what I think," Claire countered. "What do *you* think?"

Back in the hall, Ruby tried to collect her thoughts. "You said you've done some research on the house. When was it built?"

"Around 1910, I understand," Claire said. "Mrs. Blackwood drew up the plans herself, according to Aunt Hazel. That's why it looks so strange on the outside, so sort of . . . mismatched. Crooked. Like parts of it don't fit."

"So you noticed it, too," Ruby said. *And they all lived together in a little crooked house.*

"How can you miss?" Claire asked with a shrug. "But there's a reason for that. Aunt Hazel told my mother that Mrs. Blackwood had a house just like this once—a house that was destroyed. She tried to reconstruct it from memory, but she didn't get parts of it quite right. The builder attempted to fix some of the worst things as he went along, but Mrs. Blackwood knew what she wanted." She paused. "There are some old scrapbooks and papers in the library. Maybe we could sit down with them one evening. They might help us learn more about—"

"What was *that*?" Ruby whispered, startled.

Claire shook her head. "Sorry. I didn't—"

Then they both heard it. The musical sound of harp strings jangling, as if they'd been swept by light fingers. The hair rose on the back of Ruby's neck.

Claire grinned at Ruby. "I'm braver, now that you're here." With a flourish, she opened a double door. "This is the music room. Suppose we'll see our ghost?"

But to Ruby's huge relief, they saw no one. The room was carpeted and furnished with a sofa and several comfortable chairs, including a child's little red rocking chair. The space was large enough not to appear crowded by the Steinway grand piano at one end. A gold-colored silk shawl was thrown carelessly across the piano bench, the lid was open over the keys, and a piece of sheet music was spread on the rack. A silver flute lay across the piano top. The harp stood beside the piano.

Ruby stepped forward quickly and placed the palm of her hand over the strings. She jerked her hand back quickly, as though her fingers had been burned. "Still vibrating!" she exclaimed in a wondering tone. Whatever was going on here, it wasn't in Claire's imagination, or in hers, either. It was in the house.

"When I was a girl," Claire said quietly, "this room always looked pretty much the way it does now. The sheet music for Scott Joplin's 'Maple Leaf Rag' was on the piano and the shawl was on the bench and the flute was lying on the top of the piano—at least, that's how I remember it. I found the things—the music, the shawl, the flute—in a cupboard and put them back where they belonged." She frowned. "I haven't found the pipe yet, though."

"The pipe?" Ruby asked. "As in whistle?"

"As in smoke." Claire pointed to a large green glass ashtray on the table beside the sofa. "There was always a pipe in that ashtray. It struck me as odd when I was a girl, since there were no men living here."

Ruby picked up the ashtray, feeling the smooth, solid heft of it. It was engraved with an image of a columned building and the words *Galveston National Bank, a Leader for Business*. She put the ashtray back on the table.

"You said you put the things back where they belong—you said it about the china, as well. Did you start doing that before or after you heard the harp strings jangling?"

"Gosh, I don't know." Claire sounded puzzled. "Does it matter?"

"It might," Ruby replied thoughtfully. They were back in the hallway now. "I'm just wondering if you were somehow . . . well, prompted to put things back. The flute, the shawl, the china—put them back the way they once were, I mean." Like props on a stage set, she was thinking.

"Prompted—by whom?" Claire's voice was sharp and she looked frightened.

"That's the question, isn't it?" Ruby countered. They were standing at the foot of the grand staircase now, and she hazarded a look upwards into the dimness, half-expecting to see the woman in the gray skirt with the Gibson Girl hair, as she had seen her all those years ago. But the stairs, as far as she could see, were empty.

"If that's the question, I don't think I want to answer it," Claire said grimly, and threw open another pair of doors on the opposite side of the hall. She took a deep breath. "And here we have the drawing room. Aunt Hazel kept it shut up. She told me once that it was much too grand for her. She said she always felt like a servant when she went into it." She hesitated and added, with a half-defiant lift of her eyebrow, "In case you're wondering, I moved a few things around, back to the way I remembered when I was a kid. So far as I know, I wasn't prompted, but I suppose it's possible."

It was a very large, very grand room, Ruby saw, with a massive fireplace and marble mantel topped by a gilded mirror and an ornate ormolu clock that showed it was not quite three. The stained-glass windows—brilliantly colored floral patterns in shades of green and blue—were framed in green velvet swags. The light that shone through them was subtly shaded, so that a dim, mysterious glow filled the room, almost as if it were underwater. There was an elaborately upholstered and buttoned green velvet love seat with matching chairs. A half dozen other ornate chairs and footstools and marble-topped tables were arranged in various groupings, as if to entertain a large number of afternoon callers. The doilies and knickknacks and vases of silk flowers on the tables gave the look of carefully planned Victorian clutter. There was a faint scent of violet perfume in the air that made Ruby want to sneeze.

"You don't suppose," she said, "that those are genuine *Tiffany* windows?"

"Oh, I don't think so," Claire replied, surprised. "Surely Mr. Hoover would have mentioned it if they were. They'd be worth a tremendous fortune."

"If they were," Ruby replied significantly, "they would be a tremendous tourist attraction. Art lovers would come just to gawk at your windows. They'd never get around to noticing your ghost."

Claire rolled her eyes. "I wish you would cut that out, Ruby. She's your ghost as much as she's mine. In fact, you saw her first."

"But she lives in your house," Ruby pointed out with a teasing smile. "Don't you think that qualifies as—"

She was interrupted by a sudden loud tinkle. Claire clutched her arm. "It's the bell I've heard tinkling," she said, sounding frightened. "It's *here*, in this room!"

Ruby turned around. There was no one else there but the two of them. The room was empty. And then, with a merry little jingle, the bell sounded again. "It's coming from over there!" Ruby said, pointing, and went toward a green velvet wing chair in the corner, a table beside it.

The chair had white crocheted antimacassars on the back and arms and a small footstool in front of it. It was a lady's chair, Ruby thought, and could almost picture old Mrs. Blackwood sitting there in the darkening twilight. The table beside it held a lamp, several books, a basket with a small piece of delicate, half-finished embroidery, and a small brass bell with an ornate handle. The kind of bell Mrs. Blackwood might ring to summon a servant.

Ruby picked up the bell and rang it, then silenced it and put it down quickly. It was the bell they had just heard. "It's the same bell you were hearing earlier?" she asked. "The one you mentioned to me?"

"Yes." Claire's eyes were large and round. "Of course, I had no idea where the sound was coming from." She swallowed. "And the violet scent. Did you smell it?"

"When I first came into the room," Ruby replied. She sniffed. "Yes, very faint, but I can still smell it." That was what had made her want to sneeze.

Claire backed toward the door. "Let's get out of here." She shut the door behind them. And then, as they stood there, they heard the bell inside the room. It rang with an imperious tone, fell silent for a moment, then rang again, more impatiently.

"Maybe she wants us to bring tea," Claire said tentatively.

"I vote that we ignore it." Ruby lifted her chin. "I don't bring tea. Or do floors."

Claire folded her arms. "And I don't do windows." She raised her voice. "No tea, no floors, no windows—hear?" Their shared nervous laughter seemed to make them both a little braver.

The bell rang violently and kept on ringing, then stopped abruptly, as if someone had silenced the clapper.

Claire shook her head. "Do you see what I'm up against?"

Ruby took a deep breath, opened the drawing room door, and looked inside. The brass bell stood on the table where they had left it, and the chair was empty. But the violet scent was noticeably heavier and, out of the corner of her eye, she glimpsed a light, quick movement and heard the soft swish of a long skirt. She closed the door firmly.

"See anything?" Claire's voice was thin.

"Definitely haunted," Ruby replied with a shudder. She ticked off the rooms on her fingers. "The kitchen, the dining room, the music room, the drawing room. Four haunted rooms." She forced a smile. "Gosh, Claire— you could line people up at the door and sell tickets. A dollar a room, two dollars for sound effects. What's next?"

"The library." Claire laughed a little and some of the color came back into her face.

"Don't tell me it's haunted, too," Ruby said, rolling her eyes dramatically. The word itself didn't change the physical facts—the wind outside the window, the sound of the harp strings, the imperative brass bell. But now that they were able to laugh, the situation seemed a little less frightening.

"Actually, yes," Claire said hesitantly. "I've smelled pipe smoke there. Cherry flavored tobacco. I recognized it, because I had an uncle once who smoked that kind."

She opened the door and flicked a switch. They were looking into a room lined floor-to-ceiling with bookshelves filled with leather-bound books. A large globe, some four feet in diameter, sat in one corner with a brown leather chair beside it, and there was a leather sofa and other chairs and tables around the room. Under a window, a library table held a stack of what looked like scrapbooks. A collection of framed black-and-white photographs hung on the wall beside the window.

Claire pointed to another door. "That leads to a small study—handsome desk, leather chair, wooden filing cabinet, more bookshelves. A rather masculine room."

"The man of the house," Ruby muttered. She went to the wall and looked at the framed photographs—imposing houses surrounded by palm trees, beautiful gardens, beach scenes, churches, even a hospital. Each one was labeled in a spidery script. *St. Patrick's Church, Marwitz House, John Sealy Hospital, Pagoda Bath House.* All were labeled *Galveston.* All were built in an ornate, late-Victorian architectural style.

"Except that there was no man," Claire said, and flicked off the switch. "Just the two old ladies. Which doesn't explain the nursery or the play-room," she said as they went, closing the library door out into the hall.

"Nursery?" Ruby asked. "Playroom?"

"The second and third floors," Claire said with a sigh. "That's a whole other story, so to speak. I'm not up to it right now."

"The tobacco you smelled," Ruby said. "How about Mr. Hoover? He was here, wasn't he? Maybe he smoked a pipe."

"How'd you know that?" Claire asked, but didn't wait for an answer. "Actually, he and his wife stayed here for several days summer before last, back when he was considering renting the place. I don't think he smokes—at least, there's a big No Smoking sign in his law office. Still—" She paused. "I wonder if the Hoovers saw anything."

"According to local lore, they did," Ruby said ruefully, and told Claire what she had learned from Monica.

"More haunted house stuff," Claire said grimly, shaking her head.

Ruby chuckled. "Look at it this way: at least, you won't have to adver-tise. Word will get around, and all the ghost-busters in Texas will beat a path to your door." She paused. "And you might talk to Mr. Hoover and find out what really happened when they were here. Another witness, so to speak, and maybe an objective one."

"Good idea. I will." Claire paused, her hand on a doorknob. "And here, at last, the morning room—Aunt Hazel's favorite. And mine." She opened the door. "Do you remember it?"

"Oh, I do," Ruby said, smiling. The room, painted a pale yellow, was on the eastern side of the house where it would catch the first light of the morning. A table and two straight chairs sat in front of the window, the white curtains pulled back to either side. There was a small fireplace with a brick surround and hearth, flanked by a pair of comfortable upholstered chairs. "This is where I met your great-aunt Hazel. She was sitting in that yellow chair over there by the fireplace. She seemed very old to me, with her stooped shoulders and her nearly white hair. But she made me feel at home. She was nice."

"She gave us cookies and lemonade, as I remember," Claire said in a soft, reminiscent tone. "And sent us out to play. And then you—" She looked at Ruby.

And then the two little girls had gone out of this room and into the main hallway, where Ruby had felt the first shimmering of Gram's gift and looked up the stairs to see the woman in the dark skirt and the gray shirt-waist with the black ribbon. At the time, she had been so startled—yes, and frightened, too—that she hadn't caught any details. Now, in memory, she saw the image clearly, as if it were happening in front of her: the woman half-turned and fixed in place, one hand raised as if to fend off danger. Her eyes were wide, her face white, her expression terrified, as if she were looking at something so unimaginably awful that it had turned her to stone. What did she see that frightened her so? Was someone—or something—pursuing her up those stairs?

And seeing her now, in memory, Ruby could *feel* the woman's fright, which was all the more terrible because it was impossible to know why she was afraid. And all the more important because it was the sight of her on the stairs that had changed a young girl's life. After that moment, Ruby had had to learn to live with a sixth sense in a world where most people got along very well with just five. After that moment, nothing had ever been the same.

And suddenly, with a chilling certainty, Ruby knew that there was some sort of inexplicable bond, some deep and enduring connection between herself and the woman, and that it somehow transcended that single moment on the stairs. What was it? *When* was it? *Where?* What could it *mean*? But of course, to know all those things, she would have to know who the woman was and when she had lived and why she was so frightened. How had she died? Did her fear have anything to do with her death? Or with the headstones in the graveyard? Or—

Claire reached out to her. "What's the matter, Ruby?" she asked, concerned. "You look funny."

The room was spinning. Ruby groped her way to the nearest chair and sat down with a thump. She closed her eyes, then opened them again and took a few steadying breaths. Finally, she said, "Sorry. I'm okay. It's just that . . . for a minute there, I thought I must know that woman—must have had some sort connection with her, I mean."

"What made you think that?" Claire asked. "Did she look familiar to you? But judging from her dress, she's from a different time, so I don't know . . ." Her voice trailed off.

"I don't know, either," Ruby said, "and I'm not sure I want to." But that wasn't true, was it? The truth was that she wanted to know. She wanted *desperately* to know. "You . . . you didn't feel like that, those times you saw her?"

"No way." Claire shook her head emphatically. "I'd never seen anyone like her in my whole, entire life." She peered at Ruby. "You're sure you're okay?"

"Uh-huh." Ruby looked around dizzily, trying to get her bearings. She caught sight of a small television set topped by a rabbit-ear antenna on the other side of the room and was startled at how glad she was to see something so ordinary. She fumbled for something to say. "The TV—it's yours?"

Claire nodded. "It gets a couple of San Antonio network channels, but the reception is lousy. If I stay here, I'll have to get one of those satellite bundles—TV, phone, and the Internet." She gestured. "I was thinking about using this room for my office. I feel safer here than anywhere else in the house, almost as if it's protected—by Aunt Hazel, maybe." She glanced uncertainly at Ruby. "Does that sound silly?"

"Not to me," Ruby said. "I'm all in favor of protection—the more, the better. How about using this room for our meals, instead of that cavernous kitchen?" She heard herself giggle. "That way, if the pans on the rack want to hold hands and dance to a little harp music, we won't be there to listen."

"Good idea," Claire replied, looking closely at Ruby. "Listen, we need to take your stuff upstairs so you can get settled, but we've had a lot of house for the moment. It's not quite three yet. What would you say to a short walk outside?" She glanced out the window. "Before it rains, if that's what it's going to do."

Still feeling shaky, Ruby stood up. "What I'd like," she said, thinking of the row of headstones, "is to see that graveyard you told me about."

"Why?" Claire asked, frowning.

"Because I'm curious," Ruby said. "Two old ladies lived here, you said, and I suppose they're buried out there. But you mentioned a row of headstones. So who else is in that graveyard? Just seems a little odd to me."

117

"I get your point," Claire replied. "Come on. We'll go back through the kitchen."

They went down the hall, around a corner, and into the kitchen. Ruby had thought they were alone in the house and was startled to see a small, plumpish woman with shoulder-length dark blonde hair standing beside the table, dressed in jeans and a man's loose plaid cotton shirt. She straightened hurriedly, and Ruby noticed that her shoulder bag, which lay on the floor beside the table, was half-open. Had she left it open when she put her cell phone back, or had this woman been going through it?

"Oh, Ms. C-C-Conway," the woman said, stuttering a little. "I brought your friend's suitcase in—it's over there, by the door—and some stuff outta the garden." She gestured to a dish on the table. It held several carrots, a handful of radishes, some green onions, and some lettuce leaves. "Thought you might like a salad for supper tonight."

"Thanks, Kitty," Claire said. "That's sweet of you. Hey, I'd like you to meet my friend Ruby Wilcox. Ruby, Kitty is Sam Rawlings' wife, and a great gardener. Raises chickens, too."

Ruby felt a disorienting jar, as if the floor had trembled under her feet. *There was a crooked man*

Kitty ducked her head, her face turned half away. "Glad to meet you, Ms. Wilcox. Sam said to tell you he moved the yard tractor out of the garage, so you can put your car in there if you want." To Claire, she said, "I copied down the stuff on your grocery list. Yogurt, bread, milk, coffee." She nodded toward the list on the menu board. "We'll bring it back with us when we come home and save you a trip. Was there anything else?"

Who had a crooked wife

Ruby felt the beginning of a shimmer and tried to turn it off.

"Thanks, Kitty. I appreciate—" Claire broke off abruptly and went around the table. "Good heavens, Kitty. What happened to your lip? It's all swelled up! And your eye?"

"Nothin'," Kitty said, keeping her face turned. "Honest, Ms. Conway. It's okay. Like I said before, I don't want you fussin' over me."

found a crooked sixpence

"No, it's definitely not okay! Let me see it." Claire pulled Kitty around and brushed her hair back. The woman's lip was split and swollen. Her right eye was swelled half shut, the puffy skin around it colored purple and green. "That's terrible, Kitty! That must hurt!"

"It was the bathroom door this time," Kitty said, jerking away. "Gotta get me a night-light. I put some ice cubes on it when it happened. It'll be better tomorrow."

crooked man

Ruby sat down at the table, still trying to dial down the shimmer—and that stupid nursery rhyme that kept echoing in her head.

crooked cat

"Kitty," Claire began. "You really ought to get a doctor to stitch up that lip. And your eye might be—"

"I'll just put these in the fridge and get out of your way," Kitty said in a determined tone. She picked up the dish and took it to the refrigerator. "I thought you and your friend was walkin' down by the creek or I wouldn't've come in." She closed the refrigerator and started toward the door.

"Look, Kitty." Claire put her hand on the woman's arm. "I know you didn't run into the bathroom door. And I know you said you didn't want to talk about things like . . . this. But if you ever feel like you need help, you just come over here. It doesn't matter what Sam says or whether it's day or night. You just come." Her voice was urgent. "You hear me?"

"I hear, Ms. Conway," Kitty said impatiently. "Thanks."

crooked sixpence

"I mean it, Kitty!" Claire protested, still holding on to the woman's arm. "You can't go on this way, you know. One of these days, he's going to hurt you seriously. You need to get away from him. I can put you in touch with a counselor who will be glad to—"

"Thanks," Kitty said again, more loudly this time. "But I don't want to get away. He just goes a little haywire sometimes. Everything's gonna be fine. Honest."

"Kitty, please—" Claire began.

There was a furious honking outside and Kitty cast an apprehensive glance at the clock over the refrigerator. She twisted her arm out of Claire's grip. "Look, it's already after three and Sam's waitin' for me. I gotta go. We're headin' to Houston to visit some friends. We'll be stayin' overnight, gettin' back tomorrow. I penned up the chickens and left plenty of food and water. You won't have to bother with 'em." And with that, she was out of the door.

Shaking her head disgustedly, Claire came back to the table. "Wife beater," she muttered fiercely. "It's a clear case of domestic violence. I'd fire him, but that's not going to help *her*. It might just make things worse." She looked at Ruby, then frowned. "Hey, Ruby, you okay?"

Ruby rubbed her forehead. The shimmering was fading. "There's something wrong with—" She stopped. Wrong with the Rawlingses? Of course there was. The wife was a battered woman, the husband a batterer. But it was more than that, wasn't it? What else was going on here?

crooked sixpence upon a crooked stile

"Can I get you a glass of water or something?" Claire gave a little laugh. "I don't keep any booze around, or I'd offer you a stiff drink."

Ruby shivered. "I'm okay," she managed. She cleared her throat. "You're not—you're not afraid of Rawlings? Obviously, he's violent."

"Afraid?" Claire made a wry mouth. "Well, maybe a little. The day I got here, she was sporting a shiner on the other eye. Last week, it was bruises all over both arms."

"What are you going to do?" Ruby asked shakily. She bent over and took her billfold out of her bag.

crooked sixpence

Claire thought for a moment. "Maybe I should drive over to La Grange tomorrow morning and talk to Mr. Hoover. He's the one who hired Sam." She paused, chewing on her lip. "To tell the truth, I guess I'm a little apprehensive about firing him myself. He's never threatened me, but he's got such a short fuse, he might—" She broke off, frowning. "What are you doing?"

"Just checking," Ruby said. Her credit cards and cash seemed to be untouched.

"You don't think Kitty was messing around with your purse, do you?"

"If she was, she didn't take anything," Ruby replied. She put her billfold back. While she was at it, she took out her phone. She'd text China and let her know that she got her message and ask about Grace. Tonsillectomies weren't particularly dangerous, but you never knew. And she needed to know if her mother had gotten back to the nursing home safely.

Ruby flipped her phone open. "If you want to fire Sam, maybe you could get Mr. Hoover to do it. That might be the safest thing—appropriate, too, since Mr. Hoover hired him."

"That's true," Claire said thoughtfully. "But what's to keep him from coming back? Sam, I mean."

"A restraining order," Ruby replied. "Mr. Hoover would know about that." She frowned at her phone, not believing what she saw. The battery was out? Already?

"What's the matter?" Claire asked.

"Battery seems to be gone," Ruby replied. "But I charged it in the car on the way here. And it was okay when I got China's message just a little while ago."

Claire gave her a crooked grin. "Maybe your ghost has cut off your connection to the outside world."

"*Your* ghost," Ruby said emphatically, and snapped the phone shut. She retrieved the charger from her bag. "Got a plug I can use?" Claire pointed to the coffeemaker on the worktable beside the stove, and Ruby plugged her phone into the outlet. "Drat." She jiggled the connection. "It's not taking a charge. You're sure this plug works?"

Claire flipped the switch on the coffeemaker and the light came on. She chuckled wryly. "I told you, Ruby. The ghost has killed your phone. You're cut off from the outside world."

"What about your cell phone? I could try texting with that."

"Sure," Claire said. "I keep it in the kitchen, since I don't use it very often." She opened a drawer in the table and took it out. But when she flipped it open and turned it on, she frowned. "That's weird. No battery on this one, either. And I know I charged it up before I turned it off." She pulled out the charger and plugged it into the outlet. "Damn," she muttered, shaking her head. "Nothing's happening. What in the world is going on here?"

Ruby got her keys out of her purse and dropped them—and her phone—into the pocket of her yellow sundress. "How about the cars?"

"Smart idea," Claire said approvingly. "We can leave them running with the phones plugged into the chargers while we walk up to the graveyard."

It was a smart idea, Ruby thought. But she wasn't so sure it was going to work.

Chapter Nine

In Greek mythology, parsley sprang from the blood of Opheltes, infant son of King Lycurgus of Nemea, who was killed by a serpent while his nurse directed some thirsty soldiers to a spring. For centuries, Greek soldiers believed any contact with parsley before battle signaled impending death.

The Healing Herbs
Michael Castleman

In later Greek and Roman times, parsley wreaths were used to crown the winners of athletic contests. The herb came to symbolize strength and victory through competition and struggle— getting the upper hand, so to speak. Parsley growing in the dooryard meant that the woman of the house was its master— and not a kindly one, either.

In the language of flowers, parsley represents competitive victory and points to the "mistress who is master."

China Bayles
"Herbs and Flowers That Tell a Story"
Pecan Springs Enterprise

Traffic had slowed down by four o'clock, so I asked Dawn to keep an eye on both shops and let me know if somebody called or came in with a question that she couldn't handle. I picked up the trug I keep loaded with gardening tools and went out to the medicinal garden for an hour's pleasant work.

Both Brian and Caitlin take their turns in the garden: Brian under duress (what do you expect from a senior in high school?), Caitlin more or less willingly, when I can tear her away from her flock of chickens and her violin. But I got smart last year and organized a team of regular customers—the Wonder Weeders—who are willing to swap garden work for shop credits, who know quack grass from lemongrass, and who don't mind getting dirt under their nails. It turned out to be a good move, because the theme gardens are much neater now, and the plant bullies are kept at bay, more or less. The big thugs—especially the unruly mints and artemisias—live in pots or in areas all to themselves, but they still bear watching.

Today, I was replanting a section of the medicinal garden using some of the larger plants from the for-sale rack. In my tray: echinaceas (both *E. purpurea* and *E. angustifolia*); a sturdy Spanish lavender, which does well in our hot, dry climate; and several varieties of oregano and thyme, as well as our native bee balm, *Monarda punctata*, also known by the inelegant name of spotted horsemint. Oregano, thyme, and bee balm are endowed with the plant chemical thymol, which has a long tradition of use because of its antiseptic, antimicrobial properties. And I do mean "long": Some 5,500 years ago, the ancient Egyptians used oils from these thymol-rich plants to make mummies. I've designed garden labels for these plants, giving some of their history and uses; if you're interested in knowing more, there's a plant list in the shop.

I loaded a tray with a couple dozen pots and headed for the medicinal garden. I slipped on kneepads to keep my jeans decent and got to work. The sun was warm, the breeze was pleasant, and the earth was sweet, and forty-five minutes went by in a flash.

I had only a couple more plants to go when I heard my name and looked up to see Ruby's sister, Ramona. She was wearing sandals, a blue tank top, khaki slacks, and a couple of loose gold bracelets. Her red hair was cut short, her makeup subdued. She's not nearly as stylistically outrageous as Ruby. If you were looking at the two of them together, you might not guess they were sisters.

"Oh, hi," I said, straightening up. "I hope you found Doris."

"I did." Ramona laughed triumphantly. "Cornered her in the adults-only video store a couple of blocks off the square. The clerk thought she was a little weird, he said, so he called the cops—although I don't know how he could distinguish Mom's weirdness from the weirdnesses of some of his other customers." She rolled her eyes. "I never would have guessed that Pecan Springs had any cross-dressers. But there they were, two of them. Big as life and twice as natural, babysitting my mom until the cavalry showed up. She was thrilled with the attention."

I had to laugh at that. Pecan Springs may be a small town, but it faces some of the same interesting challenges that the big cities are confronting, and more, because of its location. Austin is creeping south and San Antonio is crawling north, and the spillover from these two big cities—along with the drug traffic that flows north from the border along the I-35 corridor—is changing the nature of our community.

"Well, anyway, she lost that round," Ramona added. "She's back at the nursing home. They've locked her in and promised to throw away the key." She paused. "Were you able to contact Ruby?"

"I sent her a text message," I said. "That's the best I could do. No idea if she got it. What have you heard about Grace's tonsils?"

"Amy says they're keeping Grace overnight for surgery early tomorrow morning. She should be home by tomorrow afternoon." She hesitated. "Do you have time to talk for a few minutes, China?" There was a metal garden chair nearby, and without waiting for a yes or no from me, she pulled it forward and sat down. Obviously, we were going to talk whether I had time for it or not.

Ramona shares her sister's red hair and leprechaun freckles (there must be an Irish grandmother or two on their family tree) but she's short and round and fully packed, where Ruby is tall and angular. She's also inclined toward self-dramatization in a way that I find . . . well, trying. A little of Ramona, in my opinion, goes a long way. And she's ditzy. Things happen to her that don't happen to ordinary mortals, although some of that probably isn't her fault. I don't actively dislike her (not yet, anyway). But I could probably go all day without talking to her and still fall asleep at night feeling perfectly complete and happy. But I adore Ruby and Ramona is Ruby's sister, so I make an effort to be nice.

I reached for a pot of echinacea. "Sure, we can talk," I said. "As long as you don't mind if I get these plants in the ground." I tapped lightly on the bottom of the pot to loosen the plant's roots. "What did you want to talk about?"

She cleared her throat. "Have you noticed something going on with Ruby?"

"Something's always going on with Ruby," I said. "She's one of the busiest people I know." I pulled the plant out of the pot and frowned at the mass of roots. The poor little echinacea was already root-bound—happens when a plant stays in its pot too long. "She's not having any health problems, is she? I know she said she got an all-clear on her checkup last month." Ruby had breast cancer a couple of years ago and elected to have a mastectomy. She belongs, she says, to the Tribe of One-Breasted Women. She can laugh about it, but I can't. I was afraid I might lose her, and the thought was very, very scary.

"Yes, she got an all-clear, but—" Ramona waited, tilting her head to one side, eyeing me as if we were playing some sort of game and the next move was mine. When I didn't take the bait, she said, "I guess you haven't noticed, then."

"Noticed what?" I tried not to sound irritated. If Ramona had something in mind, I wished to heck she'd come straight out and say so. I don't like people who try to get you to guess what they're thinking. It's manipulative.

"How burned out she feels." Ramona gave me a sly, smug smile that said, *You can't be much of a friend if you hadn't noticed* that. "She's been doing way too much. It's getting to her. She's dying to take a long break. That's why she wanted to go away this week."

I was nettled by the smugness in Ramona's tone, which seemed to imply that, as a sister, she had a privileged view into Ruby's inner life and knew secrets that Ruby's other friends would never be able to share. But maybe she didn't mean that. Maybe I was letting her push my jealous button.

"I know she's doing a lot," I agreed evenly. "Ruby enjoys being a businesswoman, but she's taken on quite a load, with the shop and the tearoom and the catering service. All three of us have—Ruby, Cass, me. Sometimes it's hard to keep our heads above water." It was true. We enjoy our three-ring circus, but there are days when it feels like the lions are in charge.

"I've noticed," Ramona said with an irony that bordered on sarcasm. She sat back in the chair and crossed her legs. "That's what I wanted to talk to you about, China. I'm sure you know that I've been looking around for a business opportunity here in Pecan Springs."

I pulled apart some of the plant's tightly packed roots so they would grow out into the soil. "Yeah, I know," I replied, and dug an echinacea-sized hole with my trowel a foot away from a flourishing parsley plant. Ramona's business aspirations were no secret. For a while, she'd thought she had a deal to buy half of Molly McGregor's Hobbit House Children's Bookstore next door. But the more time Molly spent with Ramona, the less Molly liked the idea, and she had finally decided it wouldn't work. Molly's rejection hadn't fazed Ramona, of course. She was also considering buying half of an advertising agency, going into the real estate business, and opening a boutique coffee bar on the square.

"She has eclectic interests," Ruby said when she told me about the options Ramona was exploring. I didn't say so out loud, but I thought that *unfocused* might be another word for it. Or *scatterbrained*.

"And you know I've gotten my divorce settlement," Ramona went on, swinging one sandaled foot. With a tiny stab of envy, I noticed that her pretty toenails were painted black and sprinkled with glitter, although I don't think I'd paint my toenails like that even if I had the time (which I don't). "I can afford to invest in a business—not just my expertise," she added expansively, "but money, as well."

"Yes, I know," I muttered, settling the echinacea in its new hole and patting the dirt around it with my bare hands. I couldn't avoid knowing, because Ramona has been bragging about it for weeks. She not only got a big-as-Dallas cash settlement out of her doctor ex-husband, the poor jerk, but a substantial monthly payout as well. The way Ramona described it, she was fixed for life. And the way Ruby described it, Ramona didn't actually *have* to go into business: she just wanted something to put her energies into. I picked up my shears, reached into the parsley plant, and nipped off a few dead leaves, neatening it up. As far as expertise was concerned, well, I wasn't so sure. Ruby says that Ramona's a very good manager with lots of administrative experience. I have yet to see her in action, though. Mostly, there's been just a lot of talk.

Ramona leaned forward. "So I've told Ruby I'd like to buy into the Crystal Cave," she said, as if she were imparting a great secret.

That got my attention. Immediately. "Buy into the *Cave*?" I asked.

Ramona heard the disbelief in my voice and narrowed her eyes. "Sounds like that surprises you."

"Yes, a little," I admitted. Actually, the idea surprised me a lot. The Cave is Ruby's baby, her pride and joy. She might complain at the amount of time she had to spend on the administrative stuff, but I would never in the world have thought she'd sell even the tiniest fraction of it. And especially to Ramona. They might be sisters, but being sisters didn't mean that they would be good business partners. Ruby doesn't like being bossed around any more than Molly does. Any more than I would. Ramona is competitive, especially where Ruby is concerned. I suspect that it's one of those sibling things, where the younger sister is continually trying to one-up the older sister.

"How does Ruby feel about this?" I asked, trying for a neutral tone.

"Oh, she *loves* it," Ramona said, and raised her chin. "After we talked about it, it was clear that she's willing to sell out entirely, which in my opinion would be a really good thing for her. She could stay on to teach classes and do consulting, while I would handle the shop, the taxes, the bookkeeping, all that administrative stuff that Ruby hates. This would give her the time she needs to do more of the things she'd really like to do."

"Which are?" I asked cautiously, wondering where Ramona got the idea that Ruby hates administration. She's definitely good at it, which might come as a surprise to some people. She is creative and imaginative and she thinks outside the box—not the hallmarks of an administrator. But under her Orphan Annie hairdo there lurks the brain of a whiz-bang accountant.

Ramona waved her hand. "She wants to teach more classes. Give more readings. Spend more time with Grace. Spend more time quilting. She's often told me that she wished she had time to do more along those lines."

I sighed. I couldn't argue with any of that, and I cared for Ruby deeply enough to want her to do whatever was best for her. I just wished she had talked to me about the way she was feeling before she came up with something as drastic as selling out to Ramona. Maybe we could have worked something out—hired a bookkeeper who would handle both the shops, for example. I'm not saying that Ramona wouldn't do a good job with the Crystal Cave, or that she doesn't have good marketing ideas. But I've been around her long enough to know that when she gets excited about something, she has a tendency to shift into takeover mode. Which was exactly the reason Molly had pulled back from their discussions about the Hobbit House. "I'm afraid I'd end up feeling like I was harnessed to a runaway bulldozer," she had told me in confidence. "I want a partner, not a boss. Especially a bossy boss, who always knows what's right, even when it's wrong."

I dropped the plant shears into the trug and reached for the last pot, a Spanish lavender. "Well," I said, "that's between you and your sister, Ramona. If you want to buy in to her shop, or even buy the whole thing, it's none of my business." Losing Ruby as a neighbor would be terrible, and I'd hate having Ramona take over the shop next door. But I couldn't stop either of them from doing it.

"Oh, it isn't just the *shop*," Ramona said with a careless wave of her hand. Her bracelets jangled. "We're talking about the whole package. The Cave, the tearoom, the catering business, everything."

"The whole . . . package?" I asked incredulously, feeling suddenly chilled. I put down the Spanish lavender I was holding and pulled in my breath. "I mean, I knew that Ruby has been feeling a little besieged. That was why I was glad when she said she wanted to take a few days off. But I had no idea she was considering selling part—"

"In fact," Ramona said, leaning forward, "I am offering to buy her out completely, if that's what she wants me to do. And I have the feeling she will, when she's had some time to weigh all her options. I can afford to make her an offer she can't refuse." Her tone became confidential. "That's why I thought you and I should have this little chat, China. If Ruby says yes, you and I will be partners. You and I and Cass, of course." She smiled. "Won't that be *fun*?"

Now, wait just a minute. Ruby's shop is one thing. She can sell all or part of it to whomever she chooses. Heck, she can *give* it away if she wants to or even close it, as long as she pays the outstanding rent on the space she rents from me. But our partnership is another thing altogether, and we have an agreement that says so. What's more, our agreement spells out what happens if one of the partners—in this case, Ruby—has an offer from somebody to buy her share of the partnership. She is required to notify the other partner in writing, giving the name of the person who is making the offer and how much that person is offering. The other partner—that's me—has thirty days to purchase her interest, at that price. There's a provision for mediation and evaluation if the offer seems unreasonably high, which it might, if Ramona was dead set on buying Ruby's share and offered her a great deal more than it's really worth. This is called the right of first refusal. It's standard boilerplate in most partnerships. I wouldn't be worth my salt as a member of the Texas Bar if I had failed to include it.

I dug a hasty hole, tipped the Spanish lavender into it, and firmed the dirt around its roots. Then I got to my feet and started unbuckling my kneepads. This was serious stuff, and attending to it took priority over garden work. I didn't intend to discuss this matter with Ramona until I sat down with Ruby and got the word directly from her.

Ramona was frowning. "You're leaving? I thought we were going to talk."

"I've heard enough for the moment," I said, and dropped my kneepads into my trug. I don't have piles of extra money lying around. In fact, things have been a little tight lately, money-wise. If Ruby was dead set on leaving our partnership, I would manage to scrape the dollars together somehow or another—how, I didn't know. But I knew one thing: if Ruby meant to leave, I was *not* going into partnership with her sister. Ramona and I wouldn't last a week together—heck, we wouldn't last an hour.

"Wait, China." Ramona pushed herself out of her chair. "Before you jump to any conclusions, I hope you'll stop and think. Think of Ruby, I mean. You might be comfortable with your workload, but I know my sister well enough to know that she's really overwhelmed. And she's still not over Colin—she thinks about him all the time. If you ask me, she needs a change of scene, something new and different to take her mind off her grief. That's really why I made the offer. I want to help."

I bet she did. Ramona wanted to come out on top, that's what she wanted. I collected my trowel and empty pots and dropped them into the trug. "I won't argue with that," I said noncommittally. And I wouldn't argue over Ruby's feelings for Colin, either. I know she's been grieving.

"I want to help, and I *can*," she went on. "I've been in the advertising business for over a decade. I have lots of administrative experience. I can see things in this operation that need to be . . . adjusted. Not huge things," she added hastily, as if she didn't want to offend me. "Just a few little things. Here and there. I really think we ought to talk about it."

"Later," I said. I picked up the trug and began walking back to the shop. I was in a hurry. I was taking big steps.

She ran after me. "I think we should talk about this *now*," she said petulantly. "We need to have an understanding. If you and I are going to be partners—"

That was enough. "Not," I said over my shoulder.

"But if I buy Ruby's share of—"

"You're not going to do that," I said. I walked faster.

"Why not?" she cried, running to catch up. "I've got the money—"

I stopped, so short that she almost bumped into me, and turned to face her. "You may have the money, Ramona," I said in my calmest, most lawyer-like voice, "but I have Ruby's signature on a partnership document that gives *me* the right of first refusal."

She pulled her brows together. "Which means?"

"Which means that if Ruby wants to sell to you, I can match your offer. I can buy her out."

Ramona's eyes widened in shock and she opened her mouth. But I lifted my hand like a traffic cop. "What's more, I intend to exercise that right—*if* she intends to sell. But all I have right now is your word for it. So let's call this conversation concluded until Ruby and I have talked." Of course, that wouldn't be for at least a week, since Ruby was out of town. Unless—

Ramona likes to have the last word, but she wasn't going to get it this time. I turned around and started walking again, leaving her behind. When I reached the shop, I glanced back over my shoulder. She was standing on the walk, fists on her hips, pouting like a little girl who has just been told that she can't have a piece of her favorite candy.

Inside, I put my things away and glanced at the clock. It was closing time. I hung up the *Closed* sign, locked the outside door to my shop, then went next door to Ruby's, where Dawn was clearing out the register. I peered over her shoulder at Ruby's bulletin board, which was plastered with the usual notices and reminders and community items.

"Looking for anything special?" Dawn asked. She stuck the deposit slip in the blue plastic bank bag and zipped it shut.

"A postcard from the friend Ruby went to visit," I said, scanning the board. "I know she pinned it here somewhere." I had happened to be in the shop when Ruby found it in the mail. She said she didn't need directions and since it had a colorful photo of bluebonnets on one side, she'd stuck it on the board.

"Hey, there it is!" I said, and pounced on it. I turned it over. "Just what I needed. Directions to Ruby's getaway destination, somewhere the other side of Round Top." That glimpse of Ramona pouting had been enough to make up my mind. I needed to talk to Ruby, and the sooner the better. If I've got to live with bad news, I'd just as soon get it over with so I can get on with whatever has to be done. The thought of losing Ruby as a partner—and having to figure out some way of working with Ramona—was just about the worst thing I could imagine. I wouldn't get any sleep until it was resolved.

"If you're driving through Round Top, be sure to stop at Royers and get some of their fantastic pie." Dawn is from San Antonio. She knows the area. "You're going tomorrow?"

"Tonight," I said. "That is, if McQuaid is okay with managing the kids." He'd probably see it as a good chance to take them out for Tex-Mex. It was a school night, so they'd be doing homework and going to bed early. "I suppose there's a chance that I won't get back tonight, though," I added. "If there's a problem, could you open the herb shop tomorrow morning? Myra Mason is scheduled to help with the tearoom, although I'm sure I'll be back before the lunch crowd shows up."

"I can do that," Dawn said comfortably. "I'll come in as soon as I get my youngest off to high school. If you're not here, I'll open up both shops and get things going. You come in whenever you get back to town."

I gave her a quick hug, feeling relieved. "Thanks, Dawn! You're a peach." I glanced at the deposit bag. "Want me to take that? I have to drop mine off, too. Might as well make both deposits."

"Sure," Dawn said, and handed it to me. "Tell Ruby I sold the last

Motherpeace tarot deck, so I went ahead and reordered—got one for myself, too. I am definitely going to learn how to use those cards. They're beautiful." She waggled her fingers at me. "See you when you get back."

I went back to the shop to clear the register and put my deposit together, stopping long enough to call McQuaid and explain the situation to him. He's teaching a course at the university this semester and he was still at the office, grading final papers and marveling at the remarkable ability of some students to torture the English language. He said he'd be glad to manage the kids' supper, although he'd rather get take-out pizza. But he had a more immediate concern.

"Are you going to try to talk Ruby out of selling?" he asked.

"No," I said. "If that's what she needs to do, I want her to do it. I can't do anything about the Crystal Cave—she can keep it, sell it, give it away, whatever. But I *can* keep her from selling her share in the partnership to Ramona, and I will. I can't work with somebody who sees every minor issue as a major battlefield and every point as a win-lose proposition. I had enough of that back in my courtroom days." I sighed. "I'm sorry, McQuaid. This could cost a bundle, and now's not the time to—"

"I'm not thinking of money," McQuaid broke in. "I'm sure we can manage that, China, one way or another. And Ruby's pretty well fixed, isn't she? She'd probably take your note."

That was true. If Ruby was dead set on selling out, we could probably make a deal. She had an income from a lottery win a few years back and from Colin's insurance.

McQuaid was going on. "It's not the money, it's the workload I'm thinking of. You and Ruby and Cass have built a pretty impressive empire. But if you buy Ruby out, where does that leave you and Cass? How will the *two* of you do what the *three* of you can barely manage?"

"A good question," I conceded. "I wish I had an answer." Once Ramona was out of the picture, I could probably find another partner. But where would I find anyone like Ruby? She was my best friend. And not just that, her knowledge and skills were truly irreplaceable. The thought of losing her—just the *thought* of it—made me want to curl up in a corner and cry.

McQuaid chuckled sympathetically. "Well, it's not an answer you need right now, babe. Just keep the question in mind, okay? You're the boss lady—I'm sure you'll come up with the right fix." He paused. "But if you're driving to Round Top, I don't think you should plan on driving back this evening. It's a four-hour round-trip, at least. And there's a storm coming. A sizeable one, the Weather Channel is saying."

I glanced at the clock. It was already five thirty. "Whoops," I said. "I've got to go. I have to drop off the deposits at the bank." The lobby windows are open until five on weekdays, the drive-through until six. "About driving home—I guess we'll have to play that by ear. If this conversation turns out badly, Ruby might not want me to stay overnight." I didn't really think that could happen. Ruby and I aren't just partners, we're buddies, friends, sisters. But just the same . . .

"Whatever," McQuaid said. "I'll leave the porch light on. Be safe, babe. Give Ruby a hug from me." As an afterthought, he said, "Hey, wait. Better give me some contact information. Where will you be?"

"You can text me, I'm sure." I scanned the postcard. "And here's an address."

"That'll work," he said, and I gave it to him. We exchanged *I love you*s, and I went back to work. I finished counting the cash, totaled up the deposit, and got the charge slips together. Ten minutes later, I was locking the door and sprinting to the car. Pecan Springs is a small town without a lot of traffic, and Ranchers State Bank is only six minutes away, so there should have been plenty of time. Seventeen minutes after I finished talking to McQuaid, I was pulling into the drive-through lane.

But that was as far as I got. A row of orange plastic traffic cones cordoned off the area, and I could see a gaggle of cop cars parked randomly around the drive-through island; a paramedic vehicle, lights flashing, uniformed paramedics standing with arms folded beside an empty gurney; and Maude Porterfield's Ford F-150 pickup truck. Maude is a justice of the peace for Adams County, which operates under an old segment of the Texas Code of Criminal Procedure called the Inquest Law. It confers on JPs the responsibility for determining the cause of death in cases of accident, homicide, or suicide. Something bad was happening here.

I stopped my Toyota and buzzed down the window, looking for my friend Sheila Dawson, the Pecan Springs chief of police. She wasn't in sight, but I spotted Rita Kidder, one of the newer officers on the force. I left the car and walked over to where she was standing, talking to another officer beside the bank's rear entrance, next to the drive-up window. Rita has been in the shop several times, both on-duty and off, and I've been impressed by her. I have the sense that she's going to be a strong officer.

The other cop—a veteran named Chico—turned away, and I stepped up. "Hey, Rita," I said. "What's going on?"

"Bank robbery," Rita said. Like a good cop, she was keeping an attentive eye on the parking lot while the two of us talked. "Inside the bank. Five minutes before the lobby closed." Rita is barely regulation height, but she's strong and wiry, all business in her sharply creased dark uniform, cap, and duty belt, which was heavily loaded with cop equipment. According to Sheila, while Rita might not have as much muscle as the other rookies, she was first in her class in defensive tactics at the academy. She has some pretty convincing takedown moves.

I wasn't surprised to hear that there'd been a robbery. The cops and paramedics obviously weren't here for a tailgate party. Five minutes before the lobby closed made it just about a half hour ago. If I hadn't stopped to find Ruby's postcard and talk to McQuaid, I might have been on the scene when it happened. There was no point in asking how much money the robber got away with. If Rita knew, she wouldn't tell me. And neither would the bank. They don't like to confess that any of their money managed to get out the door without their permission.

I nodded in the direction of Maude's truck. "A fatality, I guess." I didn't put the remark into a question because I already knew the answer. The justice of the peace wouldn't be here if somebody hadn't cashed it in—so to speak.

Rita pressed her lips together and slid me a glance, weighing how much to tell me. After a moment, she said, "Unfortunately, yes. The robber got panicked and shot a teller."

"Oh God," I exclaimed. *"Who?"* Pecan Springs may be pinched between two big cities, but it's still a small town. Everybody knows everybody else (as well as their parents, their kids, their in-laws, and their life histories). The merchants especially know all the people who work at the bank, from the president on down.

Rita looked uncomfortable. "Sorry, China. I don't think they've released—" She saw the look on my face and decided to break a rule. "Bonnie Roth. But don't go spreading it around," she added in lower voice. "It just happened. I don't know whether the family has been notified."

"Aw, *hell*," I said, very low. Bonnie and I had been friends for years, and we were both members of the Myra Merryweather Herb Guild. Since Maude was here, I didn't need to ask what had happened, but Rita told me anyway.

"My feeling, too," she said regretfully. "She died instantly, I understand. It happened so fast, she maybe didn't even have time to get scared."

I half-turned away, feeling the tears coming suddenly to my eyes. Bonnie was the bright spot of my almost daily visits to the bank. Ruby and I jokingly called her "Loose-Lips Roth." She was a reliable source of local gossip, which she cheerfully dished out as she handed you the money or took yours away from you, depending on the nature of the transaction. She was always funny, never malicious or hurtful, and sometimes she gave you some really useful information—like the time she handed me an important hint about what Sally (McQuaid's ex-wife) was up to. Bonnie's husband, Al, worked in the hardware store; Briana, her daughter, was in Brian's class and would graduate high school in a few weeks and had already been accepted to UT-San Antonio. Their lives would be changed by this horror, changed completely, changed forever.

"I hope you get him," I said between gritted teeth.

"Them," Rita said. "One did the stickup, wearing a hoodie and a mask. From the build, it could've been either a man or a woman. Somebody else was behind the wheel. A security guard got a quick shot off as the truck drove off—drilled a hole through the cab's back window. May have struck one of them."

"Description of the truck?"

"Ford Ranger, mid-'90s model, maybe gray, maybe green, with a *Protected by AK-47* sticker in the rear window of the cab. A surveillance camera picked up the license number. But Chico just told me that when they ran the plate, it turned out to be registered to a Mazda in San Antonio." She shook her head disgustedly. "You'd think if they were smart enough to put on a stolen license plate, they'd be smart enough to take that sticker off the window, wouldn't you?"

"Bonnie Roth," I muttered numbly. Sweet, funny Bonnie, who always found something nice to say about everybody, even when she was dishing the dirt. "I can't believe it."

"Now, remember what I said," Rita cautioned, frowning. "Keep this to yourself. The chief will hold a press conference in an hour or so. And I think I saw Mr. Hibler here someplace." She glanced around. "I'm sure the story will make the next issue of the *Enterprise*."

No doubt. There have been a few bank robberies in the area, mostly small-town banks without heavy security, but it's been a while since Pecan Springs was hit. This would be big news. I glanced at my watch, then at the drive-up window. "I guess it's too late to make my deposit."

Rita nodded. "The bank closed right after Ms. Roth was shot."

Well, it wouldn't be a problem if the deposit didn't go in until tomorrow. I thanked Rita and got back in the car, thinking again, sadly, about Bonnie. How many times had I driven up to that drive-through window, looking forward to seeing her and laughing at her jokes? Suddenly, I was swept by a deep, deep sadness for Al and Briana, who had got up that morning believing it would be an ordinary day, that the three of them would be together for supper this evening. But they wouldn't. They would have to face life without mother, wife, lover, and best friend.

But my sadness was laced with a savage anger at the person who had pulled the trigger. I knew Rita was right. The cops would catch him—95 percent of bank robbers are male—and he'd be charged with capital murder, intentional murder in the commission of a felony offense, which would likely get him the death penalty here in Texas. I'm not in favor of that: too many innocent people have been executed in this state. But when he was convicted and sentenced, I'd bet that the whole town of Pecan Springs would stand up and cheer.

I put the Toyota in gear and drove east on Navarro, heading for the I-35 on-ramp. Far to the southeast, against the horizon, I could see a rising tier of cumulous clouds, and I wondered if they were a portent of some kind—a metaphor, maybe, of the stormy night ahead if it turned out that Ruby was as serious about selling out as Ramona claimed. I also thought of Hark's warning about the tropical storm. But there was nothing to worry about on that score. However powerful Amanda turned out to be, once inland, she would likely follow Allison's path, re-curve sharply to the north, and hightail it for East Texas. Houston would probably see some rain—welcome rain, actually. It's been a dry spring.

Had I but known . . .

Chapter Ten

Galveston
Early evening, September 8, 1900

At 6:30 p.m., Isaac [Cline], ever the [weather] observer, walked to the front door to take a look outside. He opened his door upon a fantastic landscape. Where once there had been streets neatly lined with houses there was open sea, punctured here and there by telegraph poles, second stories, and rooftops. He saw no waves, however. The sea was strangely flat, its surface blown smooth by the wind. The Neville house across the way now looked so odd. It had been a lovely house: three stories sided in an intricate pattern of fish-scale shingles and shiplap boards and painted four different colors. Now only the top two-thirds protruded from the water. Every slate had been stripped from its roof.

Issac's Storm: A Man, a Time, and the
Deadliest Hurricane in History
Erik Larson

Isaac Cline, whose house stood on Q Avenue very near to the Blackwood mansion, was deeply puzzled by the flat surface of ocean that stretched from his front gallery as far as he could see through the sheeting rain. He could not know the reason for this strange calm: that the hurricane-powered waves had pushed up a massive levee of debris dozens of yards wide and nearly three stories high, stretching for miles along the beach. This temporary barrier was constructed of the walls and roofs of buildings, barrels, bathing machines, banisters, buggies, benches, bales of cotton, boxes and crates, broken boards, empty boats, and bodies, uncounted, countless drowned creatures: cows, pigs, horses, chickens, dogs, cats—and humans. The gigantic wedge, fronted by long sections of wrecked streetcar trestle, was being shoved by the waves toward the north and west, a giant bulldozer obliterating everything in its path.

But as Cline stood in the open door, marveling at the eerie calm before him, part of the barrier suddenly gave way and the ocean poured through the gap. He was nearly lifted off his feet by a sudden rise in the level of the water, which in the space of four seconds rose an incredible four feet. He was up to his waist in salt water before he could pull in a deep breath. It was not a lashing wave but a gigantic swell, like some maddened Leviathan rushing toward the city: the "storm wave," it was called then—the *storm surge*, meteorologists call it now, to distinguish it from the wind-driven hurricane waves. Calculating its height against the interior walls of his house, he saw that the water was now an unbelievable 15.2 feet deep on Q Avenue and still rising.

As he ran up the stairs to the second floor of his house, he must have remembered that just nine years before, he had ridiculed hurricane fears as "an absurd delusion." With a supremely arrogant hubris, he had written, "It would be impossible for any cyclone to create a storm wave which could materially injure the city."

Now, Isaac Cline's city was being destroyed by the relentless, ruthless reality of his "absurd delusion," at this moment making its mark on his dining room wall.

CLINE's wasn't the only proud boast being annihilated by the storm. Galveston thought of itself as the New York City of the Gulf, the equal of

New Orleans, certainly, and perhaps even of San Francisco. It was the largest cotton port in the country and the third busiest of all.

But on this terrible day, the city's claims to fame were falling like ninepins. By mid-afternoon, the celebrated Pagoda Bath House, a Victorian frivolity, had been ripped apart by the waves, as had the Bath Avenue and Beach Street trestle that carried sightseers out over the surf. The three railroad bridges that linked the island and the mainland were underwater. And the longest two-lane wagon bridge in the United States was impassable. Galveston had been proud of its unique island location. Its vulnerability was now apparent to all.

There was more to come. In late afternoon, the brick smokestack that towered over the Brush Electric Company powerhouse came down with a roar across the roof, crushing it and killing the men inside. At about the same time, the Celtic cross perched on the spire of Saint Patrick's Church was blown down. (Saint Patrick's, like John Sealy Hospital, the Ursuline Academy, and many other grand buildings in Galveston, was the work of architect Nicholas J. Clayton, who loved to execute his fanciful Gothic structures in brick—not the best choice for a hurricane-prone city.) At two hundred feet, the spire, topped by a massive gilded cross, was the tallest structure in the city. According to church records, the electrically illuminated cross was designed to be "the first and last object visible to mariners or travelers approaching Galveston Island from the deep blue waters of the Gulf of Mexico." The shriek of the wind was so great that it blotted out the noise of its collapse. Nobody heard it fall.

A half hour later, the Angelus rang out for the last time from the great bell at St. Mary's Cathedral, the first church to be named a cathedral in the new state of Texas. To the rector, Father James M. Kirwin, the Angelus was "not like a salutation of praise but a warning of death and destruction." Moments later, the cathedral towers began to sway ominously. The two-ton bell was ripped loose from its moorings and crashed to the floor. Gathered with the priests in the nave, the bishop of Galveston turned to the rector and said quietly, "Prepare these men for death."

Just before six thirty, the Weather Bureau's anemometer atop the four-story Levy Building was blown away. Its last recorded wind speed: one hundred miles per hour. After that, there could be only estimates—120 miles per hour by contemporary reports; later estimates determined that the wind speeds must have reached Category Four on the Saffir-Simpson scale: 131-155 miles per hour. The first mate of the *Comino,* a British steamship tied up at Pier 14 on the west side of the island, noted that the barometric pressure had fallen to 28.30 inches and wrote in his log book. "Wind blowing terrific, and steamer bombarded with large pieces of timber, shells, and all manner of flying debris from the surrounding buildings." A few moments later, a board four feet long and six inches wide was hurled like a huge javelin through the inch-thick iron plate of the *Comino*'s hull. And at the corner of Twenty-second Street and the Strand (known to proud Galvestonians as the "Wall Street of the Southwest"), the wind tore off the entire fourth floor of the W. L. Moody Building, as neatly, some said, as if a butcher had sliced it off with his cleaver.

Nobody in Galveston could have told you how hard the wind blew that night. They just knew that no man could stand against it, and that the air was so thick with whirling debris and sword-sharp slates that to step outside was to face certain death.

AT the Blackwood house on Q Avenue, Rachel had given up all hope that Augustus would be able to make his way home before the storm ended. The howling wind was too fierce and the water, rushing up the street like a foam-flecked river in flood, too impossibly high. His absence was a hollow in her heart, but she was too busy—and too frightened—to dwell on it. She could only thank Providence that Colleen O'Reilly, for whatever reason, had come back. Until Rachel had heard Matthew's shout and turned to see Colleen standing in the door, she had not known how desperate for help she was. It was only later that she would remember the sweet sympathy in the other woman's eyes and wonder whether she had heard of Augustus' death and could somehow see the terrible fate that waited for the rest of them.

But that was to come. Their first order of business was to finish Matthew's birthday party, with candles and a song and his present, a little army of painted tin soldiers, with extra-large pieces of chocolate cake for everyone. When they finished, Rachel proposed a new game. While they were waiting for their father to come home from the bank, they would have a parade up the stairs to the second floor. Each child could carry something important to the family—"just in case"—and when they had taken their precious burdens up the stairs, they could march down for something else. Mrs. O'Reilly volunteered to be "Parade Supervisor," making sure that everyone had something to carry, and Patsy was sent upstairs to find safe places for all the items. Rachel, as "Music Master," went to the Steinway to play some rousing Sousa marches—"The Stars and Stripes Forever," "The Liberty Bell," "The Washington Post"—while Angela sat in her little red rocking chair beside the piano, happily beating a spoon against a tin pan.

Matthew was given the honor of carrying his father's spare briefcase stuffed with papers. Ida carried the family's silver forks, done up in a tea towel; Peter carried the spoons, and Paul the knives. On their second trip, Matthew had his father's coin collection, Ida a piece of wedding crystal, and the twins brought the photograph albums. But while the children sang and shouted and marched and Rachel played as loudly as she could, their noise could not drown out the pounding of the rain and the rising shriek of the wind, like a hundred banshees howling around the house and down the chimneys.

Of course, there could be no hope of saving the fine rugs and heavy furnishings—the Steinway piano, the mahogany dining table, Augustus' walnut desk—although all over Galveston, people were trying to do just that. But several of Rachel's favorite crystal pieces were paraded upstairs, and the lavishly engraved silver trays that had been wedding presents, and some of the Haviland china, as well as Augustus' most precious books and the big globe from the library, where Matthew and his father spent long winter evenings tracing out the journeys of Christopher Columbus and Ferdinand Magellan and the lost Henry Hudson.

Before long, though, it was clear that the parade would have to end. The water that had risen to the fifth gallery step while Rachel had been talking to Mr. Cline had reached the seventh step before Matthew blew out his candles. It was sweeping across the gallery as the parade got underway and beginning to flow under the front door as Rachel swung into the second march, "The Liberty Bell."

But they bravely kept on. When the water flooding across the main hallway was several inches deep, Mrs. O'Reilly clapped her hands and called out, in her rich Irish brogue, "Let's all take our shoes off an' play like we're at the beach!"—which of course delighted the children, who were having too much fun to notice that the walls were shaking constantly now under the brutal cannon-like battering of the wind and that the *ocean* was rising inside their house.

The parade continued for another little while, and on the last trip, Matthew carried little Angela in his arms. When all the children were upstairs, Mrs. O'Reilly appeared in the doorway of the music room. By this time, the water on the first floor of the house was knee-deep and still rising. Mrs. O'Reilly was barefoot, and her skirt—the one Rachel had loaned her—was tucked up into her waistband. She had an ax in each hand.

Rachel stopped in the middle of "The Washington Post" and stared, her heart in her mouth. "Axes?" she whispered. "Whatever *for*?"

"Chop holes in the floors," Mrs. O'Reilly said in a matter-of-fact tone, holding out an ax. "I helped my mother do this in the Indianola hurricane. The water comin' up through the holes will weigh down the house some—hold it on its foundation, maybe enough to keep it from gettin' lifted up and pushed over."

Rachel got up from the piano and closed the lid carefully. She ran her hands over the smooth, shining wood one last time, then raised her voice. "Patsy," she called, "please keep the children upstairs now. Tell them that Mrs. O'Reilly and I will bring the rest of the sandwiches and cake and we'll all play another game."

"I think we'd best hurry," Mrs. O'Reilly said urgently. "Might not be much time left."

"Thank you," Rachel said, and reached for the ax. At that moment, with a splintering crash, the front gallery was ripped from the house.

Upstairs, little Angela began to wail.

Chapter Eleven

Widow's tears is a name shared by two plant cousins in the family *Commelinaceae*. These cousins also share another common name: dayflower. Both are beloved by bees and other pollinators; both are invasive.

One of the plants called widow's tears is found in the genus *Commelina*. Its showy flower is made up of two larger symmetrical petals above (usually blue—some people think they look like mouse ears) and a tiny white petal below. Around the world, *Commelina* is used as food, medicine, dyes, animal fodder, and in the production of paper.

The other widow's tears (also called spiderwort) belongs to the genus *Tradescantia*, a New World native named for the sixteenth-century English naturalist John Tradescant. The blossoms range from pale pink and lavender to purple, and usually have three symmetrical petals. Spiderworts have been used for both food and medicine.

Widow's tears flower in the morning and fade by day's end. When you squeeze the bract that surrounds the flower stalk of a *Commelina* blossom, a drop of tear-like mucilaginous sap oozes out. *Tradescantia* flowers wilt into a fluid jelly. Some people are reminded of the tears of a truly grieving widow—or of a widow who is making a show of grief.

In the language of flowers, widow's tears represent grief.

China Bayles
"Herbs and Flowers That Tell a Story"
Pecan Springs Enterprise

Ruby's car was parked beside the frame double garage, not far from the Rawlings' cottage. Her phone in one hand, Ruby opened the door and slid onto the seat, then put her key in the ignition and turned it.

Click.

She turned it again, with the same result. And again. And again.

"Rats," she muttered, remembering that the car had behaved the same way—refusing to start—on the hill, at the same time she had seen the woman with the basket of flowers. Was there a connection?

"Uh-oh," Claire said softly, standing beside the car. "Sounds like a dead battery."

Ruby tried again, then gave it up and got out of the car. "I just replaced the battery a couple of months ago. I don't think that's the problem, Claire."

"Well, then, what is it?"

Ruby looked over her shoulder. They were some distance away from the house. Seen from this angle, its odd angles and out-of-proportion, out-of-kilter hodgepodge of towers and turrets were once again apparent, silhouetted against the gathering of dark clouds, the color of bruised flesh, that filled the sky to the southeast. Somehow, the house seemed closer than it was, seemed almost to lean toward her, watchful and expectant. And sad, bitterly, hopelessly, desperately *sad,* as if it were built not of wood and stone and slate but of the wreckage of broken dreams.

Ruby felt the gooseflesh break out on her arms. She shivered and turned back to Claire, trying to sound casual. "Let's try your car."

"Sure," Claire said, taking her keys out of the pocket of her jeans. "We can charge your phone first if you want, so you can text your message." She headed toward the garage.

But Claire's car—a beat-up, old gray Ford Focus—wouldn't start, either.

"I don't understand this at all," Claire muttered. "It was running just fine two days ago when I went for groceries." She looked up at Ruby, suddenly understanding. "Really, Ruby, it's got to be the gh—"

"Don't say it," Ruby interrupted grimly. "Just . . . don't say it."

Claire tried several more times, then got out of the car. "Not saying it isn't going to make it not true." She was making an obvious effort to stay calm. "Something—the ghost or something else—doesn't want us to use our phones. Or our cars."

Ruby frowned, thinking that if China were here, she'd suggest a more mundane and logical explanation. "It could be Sam Rawlings," she said. "Maybe he jimmied a wire or something."

"But why?" Claire asked, closing the car door. "I mean, he no doubt has his reasons—sick or stupid or whatever—for beating up on his wife. But he has no reason at all to monkey with our cars. And anyway, Sam couldn't be responsible for the phones not charging." She shook her head ruefully. "Sorry. Afraid we're back to the ghost. And I don't know about you, but I'm more than a little nervous about being out here without a way to go for help, if we had to. The county road is seven miles away and the main road is farther than that. And none of these roads are high traffic. We could wait for hours and not see a single car."

Ruby didn't like the idea of being isolated, either. And Claire was right about Sam Rawlings. He might have disabled the cars, but the cell phones were another matter entirely.

The two of them had left the garage and were walking down the gravel path toward the Rawlings' house. The place might have been nice once, and with a coat of paint and some shutters, it could be nice again. But the front yard was full of ragged weeds, and the window blinds were drawn down to the sills, giving the house a lonely, dispirited look. A junked riding mower, minus its wheels, crouched in the dirt. From the direction of the chicken coop came the sound of a hen cackling, celebrating the laying of another egg. Not far from the fenced coop was a garden. A row of hollyhocks was blooming along the fence—the only cheerful thing in sight.

Claire cast a disgusted look at the house. "When the Rawlingses get back, I'm going to tell them they've got to do some cleaning up before I put any money into paint and repair. This place is a mess." She sighed. "But I really think you're right about getting Mr. Hoover to fire Sam, Ruby. It seems like the best thing to do—for me, at least. For Kitty, it'll probably be a different story. Getting fired is likely to make Sam's problems even worse, and he'll take out his frustrations on her. He might not find another job right away, either. Mr. Hoover can give him a recommendation if he wants to, but not me. Not after the way he's treated his wife."

At this point, the path forked, one branch curving back to the Rawlingses' house, the other heading up the hill toward the woodland. Claire gestured in that direction. "If we're going to the cemetery, that's the path we need to take. You can see the iron gate from here. That's where I saw the ghost that morning, with her basket of flowers."

Ruby cleared her throat. "I guess maybe it's time we gave her a name. 'The ghost' seems a bit too generic." She glanced at Claire. "We know for a fact that she isn't your great-aunt Hazel. Right?"

Claire nodded. "Right. She couldn't be, because the first time you saw her, Aunt Hazel was still alive. She wouldn't be dead for another twenty or twenty-five years. Old Mrs. Blackwood is the only other person who has ever lived in this house—at least, so far as I know. Unless we find out differently, we could call her Mrs. Blackwood." She smiled wanly. "If that's wrong, maybe she'll tell us who she is."

They were walking up the path now, away from the house, toward the cemetery. Ruby thought about ghosts for a minute, wishing she knew more about them. Were there general rules for the way they behaved? Or did every ghost—or spirit, or entity, or manifestation, whatever it was called—make its own rules to fit the situation in which it found itself? What about appearance, for example?

"You said that Mrs. Blackwood was in her nineties when she died," Ruby said. "But the woman we've seen is much younger. I couldn't see her face, but I'd guess her to be in her thirties. If she's the ghost or the spirit or whatever of old Mrs. Blackwood, you'd think she'd be stooped and walk with a cane and her hair would be white, not dark. This one goes around looking like a Gibson Girl."

"True," Claire said thoughtfully. "Judging from her clothing—the big sleeves of that blouse and the length of that skirt—I'd say early 1900s, wouldn't you? Maybe even the 1890s."

Ruby nodded. "And I'm wondering why she's making all this fuss now—the appearances, the harp, the pans in the kitchen, all that stuff. Is there a reason for it, or is it just something she likes doing?"

"Or maybe she's been doing it all along," Claire suggested, "but the house has been empty. Nobody's been around to hear."

"Except Mr. and Mrs. Hoover," Ruby said, remembering what Monica had said. "Maybe she doesn't *want* anybody around. Maybe she's trying to get everybody to leave, so she can have the place to herself."

"Or maybe she's trying to get our attention," Claire replied, "and she's like . . . well, waving a flag. Ringing a bell, playing a harp, banging pans. Maybe she wants something from us. Or needs something." In a helpful tone, she added, "I suppose you could ask her. Since you're the one who saw her first. And since you're psychic."

"Since she lives in *your* house," Ruby replied pointedly, "it would be good if you could do the asking. Anyway, you've seen her, too, which means that you must be psychic as well. I told you, Claire. I've never tried to communicate with the dead—or the undead."

"Dead, undead." Claire shoved her hands into the pockets of her shorts and hunched her shoulders. "I'm not sure I understand the difference."

"The dead are dead and they know it," Ruby said. "They stay dead. The undead are a different story, at least from what I've read. Some of them were taken by surprise and they haven't yet figured out what happened. Or maybe they're stubborn and simply refuse to accept the fact that they're dead. Or they have a job to do, or a mission, and they can't be at peace until they've finish it." Her attention was caught by a half dozen wheeling turkey vultures spiraling upward in the darkening sky, carried on a thermal ahead of the coming storm. "And some are just plain stuck. Betwixt and between, as it were—between there and here, then and now. We think time is linear—that it's always moving forward—but maybe that's not always true. Maybe time sometimes loops back on itself and repeats. Or gets trapped in a loop, so that the same thing happens over and over again."

Claire shuddered. "That's the worst hell I could imagine. To get trapped, I mean. To get stuck in something and keep repeating it over and over, for all eternity."

For a moment, Ruby wondered whether Claire might be thinking of her own situation. She had said herself that she wasn't able to get over her husband's death, that she'd gotten stuck and couldn't break away from the past, from losing Brad.

But she seemed to be thinking only of the ghost, not of herself. She went on. "I wonder, Ruby . . . maybe the problem is that Mrs. Blackwood is trapped *here*. Not in time, I mean, but in this place. Or rather, in this house." She stopped in the path and turned to look back at the mansion and the *maybes* began to tumble out. "Maybe the house won't let her go.

Maybe something really bad happened here when she was in her thirties. Maybe that's why she appears to be so much younger than she was when she died."

Ruby turned to look, too. They were far enough away so that the house no longer looked terribly threatening. But it still looked terribly *wrong*. "This poor house," she said, shaking her head. "It seems almost tragic to me, as if something happened here that was so utterly awful that it left its imprint on the structure itself." She gestured. "Perhaps it even . . . you know, wrenched the house out of alignment. Distorted it. Unbalanced it. Made it *crooked*. Does that sound crazy, Claire?"

"Not at all." Claire tilted her head, squinting. "The house does seem crooked. It's not so bad on the inside, at least not on the main floor. On the outside, though—" She broke off. "But what could have happened that was so horrible that it could have such a strong physical effect?" Her voice dropped. "A murder, do you think? And Mrs. Blackwood survived it?"

"Or more than one murder," Ruby said, thinking of the multiple headstones in the graveyard up ahead. "And Mrs. Blackwood herself was the . . . murderer."

"Oh no!" Claire exclaimed, horrified. "I . . . I didn't get that impression at all—when I saw her, I mean. She didn't seem malevolent or evil. She just seemed terribly *sad*, especially when she was standing up there on the widow's walk, looking out to the horizon."

"You're right about that," Ruby conceded. "When I saw her, I didn't get the impression of anything sinister. So maybe there was a mass murder here and she was the only survivor." She frowned. "But surely your aunt Hazel would have known about that, wouldn't she? She would have passed the story along, if not to you, then to your mother."

"Not necessarily," Claire said. "Aunt Hazel didn't come here until she was sixteen. And while she was very sweet, she wasn't a curious sort of person—certainly not the kind who goes digging into somebody else's secrets. Anything could have happened in this house before she arrived, and she wouldn't have known." She smiled a little. "You could add that to your list of questions to ask Mrs. Blackwood when you talk to her."

"*We* could add that to our list," Ruby said pointedly. "And if we have to communicate with her, I think I'd prefer something a little less formal than 'Mrs. Blackwood.' What was her first name?"

"Aunt Hazel never mentioned it. But I'm sure it's on her headstone in the cemetery. Aunt Hazel pointed it out to me—the headstone, I mean—the one time we went there together, but I didn't go over and look." Claire chuckled wryly. "I was just a kid, what did I know? Cemeteries always creeped me out—still do. Anyway, at the time, I had no reason to be especially interested in Mrs. Blackwood. She was only the little old lady who'd built the house and lived here until she died. I didn't connect her with the woman you saw on the stairs."

"If you weren't interested, why did your aunt take you there?"

"Aunt Hazel had found a hawk's nest in the woods and wanted to show it to me. I saw the angel and asked what it was."

"The angel?" Ruby asked, then remembered. "Oh, right. The Victorian marble angel. In the cemetery."

"Yes. On a pedestal, overlooking the row of headstones."

The sky was darker, and the freshening breeze carried the scent of rain. "You mentioned those headstones before," Ruby said. "Who is buried there?"

"I have no idea," Claire replied, "except for Aunt Hazel, that is. Mom wanted to put her with the rest of the family over in the cemetery at Smithville, but Hazel insisted on being buried here. I didn't come to the funeral," she added. "I think it was just my mother and my uncle and the caretaker. Nobody else knew her."

Ruby shook her head, thinking how it would be to live your whole life so utterly alone that only three people were aware of your death. The path was considerably narrower now, climbing up the hill. As they drew closer to the small cemetery, Ruby could see that it was surrounded with a tall, Gothic-looking iron fence topped with a row of pointed iron finials along the top rail, which was decorated with a skein of old wisteria vines bearing lush purple blooms. A pair of stern stone lions flanked the head-high gate, twins of the pair on either side the front steps of the house, and a brick path led beyond the gate into the graveyard. In a nearby tree, a redbird sang, *cheer-cheer-cheer*. A mockingbird returned the call, with amused irony, from the other side of the fence.

There was an old-fashioned cast-iron lock on the gate, but when Claire tried to turn the handle, it wouldn't budge. "Looks like it's locked, and I don't have a clue where the key is—maybe in the kitchen somewhere." She turned away with a discouraged sigh. "Sorry, Ruby. I guess we're out of luck."

Ruby stood for a moment, very still. Then, without thinking of it, without willing it, she felt her glance being pulled in the direction of a large gray rock beside the gate. She went to the rock, pushed it aside with an effort, and there was a large brass skeleton key.

"Do you suppose this is it?" she asked, holding it up.

Claire frowned. "How did you know where to look?" she replied. "Oh, duh," she said, rolling her eyes, and put the key in the lock. After a moment, she gave up. "Feels like it's the right key, but the lock is just too rusty. Maybe if I brought some oil—"

"Let me try," Ruby said, and put her hand to the key. It turned easily.

Claire chuckled wryly. "I guess you've got the magic touch, Ruby. Or somebody wants you to see what's here."

159

Ruby frowned. "Maybe it was too easy," she said. The gate, though, was a different matter. It took both of them, shoving hard, to push it open. But it finally yielded with a rusty screech, and they went in.

At one time, the little cemetery must have been well kept and even beautiful, for there were oleanders and gnarled hollies all along the fence, as well as a couple of stone benches and flower urns placed along the walk. But from the looks of the rampant undergrowth, it hadn't been touched in years. The shrubbery was a jungle and the weeds and grass were knee-high. The red bricks in the path were uneven and some were broken and crumbling. Everywhere there was a profusion of small blue flowers, faded and wilted as if by the sun. Ruby recognized them as the same wildflowers that volunteered along the fence behind her shop in Pecan Springs. Widow's tears, they were called.

Somehow the little flowers seemed appropriate here, for in the far corner of the little graveyard stood the marble angel that Claire had mentioned. It was the very image of grief, standing fully seven feet tall on its rough stone pedestal, wings folded, head bent, eyes cast down. The stone from which it was carved was gray with age and exposure to the weather, and green and gray lichens were growing in the folds of its stone robe. A sweet, fragrant tangle of blooming honeysuckle was draped around it, and a black crow perched carelessly on the angelic shoulder. At its feet, nearly hidden in the grass and wildflowers, was a row of seven stone crosses.

Ruby's skin prickled. The breeze had gone still, the birds had stopped in mid-song, and there was an almost electric feel to the air. She had the strong sense that she and Claire were not alone in the graveyard, and her heart began to beat fast. She looked back and was startled to see the rusted iron gate, with a loud screech of its rusty hinges, begin to swing shut.

Claire saw it, too. With a cry of alarm, she sprinted for it, catching it just before the latch clicked shut.

"Thank God," Ruby said, swept by relief. "The key is still in the lock on the *outside* of the gate. I don't think we could reach it through the bars. We could have been locked in here!"

Claire was pushing the gate open again. "I don't see how this could swing shut," she said, panting. "The hinges are so rusty."

"Yeah." Ruby went to help her. "And it's *heavy*. If our ghost pushed it shut, she's a better woman than I am."

"You hold it, Ruby," Claire said. "I'll get a rock." She found the large rock that had hidden the key and rolled it into place. "There," she said firmly, dusting her hands. "I don't know about you, but I do *not* intend to be locked in here. I'm not in the best shape, and with those spiky doodads on top of that fence, I'm not sure how I'd climb over it. And with the Raw- lingses gone, we might have to spend the night, which I would definitely *not* enjoy." She glanced apprehensively toward the darkening sky. "Looks like it's about to rain. Maybe we should just head back to the house."

"Not yet," Ruby said. The closing gate made her nervous, and she wasn't any more anxious to get rained on than Claire was. "Now that we're here, I think we ought to at least take a look." She didn't want to say it out loud, but she felt compelled to find out just who was buried in those graves—who they were and when they were buried.

"Well, okay," Claire said, sounding resigned. "But let's make it quick." She gave another nudge to the heavy rock to make sure it would stay put and followed Ruby down the brick path.

The graves were lined up in a row to the left of the path. Mrs. Black- wood's was first, the coffin-shaped mound obscured by the tall grass. The stone cross at the head of the grave was carved with her name, *Rachel Blackwood,* and the words *Wife and Mother.* There was no date.

"Rachel," Ruby murmured. A gentle breeze lifted the leaves of a nearby tree, and the grasses on the grave bowed in a soft ripple.

"Rachel," Claire repeated softly, coming up behind her. "Well, at least we know what to call her. What about the others?"

"Looks like they're children," Ruby said. "There's a name and an age on each stone." These crosses—some of them were tilted crookedly—were smaller than Rachel's, and an angel was engraved at the top of each. Ruby read the inscriptions as they went along the path, stepping to the crosses and bending over to pull the grass aside. "Angela, age three. Peter, five; Paul, five." She paused. "Peter and Paul. Twins, maybe?" The next one was Ida, age eight; then Matthew, ten.

She straightened with a long, regretful sigh, and the thought of it clutched at her heart. Five children, a whole family of brothers and sisters, buried here together. When had they died? All at the same time? And *how* had they died?

Beside her, Claire broke the silence. "I guess this explains the nursery," she said quietly. "And the playroom. They must have been the children's rooms." After a moment, she added, "You know, I'm thinking that Rachel's children could have died in an epidemic—diphtheria or whooping cough, scarlet fever, even. Back in the day, when kids got sick with something like that, it was hard to treat them, especially if they lived miles away from a doctor." Her voice softened. "I just wish there were dates on the grave markers. That way, we'd know for sure whether they all died at the same time."

"There's another marker here," Ruby said. She took a few more steps down the path. Next to Matthew's cross was a larger one, the same size as Rachel's. It bore the name *Augustus Blackwood* and the words *Husband and Father*.

"My gosh," Claire said, staring down at Augustus' marker. "Not just mom and kids, but the whole family buried here. Rachel, Augustus, and five little ones. How sad. How terribly, terribly sad. Do you suppose they died at once, all of them?"

"Six of them, maybe," Ruby said, "but not Rachel. Rachel survived."

"True," Claire said, and frowned. "But something is bothering me, Ruby. I was only a kid when Aunt Hazel told me this, but I remember it very clearly. She said that nobody else had ever lived in the house except her and Mrs. Blackwood—she was really definite about that. But she must have been wrong. For one thing, there's the little rocking chair in the music room, and the nursery and the playroom upstairs." She pointed down the row of crosses. "And this. It's evidence that the whole Blackwood family— all seven of them—must have lived in the house. And at some point, maybe all at the same time, the father and children died and were buried here."

"Makes sense," Ruby said distractedly.

"Exactly." Claire was going on, trying to work it out. "But what's puzzling me is that Aunt Hazel must have known about this . . . this whatever, even if it happened before she came here. She lived and worked in the house all her life, so she had to know about the rooms upstairs—unless they were kept closed up and she was forbidden to go in them. But after old Mrs. Blackwood died, she often came to this graveyard to put flowers on her grave, so she had to know about the graves. And the house was hers, so nobody could forbid her to go into any room she liked." She shook her head, frowning. "So she had to have known about the children, at least. Then why did she tell me that she and Mrs. Blackwood were the only people who had ever lived in the house?"

Ruby wasn't really listening. An Old Testament phrase had slipped into her mind. *Rachel, weeping for her children, refusing to be comforted for they were dead.* Rachel, who had survived the awful thing that had destroyed her family, whether she had lost them one by one over months or years or all at one terrible time. The children had died so young—Angela just three, Matthew only ten—so Rachel herself must have been in her thirties when she was left childless, perhaps widowed at the same time.

And Rachel had survived. She had lived into her nineties, another sixty-some years, with no life outside this house, with nothing to do but weep and refuse to be comforted, with only Hazel to keep her company and a caretaker to manage the chores. Perhaps that was why her ghost haunted this place. Perhaps Rachel could not bear to leave the house where all she had loved in the world had lived and died. She wanted to go on grieving, to go on possessing this place until the end of time, to go on bringing white roses to this lonely cemetery, touching harp strings, ringing bells. That's why she had included the odd stipulation in her will, requiring the person who inherited the house to live in it and keep it up—and if they didn't, it would be torn down.

Somewhere nearby, thunder growled. Nearer at hand, the mockingbird offered a staccato barrage of skeptical chirps. Of course, Ruby thought, the situation might be entirely different. Perhaps Rachel's spirit, her ghost, was actually *stuck* here. Maybe she wanted to leave, would leave if she could, but the house—the crooked, misaligned, misshapen house—held on to her and refused to allow her to go. Ruby remembered what Claire had said a little earlier: that it would be the purest hell to be trapped inside a time or a place, to keep repeating something over and over, forever and ever, for all eternity. Was Rachel's ghost being held a prisoner, drowning in an overwhelming grief from which there could never be any rescue? Or was it the other way around? Was she voluntarily, willfully, stubbornly holding on, refusing release?

Ruby shivered, hearing those questions pounding on the walls of her own heart. She knew how it felt to grieve, yes. She still grieved for Colin.

But would she want to grieve for dozens of years, for decades? To grieve for the rest of her life, and beyond? No. No, of course not. She couldn't want that. It had already been too long. She wanted to stop grieving now, and get on with the rest of her life. Maybe she needed to let Hark pull her out of her own stuck place. Or pull herself out. Either way, she didn't want to let herself stay stuck.

She wrapped her arms around herself. It might be her imagination, but the air seemed colder. Nervously, she glanced over her shoulder. She had the feeling that someone else was here in the graveyard with them, standing not far away, listening to what she and Claire had been saying, listening to what she had been *thinking*. She raised her voice.

"Are you there, Rachel?" she asked tentatively. She felt a little foolish, talking to a ghost, talking to something she couldn't see. "Rachel, if you're there, tell us—tell me—what you want? Do you want to stay or go?"

For an instant, Ruby thought she heard a soft sob, the faintest sound of anguished weeping, coming from a distant place. But the mockingbird chose that moment to set up a cheerful, noisy chatter, and when he stopped gossiping, the weeping was gone, or perhaps it had never been, or had been only in her mind.

Still—Ruby cast an apprehensive glance over her shoulder and was absurdly relieved to see that the iron cemetery gate stood open, propped by the solid rock Claire had put there. She comforted herself with the thought that it would take a hefty ghost to move that rock, although maybe the undead weren't bound by the same physical laws that held the living.

But then her eye was caught by something lying on the brick walk a few paces away from the open gate, a white silk handkerchief maybe. That's odd, she thought—I don't remember seeing that when we came in. She went back along the walk to pick it up and saw, to her astonishment, that it was a perfect white rose, so fresh that there were crystal drops of dew, like tears, on the petals. She was holding it in her hand, staring at it and hardly daring to breathe, when Claire called out to her.

"Ruby, I've found Aunt Hazel's marker."

Ruby went toward her, carrying the rose in her open hand. "Claire," she said shakily, "Claire, tell me that you dropped this when I wasn't looking." She held it out.

"Dropped that rose?" Clair shook her head, frowning. "No, of course I didn't. I've never brought any flowers up here. I—" She looked up and saw Ruby's face. "Why are you asking? Where did you find it?"

"Lying on the brick walk, just inside the gate. I'm sure it wasn't there when we came in—or when we went back to keep the gate from closing."

"It wasn't." Claire's voice was flat and matter-of-fact. "*She* dropped it, Ruby. Rachel. She left it for us, so we'd know she was here."

Ruby bit her lip. She herself had seen Rachel's ghost this morning, carrying a basket of roses. It shouldn't be hard to believe that Rachel had followed them into the cemetery and left the rose for them to find. No, it wasn't *hard,* it was unsettling, unnerving. Just another small testimony to the frightening strangeness of this place.

Ruby bent over and laid the rose at the foot of Augustus Blackwood's cross. *There you are, Rachel,* she said silently. *I've left it for him. I hope you approve.*

She straightened up. "You found your aunt's marker, you said?"

"Over here," Claire said, taking her arm. "No wonder I didn't see it right away. It's totally buried in green stuff."

The three stone crosses lined up in a row along the back fence were almost completely hidden in a tangle of weeds and widow's tears, its blue blooms spilling everywhere.

"Mother always said she didn't want to leave Aunt Hazel here alone,"

166

Claire said quietly. "She thought it was a lonely place." She turned to look at the row of Blackwood graves. "But now I'm not so sure. Hazel loved old Mrs. Blackwood, and this place—especially the woods." In a lower voice, she added, "Maybe she loved Rachel's children, too, and her husband, even if they died before she came here."

The first of the three crosses stood at the head of what was still a visible gravesite. It bore the name *Hazel Penland* but no date.

"Hazel wanted her marker to look like the others," Claire said. "I didn't understand that, then. Now I think I do." She pointed. "That's the family, there—all seven of them. These three, they're the servants, or helpers, or whatever. Aunt Hazel didn't like to think of herself as a servant, but I suppose that's what she was. And that's probably what Patsy and Colleen were. Servants."

Those were the names on the remaining two crosses: Patsy Hill and Colleen O'Reilly. Both names were barely legible, the stones battered by the elements and covered with lichen and moss. Colleen O'Reilly's cross bore something else, but whatever it was, it was so weathered that it could not be read.

Colleen O'Reilly. Ruby frowned, feeling an odd tug at her memory. Gram Gifford's mother, Ruby's great-grandmother. Her name was Colleen, wasn't it? Or was it Corinne? No, Colleen, it had been Colleen. And her last name might have been O'Reilly. But it had been a long time since Gram had mentioned it, and Ruby couldn't remember for sure. Kids don't pay a lot of attention to family history. Perhaps it had been O'Ryan. Of course O'Reilly (O'Ryan, too, for that matter) was a common Irish name, as common as Jones or Smith. And Colleen—well, every Irish family had to have at least one Colleen among the girls. Still, the longer Ruby stared at the cross, the more certain she felt that her great-grandmother's name had been Colleen, not Corinne. Colleen O'Reilly.

Anyway, Gram had told her once that her mother had been carried out to sea in a great storm and drowned, when Gram herself was so young that she barely remembered it. Gram and her grandmother, whose name Ruby had never heard or didn't remember, had lived through the same storm. After that, the two of them had moved to San Antonio, where her grandmother had done her best to bring her up, working at two jobs so Gram could go to college, back in the day when a young woman was only encouraged to get married. But Gram's eyes always filled with tears when she talked about the last time she saw her mother, going bravely back out into the storm to help someone she cared for. Ruby, still a little girl, hadn't wanted to make her favorite grandmother unhappy, so with a child's tact, she had never asked for the whole story.

Maybe the story was here, Ruby thought. *But how could that be? Colleen O'Reilly was lost at sea, not buried in a lonely Texas graveyard.* She stood very still, looking down at the cross. The graveyard, which had been full of birdsong a moment ago, suddenly seemed to go silent. She felt colder, more remote. She was beginning to feel a shimmer. There was something about the cross, something that pulled her, something that could tell her—

"Ruby," Claire called. "I've found something, here on the angel. Come and take a look. I can't quite read it. Maybe you'll be able to make it out."

Ruby felt the shimmer disappear—for the first time, regretfully. Claire was kneeling down, examining the pedestal. Then she picked up a stick and began scraping away some of the moss.

"What is it?" Ruby asked, going over to her.

"Don't know," Claire replied. "The carving is almost worn away. All I can make out are two words. Looks like *My Angels*."

"My angels?" Ruby repeated.

"Yeah. There's more engraving, but I can't read it. Can you?"

Ruby bent over and peered at the rough-cut stone. She could decipher the shapes of letters and some numbers, but not clearly enough to know what they were. "Sorry," she said, straightening up. "All I can make out are those two words.'"

Claire stood up. "Now I'm really curious. I think if I bring a knife or a paint scraper or something like that, I can get some more of this stuff off. There might be a date under all this moss. And if we knew the date, we might be able to figure out what—"

Claire's words were obliterated by a simultaneous, blinding flash of lightning and a teeth-rattling, ear-splitting clap of thunder. About fifty yards away, along the edge of the woods, a tall pine tree was split by a bolt of lightning. It exploded like a detonating bomb, hurling showers of sparks and huge chunks of broken, splintered wood in every direction. The iron fence around the cemetery seemed to vibrate, and the air was filled with the smell of smoke.

For a second, Ruby and Claire froze. "Holy cow," Claire breathed. Her eyes were huge and staring in her white face. "Ruby, I've never seen anything like that before. That was *close*! We could have been killed!"

Ruby's ears were ringing and her heart was pounding like a trip-hammer. "Come on, let's run," she said urgently, heading for the gate. "If our ghost is throwing thunderbolts, I'd rather be a moving target."

Chapter Twelve

Herbs and flowers often figure in both personal and political history. Napoleon Bonaparte's wife Josephine loved violets. She wore them on her wedding day, and Napoleon sent her a bouquet of purple violets every year on their anniversary. He adopted the violet as his political emblem, and when he was banished to Elba, he promised to "return with the violets." While he was in exile, his followers defied the law by wearing the flower as an emblem of their faithfulness to him. After Waterloo, Napoleon reportedly visited Josephine's grave, picked a few violets he found growing there, and kept them in a locket he wore until his own death.

In the language of flowers, the violet represents love and faithfulness.

China Bayles
"Herbs and Flowers That Tell a Story"
Pecan Springs Enterprise

The sky remained ominously dark and threatening, especially toward the east and south, where heavy gray clouds were dropping sheer curtains of silvery rain. There was another lightning strike on the other side of the creek, another flash and loud crash. But only a few large, warm splatters came down on Ruby and Claire as they ran to the house, and they managed to get back without getting very wet.

Ruby picked up her bag from the kitchen and Claire showed her to her room upstairs. After the grandeur of the rooms on the main floor—and the ghostly presence—Ruby didn't know quite what to expect. Something dark and frightening, maybe, or somehow misaligned in its dimensions, like the outside of the house. In which case, Ruby had decided, she would suggest that she and Claire sleep together, for company, and comfort.

But there was nothing out of the ordinary about the room, and nothing very personal about it, either. There were no pictures on the wall, nothing to indicate who might have slept here. It was simply a large, high-ceilinged bedroom pleasantly wallpapered in light blue flowers above a white-painted beadboard wainscot, a pair of twin beds spread with blue coverlets against one wall, and a blue rug on the polished wooden floor.

"Nice," Ruby said approvingly, looking around. The room was furnished with an old-fashioned white-painted dresser and mirror, a chifforobe, and a rocking chair with a blue print cushion. The chair sat in front of a tall, white-curtained window, which looked out over the creek running through the green meadow at the foot of a long, low wooded hill.

"I thought you'd like the view from this window," Claire said, going to the door. Carelessly, over her shoulder, she said, "In case anything bothers you in the night, my room is right through that door." She pointed to a white-painted door in the wall beside one of the beds. "Just come on in and wake me up—if I'm not awake already."

"Bothers me?" Ruby asked, frowning apprehensively. "Like . . . how?"

"Well . . ." Claire hesitated. "I sometimes hear sobbing. And water dripping. And the wind."

Ruby thought of the sobs she had heard—well, almost heard—in the cemetery. "What else?"

Another hesitation. "I don't think there's anything that will hurt you, if that's what you're asking," Claire said, a little stiffly. "If I did, I probably wouldn't be here myself. And I certainly wouldn't have invited you to come."

"I didn't mean that, exactly," Ruby said, although she had been wondering, a little nervously, if there was any danger. So far, the manifestations hadn't seemed threatening, but—

"It's all very scary, I know." Claire sighed. "But I've never sensed anything malicious or evil about any of it. I think we'll be okay." She added, "The bathroom is two doors down on the left, just past my room. Come down to the kitchen whenever you're ready. I was thinking spaghetti for supper—store-bought sauce and definitely non-gourmet, but it's easy. And we have the salad fixings that Kitty left, and some hard-boiled eggs." She gave a short laugh. "I'd offer you some wine, but I don't keep it in the house, for obvious reasons."

"I can do without wine," Ruby said. "But don't forget the pie. Oh, and let's eat in the morning room, if it's okay with you. There's something about that kitchen—" She shivered.

"What's the matter?" Claire asked, making a comic face. "You're afraid Rachel might whap us over the head with a skillet?"

"I agree—she doesn't seem to be the malicious type," Ruby replied lightly. "But that's what people said about Lizzie Borden. And don't forget that we were very nearly fried by that lightning bolt." They both laughed as Claire left the room.

As Ruby unpacked, she glanced out the window and saw a white-tailed doe with a pair of twin spotted fawns at her side, coming down to the creek to drink. Mother and babies—a reminder, somehow, of the mute cluster of small, sad stone crosses in the cemetery. What had happened here? How had those children, and their father, died? Had Rachel herself committed some unthinkable crime and been sentenced to mourn forever in this house?

And what about the three other people who were buried in the cemetery? Hazel Penland was Claire's aunt—there wasn't much mystery about

173

her. But who were Patsy Hill and Colleen O'Reilly? Had they lived here, servants in the house before Claire's aunt came? Which would have been when? What year? Ruby realized that she didn't know, and made a mental note to ask Claire.

Colleen O'Reilly. Ruby stood still in the middle of the room, feeling suddenly that she needed to know who that person was. She focused, trying to remember what Gram Gifford had said about her mother—whose name, Ruby was now sure, had been Colleen O'Reilly. But the conversations had been so long ago, in another life almost, and nothing came, nothing more than the recollection of hearing Gram say that her mother had died in a storm—swept out to sea when she went to help a friend. And there wasn't anybody left on that side of the family who could fill in the blanks.

Still thinking, Ruby pulled off her sundress and hung it in the closet, then changed into a pair of comfortable jeans and a green-and-peach striped pullover and went out into the hall, where she stood for a moment getting her bearings. Claire was busy in the kitchen—maybe now would be a good time to do a little exploring. If she remembered right, Claire had said the nursery was on the second floor.

Ruby's room was at one end of the hallway, opposite the stair. Along the hall, there were four doors on each side, eight altogether. Claire had said her room was the next door on the left, so Ruby skipped that one, then opened the other doors one by one. She didn't have to turn the lights on. A strange, pearly gray twilight hung over the house, and the windows in each room and at the ends of the hall let in enough light so that she could see.

On the other side of Claire's bedroom, the bathroom was large and old-fashioned, with a deep claw-foot tub, a white tile floor, and a porcelain sink with a medicine cabinet and mirror over it. The walls were the same pale yellow as the morning room downstairs, and the room smelled of fresh paint—one of Claire's fix-up projects, Ruby guessed.

174

The four bedrooms on the other side of the hall were about the same size as Ruby's, but with green wallpaper, or lavender, beige, or yellow, each one furnished with a bureau, a chair, and a bed with a coverlet in the same color as the wallpaper. But none of them felt occupied or personal—no pictures on the wall, nothing but the minimum of furniture. If anyone— the children, especially—had slept in these rooms for any length of time, they had left nothing of themselves behind. But then Ruby remembered Claire saying that Mr. Hoover had packed up the china from the dining room and some of the things in the music room, with the idea of renting the house. Maybe any personal items from the bedrooms had been packed, as well.

The bedroom on the other side of the bathroom was more spacious and much better furnished, with a huge arched headboard and footboard carved out of some sort of dark, highly polished wood. There was a mir- rored dresser and a matching bureau to match, a gilt-framed full-length chevron mirror in the corner, and an ornately patterned rug in shades of red and blue covering most of the floor. It had to be the master bedroom, Ruby thought, where Rachel and Augustus had slept, although this room, like the others, had been stripped of anything personal. There were no family photographs, no toilet articles, not even a doily. She stood in the doorway for a moment, waiting for—what? She didn't know, except that even though there was a kind of bleak emptiness to the room, she was be- ginning to feel uncomfortably like a voyeur, as if she were intruding on the privacy of the people who had slept together here, made love here, con- ceived their children here. She closed the door very quietly, not even allow- ing the latch to click.

There was one room left, the last room on the left, just past the master bedroom. She guessed, as she put her hand to the polished brass doorknob, that it was the nursery. Remembering Claire's nervousness about the room, she opened it an inch, then wider, and finally stepped inside. The room was painted yellow, with a low, narrow, white-painted bed beside the window, a ruffled pillow at the head, a ruffled yellow-and-blue quilt spread over it. In the wall across from the bed was a connecting doorway into the master bedroom, Ruby thought. Beside the door was a white chifforobe decorated with painted baby animals and flowers. Next to the window stood a child's red-painted rocking chair, twin to the one in the music room downstairs.

But unlike the other rooms, this one seemed to hold a number of personal things, for under the window, white-painted shelves displayed a trio of small stuffed brown bears, a red-and-blue ball, a box of wooden alphabet blocks, a painted metal box with a handle on the side—a jack-in-the-box, likely—and several books. But the toys and the books were all new looking, Ruby noticed. Not new in the sense of *modern*, for they definitely had an old-fashioned, Victorian look. They were new in the sense of *unused*.

That's odd, Ruby thought. Frowning, she went over and picked up a small brown bear. Then, suddenly, she felt the shimmer begin, felt herself being pulled, involuntarily, into the bear. But this time she didn't raise her defenses. Instead, she went with the feeling, letting herself go, trying to get a sense, through the little bear, of the child to whom it had belonged, the child who loved it. Little Angela, perhaps? As the baby of the family, just three when she died, Angela would surely have slept in this room, where her mother could hear her and comfort her when she cried. But there was no one who could comfort Rachel. *Rachel, weeping for her children, refusing to be comforted for they were dead.*

Ruby turned the bear over and over in her hands, attempting to learn something about it, attempting to *feel* it. But after a moment, she gave up. The bear seemed lifeless, entirely empty of energy, nothing but a cloth shape stuffed with cotton, with two shiny black buttons for eyes and a stitched-on red mouth. Was she getting this feeling because she had for so long refused to use her gift in any important way, and now that she needed it, *wanted* it, it wasn't available?

Well, maybe. But even as she considered that possibility, she knew that wasn't what was happening here. The poignant truth was that the bear had spent its whole lonely existence, not in the hands of a child, but sitting on a shelf, on *this* shelf. She knew with a sad conviction that Angela had never loved this little bear, had never slept with it, had never even touched it. Regretfully, she put it back in its place on the shelf, and then, one after the other, picked up each of the toys: the other bears, the ball, the blocks, the jack-in-the-box. They all had the same blank and lifeless emptiness. They had never been played with. They had never been loved.

By now feeling deeply perplexed, she turned to the bed and picked up the child's pillow, holding it against her and feeling the same lifelessness. On the top of the bureau, she found a pair of child's white leather shoes, high-top, lace-up little Victorian boots. But the soles were immaculate and the leather showed no signs of wear. And when she opened the drawers of the bureau, she saw tidy stacks of clothing for a little girl of two or three— underclothes, play clothes, little dresses and pinafores, all well-made clothes and beautiful, in the old-fashioned style of a century before. Old-fashioned, yes, but new-looking, never worn. She picked up one of the little pinafores and saw, with a shiver of recognition, the name *Angela* embroidered on it in loopy pink letters. Now she was sure. This had been Angela's nursery for the first three years of her life—the *only* three years of her life.

But there was something wrong with that idea, Ruby knew, for despite all the personal items that made the room look as if a child had once played and slept here, it was no more lived-in than the other rooms on the floor. It was like a stage set, with toys for props and drawers full of costumes. She stood for a moment, looking around, feeling bewildered, trying to puzzle it out. On the one hand, Claire's aunt had insisted that only she and Mrs.

Blackwood had ever lived in the house. On the other, there were five head-stones in the graveyard, Angela's among them. And this was Angela's nurs-ery. So why hadn't her pillow been *used*? Why hadn't her boots and little dresses been worn, her stuffed bear loved?

Ruby's shoulders slumped. Well, it was still possible that *she* was the problem. It had been a long day. She was tired and hungry, and she had barely missed being struck by lightning an hour before. And while she was psychic, she wasn't very skilled at it—skilled, that is, in using her gift to pick up information from people's possessions. And since Angela's mother had been in her nineties when she died, over thirty years ago, Angela her-self must have been dead for longer than that, a hundred years, perhaps. And surely, in the decades since, the vibrations would have faded.

"When?" Ruby whispered into the twilit air of the empty room. "When did you die, Angela?" She was surprised when she heard her voice—she had thought she was just *thinking* the question, holding it in her mind. But now that the words were out there and audible, hanging in front of her like pale breath on a chilly morning, she went on.

"And *how*?" she persisted. "How did it happen? Did all five of you go at once, or over time? And what about your father? Was it an illness, an epi-demic? An accident, or some sort of violent death? *How*?" She paused, and the question echoed eerily in the silence. "Hey, Rachel," she said softly, "how about a little help here, huh?"

She stood listening for a moment, the aching loneliness of the five little graves in the cemetery, the sadness of the unloved toys, the emptiness of the small, silent bed—all of it washing over her like a chilling wave. But there was nothing more to be learned from this room, and Claire was wait-ing for her downstairs. She turned toward the door with a sense of some-thing like resignation.

But just as she put her hand to the doorknob, she smelled the faint scent of violets, the same fragrance she had smelled in the drawing room, and heard the sound of choked sobbing, a woman's hopeless, despairing weeping, just on the other side of the door.

The room had been warm, like the rest of the house, but all of a sudden, the temperature plummeted, as if an icy polar wind had suddenly breezed into the room, sweeping out all the warmth. Ruby stood trembling, cold inside and out, wanting desperately to open the door and comfort the crying woman, yet desperately afraid of what might happen if she did. She would come face-to-face with Rachel, or whatever the thing was that she and Claire had named Rachel. And if she did . . .

And if she did? She bit her lip until she tasted salty blood. She wasn't sure what would happen, but she knew what she feared. She would be drawn into that restless, unmoored spirit, she would become sister to that undead soul of grief and lost to herself forever.

Feeling the almost irresistible, magnetic attraction, Ruby pressed her forehead against the door, tightening her muscles and her hold on the doorknob, pushing back with all her will and physical strength against the pull of whatever was on the other side, knowing with the most awful certainty that the closed door between her and Rachel was all that was saving her. Saving her from *what*? She didn't know. But she knew that if she opened the door, if she stepped out into the hall, Rachel would take possession of her, would draw her into that terrible grief, would *drown* her in it. And that would be the end of her life as she knew it.

The sobbing went on, growing louder to a tremulous crescendo, then softer, as if muted by an unbearable grief. But loud or soft, the sound seemed to vibrate through Ruby's flesh and bones, filling her, as if she were an empty vessel, with Rachel's despairing bereavement and loss. She wasn't sure how long she stood there—five minutes? Ten? A half hour? As she clung to the doorknob, feeling her knees weaken, her resolve falter, even as the cold seemed to wrap around her more intently than ever, its icy tentacles probing her veins, freezing her blood.

But as the moments passed, the contest—if that's what it was—seemed to turn in Ruby's direction. The power of the attraction seemed to diminish, lessening its pull on her, as if Rachel were yielding, reluctantly but at last, to Ruby's strength, and to the fact that Ruby was firmly rooted in her own life and refused to be pulled into Rachel's spectral existence.

But even as the tug-of-war eased, it seemed to shift its terms, as if Rachel had been taking the measure of Ruby's physical and psychological strength. Understanding that she had met her match and realizing that she could not pull Ruby into herself, she would use her in another way. It was as if she had become practical. She was saying, *Well, then, if not that, then this.*

And then, just when it seemed that the balance of power had shifted in Ruby's favor, an idea slipped, specter-like and seductive, into Ruby's mind. She didn't know how she knew, but she knew that it came directly from Rachel, and that Rachel was telling her what she wanted, what she *needed*. Ruby couldn't quite give words to the idea—it was more like a glimmer of a faraway lamp in a fog, a feeling-glimpse of an intention or a whisper of a prayer, too distant to quite catch. She closed her eyes and put her ear against the door.

What is it, Rachel? she cried silently. *What? What do you want? What would ease this pain? What would release you from this—*

At that moment, there was a loud metallic whir from the other side of the room. She turned, startled, to see the jack-in-the-box lid snap open. The jack itself—a sailor doll with a painted-on smile, wearing a blue uniform jacket and a white sailor cap—jumped up and began to wave his arms, accompanied by a tinny hurdy-gurdy melody, very loud, impossibly

180

loud, so loud that Ruby had to put both hands over her ears. *Sailing sailing over the bounding main For many a stormy wind will blow ere Jack comes home again Sailing sailing over the bounding main For many a stormy wind*

The fun-house music stopped abruptly. The sailor jack disappeared back into his box, and the lid snapped shut. Ruby dropped her hands and sucked in her breath. Then, quite suddenly in the silence, she heard a child's sweet giggle—sweet, yes, reminding her of Baby Grace's sweet laugh. To her horror, she saw that the little red rocking chair was rocking steadily, as if Angela herself were sitting in it, delighting in the musical antics of Sailor Jack.

And then, as if on cue, the tinny music-box melody came again, *Sailing sailing*, and Jack popped up again and saluted until the music ended and he dived back into his metal box. *Sailing sailing over the bounding main For many a stormy wind will blow ere Jack comes home again Sailing sailing over the*

Ruby watched, trying to catch her breath. The room was as empty and bare of life as it had been. But there sat the rocking chair, silently, steadily rocking. And in the quiet, the child's happy giggle continued until, outside the door, Rachel's sobbing began again, rising to a wail of unspeakable loss and grief.

Then it was over. The chair stopped rocking. The giggle ceased abruptly. The sobbing gradually faded into the distance, as if the weeping woman had walked to the end of the hall and turned to go down the stairs, carrying her grief with her. Then it, too, was gone, and there was absolute silence.

And at that moment, with a sound that seemed louder than it was in the stillness, a book slipped off the shelf and fell, open, onto the floor. Ruby fought against the urge for a moment, then crossed the room and bent to pick it up. It was a book of nursery rhymes illustrated with colorful Victorian drawings. It had fallen open to a page that bore the rhyme that had haunted her all day.

> *There was a crooked man and he walked a crooked mile,*
> *He found a crooked sixpence upon a crooked stile.*
> *He bought a crooked cat, which caught a crooked mouse.*
> *And they all lived together in a little crooked house.*

She stared at the page, her chest tightening, the pulse in her throat pounding. What was this supposed to *mean*? What did it have to do with this place? What was going on here?

Hurriedly, she closed the book and put it back on the shelf from which it had fallen, then went to the door. The jack-in-the-box, the rocking chair, the child's sweet giggle, the anguished sobbing, the book. It was all too much, just too much. Moving like a woman clutched in the vise of a nightmare, fighting a wave of light-headed nausea, she left the room and groped her way down the shadowy hallway, which was still filled with the faint scent of violets.

But the glimmer of an idea that had slipped into her mind as she'd stood on the other side of the door was still with her as she went down the stairs.

In the kitchen, Claire had taken the salad fixings out of the refrigerator and opened a package of spaghetti. It wasn't quite seven yet, but outdoors, the dusky twilight had deepened. As Ruby came into the room, Claire flicked on the kitchen light. It didn't work.

"Uh-oh," Claire said, trying it again. "Were the lights working upstairs?"

"I didn't try," Ruby mumbled. "It wasn't that dark." She took a deep breath, trying to steady herself. "Listen, Claire, I've been in the nursery. Have you spent any time there? Do you remember that little jack-in-the-box on the shelf under the window? Have you ever heard—"

But Claire wasn't paying attention. "Might be a circuit breaker," she said worriedly, taking a flashlight out of a drawer. "Maybe there was some kind of surge on the power line when the lightning struck that tree. It could have knocked the breakers off. The breaker box is in the storeroom. I'll go check."

"I'll go with you," Ruby offered. She didn't want to be alone right now. She would wait to tell Claire what had happened until after they had dealt with the lights. And by that time, maybe that glimmer of an idea would seem more clear. Right now, it was so shapeless, so amorphous, that she couldn't put words to it.

"Sure, come along." Claire clicked the flashlight in her hand, testing it. "Well, *hell*," she said disgustedly. "I just put these batteries in last week. I—" She stopped and looked at Ruby. "You don't think—" She clicked the switch again. "Rats," she said disgustedly. "Just like the cell phones."

"And the cars," Ruby said, feeling resigned. She took the candle and matches that Claire handed her. "I'm afraid I don't hold out much hope for the circuit breakers, either."

She was right. The breakers were all on, although the power was indisputably off. Whatever the problem was, it wasn't in the breaker box.

"Maybe this doesn't have anything to do with Rachel," Claire said as they made their way back to the kitchen through the dark hallway, Ruby carrying the flickering candle. "It could be a transformer out on the main road. In fact, for all we know, the power could be off all over this part of the county. It's not like we can phone the electric co-op and ask whether the service is down."

"Has this happened before?" Ruby asked.

"No, but there's no reason it couldn't. If I turn this place into a B and B, I should probably plan to buy a generator for backup power. It's not going to be a big problem for just you and me, but if we had a houseful of guests, it would be another matter entirely." She sighed. "Although I really wanted to watch the weather forecast on TV to see if we're under some kind of alert. This morning, the forecasters on the San Antonio channels were talking about a tropical storm making landfall this evening. We're so far inland, I wouldn't think it could be a problem, but you never know. Sometimes those storms spin off tornadoes. That's all we'd need—to get hit by one of those."

"You don't have a battery radio?" Ruby asked, as they came into the kitchen. She put the candle on the table. "Well, that's dumb," she said with a wry laugh. "If Rachel doesn't want us to use our cell phones or the flashlight, she'd probably draw the line at the battery radio, too."

But *why*? she wondered, even as she made the remark. Assuming that there was some kind of logic to cutting them off from the rest of the world in this way, what *was* it? But maybe ghosts didn't need logic, or at least the kind of logic that would make sense to someone who wasn't a ghost. She thought about the sobbing, the giggle, the sailor jack-in-the-box, and felt cold in her bones.

Claire, meanwhile, was thinking practical thoughts. "Here's something else we have to consider, Ruby. Without electricity, the water well pump doesn't work. There's probably enough water in the pressure tank for flushing, if we're careful, and there's some in the fridge for drinking. But we'd better skip our showers tonight. If the power hasn't come on by the time Sam gets back tomorrow, I'll have to send him to find out what's going on."

"Assuming his truck will run," Ruby remarked in a light tone, and managed a scrap of a smile.

Claire rolled her eyes. "Let's not go there, shall we? At least we'll have plenty of light tonight." She went to one of the kitchen cupboards, took out two lamps and put them on the table, then stood staring at them. "I hope you know how to operate these things. I don't."

"Actually, I do," Ruby said. "I have a couple at home, in case of emergencies. Do they already have lamp oil in them?" She saw that they did, so she took off the glass lamp chimney, turned up the wick, then lit a match and touched it to the wick. When it caught, she turned the wick down slightly so it wouldn't smoke, and put the chimney back on.

"Voilà," she said, setting one of the lamps in the middle of the kitchen table. "A little pioneer magic."

"Laura Ingalls Wilder would be proud of you," Claire said with a laugh, and blew out the candle. "Now, how about supper? The gas stove is working, so we can cook our spaghetti." She stepped to the small stove and turned on a burner. "See? I guess Rachel didn't think to zap our propane tank. Either that, or she can't figure out how." She put the lamp on the pine table next to the stove and took down a pan from the rack on the wall.

Ruby froze. "Claire," she said. Her chest felt tight. Her voice sounded as if it were strangling in her throat. "Claire, *look*."

"Yeah?" Claire turned, the pan in her hand. "Look where?" Her eyes widened as she saw the look on Ruby's face. "Are you okay, Ruby? What's wrong?" She turned to look in the direction of Ruby's gaze, and gasped. "Oh my *God*," she whispered.

They were staring at the black chalkboard that hung on the wall next to the rack of pots and pans, with *Menus* printed across the top in an old-fashioned script and a chalk tray with a small eraser at the bottom. Earlier, the board had displayed Claire's perfectly ordinary grocery list—bread, milk, yogurt, coffee. But in the flickering light of the oil lamp, they saw that the list had been erased, and in its place was a date, scrawled shakily across the width of the board. *Sept. 8, 1900.* And beneath that, four words, four nonsense words.

> *crooked*
>> *man*
>> *crooked*
>> *sixpence*

Chapter Thirteen

Santolina (*Santolina chamaecyparissus*) is a shrubby gray or green plant twelve to eighteen inches tall, with yellow button-like flowers in summer. It does especially well on arid hillsides and in dry gardens. A moderately fast grower, a single plant is likely to spread three to five feet, rooting along the lower branches. It is often used as a border plant, and clipped. Medicinally, it was used as a children's vermifuge. The dried leaves are strongly aromatic and were often placed in drawers and chests to protect clothing against moths.

In the language of flowers, santolina represents protection against all evils.

China Bayles
"Herbs and Flowers That Tell a Story"
Pecan Springs Enterprise

I had plenty to think about on the drive from Pecan Springs to Round Top. Under ordinary circumstances, I wouldn't barge in on Ruby's well-earned vacation. But this didn't qualify as an ordinary circumstance, at least as I saw it. Maybe I was being selfish (yes, there's always that possibility) but I didn't want to wait a whole week to find out whether Ramona was telling the truth or handing me a big bunch of baloney.

Was Ruby *really* thinking of selling her shop to her sister—and hoping to sell her share of the partnership, as well? I was aware that she was overdoing it and needed a vacation, but I hadn't suspected anything so drastic. Maybe I was being selfish about this as well, but the thought of having Ramona as my next-door shop neighbor did not fill me with rejoicing. And as McQuaid pointed out, if Ruby left the partnership, it would be very hard for Cass and me to keep all of the lions at bay. The catering service would probably have to go—and how would we manage the tearoom?

The thing that was bothering me most, though, was that I had failed to see any of this coming. Had I been too preoccupied to notice? Too self-absorbed, too busy with my own affairs? Was I guilty (as Ramona implied) of not paying attention to my best friend's feelings? I had to admit that this was entirely possible. McQuaid has pointed out to me more than once that I have a tendency to get overly involved with whatever I'm doing and forget about everything—and everyone—else.

Of course, Ruby doesn't always let on what's going on inside her, especially if she thinks it might worry me. She might have been deliberately keeping her thoughts to herself until she had come to some sort of conclusion. All I knew was that the past few weeks had been difficult for her, and that the invitation from Claire Conway had given her a break from her usual routine, which to my mind was a good thing. No doubt she and Claire were lounging around in their negligees, sharing a bottle of fine wine, nibbling on some great gourmet goodies, and trading girl-talk, catching up the events of their lives since they had last seen each other. I hoped they wouldn't be too irritated by my interruption. I had thought of texting Ruby to tell her that I was coming, but my concern was impossible to explain in a text, so I had decided against it.

And now it occurred to me—belatedly, I'm afraid—that she might have had another reason for wanting to go away. For all I knew, she might not just be taking a break from her shop and our partnership, but a break from *me*.

At the thought, I felt a terrible sinking feeling in the pit of my stomach. Well, I wouldn't take more than an hour of her time. I wasn't asking for a yes or a no on the spot. I just needed to find out whether Ramona had described the situation accurately. And whatever the outcome of our conversation, my feelings for Ruby wouldn't change, I knew that much for sure. We would still be best friends and I would do whatever I could to support her choice and make her happy. And if the news was bad—well, at least I would know where I stood and could start making plans, which would definitely *not* include Ramona. That was another thing I knew for sure.

But I was already wishing I had taken the time to stop at home and pack my toothbrush and nightie before I left town. From the looks of the weather, it might be a good idea to stay over, if Claire had room for me. By sunset, the clouds that had hugged the horizon when I left Pecan Springs had grown to towering heights and seemed to fill half the eastern sky, billowing in delicate pastel shades of lavender, purple, and gray. Lightning slashed like jagged knives, and the radio crackled with static. When I managed to tune in to a weather forecast, the announcer, breathy with excitement, reported that Amanda had made landfall near Corpus Christi and was heading inland faster than expected. The winds had already peaked at gale force, around fifty miles an hour. Amanda obviously wasn't a big wind threat. But a cold front was stalled out across the middle of the state, which would slow Amanda's advance overnight. She was going to be a rainmaker, with a predicted seven or eight inches or more across the southern tier of Texas counties. This wasn't a bad thing, since the lakes and reservoirs were seriously depleted and a huge chunk of the state was officially parched. But the real danger would be the roadway flooding. It's not a good idea to drive in heavy rain, after dark on strange roads, where you don't know the terrain—especially in Texas, where flash-flooding kills a couple dozen people every year. "Turn around, don't drown" has become the newscasters' mantra, and with very good reason. Slide off the road and into a roaring stream in the dark, and unless the swift-water rescue helicopter happens to be hovering overhead, you're a dead duck.

All of this was going through my mind as I hung a right off Highway 290 and headed south toward the little town of Round Top. I drive this way fairly often, because the Pioneer Unit of the Herb Society of America (of which I'm a member) holds its Herbal Forum every March at the Round Top Festival Institute. I hadn't had any supper, so I dropped in at Royers Cafe and ordered a burger. On impulse, I bought one of their great pecan pies to take along with me, as an apology for barging in on Ruby and her friend unannounced. If they hadn't bothered with dessert—or even if they had—they might be glad to see me arrive with a pie in my hand.

In the café, the television was turned on, and the crawler across the bottom of the screen carried a bulletin about the storm, as well as a short bit about the bank robbery in Pecan Springs. It was a painful reminder that Bonnie's husband and daughter were facing their first night without their wife and mother. I still couldn't get over it. And Ruby knew Bonnie as well as I did. She would be devastated by the news.

As I said, I've been to Round Top often, but I had never driven Texas 237 south of town, so I took it slow. By now, it was past eight o'clock and the rain was beginning to come down hard enough to make me wish I had not only brought my nightie and toothbrush but a poncho and boots as well. But I had Claire's sketch map on the back of the postcard she had sent to Ruby, and her directions were pretty clear. It was so dark that I almost missed the church camp sign that marked the road where I was supposed to make a right turn, but I saw it at the last minute. After that, it was a matter of spotting the black mailbox and the twin brick pillars on the left, and then all I had to do was peer through the sweeping arc of the windshield wipers and into the rainy cone of the headlights as I followed the twists and turns of the narrow lane that led to the Blackwood house and Ruby. I fervently hoped that was where it led, because if it didn't I was probably lost. And from the looks of the road, which was getting muddier by the minute, turning around and driving back the way I had come might not be an option. Already this was beginning to seem like *not* the smartest idea I had ever had.

It was a long, dark, slippery seven miles, and in the end I was creeping along at about fifteen miles an hour. But just when I was about to despair, I found myself topping a hill and heading down a rutted incline so steep and slick that I had to shift into first gear and keep one foot on the brake all the way down. The car skidded in a couple of places and I clutched the steering wheel, biting my lower lip.

But I finally made it. At the bottom, the lane made a sharp dogleg turn and I crossed a narrow concrete bridge, so low that the water was already rushing hubcap-deep over the top of it. The hill and the bridge were shown on Claire's sketch map, so I allowed myself to hope I had come to the right place—because if I hadn't, I was in serious trouble. Off to my left loomed a bulky black silhouette—the Blackwood house, I guessed, although it was too dark to see much of it. I followed the curving lane around the back of the house, where Ruby's car appeared in my headlights. As I parked beside it, I breathed a relieved, heartfelt sigh. I wouldn't have to test my Toyota's traction by trying to climb back up that dangerously slick hill. And it wouldn't take much more rain to make that bridge impassable.

The rain had temporarily slacked off, and I could get to the house without getting soaked. But the place was dark as the inside of a tomb—no lights in any of the rooms, no outdoor light. Maybe Ruby and Claire had gone somewhere for the evening, I thought. But why hadn't they left the yard light on? I was going to need my flashlight, which I usually stash under the driver's seat. But when I found it, I said one of those words that

191

Brian and Caitlin are forbidden to utter. The flashlight wasn't working. The batteries must be dead, I decided.

I left it in the car, picked up the pie box, and groped my way through the gate and up the back walk. I didn't have much hope that anyone was home, but I knocked at the door just the same, and then for good measure, knocked again, louder. As if in answer, from somewhere deep in the house, I heard the sharp silver sound of a bell.

Well, that was promising. Where there was a bell, there was likely a bell-ringer. I knocked again. Then, just as I was about to give it up and go back to the car to wait for Ruby and Claire, a thin, quivering voice spoke up on the other side of the door.

"Sam, is that you? Kitty? Who is it?" The voice sounded afraid.

"It's China Bayles," I said, in my most reassuring tone. "Ruby knows me. May I come in?"

"Ruby," the voice said, "it's your friend. China Bayles." I heard the sound of footsteps and then the clicking of a lock.

"China!" Ruby cried, flinging the door wide open. She sounded hugely relieved. "Oh, China, it's really, truly *you*! Oh, I'm so glad you've come!"

It wasn't quite the welcome I had expected, even if I was bringing a really good pie. Nor had I expected to see Claire—that's who I thought she must be, anyway, dressed not in a negligee but in ragged denim cutoffs, a pink shirt, and sneakers—with a flickering oil lamp in one hand and a wicked-looking iron fireplace poker in the other. Beside her, Ruby was brandishing a rolling pin. A *rolling pin*?

"Wow," I said mildly, stepping into what I took to be a large, old-fashioned kitchen. "You guys are loaded for bear. You're expecting trouble?" I was going to ask whether those were appropriate weapons for ghost-busting, but something stopped me.

Ruby lowered the rolling pin and closed and locked the kitchen door.

Claire's lamp cast flickering shadows across her pale face, and I saw that she had changed out of the yellow sundress she had worn that morning and into jeans and a green-and-peach striped pullover.

"We saw your lights coming down the hill, and we weren't expecting anybody," she said. "Given everything that's been going on, we decided that we'd rather be safe than sorry." She turned the lock and slid the dead bolt firmly into place, then tested the door to make sure it was locked. "What are you *doing* here, China?" She was trying not to show that she was scared, and it occurred to me that my arrival might have frightened her. She was probably thinking that I was here because of a family emergency—in *her* family.

"Not that we're complaining," Claire said hastily. "We're really glad you came." She raised the lamp and gave me a brave smile. "I'm Claire, in case you haven't guessed. And I really have paid the electric bill."

Well, then, what's up with the lights? I wanted to ask. And why are you locking the door? Afraid of the boogeyman? But I was too polite. Instead, I said, "I apologize for barging in on you like this, but something came up back home and I needed to talk to Ruby." To Ruby, I added hurriedly, "I hope I didn't frighten you, showing up like this. You got my text message about Grace? I talked to Amy on my way out of town and our little girl is fine—or she will be tomorrow, once she's minus a pair of nasty old tonsils."

"Thank God." Ruby's eyes were large and dark. "Then it must be Mom. Something's happened to my mother? They haven't found her yet?"

"Oh, they've found her." I shook my head, grinning crookedly. "Doris the Daring is safely back in the arms of her nurses. She was nabbed at the adults-only video store, in the tender care of a couple of cross-dressers who looked after her until Ramona and the Pecan Springs gendarmerie arrived on the scene and took her into custody. You know Doris. According to Ramona, she was thrilled with the attention."

Ruby rolled her eyes. "Well, *that's* a relief." She gave me a suspicious look. "If it isn't Grace and it isn't my mother, then why *are* you here? Dawn didn't have any trouble at the shop today, did she?"

"Dawn never has any trouble. Oh, and she said to tell you that she re-ordered more of the Motherpeace tarot." I hefted the pie box. "I've brought dessert," I added helpfully. "If you could rustle up some coffee, we could have a piece of Royers' world-famous pecan pie and I'll tell you why I've come."

Ruby and Claire exchanged glances, then Ruby said, "We've already had supper, and some world-famous pie for dessert. But if you haven't eaten, we could warm up some leftover spaghetti for you. Totally non-gourmet, though."

"And the coffeemaker is electric," Claire said apologetically, "so I'm afraid coffee is out. I don't keep wine, because I'm a recovering alcoholic. Will you settle for some cold tea—without ice? I'd just as soon leave the ice cubes in the freezer. They might help to keep things cold. There's no telling when the electricity will be back on."

Well. So much for my imagined scene where Ruby and Claire, *en negligee*, sipped a fine wine and gorged on gourmet goodies. Thankfully, my supper was a very recent memory, so I could pass on the spaghetti. But I accepted a glass of tea and followed Claire and Ruby down a dark hallway. A few moments later, we reached a small but comfortable old-fashioned parlor, which Claire called a morning room. Outside, the rain was beginning to pelt down hard again, rattling against the window. But there were oil lamps on the tables, and the yellow-wallpapered room was cozy in the flickering light.

We sat down on either side of a small fireplace and I got straight to the point. It took me about five minutes to tell Ruby why I had come, and about half that time for her to tell me that I needn't have worried.

"Yes, of course, Ramona's offer to buy me out of the store is tempting," she said. "And every now and then I think there's nothing I'd like better than a little place in the country where I could raise chickens and have a garden and just be alone and *quiet*." She sighed. "But I can't do that. I need to be close to Mom, and I want to spend lots of time with Grace. Anyway, it wouldn't be healthy for me, in the long run." She made a face. "If I were alone too much, I'd probably drown in all that Colin stuff."

"No, you wouldn't," Claire said, and patted her hand. "You're stronger than that."

"I don't know about that," Ruby said. "I've already started letting it narrow my relationship options." She turned to me with a repentant look. "I'm sorry about letting Ramona think I might take her up on her offer, China. I know better. She would drive all the Cave's customers away in a matter of weeks, and she'd be a terrible partner for you and Cass. She's too dictatorial. She wants to be queen of the world."

Dictatorial. I couldn't have chosen a better word. I let out a gusty sigh, feeling as if the weight of the world had just rolled off my shoulders. "Ruby, I am *so* relieved to hear you say that. I couldn't tell whether Ramona was telling it straight or making things up. I even thought that she might be testing to see how I would respond to the idea that she might buy into the partnership. That idea wasn't working for me, and I came because I just had to find out how much of it was true. I'm sorry."

"Don't be sorry," Ruby said. "I love my sister—most of the time, anyway. But she can be very pushy when she decides she wants something. I should have told her no, right from the start."

I was relieved to know I wouldn't be taking bad news back to Pecan Springs with me. But I still had some to deliver. "I'm sorry to tell you this, Ruby," I said gravely, "but Bonnie Roth was killed this evening. She was shot during a robbery at the bank, just before it closed."

195

Ruby stared at me, incredulous. "Bonnie!" she whispered. Her hand went to her mouth. "Not Bonnie! Oh, China, not Bonnie!"

"I'm afraid so," I said soberly. "I went to the bank to make the deposit, yours and mine, but the drive-through islands were closed and the parking lot was full of cops and patrol cars. EMS was there, too. As soon as I saw Maude Porterfield's truck, I knew there'd been a fatality. Rita Kidder told me who it was."

Ruby shook her head, pressing her lips together. "Did they get the guy who did it?" she asked bleakly.

"Not when I was there," I said. "The getaway vehicle was wearing stolen plates. They got the make and model from a surveillance tape, but there must be a gazillion Ford Ranger trucks in Texas."

"A friend of yours, I guess," Claire said sympathetically. "I'm so sorry." She frowned. "I wonder if it's the same gang that's been robbing the banks around here. The Fayetteville bank got hit last week."

"Terrible," Ruby muttered. "Just terrible."

The silence stretched out for a long moment. Then, just as I heard the shimmering sound of that silvery bell again, Ruby spoke up, obviously making an effort to be cheerful. "Well, whatever brought you down here tonight, Claire and I are glad you came. Aren't we, Claire?"

"You said it," Claire replied fervently.

"Thanks." Curious, I added, "Say, what was that little bell just now? I heard it before, when I was knocking on the back door."

"Bell?" Ruby asked innocently. "I didn't hear a bell. Did you, Claire?" She and Claire traded secret glances and Claire, wide-eyed, shook her head.

"Not I," she said.

I laughed a little uncomfortably. "I must be hearing things." Lightning flared blue-white outside the window. There was a smashing crash of thunder and all of us jumped. "Listen, I don't want to interrupt anything the two of you had planned for tonight, but I hope you've got room for another guest. They're forecasting heavy rain from this tropical storm—as much as eight or nine inches in this area. I'd rather not drive back to Pecan Springs until Amanda's blown over. And I would definitely *not* like to try that steep hill in my Toyota. I don't have four-wheel drive. I'd probably end up in the creek."

"Amanda?" Ruby looked puzzled for a moment, then threw back her head and laughed. "Oh, now I get it! That's what you meant by TS Amanda in your text message. Tropical Storm Amanda!"

"Actually, we were going to suggest that you stay all night," Claire said slowly, trading another secret glance with Ruby. "In fact, you probably wouldn't be able to leave even if you wanted to. And not because of that hill."

"I couldn't?" I frowned. "Because?"

There was a silence. "Because your car probably won't work," Ruby said uncomfortably.

"I don't understand. My car was working okay when I got here. I mean, it didn't much like that hill, but otherwise it was fine. Why won't it work now?"

"We don't know," Claire said helplessly. She looked at Ruby. "Do you think maybe she should try it and see?"

Ruby looked at the rain beating against the window. "I guess," she said hesitantly. "Then we'd know for sure. If China's car works, then it must be a matter of . . . us. You and me."

Claire nodded. "It would settle the question."

"I'm sure there's a plot here somewhere," I said, looking from one to the other. "Is somebody going to tell me what it is, or do I have to keep guessing?"

197

Ten minutes later, I had some of the story, or at least enough to understand that something weird had happened to their cell phones, their flashlight batteries, their car batteries, and the electricity. They were about to tell me more—something about a ghostly apparition in Victorian dress and pans clanging and balls bouncing and harps playing—but I suggested that we take a break. We could save the supernatural stuff for later.

"You might be right about my car," I said, getting out of my chair. "I tried to use my flashlight so I wouldn't fall over something in the dark and smash our pie, but the dang thing refused to work. It would be a good idea to give the car a try, though, just so we know what's what. And I want to check my cell phone. Does somebody have a raincoat, or maybe a poncho?"

"You're not going out there alone, are you?" Ruby asked nervously. "It's dark out there, China. I don't think—"

"Then make that two raincoats," I said. "And we'll take a lamp."

Claire fetched a raincoat and a poncho while I covered the top of the lamp chimney with a piece of aluminum foil to keep the wick dry, and then Ruby and I dashed through the pouring rain to my car. The ground must have been pretty well saturated, because the rain wasn't soaking in. There were spreading puddles everywhere, impossible to avoid. Our errand didn't take long, and we didn't linger. Four minutes later, we were back in the house.

"You can say, 'I told you so,'" I said to Claire, who was standing inside the kitchen door with the oil lamp. I pulled the poncho over my head and hung it on a wall peg, then bent over to unlace my wet sneakers. "The car battery is totally dead. It won't even power the headlights. My cell phone is a goner, too."

"Well, at least it's not just us. Claire and me, I mean." Ruby had found a towel and was drying her hair. "Which means that the three of us are here for the duration, however long that is." She dropped the towel and looked at Claire. "Which also means that we have to tell China the rest of the story—as much as we know, anyway."

"The part about the ghost, I suppose," I said, resigned. "And the harp and the ball and the dancing pans. All that weird supernatural stuff." I thought of what I had said that morning, showing off, trying to be funny. *Bust those ghosts. Purge those poltergeists. Get rid of those ghouls.* I still wasn't convinced that we were up against something supernatural here, but I certainly couldn't explain all those dead batteries. And it was daunting to think that we were stuck in this house, miles from anywhere, in the middle of a tropical storm, with no means of summoning help and no way to leave unless we wanted to hike seven miles to the county road and hope to catch a ride to the nearest phone. My efforts to be funny didn't seem at all funny now.

"Yes," Ruby said with a sigh. "All that weird supernatural stuff. I know you're a skeptic, China. But there are some things about the world that your mega-logical legal mind just has to learn to accept. Like the bell, for instance."

I was wary. "The . . . bell?"

"It's a little brass bell on a table in the drawing room," Claire replied helpfully. "Designed to be rung when the mistress of the house wanted something."

"But it rings all by itself," Ruby added. "When nobody else is in the room." She gave me a telling look. "You heard it yourself. I know you did. Twice."

"Well, yes," I said. "I admit to hearing the bell, but that doesn't mean—"

"And just in case you suspect that either Claire or I rang it," Ruby went on, "I would like to point out that the second time you heard it, we were all together in the morning room. And there is no one else in the house." She dropped her voice. "No one *living*, that is."

"If you say so," I said. "But—"

"And there's the menu board," Claire put in. "Ruby, we need to show it to her. Maybe that will convince her that we're not making things up."

"Good idea." Ruby took my arm and led me to the wall, while Claire brought the lamp. I saw two stoves, one old-fashioned cooking range and a smaller gas stove. Next to the gas stove was a table and a rack of pans.

I suppressed a dry chuckle. "Those are the dancing pans, I suppose."

"Actually, yes," Claire said. "Sometimes they bang against one another." She glanced at Ruby. "I've heard it often. And Ruby and I both *saw* it, just this afternoon."

"But that's not what we want to show you," Ruby said. "It's the menu board, China. When I got here this afternoon, Claire's grocery list was written up there. But when we started to make supper, we saw that the list had been erased and *this* was written in its place."

Claire held up the lamp. In the circle of its light, I saw that next to the rack of pans hung one of those old-fashioned menu boards that you sometimes see in funky restaurants. Something was written on it—not Claire's grocery list, I assumed. Anyway, it wasn't a list. It was phrases and words, written at odd angles all over the board in a spidery Spenserian script, the kind of writing you see in your great-grandmother's letters.

"Read it out loud," Ruby commanded.

I leaned closer, and read what I saw. "*Crooked man, crooked cat, crooked house.* And then there are three words kind of scattered around: *roof hole clown.*" I frowned. "No," I corrected myself. "That's not *clown.* The handwriting is a little hard to read. It's *drown.*"

Behind me, Ruby gasped. "But that isn't what we saw, is it, Claire?"

"No," Claire said, very quietly. "When we saw it before supper, there were four words: *crooked man, crooked sixpence.* And there was a date.

That's been erased and this is written in its place." She read the board again, almost whispering the words. *"Crooked man, crooked cat, crooked house. Roof, hole, drown."*

"You're sure there's been nobody else in the house?" I asked. "Nobody in the kitchen today? Nobody could have come in while you were in the morning room and written this, for a joke or something?"

"Just Kitty," Claire said slowly. "She's Sam's wife. He's the caretaker. She was here this afternoon. But I know I looked at the board when she was leaving, because she and Sam were on their way to Houston and she said she'd pick up the things I had on my grocery list. Bread, milk, yogurt, coffee. That was what was on the board when she left. But the next time I looked, a couple of hours later, it was *crooked man, crooked sixpence*. And a date."

"We know who wrote it," Ruby said. "It was Rachel."

"Rachel?" I asked, frowning. "I thought Claire just said that Kitty was the only one who—"

"Rachel is our ghost," Claire said. "Rachel Blackwood."

To give myself credit, I did not roll my eyes. I was about to ask the logical next question—*Who is Rachel Blackwood?*—but Ruby interrupted.

"China," she said urgently, "this is all the more weird because I have been hearing those lines in my head all day—*before* I saw them on that board. And before I saw them in a book in the nursery upstairs." She shook her head. "I know that sounds crazy, but it's true."

"All day?" I asked. "Starting when? Before you left Pecan Springs?"

Ruby frowned, concentrating. "No. It started when I was driving down the hill and caught a glimpse of this house, which reminded me of the title of an Agatha Christie story. Wait until you see it in the daylight, China. It really is sort of *crooked*, like the parts of it were just put together,

201

helter-skelter." Her frown deepened. "And the words *crooked man* popped into my head when I saw Sam for the first time. Sam Rawlings," she added. "Claire's caretaker. He stopped me on the hill."

"*Crooked man* fits him," Claire said. To me, she added, "The jerk beats up on his wife. In my book, that makes him crooked."

Ruby was peering at the board. "*Roof, hole, drown,*" she muttered. "That reminds me of something else, but I can't think what."

"It's from an old song," Claire said. She began humming and snapping her fingers. "I can't remember all the words, but that nursery rhyme is the verse—*There was a crooked man*—and he's trying to fix his roof with crooked nails. The chorus is about a roof with a hole in it and everybody might drown. Or something." She hummed another few bars.

"It's called 'Don't Let the Rain Come Down,'" I said ironically. "Appropriate," I added, as the thunder boomed.

"I wish Rachel would stop writing nursery rhymes and song lyrics on the board and just come out and tell us what we're supposed to know," Ruby grumbled.

"Rachel again," I said plaintively. "Is anybody going to tell me who this Rachel person is and why you think she's haunting this place?"

Ruby and Claire traded looks, then nods. "This calls for some of that pecan pie you brought," Claire replied. "No coffee, but we do have milk. How about some hot chocolate?"

Outside, there was grumble of thunder and we could hear the rain beating against the windows.

"If we're going to be telling ghost stories on a rainy night," I said, "pie and hot chocolate would be a big help." I paused, remembering something we'd skipped over. "You said that this afternoon's message contained a date, didn't you, Claire? But you didn't say what it was."

Claire took down a box of chocolate mix from a shelf. "September eighth, I think. There was a year, but I don't remember what it was."

"It was 1900," Ruby said. She looked at me. "I keep thinking I know what that is, but I can't quite get it. Does that date mean anything to you, China?"

September 8, 1900.

"Yes," I said. I closed my eyes. "I'm afraid it does."

Claire got the milk out and went to get a pan from the rack to make our hot chocolate. As she touched the rack, the pans began to dance.

Chapter Fourteen

Galveston
Early evening, September 8, 1900

Queen of the Waves, look forth across the ocean
From north to south, from east to stormy west,
See how the waters with tumultuous motion
Rise up and foam without a pause or rest.

But fear we not, though storm clouds round us gather,
Thou art our Mother and thy little Child
Is the All Merciful, our loving Brother
God of the sea and of the tempest wild.

"Queen of the Waves"
sung every year on September 8
by the Sisters of Charity of the Incarnate Word

The Galveston Hurricane of 1900 was thought to have begun life as a tropical wave moving off the west coast of Africa around the middle of August. It strengthened as it slowly crossed the sun-warmed Atlantic, breezed past the Windward Islands on August 27, skipped through the Leewards on August 30, drenched Cuba as it grazed the south shore and bounced across its midsection on September 3, and emerged into the Florida Straits two days later, weakened by its tussle with the Cuban mountains.

From that point on, the storm gathered strength and momentum, setting a steady track for the Texas coast. The Gulf waters had been warmed by the extraordinarily hot summer, the wind shear was light, and the steering currents were favorable, all of which made the Gulf a perfect nursery for the adolescent hurricane. What's more, a huge low-pressure area was building in the center of the country from Canada to Texas: a giant vacuum pulling everything, irresistibly, into itself.

Propelled by these energies and growing to an almost supernatural size and strength, the storm barreled straight across the Gulf basin. It made landfall on the southwestern end of long, low Galveston Island, and its right front quadrant—the most powerful part of the storm—smacked into the city like a balled-up fist, striking at a straight-on 90-degree angle, propelled by all the pent-up ferocity of its long passage. Its trajectory thrust the wind-powered waves straight into the low-lying city, whose highest point was only 8.7 feet above sea level.

But the storm's route and the size of what modern meteorologists call its wind field would create another deadly outcome. All day Saturday, the winds had blown out of the north, produced by the counter-clockwise circulation around the approaching storm. By noon, they had reached gale force, prying the roofs off downtown buildings (like Ritter's Café) and pushing the water out of Galveston Bay and into the city, flooding it from the northwest. Then, around seven in the evening, the winds shifted to the southeast, blowing at an incredible 150 miles an hour with gusts much higher than that. They shoved a fifteen-foot storm surge onto the Gulf side of the island. The bay waters met the Gulf waters over the heart of the drowning city. The barrier island that was Galveston was completely submerged.

It had earned the name given to it by the unhappy Cabeza de Vaca when he was shipwrecked on its sandy shore.

Malhado. Misfortune.

* * *

THREE miles west of the city, rising like a brick-and-stone stronghold above the beach, was St. Mary's Orphanage. Like St. Mary's Infirmary in the city, it was in the charge of the Sisters of Charity of the Incarnate Word, who were deeply dedicated to the care of orphaned children. At first, the children lived at St. Mary's Infirmary, at Tenth and Market Streets, but after a time an orphanage was established on a beachfront property on the estate of Captain Farnifalia Green—a healthy location, it was thought, open to the sky and the sea, remote from town and the omnipresent threat of yellow fever. The facility consisted of two large, two-story dormitories with open galleries facing the Gulf and rows of windows to catch the cooling ocean breezes. It was protected from storm tides by a natural barrier of sand dunes, anchored in place by beach grasses and salt cedar. In September of 1900, the orphanage was home to ninety-three children and ten sisters.

The summer had been abysmally hot, and the sisters must have been miserable under their heavy habits and veils of coarse black serge. Saturday morning's north wind had been very welcome, and anyone listening to their pre-dawn prayers that morning might have heard them thanking the good Lord for sending the cooler weather, even though it seemed that He was sending a storm as well. After breakfast, Mother Superior Camillus sent Sister Elizabeth Ryan with a wagon to get supplies from the infirmary in the city. The weather was indeed growing stormy, and Mother Gabriel, at the infirmary, tried to persuade her to stay until it cleared. Sister Elizabeth refused. Mother Superior was expecting her, she said.

The beach road often flooded, but this morning it was worse than usual—in places, entirely underwater, so that Sister Elizabeth had a great deal of trouble getting back to the orphanage with the supply wagon. By the time she finally returned, the waves were eating away at the dunes "as though they were made of flour," one of the older boys would say later. Soon the dunes had disappeared and the orphanage was completely surrounded by water, so that even the youngest novice could see that the storm would pose a significant peril by nightfall. The sisters prayed, consulted, and decided that God had given them no other choice: they had to remain where He had put them and trust to Him and the Blessed Virgin to keep the children safe.

In mid-afternoon, Mother Superior and the nuns herded their charges into the chapel on the first floor of the girls' wing, the newer and stronger of the two buildings, where they led the children in prayer and in song—one of their favorites, an old French hymn called "Queen of the Waves." But the wind and the waves battered the building relentlessly, and by six that evening, the rising water forced them upstairs. Still trusting the Blessed Mother but knowing that they had to do the best they could for the children, Mother Superior sent one of the workers, Henry Esquior, to collect all the clothesline he could find. With that, the sisters tied the children together in groups of six and eight. Then they tied one group to the cincture each sister wore around her waist, promising never to let go.

The sisters were gathered in a protective circle around the children when they heard a great, bone-rattling crash. The boys' wing had collapsed and some of the debris had struck their building. Frightened but firm in their faith—and "very brave," one of the three surviving boys would say later—they continued to sing.

Help, then sweet Queen, in our exceeding danger,
By thy seven griefs, in pity Lady save;

Think of the Babe that slept within the manger
And help us now, dear Lady of the Wave.

Then joyful hearts shall kneel around thine altar
And grateful psalms re-echo down the nave;
Never our faith in thy sweet power can falter,
Mother of God, our Lady of the Wave.

They were still singing when the building broke apart and the children and the sisters were flung into the wind-driven deep.

AUGUSTUS Blackwood had built well. His house stood on sturdy piers that rose eight feet above the island's sandy surface, its walls were stout, its slate-covered roof was firm. At least, that's what Rachel Blackwood told herself as she and Colleen (in such a dire circumstance, they could hardly be Mrs. O'Reilly and Mrs. Blackwood) and Patsy retreated with the children to the nursery, which overlooked what had once been the garden and was now a surging, foam-flecked sea. The room was at the rear of the second floor, away from the Gulf, and seemed somehow safer, although the gallery that had been wrapped around the back of the house had gone the way of the front gallery, ripped off almost playfully by the giant hand of the wind.

Before they fled up the great staircase, Rachel and Colleen had chopped holes in the floors of the dining room, the drawing room, and the music room, then opened the front and back doors to relieve the pulsing pressure of the water. Now, they were standing at the second-story window, looking out across the neighborhood. There was still enough light so that Rachel could see the houses on the street behind them breaking up and washing away, the wreckage turning into battering rams and demolishing other houses as it was swept about by the waves. The Nevilles' house next door had been among the most splendid in the city: large, three-storied, sided in an intricate pattern of shiplap boards and fish-scale shingles, painted in a colorful medley of greens and blues with red trim. But the piers on which it was built were several feet shorter than those beneath the Blackwoods' house. Now, the Nevilles' first floor was completely underwater, every slate stripped from the roof, the widow's walk torn away by the wind. Rachel shuddered, wondering what their own roof looked like—and what horrors she would see from their widow's walk, if she were able to stand there now.

Colleen clutched her arm. "Look!" she whispered. Just below them, past the window, a woman lashed with a rope of bedsheets to a wooden door was being whirled along by the waves. She lay limp and lifeless, her long hair trailing in the water like Ophelia's, and Rachel knew she must be dead. Behind her was the body of a dead horse, grotesquely rolling over and over like a barrel whirled by the flood. For an instant Rachel wondered about Augustus. If he were alive, surely he would have braved even the worst of the wind and flood to come to her. He would not, *could* not abandon her and the children to face these terrors alone.

Then, just at that moment, Matthew ran from the hallway door and flung himself at her. "Mama, Mama!" he cried, clutching her around the waist. "The water has climbed to the top of the stairs! It's coming across the floor!"

Rachel held him as tight as she could, her heart in her mouth. To the top of the stairs? How much farther would it come? How fast? The windows rattled and the floor shuddered under her feet, bricks from the chimneys were thumping down onto the roof, and wooden blinds slammed against the casements of the broken windows. Around her, the house was creaking and groaning, crying out as if it were in agony—as it was, she thought despairingly, as they were, as *all* were on this island, on this horrible night.

For Rachel, seeing that horrid black water sloshing across the upstairs hallway in her lovely house, the house that held everything that was dear to her, it was as if all that was good and true and beautiful in this world was being washed away.

Chapter Fifteen

Elecampane (*Inula helenium*) is a perennial plant common in Great Britain, Europe, and western Asia. The species name, *helenium*, is thought to commemorate Helen of Troy, from whose tears the herb was said to have sprung as Paris abducted her. The seventeenth-century herbalist John Gerard advocated a tea of elecampane for "the shortness of breath" (congestive heart failure); contemporary herbalists recommend it as a diuretic and expectorant. Recent research suggests that extracts from the herb are strongly antibacterial.

In the language of flowers, elecampane means "I cry for you."

China Bayles
"Herbs and Flowers That Tell a Story"
Pecan Springs Enterprise

The clattering pans stopped dancing when Claire took one down and poured milk into it. She put it on the gas stove and turned on the burner, stirring it to keep it from scorching while Ruby took the pecan pie out of the box and got out three small plates and forks.

"The date," Ruby said. She found a knife and cut the pie. "September eighth, 1900. You said it meant something to you, China."

"It does," I replied. "It's the date of the Galveston Hurricane." It was the deadliest American natural disaster ever—eight to ten thousand dead, according to most estimates. It was impossible to come up with an accurate count because so many victims were swept out into the Gulf or buried beneath the wreckage that littered the island. Unfortunately, the citizens had been encouraged—by their local weather expert, of all people—to believe that they didn't need the protection of a seawall. They built the seawall, of course, too late to save themselves from the 1900 hurricane, but soon enough to protect them from the hurricane of 1915 and from Hurricane Ike, the second most destructive hurricane ever to hit the United States.

"I saw a TV documentary about that." Claire frowned. "It must have been horrible. But I don't see what that has to do with us. Here and now, I mean."

"I do," Ruby said, putting slices of pie on three plates. "Those framed photographs on the wall in the library, Claire. They're all Galveston scenes, aren't they? And if I'm not wrong, the photos were taken *before* the 1900 hurricane. Do you think maybe Rachel lived in Galveston at one time?" Without waiting for an answer, she handed me my plate. "Let's not talk here," she said. "Let's go to the morning room."

"How about the library instead?" Claire countered. "The chairs are comfortable there, and after we've filled China in on what's been going on, we can look through those old scrapbooks. They might have something to tell us about Rachel. Where she lived before she built this house, for instance."

Plate and mug in hand, I followed Claire's and Ruby's flickering oil lamps down a passage that probably seemed much longer than it was because I had no idea where we were going, and also because it was very dark and spooky. The lamplight cast shape-shifting shadows on the walls and high ceiling. It didn't take a lot of imagination to see shrouded, misshapen ghosts in those hovering shadows, and it occurred to me that some of what was going on in this house could very easily be the product of Claire's and

Ruby's imaginations. The house was that kind of place, especially with the lights off and the storm howling outside.

But still, there were the dead batteries and the ringing bell and the dancing pans and the writing on the menu board. I had personally witnessed all of that, and I can't lay claim to an exceptionally lively imagination. Whatever was going on here must have some sort of reality to it, although it was an eerie, inexplicable reality. And Ruby and Claire had been deeply frightened—I could judge that from their grateful relief when I'd showed up at the door.

Was *I* frightened? Well, not then, I wasn't. At least, my hair wasn't standing on end and my blood hadn't turned to ice water and I don't think I had gone white as a sheet—all those physical symptoms of anxiety and fear that you read about in ghost stories. But I will certainly admit to a knot in the pit of my stomach and a few shivers of apprehension.

And although I couldn't have known it at that moment, I was right to be afraid, although I could not have guessed why. What was yet to come— and soon—was more terrifyingly real and much more threatening than anything I could have possibly imagined. And there was not a thing in the world that I could have done to keep it from happening.

The book-lined room was large and deeply shadowed with a faint odor of flavored tobacco smoke in the air—another ghostly manifestation, Claire said, because so far as she knew, nobody had ever smoked a pipe in this house. Certainly not the two old ladies who had lived here.

Like the morning room, the furnishings of this room looked as if they were a century old. Claire closed the hallway door and we pulled three cushioned leather chairs into a circle around a low table, where we put the lamps, almost as if we were gathering around a hearth fire. There was something very comforting about our little circle, for the tall wingbacks of the chairs were turned away from the uncurtained windows and our plates of pie and mugs of hot chocolate were on the table in front of us. Of course, pecan pie and hot chocolate are comfort foods at any time, but on such a wild night, they seemed especially consoling. We settled down to our dessert, eating in silence while the wind howled in the eaves and shadows lurked like lost souls in the room's dark corners.

Ruby tilted her head, listening. "That's some wind," she said. "I'm glad you're not driving back home tonight, China. You could be blown right off the road."

"I'm glad, too," I said. "But I'm a little surprised. At six thirty, the weather forecast said that Amanda's winds peaked when she made landfall, which must have been hours ago. But these early storms aren't always entirely predictable, I guess." Something loose banged against the wall—a shutter maybe, or a gutter pulled down by the wind—and we could hear the rain pelting down, harder now. It sounded as if it was mixed with sleet, or even hail. "They were warning of eight or nine inches. There's likely to be flooding everywhere."

"Or not," Claire said. She finished her pie and pushed back her plate. "It might be this house. The wind howls like a banshee around here even when the wind isn't blowing. Doesn't it, Ruby?"

"I think I don't quite get that," I said around my last mouthful of pie.

Ruby nodded soberly. "It's true, China. I saw it myself—phantom wind. I could hear it howling a gale, rattling the windows, banging something loose against the house." Just as she said that, there was another sharp bang. "But when I looked outside, there wasn't a leaf stirring on the trees."

"There are phantom rains, too," Claire said in a matter-of-fact tone. "It can be dry as a bone outdoors, not a trace of moisture anywhere. But I'll find puddles of water in the first-floor hallway, just inside the front door, and on the second floor, at the top of the stairs. And the ceiling in one of the third-floor bedrooms has been wet since I arrived, even though there's been no rain to speak of until today." She added, thoughtfully, "It's almost as though the house creates its own climate." In the distance, I heard the bell ring. Odd how that bell seemed to have taken on the qualities of a voice. This time, it sounded bright and cheerful, like an affirmation of Claire's statement. Claire and Ruby heard it, too, and the three of us traded glances.

"I don't know about that," I remarked, almost defensively, "but what's going on out there right now is no phantom. I had to drive through it on the way here. It's a tropical storm, for real." I put my fork down, picked up my mug, and leaned back in my chair. "Maybe you'd better tell me about it," I said. "Start at the beginning and don't leave anything out."

"It's a long story," Claire cautioned. "It's going to take a while."

"We've got all night," I said, and cocked an ear to the rain, which was coming harder. Thunder was booming almost constantly. "I don't think any of us is going anywhere."

Even if we wanted to, I added to myself. For better or worse, we were here, at the whim and will of whatever force, natural or supernatural or both, had disabled our vehicles and our cell phones. I wished fervently for a radio or a television set so we could get the ten o'clock weather report. There was no telling what was developing out there. Lightning was putting on a spectacular light show outside the windows, and even though the floors and walls of the old mansion seemed solid, I could hear a mixed chorus of groanings and creakings, as though the house had its own story to tell and was anxious for us to hear it.

"It's as if we were all brought here together for a purpose," Ruby said in a musing tone. "Like one of those Agatha Christie locked-room mysteries. I wonder what we're supposed to—"

The bell rang. It sounded closer now, as it had moved from the drawing room out into the hall. Then it was abruptly silenced, as if a hand had grasped it to keep it from vibrating. The hair rose on the back of my neck. Whose hand? *Whose?*

"I think we're supposed to hear the story," I said.

IT *was* a long story, which is entirely understandable, given the age of the house and its complicated ownership history. When Claire had finished (with several interruptions from Ruby, and one sharp ring of the bell), I set down my empty mug and said, "Now I understand why you wanted to have Ruby here, Claire. She's the one who saw the ghost in the first place, when you were both here as children."

"Saw *Rachel*," Ruby corrected me. "This isn't a generic ghost, China. Her name is Rachel Blackwood—at least, that's who we think she is, based on the evidence in the graveyard. Her five children and her husband must have died here, perhaps all at the same time and along with their two servants. It could have been illness or some sort of violent tragedy, an accident—a fire, maybe?—or even murder. Whatever the tragedy, Rachel survived it and lived decades past it, lived to be a very old woman. But even her death didn't allow her to escape this place. She seems to be deeply attached to it, and especially to certain rooms. The nursery, for instance."

Ruby had already told Claire what had happened there that afternoon, and now she told me, ending with a shudder. "What I saw and heard—it was frightening. The jack-in-the box, the nursery rhyme book, the rocking chair, the giggle, the violet perfume, the sobbing. While it was happening, I was scared half to death. But afterward, I couldn't think about being scared. I could only remember how sad I felt. Just terribly, terribly sad." She looked at me, reading the skeptical expression on my face. "I know it's hard for a lawyer to accept all that, China, but you'll just have to take my word for it." She lifted her chin half-defiantly. "I am *not* exaggerating. And I am not making it up."

"I believe you, Ruby," I said quietly. It was true. Ruby may worry that she doesn't use her gift to advantage, or even that she doesn't know how to use it at all. But I've seen her in action more than once, and I know that she's in touch with something in the universe that the rest of us ordinary mortals are oblivious to. I don't pretend to know what it is—to tell the truth, I don't want to know. But whatever it is, it's *real*."

"I've heard some of it, too, China," Claire said, "although not as strongly as Ruby. Sometimes it seems as though the place is inhabited, except that the inhabitants are invisible. And I suspect that anybody who has even a touch of ESP is likely to hear and see scary things in this house." She leaned forward, her face intent. "I don't have any idea what happened to Rachel's family and I don't want to be inhospitable, but that ghost really has to go. I need this house, but I can't live here—and I certainly can't have guests here—as long as she's making cameo appearances and weird noises and leaving puddles on the floor." Her mouth tightened. "And especially killing cars. People don't want to get stuck here. They have to be able to leave when they need to."

"I get it," I said ruefully. "But I'm afraid I can't make any suggestions about how to convince your ghost to leave." I looked at Ruby. "Ruby, you're the one with the gift, so this is your department. Any ideas?"

Ruby sighed. "Well, maybe. This afternoon, when I was in the nursery, I . . ." She stopped. "I don't really know how to describe it. I felt that Rachel and I were engaged in some sort of tug-of-war, and that when it was over, I had . . . well, not won, exactly. But I hadn't let myself be taken over, physically, anyway."

"What would that have meant?" Claire was apprehensive. "What do you think might have happened to you?"

219

"I don't know." Ruby shuddered. "I don't even want to *think* about it. I can't say why, but it felt very dangerous. And I'm not saying I came out on top," she added. "I just didn't give in, if that makes sense."

"Yeah, maybe," Claire conceded.

"Anyway, when the tug-of-war was over," Ruby went on, "Rachel seemed to sort of slip into my head."

She paused, and it occurred to me that perhaps—to use Ruby's own terms—Rachel had won, after all. If she had infiltrated Ruby's consciousness . . . But I wasn't sure what that would mean.

"At the time this happened," Ruby went on, "I couldn't put words to it. Rachel wasn't speaking to me, at least not in words. It was more or less a glimmer, and certainly not a full-blown idea. But while we've been talking here tonight, it's been . . . well, pushing its way into my thoughts. It's coming clearer, and I think I'm beginning to understand." Ruby turned to her friend, her face intent. "Claire, I think I know what she wants. What Rachel wants."

Outside, there was a loud crash, like the sound of a heavy tree limb coming down against part of the roof. The house groaned and shifted slightly on its foundation, as if it had been nudged by the falling tree. I thought of the five little graves out there in the cemetery, in the wild night, the father's grave, the graves of the servants. What had happened here? How had they died? Why?

The room was illuminated by a sudden glare of lightning, and when it went dark again, I caught the scent of violets, or thought I did. I gave myself a stern mental shake. Violets, schmiolets. I know for a fact that the power of suggestion can be very strong. I have employed suggestive strategies often enough myself when I've argued cases in front of a jury. I haven't used perfume, though. Words are stronger.

Claire was leaning forward, intent on Ruby. "You know what she wants?" she asked eagerly. "What is it, Ruby? What does Rachel want?"

The wick in one of the lamps flamed up ardently, smoked, and extinguished itself. The room dimmed and the shadows in the corners thickened. Ruby was silent, her head tilted slightly, as if she were listening to something that came from somewhere deep inside her.

"I think," she said slowly, "I think we're here because Rachel is ready to let go of all this." She spoke as if she were hearing the words, weighing and measuring them, wondering, even as she spoke them, if they were true. "She's ready to leave—if she could. But she can't."

Once more, for the record, I do not believe in spooks, and the rational, legal-eagle part of me—if I'd let her—would have jumped straight out of her chair, announced that she had heard enough of this mystical claptrap (to use one of McQuaid's favorite phrases), and stalked out of the room. That's exactly what I would have done if this were anybody else but Ruby.

But the fact of the matter is that I believe in Ruby. Which means that I believed that she believed in what she was saying—that she wasn't imagining it or making it up. For her, Rachel was real, which made her real for me, as well. (And then, of course, there was that inexplicable bell and that writing on the menu board, neither of which were produced by the power of suggestion.)

I waited for her to go on. When she didn't, I prompted her with a question. "Why can't she leave?"

Ruby didn't answer for a moment, and in just that narrow space of time, I felt the temperature in the room drop by several degrees. There seemed to be a draft coming from someplace, eddying around us. My bare arms broke out in goose bumps. I shivered—and not entirely from the cold. I'm the kind of person who likes to know what's happening, and right now, I didn't have a clue.

Ruby's fingers were laced tightly together as if she were praying. Her knuckles were white and in the lamplight, her face was strained and intent.

"She wants to leave but she can't because she's held on too long, too tight, too . . ."

Her voice trailed off, blurred, as if her lips had gone numb. She pulled in a ragged breath, then let it out in a lengthening sigh. "She built this house to indulge her grief. She wanted to create a place to live with it. And now she's a prisoner of it."

"A prisoner of this house?" I asked.

"Yes." Ruby drew out the word in a long sigh.

Claire was frowning. "Really, Ruby, I don't understand any of this. How could a house *indulge* her grief? What about those graves? Her kids, her husband? Did she have something to do with their deaths? And how do you know all this, Ruby?"

There was a silence, as if Ruby were asking herself these questions. At last, she shook her head. "I don't know, Claire. I don't know. I just—" Her voice was now low and uninflected—the voice of a sleepwalker, trance-like, not Ruby's voice at all. Her shoulders were slumped, her hands loose in her lap, her eyelids half-closed. She looked and spoke as if she'd been hypnotized.

"Ruby?" Obviously frightened, Claire started to get up. "Ruby, are you all right? What—"

I put out my hand to stop her. I couldn't even pretend to guess what might be happening here, but I've occasionally seen what Ruby can do when she puts her mind to it—or rather, when she connects with the in-tuitive part of herself, the knowing part that doesn't have anything to do with her mind. Before, I had seen it happen with the help of her Ouija board or as she read the tarot cards. Once, I even watched her read a Honda Civic in a parking lot in the little town of Indigo—and what she learned led us to the body of the car's owner, hidden in the basement of an abandoned school. It was happening again but without any help, except perhaps from the entity that Ruby thought of as Rachel.

And while there's not a wisp of the psychic in me (and a very healthy hunk of the cynic), I knew that if I were to ask Ruby, she would say that the three of us were not alone in this room. Rachel, or whatever collection of energies wore the name of Rachel, was with us, speaking to us.

And Ruby was giving her a voice.

Chapter Sixteen

Galveston
Night, September 8, 1900

Sweet and low, sweet and low,
Wind of the western sea,
Low, low, breathe and blow,
Wind of the western sea!
Over the rolling waters go,
Come from the dying moon, and blow,
Blow him again to me;
While my little one, while my pretty one, sleeps.

"Sweet and Low"
Alfred, Lord Tennyson

At St. Mary's Orphanage, three miles west of the city, the sisters and their charges sang and prayed while they waited for what was about to happen. The boys' dormitory was completely gone now, and the front of their building was going, too, devoured in huge bites by the ravenous waves and the roaring wind. The windows were blown in, the roof fell in pieces, one brick wall after another collapsed with a thunderous roar, and at last all was swept into the churning maelstrom.

The three oldest boys, left untethered to fend for themselves, were flung through a window and survived by clinging to a tree that was lodged in the masts of a four-masted wooden schooner, the *John S. Ames*. "The sisters were very brave," the boys said later. Their bodies, still lashed to their children, would be buried where they were found.

SISTER Elizabeth would likely have been no safer had she listened to Mother Gabriel and stayed at St. Mary's Infirmary, on Avenue D in Galveston. This imposing brick building, another one of Nicholas J. Clayton's fanciful designs, was no match for the winds. Once the windows and roofs were gone, the brick walls were next. Of the many, perhaps hundreds, who had taken refuge there, just eight survived.

Only a few blocks away, another of Clayton's projects was coming to pieces. The fantastic Victorian towers and turrets and chimney pots of John Sealy Hospital were raining down in showers of brick and slate. The nurse letter-writer added one last frantic paragraph to her note:

"Darkness is overwhelming us, to add to the horror," she wrote. "Dearest, I reach out my hand to you—my heart—my soul." Her letter was unsigned.

Nicholas Clayton declared bankruptcy three years after the hurricane. He never received another major architectural commission.

AT Twenty-fifth and Q, Weather Bureau chief Isaac Cline and his family—his heavily pregnant wife, Cora; his daughters Allie and Rosemary, twelve and eleven; and six-year-old Esther—had taken refuge on the second floor, together with a large group of refugees who had banged on the front door, pleading for entry. The water had risen to the height of the ceilings of the first floor, but Cline still believed that his house was built high and strong enough to survive any amount of battering by wind and wave—and he might have been right. He did not, however, reckon with the mountain of debris that was being shoved north and west through the city like a gigantic scraper blade, demolishing every structure in its path.

Joseph Cline no longer shared his brother's confidence. As assistant weatherman in the Galveston Bureau, he remembered and resented Isaac's self-assured prediction that the city would never be inundated by a storm surge, and was now certain that the house was no secure refuge, either. As Joseph later told the story in his book, *When the Heavens Frowned*, he urged Isaac and the others to gather in a room on the windward side, the Gulf side, so that when the house tipped over (as he was convinced it would), they would not be trapped beneath it. The best hope, he said, was to jump out of the building as it went over and grab and hold on to whatever pieces of debris could be found.

And that is what he did. The moving mountain of debris, topped by a long section of broken trolley track, finally reached Q Avenue. It struck the two-story Cline house so hard that the house was knocked off its piers. For a few terrifying moments, the building listed sharply to leeward like a stricken vessel, as the people and the furnishings in the room slid down the sharply tilting floor to land in a heap against the opposite wall. As Joseph told the story, he seized the hands of his nieces, Allie and Rosemary, and lunged backward through the front window, crashing through casement and glass and storm shutters and landing on the outside wall of the capsized house, now lying on its side.

It was dark now and the wind was still a wild gale, lashing the waves into a seething frenzy. But the clouds had broken and the moon's fleeting glimmer was enough to show Joseph and the girls that they were alone. None of the others in the room with them had managed to escape when the house went over. The raft on which they rode, it seemed, was also a floating coffin.

* * *

ON the other side of Q Avenue and a few doors up from the Cline house, Augustus Blackwood's house was still standing firm, a bulwark in a black expanse of wind-tossed water. The wind still shrieked like a banshee and the waves thundered against the house, with the occasional reverberating crash of a large piece of wreckage like a cannonball against a wall. But it seemed to Rachel, listening to the deafening din with the ears of hope, that the storm was at last abating.

When the water reached the second floor where the children could see it, they were frightened and began to cry. So Rachel and Colleen took them with Patsy to the third floor, where they all cuddled together on the bed in the back bedroom, on the side away from the Gulf. It was night now and late, although Rachel was so dizzy with fatigue that she had no idea of the time. Outside the window, the moon was beginning to flicker through the clouds, shining fitfully on the plunging seas and pitching wreckage around their refuge. But inside, in their small oasis of a room, there was the warm glow of the kerosene lamp that Colleen had brought upstairs, along with the plate of sandwiches and cake left from the party and even a jug of lemonade. The wind had blown out the windows in most of the other third-floor rooms and was shrieking madly through the hallway and pounding against the closed door so hard that it would have buckled and burst open had it not been for the chiffonier wedged against it. But even though she could feel the walls shuddering around her, this room felt safe, and she let her mind drift to tomorrow and the work that would have to be done when the storm had passed. She knew that some of the slates were gone from the roof, because she could see large damp spots in the ceiling and the plaster was beginning to sag. But let it fall, she told herself. When this was over, a little fallen plaster could be easily mended.

228

The children had eaten the rest of the sandwiches and cake and then, exhausted by the excitements of the day, had fallen asleep, Ida and Matthew close against Rachel, Angela in her arms, and the twins in Colleen's lap. Their sleep was a blessing, Rachel thought, smoothing the damp golden curls from Angela's forehead. When they woke to the bright sunshine of a new day, all these nightmare horrors would be gone. After a little time, they would forget—especially when their father managed to get home from the bank (surely one of the most secure buildings in the city) and they were all together at last. She was glad that she had forced herself to follow Colleen's example and stay calm, keeping the little ones busy. Even Patsy, hardly more than a child herself and terrified at the thought of never seeing her parents and sisters again, was dozing now. The lamp cast shadows on their peaceful faces. Somewhere, there was a crash of glass. Another window had gone.

"'Twon't be long now," Colleen said softly, and reached for Rachel's hand.

"I'm sure it won't," Rachel replied, almost giddy with relief at the idea that this ordeal would soon be over. "The storm has to pass soon and the winds will die down. And then the water will recede." She had faith in the house that Augustus had built for her. Now, more than ever, it felt like a dear and constant friend, a sturdy sanctuary in the center of an unimaginable hell of wind and water. It sheltered her and the children within its loving walls, and even though the stone lions at their door were underwater, they still stood watch.

Of course, there would be a terrible mess when the water went down. Augustus would be appalled when he got home and saw the damage to their beautiful home. The first-floor furnishings and draperies and carpets were doubtless a complete loss and would have to be replaced, and the carpets and some of the furniture on the second floor. The Tiffany windows were utterly smashed, she was sure, and the Steinway and Ida's

229

harp and Augustus' favorite leather chair were ruined, although the crystal chandelier in the dining room might be salvaged. But whatever had been lost could be replaced, and replaced exactly. It was just a matter of money. They would all be together, she and Augustus and the children. And Colleen, too, of course—what would she have done if kind, strong Colleen had not come back to help? Rachel wasn't sure she could have managed. No, she was quite, quite sure that she could *not* have.

Smiling, she began to rock Angela, holding the child's warm, sleeping body against her breast. *"Sweet and low,"* she sang. It was the sweet, soothing lullaby that the children always begged for when they were sick or very tired. *"Sweet and low, wind of the western sea. Low, low, breathe and blow, wind of the western sea."* She touched the tip of Angela's sweet, turned-up nose and smiled at Matthew and Ida, close beside her. They were all together now, and safe—except for Augustus, who would be with them when the storm had passed, soon now, very soon. *"Over the rolling waters go, come from the dying moon and blow, blow him again to me. While my little ones, while my pretty ones, sleep."*

Beside her, Colleen bent over the twins, cradling them in her strong, freckled arms, dropping kisses on their sleeping faces. "Sleep well, my angels," she whispered. "'Twon't be long now."

And at that moment, the mountain of wreckage that had toppled the Clines' house hit the Blackwoods' with an implacable force, jolting it completely off its foundations. The house tilted sharply to one side and began to topple, the bed and the chiffonier and Rachel and her children and Colleen and Patsy sliding with it. And in that one last, eons-long moment, Rachel realized with a burst of bone-freezing horror what Colleen had known all along.

'Twon't be long now, my angels.

'Twon't be long now.

Chapter Seventeen

At one time the holy water was sprinkled from brushes made of
Rue . . . for which reason it is supposed it was named the Herb of
Repentance and the Herb of Grace.

A Modern Herbal
Maud Grieve

Here in this place I'll set a bank of rue, sour herb of grace;
Rue, even for ruth, shall shortly here be seen . . .

Richard II
William Shakespeare

What savor is better, if physicke be true
For places infected than Wormwood and Rue?

Five Hundred Points of Good Husbandry
Thomas Tusser

In the language of flowers, rue represents grace and understanding, repentance, and forgiveness.

China Bayles
"Herbs and Flowers That Tell a Story"
Pecan Springs Enterprise

"Do you think she's all right?" Claire whispered apprehensively,
looking at Ruby.

I nodded (although I wasn't so sure myself), and Claire sank back
down in her seat.

Ruby sat silently, her eyes half-closed, her head fallen a little to one side against the chair's wing. Outside the window, a wild quicksilver flash lit up the sky and an almost-simultaneous crash seemed to reverberate in the floor beneath my feet. Startled, Claire and I both flinched. Ruby didn't move. Wherever she was, she wasn't with us—at least, not entirely.

We sat, silently watching her in the flickering light, while the wind howled like a mad thing around the house. Claire and I seemed united in a strange and heightened awareness that was centered on Ruby, as if all three of us had slipped into a world of different dimensions than our own, a world that had shrunk to our small circle of chairs around the flickering lamp. Ruby's eyes were completely closed now, her breathing almost imperceptible. Her carroty hair was disheveled, her face as still as carved marble and so white that each sandy freckle stood out distinctly.

"She wants . . ." Ruby said. Her voice was flat and low, whispery, almost inaudible, and I remembered my thought: she was giving voice to Rachel. There was another long silence. Then: "She's been waiting. Waiting a long time. Waiting for . . ." Her voice died away, as if the energy that powered her was waning.

Claire cast a questioning look at me. I read her glance and nodded. Somebody needed to ask a leading question or two, and Claire knew a great deal more about this situation than I did. I wouldn't know where to start.

Claire leaned forward. "What's she been waiting for?" Her voice was soft and neutral, and I nodded my approval.

Ruby shifted in the chair as though the question made her uncomfortable. Her answer came slowly and with a frightened reluctance. "For . . . me."

Claire and I traded startled glances. It wasn't the answer that either of us expected.

"For *you*?" Claire asked. At my slight head shake, she gathered herself together and smoothed out her voice. "Why was she waiting for you, Ruby?"

"Because of . . . because of Colleen." When she spoke the name, Ruby turned her head a little and her muscles tensed, as if the sound of the name puzzled her, or perhaps troubled her. "Colleen." She murmured it again, testing, questioning, probing. "Colleen. Colleen."

I leaned toward Claire. "Who's Colleen?" I asked in a low voice.

Claire was frowning, trying to make the connection. In an answering whisper, she said, "Colleen O'Reilly. She's buried in the graveyard at the edge of the woods. We saw her gravestone this afternoon. We were thinking that she might have been a servant in this house back in old Mrs. Blackwood's day, but we really don't know who she is."

Ruby, or Ruby/Rachel, had heard us. "Not in *this* house," she replied indistinctly. "The house in Galveston. The house Augustus built." She sighed, and there was a musical jumble of words, in what sounded to my untutored ear like Gaelic. Then, clearly and distinctly and almost in wonderment: "Colleen O'Reilly was my grandmother's mother. Gram Gifford's mother."

Now I was really surprised. I knew about Gram Gifford, Ruby's favorite grandmother. She had lived in nearby Smithville, and Ruby and Ramona had stayed with her during the summers until Ruby was ten and her parents divorced. But I had never heard Ruby mention her great-grandmother's name, and I couldn't even begin to guess why Colleen O'Reilly was buried in the private cemetery here. Obviously, Ruby's connection to this place went very deep into the past, perhaps even deeper than Ruby herself could comprehend. And what was this about a Galveston house?

"But I don't understand." Claire was frowning, puzzled. "You're saying—" She took a breath and corrected herself. "Rachel is telling you that Colleen O'Reilly was your *great-grandmother*? The same Colleen who is buried up there by the woods?"

Shadows from the flickering lamp washed across Ruby's face. "Yes. Colleen had a little girl named Annie. Gram was Annie." A broken sigh, as if Ruby—or perhaps it was Rachel—despaired of conveying to us all that she knew or felt. "Colleen took care of Rachel and her children for many years. Rachel loved Colleen and needed her. But Colleen isn't buried here."

There was a long pause, and tears seeped silently out from under Ruby's closed eyelids. Her voice was raw and unsteady, so heavy with anguish that it sounded like someone else's voice. "She was carried out to sea . . . in a great storm."

A great storm. The Galveston Hurricane? Ruby's great-grandmother had drowned in the 1900 hurricane? Perhaps the others, the children, the husband, had drowned as well. But not Rachel Blackwood, apparently. She had lived to build this house. She had lived in it until she died, in her nineties. And lived in it still—a prisoner, if I were to believe Ruby.

"But the *grave*!" Claire shook her head, not understanding. "Colleen's *grave* is here! I *saw* it, Ruby. *We* saw it, just this afternoon. It's here, with the childrens' graves, the whole family."

"Empty," Ruby said, her voice a little louder. The word had a bleak, hollow sound. "Empty, empty." She shivered, and I did, too. Before, it had been cold in the room. It was even colder now, and in the silence the low, grieving wail of the wind filled the air.

Claire turned to me, wide-eyed. "Empty graves?" she whispered in dismay. "Did somebody steal the bodies? What *happened* to them?"

I was beginning to understand—a little, maybe. Beginning to understand what Rachel Blackwood might have been about all through the unending, inescapable years after September 8, 1900. And beyond, if I could accept what Ruby was telling us.

"Just because there's a marker on top of a grave, it's no guarantee that there's a coffin and corpse underneath," I told Claire in a low voice. I was remembering a case I had read about some time ago, where friends of a man who they thought was deceased had held a closed-casket funeral, interred an empty coffin, and were dismayed to find, two years later, that they had been the victims of an elaborate fraud.

There was no fraud here, I suspected, and no intent to deceive others. But there *was* delusion and self-deception: a grieving Rachel pretending to the end of her life that all those she loved lay safely inside the fence of that little graveyard beside the woods. Or more likely, pretending until she convinced herself that they did, and that she could not leave them. And now she couldn't, Ruby was saying. Now she was a prisoner of her grief, contained in the house she had built to indulge it, in the graveyard where she had buried her heart.

Claire turned back to Ruby. "But what about my great-aunt Hazel?" she asked, bewildered. "And Mrs. Blackwood? Those graves are real, aren't they? I'm positive that Aunt Hazel is buried there. My mother saw it happen."

The lamp flickered, and I darted a look at it, hoping it wasn't about to run out of oil and leave us in total darkness. Somewhere in the house a door slammed. Behind us, around us, the shadows danced and swirled like silken scarves.

"Yes," Ruby said. "Your great-aunt is buried here. And Rachel. And Augustus."

Augustus. The husband, the children's father. So he hadn't died in the storm, after all. Had he lived here, too?

Claire still wasn't getting it. "But I don't understand, Ruby—the children, all *five* of them? And the servants. If they're not buried here, where are they?"

I knew the answer to that one. "The hurricane," I said.

Ruby let out a long sigh, and in it I heard an unspeakable, inconsolable grief—Rachel's grief. "The hurricane," she said. In a low, sad voice, she sang a snatch of haunting melody that I remembered from my own childhood. *"Low, low, breathe and blow, wind of the western sea . . ."* The words slid like clots of foam down the slopes of the eddying cold.

Into the silence, I said, "But Augustus survived. He lived here with her, then?"

"No, no." A listening pause. "He died in the storm." There were tears in Ruby's voice. "He died in the storm, but elsewhere. His body was found under the rubble of a collapsed building, and buried. She—Rachel— brought him here, afterward."

"So she came here and built this house," Claire said wonderingly, "after the hurricane. And reburied her husband here." She paused, frowning. "Wait a minute. Aunt Hazel said that Mrs. Blackwood built this house as a *copy*—although not a very good one—of a house that had been destroyed. So the original house, the Galveston house, was destroyed in the hurricane? Is that it?"

"Yes. Gone, in the hurricane, with the children, with Colleen and Patsy." Ruby's voice was ghostlike. There seemed to be a dim glow around her, embracing her. "Swept out to sea, all of them. She built this house for them. For Augustus." The glow brightened, then softened, and the scent of violets lay warm across the chill air. "Their home."

"Oh, now I see!" Claire exclaimed, scooting to the edge of her chair. "The music room, the nursery, the playroom! They must be . . . reconstructions! She furnished them as nearly like the Galveston house as possible!" She stopped, then shook her head. "No, not just those rooms, but the whole house. The kitchen, the dining room, the drawing room, this library—everything. As much like the Galveston house as she could make it. I understand now. Eighteen chairs around the dining room table, enough dishes and linens for a huge household, way too much stuff for one woman or two, living alone. Now it makes sense!"

Did it? Did it make sense? Perhaps—but a certain kind of blood-chilling, spine-tingling sense. Rachel, still a young woman, had exiled herself to this remote place and attempted to replicate the life she had lived before the storm, imagining her husband and children and servants with her in this house until imagination created a kind of reality and the encircling reality of her grief bound her to this place.

But she'd had help, of course. Claire's great-aunt Hazel, for one, who had also come here as a young woman. I couldn't help wondering how Rachel had managed to persuade (or entice or perhaps even intimidate or manipulate) Hazel Penland into joining her in her nunlike life of suffocating grief and sadness. But we would probably never know Hazel's story, at least not for certain—unless her ghost appeared and let us in on why she had joined Rachel in her futile and crazy effort to capture and contain a moment in time, or unless she had left a journal of her life in this house.

But for all its psychotic grotesquerie, Rachel's story wasn't unique. People have gotten stuck in the past and acted out their sense of loss and grief in many obsessive ways, in life and in literature—Miss Havisham, for instance, in *Great Expectations,* who stopped all the clocks in her decaying mansion at twenty minutes to nine, the moment she learned that her fiancé had jilted her. Rachel, it seemed, had stopped her life on September 8, 1900, even though she had continued to live until well into her nineties. The rest of it, the life beyond the end of life—well, that wasn't something I could understand with my rational mind, and I didn't care to try.

But I do care about Ruby, and I was beginning to worry about her. As

I said, I have seen her with the tarot cards and her Ouija board. She stays pretty much on the surface of whatever psychic experience she's involved with. At least, that's the way she's described it to me. She'd prefer to dabble. She's afraid of "going deep," as she puts it, afraid of getting sucked into the depths of something dangerous, something she can't pull herself out of. I hoped that wasn't happening here. She was very pale, and as I watched, she sank deeper into her chair, and the faint glow that surrounded her seemed to dim. A little while ago, she'd said that she had resisted Rachel's efforts to win her over physically—whatever that meant. But what if this Rachel-thing had somehow gotten its tentacles into her psyche and was manipulating her, perhaps in the same way Rachel had manipulated the young Hazel? Ruby is tough, but she's also exceptionally sensitive. If her emotions were engaged, she might be seduced and overtaken by a stronger psychic power.

I leaned forward. "Ruby," I said quietly, "maybe it's time to take a little break. You can come back and do more of this later. How about it?"

But Claire had an agenda. She didn't want to interrupt this . . . this sé-ance or whatever it was. "Okay," she said urgently. "Okay, I get it, or part of it, anyway. But if this is all true, how do I get Rachel to leave? What does she want?"

If she heard me, Ruby didn't give any sign of it. In a thin, reedy voice, she replied, "She's been waiting for someone to live in the house and help her."

I shivered. Did that mean that Ruby thought that this ghost wanted *her* to come and live in this house? If so, that was the scariest thing I'd heard in a long while.

But Claire heard it differently. "Help her? Me, help that ghost?" Claire gave a short laugh. "Well, if *that's* what she wants, I somehow missed it. She might have been a little clearer. What kind of help?"

Ruby sighed, and I saw that her lips were trembling. She was on the verge of exhaustion. Whatever was going on here, whatever she thought she was doing, the effort was costing her a great deal. "Ruby, please," I pleaded. "Let's take a break."

Ruby wasn't paying any attention to me. "She wanted Hazel's help, but Hazel wasn't strong enough."

"Not strong enough?" Claire spoke almost sarcastically. "What kind of heavy lifting does she have in mind?"

I thought that it might have been psychic strength that Ruby was talking about. Hazel had apparently been very young when she came here. Perhaps she had simply given in to Rachel's grief—perhaps had even enabled her, in the same dysfunctional way that families can enable an addict.

Ruby went on as if Claire hadn't spoken. "She wanted your help but she couldn't get through to you. She's been trying to get your attention, but she couldn't make you understand."

Claire's sarcasm became irritation. "Get my attention?" she repeated sharply. "You're telling me that all that pan banging and harp playing and bell ringing is her way of getting my *attention*?"

"And the puddles." The light around Ruby seemed to become a little brighter. Her voice sounded stronger, too, as if this exchange with Claire was somehow giving her more energy—and perhaps more confidence. It occurred to me that there might be more going on here than I had realized.

"The leak in the ceiling, too," Ruby added. "And the wind. But instead of getting your attention, it just made you angry."

Claire huffed out her breath. "Oh, come on, now," she said, sounding annoyed. "That's a bunch of horse pucky. I wasn't angry. Frustrated is more like it." She had found a word she liked. "Yes, that's it. I was *frustrated*, especially after I had to spend all that time mopping up those stupid puddles and trying to figure out what to do about that damp ceiling."

"Claire," Ruby said gently. Just that one word. *Claire*. It was an admonition.

Claire laced her fingers together, and her voice softened. "Well . . . okay, maybe it was more than frustration. But wouldn't you be angry if all your wonderful plans for a place to live and work were being thwarted by pans rattling and bells ringing? After all, it's not like I have a gazillion options. I don't have anywhere else to live, and finding a good-paying magazine job in this economy is pretty nearly impossible. If she was going to behave that way, I—"

"Claire," Ruby said again.

"Okay, okay." Claire sighed. "If I'm being totally honest, I guess I have been pretty pissed off, ever since Brad died, actually. My shrink said that was a lot of what was behind the pills and the drinking. I was angry at Brad for dying. For dying and leaving me all alone, with a mountain of bills." A tear trickled down her cheek, and she swiped at it with the back of her hand. "I loved being Brad's wife. I never planned on being his widow."

"Yes," Ruby said. "And then this house came along. 'A gift from heaven.'" A wisp of a half smile passed across her lips and was gone. "A gift from one widow to another, but with strings attached. Rachel tried to let you know what she needed from you, but you were so angry, she couldn't get through. She didn't want to give up, though, so she—" She stopped. "Do you see now?"

A lot of this was going right over my head, but Claire seemed to understand. "So she got me to bring *you* here," she said. "Is that it?"

"What do you think?" Ruby countered. It was her own voice, and her eyelids were lifting. She was coming awake.

"I think that's right!" Claire leaned forward. "I think she knew that you saw her years ago, when you were a child. She maybe even knew that you were Colleen O'Reilly's great-granddaughter."

240

"Yes. She knew then that I could help—someday. But not then. I was just a kid. I had to grow up and . . ." Ruby's voice grew sad. "I had to suffer my own loss. I had to know what it was to grieve, too."

Know what it was to grieve? Ah, I thought. Colin's death. The loss of her love, her lover, from which she had not yet fully recovered.

Claire chuckled ruefully. "So I suppose the last time I saw Rachel—on the widow's walk—her message finally got through. She was telling me to call you and ask you to come."

"You could say that," Ruby replied. Her eyes were open now, and she was sounding like herself, not nearly as spacey as she had a few moments ago. I breathed a silent sigh of relief. "You're not sorry you called, are you? You're not sorry I came?"

"Sorry?" Claire's eyes widened. "Oh *no*, Ruby. Calling you was the best thing I've done since I've been here. You've changed the way I see everything, in just a few hours." She gave Ruby an expectant look. "Okay. So now that we've got that straightened out, what does she want us to do? If we do it, will she go away and leave us alone?"

"Not us," Ruby said. "You."

"*Me*? But I can't—"

"Yes, you can. And if you do, she'll finally be able to let go. She'll be able to leave this place." Ruby paused, half-turning her head as if she were listening to a correction, then nodding. "Well, not leave—at least, not entirely, and not right away. But she will agree not to intrude on your use of this place. She'll stop trying to get your attention."

"Coexistence with a resident spirit." Claire made a face. "Not exactly what I had in mind."

"We coexist with them all the time, Claire," Ruby said. "Not always like *this,* it's true. But they're all around us, and sometimes they need us. When that happens, we must do what we can. Like now."

241

Coexisting with the dead? Well, maybe. But I wasn't scoffing. I could hear the conviction in Ruby's voice and had to respect her belief, which comes from a dimension of experience that I have no knowledge of—not personally, that is. I watched her carefully, wondering whether this experience, this encounter with Rachel, might mark a turning point for her, as it apparently did for Claire.

"Well, I suppose." Claire sounded as if she, like me, was not convinced. "But I still don't know what I can actually do."

"You can do this," Ruby said comfortably. "In fact, you're exactly what she's been looking for, which is why she's been so . . . well, pushy, I guess you'd say. You're a writer. You have lots of publishing experience. And you've been planning to write a book, haven't you?"

"That's true." Claire frowned. "But I'm not sure what kind of book I—"

"No buts." Ruby sat up straighter. "Rachel has a book in mind."

"A book!" Claire exclaimed blankly. "A book about *what*, for Pete's sake? What could a ghost possibly—"

"A book about the hurricane. About what happened to her family, her neighbors, the whole city of Galveston. She wants you to tell her story."

"But I don't *know* her story," Claire protested. "And if she thinks she's going to set up shop in my head and start dictating—"

"No, no, nothing like that," Ruby said hurriedly. "No dictation. But she *has* made some notes. In fact, she's made quite a lot of notes. And there are clippings and photos and old letters." She gestured toward a table against the wall. "It's all in that stack of scrapbooks and papers over there—a treasure trove of historical material, most of which doesn't exist anywhere else. Hazel was supposed to be helping her with it, but she just didn't have the writing skills. And Rachel didn't, either. She tried, back when she was still alive, but her feelings about the story just kept getting in her way—and anyway, her spelling is atrocious. So she wants you to do it for her."

"Oh no," Claire groaned. "Don't tell me this is all about my being a *ghost*writer?"

It was too much. I couldn't help it. I snickered.

Ruby gave me a long, hard, and very dirty look. "Rachel doesn't think it's funny," she said stiffly.

"And neither do I," Claire said in a huffy tone. "Ghostwriting is serious business. Nobody does it for fun."

"Sorry," I sputtered. "I apologize. But this is just too crazy for words, Ruby. I think all three of us must be certifiable. We're sitting here acting as if we've been communicating with a ghost who wants to employ a writer to tell her story because she—"

"Stop, China," Ruby said firmly. "You have already apologized. Don't make it worse." She turned back to Claire. "Rachel would like you to know that you can handle this any way you want."

"What are you?" Claire asked wryly. "Her agent?"

Ruby paid no attention. "She says that you could fictionalize it—turn the whole story into a novel about the storm. Or you could write something more factual, with photographs and newspaper clippings. She saved everything she could find. She even wrote to relatives and collected the photographs of the family and the house that she'd sent them before the hurricane." Ruby leaned forward. "Personally, I think she might have been a bit obsessive about it, but I suppose that was part of her problem. Anyway, you'll find plenty of research material, already organized."

The wind had momentarily calmed, but the rain seemed to be coming down harder, thudding against the walls and the windows with that steady, relentless thrumming that people in the Gulf states are far too familiar with. When you're outdoors in one of these tropical downpours, it feels like you're standing under a waterfall. You're drenched to the skin in seconds. If you're caught on the highway, your windshield wipers will give up in despair. The only thing you can do is pull as far off the road as you can get and turn off your lights to lessen the chance that you'll be rear-ended.

"Research materials, already organized." Claire's laugh was ironic. "Sounds like she has it all planned. But I don't suppose I should be surprised. Any ghost who goes around hurling lightning bolts at trees to get a writer's attention—"

"She didn't have anything to do with that," Ruby protested. "It wasn't *her* lightning bolt. Not all natural phenomena are *super*natural, you know. Some are just . . . well, just ordinary. Just natural."

"Oh, *right*," Claire said, adding skeptically, "Maybe it would be a good idea if I had a contract. Do you think? I mean, how do I know that if I write her book, she'll go away and—"

"Not go away entirely," Ruby corrected her. "It might take a while to release herself from this place, and even then, she would like the freedom to come and go."

I refrained from rolling my eyes at the thought of a roving ghost traveling here and there.

Ruby went on. "But she does agree that she'll stop trying to get your attention. You can go on with your plans for the bed-and-breakfast."

"Well, sure," Claire replied argumentatively. "She can *agree* to it while we're sitting here. But that doesn't mean she won't start ringing bells and crying in the night once you've gone back to Pecan Springs. How do I know I can trust her?"

Ruby lifted her shoulders and let them fall. "I guess you'll just have to get started on the project and see what happens. If there's a problem, I'd be glad to come back and—"

She didn't get to complete her offer. She was interrupted by the loud crash of smashing glass, very close. Claire almost jumped out of her skin.

"That sounded like the window at the end of the hall," she said, resigned. "I need to find something to put over it, so the rain doesn't flood the hall and ruin the beautiful wood floor." She gave Ruby a chiding look. "That's why I always had to mop up after Rachel. I'd hate for that floor to get damaged, even if it was only 'phantom' rain." Under her breath, she muttered, "Sure looked wet to me."

"I'll help," I said. "Do you have any plywood?"

"There's a piece on the back porch that will probably fit," Claire replied, getting up. "I'll go see."

"I'll help, too," Ruby said decidedly. "I saw a hammer and some nails in one of the kitchen drawers. Anyway," she added, nodding at the lamp that had extinguished itself, "we only have one light. I'm not staying here all by myself in the dark." If she was any the worse for wear after her ghostly experience as a voice for Rachel Blackwood, she didn't show it.

We were all three standing now, and I noticed that the quality of the air in the room had changed dramatically. It was fresher, more moist, but with an odd, sour smell—blowing into the house from that broken hallway window, no doubt. It would be a good idea to get it covered as soon as we could.

Claire picked up the lamp. "Let's all go back to the kitchen and get another couple of lamps," she said. "Then we can—"

"Wait," I said, raising my hand. "Do you hear something? It sounds like—" I stopped, and we all heard it. A low, ragged groan, like a creature in pain, and a dragging sound, as if—

Claire gasped. "Something's out there," she said. Her eyes were wide and frightened, and she clutched at Ruby's arm. "It's coming down the hallway, toward this room! Do something, Ruby!"

"Me?" Ruby cried frantically. "What can I do? I can't do anything. This is *your* house!"

Claire was grim. "Yes, but you're the one who talks to ghosts. What does Rachel say about—"

245

She stopped. The sounds in the hallway were louder, rustlings, as if whatever-it-was was feeling its way along the wall in our direction, accompanied by that awful dragging noise and a low, keening cry that seemed to cut to the bone.

I sucked in my breath. "Come on, guys, don't panic," I said, as much to myself as to them. "It's probably an animal that got scared and jumped through the window. A dog or a cow or—"

"A mountain lion," Ruby moaned, and we all three huddled together.

CRASH!

On the other side of the room, the door to the hallway flew open, banging like a gunshot against the wall. A sudden blast of rain-wet cold air filled the room. A hulking, hooded figure, hardly recognizable as human, raised itself up in the doorway, dragging one leg, holding one crooked arm against its chest. In the flickering light of Claire's lamp, I gasped as I saw that its face—or the place where its face would be if it had a face—was covered with mud and slimy ropes of brown and green weeds and hanks of dark, bloody hair. On one side, the skin was hideously flayed to the bone, hanging in a bloody flap from cheek to jaw like a hunk of raw meat. I could almost see eyes, too, although they were hardly human, glaring red and wild: an animal's eyes. Water, mixed with blood, streamed over its hunched shoulders and dripped onto the floor in a bloody puddle. The smell of fetid mud and decayed river weed clung to the thing as though it had just emerged from a flooded grave.

Claire screamed and turned her face away. I was frozen, staring.

Ruby gasped. "What?" she cried. "Who . . . what *are* you?"

The creature made a horrible, unholy gurgling sound. Then, with a threatening wild-animal growl and a roar of rage, hate, and pain, it lurched toward Ruby, raising its one good arm, brandishing an iron rod with a wicked, spear-like point.

Beside me, Claire screamed again and dropped the lamp with a crash of glass and a splatter of lamp oil. The light went out, and the room was plunged into darkness—except for a flickering tongue of flame that began to lap hungrily at the spilled oil.

"Fire!" Ruby cried. "Fire!"

The word slashed through the dark like the jagged neck of a broken bottle.

Chapter Eighteen

Galveston

At 8:30 p.m. my residence went down with about fifty persons who had sought it for safety, and all but eighteen were hurled into eternity. Among the lost was my wife, who never rose above the water after the wreck of the building. I was nearly drowned and became unconscious, but recovered through being crushed by timbers and found myself clinging to my youngest child, who had gone down with myself and wife. Mr. J. L. Cline joined me five minutes later with my other two children, and with them and a woman and child we picked up from the raging waters, we drifted for three hours, landing 300 yards from where we started.

"Special Report on the Galveston Hurricane"
by Isaac M. Cline, Chief Meteorologist
Texas Section, U.S. Weather Bureau

All Rachel could remember was the horrible, bone-shattering shriek of the house—the cry of a living thing dying in agony—as it was shoved off its foundations by the battering ram of debris. It listed sharply, and the bed, the furniture, lamps, and children slid into utter darkness. The house went down like a stricken ship. She didn't know what happened after that.

When she woke up, her long wet skirt was wrapped around her like a leaden shroud, and she was lying on a piece of wreckage that bobbed alarmingly in the water, tilting at such an angle that she had to cling to whatever she could grasp to keep from sliding off. With her were her neighbor Mr. Cline, his three young daughters, his brother Joseph, and a little boy so terrified that he could not remember his name, neither his first nor his last. All he could do was cry for his mother, terrible cries that ripped Rachel's heart to pieces, for she had no idea whether her own children had drowned when the house went down or were clinging to wreckage in the water and crying for her, like this poor little boy.

Ice-cold and shivering, they drifted on their storm-tossed raft through the wild night, Rachel holding the weeping child tight against her, the others clutching each other and holding on to the salvation of their slab of debris as best they could. They were bombarded by flying planks and scraps of wood and the floating corpses of drowned cows and horses and even people. Buffeted by breaking waves and frozen by wind as cold as if it blew straight off the polar ice, they were swept out to sea and then—although by this time Rachel scarcely knew it—swept back toward the land again. After what seemed an eternity of howling winds, their raft beached itself at last against the half-standing wreckage of a house. Their nightmare voyage over, another nightmare about to begin, the exhausted survivors stumbled onto solid ground.

Scarcely knowing what she was doing, knowing only that she was frantic for rest, Rachel crawled under the partial shelter of a canted roof. She curled up on the wet ground, arms around the little boy, and fell into a desperate sleep. When she woke and crawled out from under their shelter, the child was gone. She never saw him again and never knew what became of him.

As the storm blew itself out, the water receded almost as quickly as it had risen. The wind had died down to a soft breeze, and when the sun rose on that Sunday morning, the ninth of September, it splashed its customary careless brilliance across the landscape just as though nothing at all out of the ordinary had happened the day and night before. It was a beautiful day in Galveston, where beautiful days were the normal state of affairs.

But for Rachel, nothing that she saw was normal, and never would be again. Dazed, scarcely knowing who or where she was, she picked her stumbling way around and over mountains of broken lumber laced with fragments of curtains, clothing, bedsheets and blankets, electrical and telephone wires, fishing nets, and rope, all pushed up by the storm in a giant windrow that snaked across the ruined city for miles. Then she emerged onto a broad, sloping plain that reached down to the blue waters of the Gulf, bladed completely clean by the moving mountain of debris. The earth was covered with a thick layer of mud, and she recognized not a single familiar landmark until she came upon her iron gate with the ornate letter *B* in the center, wrapped around the short, broken stub of a palm tree. There was no fence in sight, and no house, just the twisted gate. But there were the twin stone lions, their ears chipped and broken, lying forlornly facedown in the mud a little distance away. And all by itself, a child's red rocking chair.

It was the sight of that empty chair that broke Rachel's heart.

THE Associated Press began its story about the hurricane with a striking and deeply heartfelt image. "The city of Galveston is wrapped in sackcloth and ashes. She sits beside her unnumbered dead and refuses to be comforted. Her sorrow and suffering are beyond description. Her grief is unspeakable."

And so it was. Galveston mourned as it began to gather up its dead and bury as many as possible in the local churchyards. Augustus Blackwood was among the lucky, for his body was recovered from the wreckage of

Ritter's Café, identified, and interred in St. Mary's Cemetery, with a headstone to mark the place. Other bodies, unidentifiable, would be buried without a marker where they were found—until even that terrible recourse proved impossible. Then the dead were carted to the shore, where they were piled on barges and towed out into the Gulf, to be weighted with stones and buried in the pitiless waters that had robbed them of their lives.

But the ocean, even more pitiless now, refused these flawed offerings and returned many of the dead to the shore, where the living, now desperate to quell the stench of putrefaction and the poisonous threat of disease, burned them on pyres of wooden wreckage. For weeks, the smell of smoldering human flesh hung over the city like a smoky pall, and the ash from the cremation fires drifted on the wind. The surviving citizens—now under martial law—tied camphor-scented rags over their faces to keep out the stench. The Associated Press' metaphor of a mourning city clothed in sackcloth and ashes had become real.

The number of dead on the island was at first reported to be modest, since the surviving leaders of the city did not want to confess to the world that Galveston had been destroyed. But within a day or two, the death count grew to three thousand, then double that, then eight thousand, and even (some said) as many as ten thousand on the island, not including the hundreds who had died on the mainland. Whole families were lost, entire blocks of homes razed, their occupants gone forever. Isaac Cline's pregnant wife was found in October, a month after the storm, buried under the wreckage of her house. The bodies of most of St. Mary's orphans were never recovered, but a searcher found the corpse of a small child on the beach. He tried to pick it up, but when he did, he discovered that it was tied to another child, and another. He pulled the bodies of eight children and a nun out of their sandy grave.

And as far as property values could be measured, it was reported that nearly half of the city's real estate had been destroyed, at a cost of some twenty-eight to thirty million dollars, very little of the loss covered by in- surance. As well, some 150 acres of Galveston Island's beautiful shoreline had been chewed up and swallowed by the greedy ocean. "And the beach?" lamented the *Galveston Daily News* of September 13, 1900. "That once beautiful beach with its long stretches of white sand—what had become of that? Shoreward as far as the eye could reach were massive piles of houses and timbers, all shattered and torn."

The uncountable losses of life and property seemed to pile as high as the massive mountains of rubble. They marked for many the bitter end of Galveston's dreams, for surely no man or woman would dare to trust their futures and those of their families to such a vulnerable place. But Galveston's city fathers were determined and still ambitious. Refusing to be cowed by a mere hurricane, they set about rebuilding their city and protecting it from any future storm.

The first order of business was the construction of a seventeen-foot- high concrete seawall, almost two feet higher than the storm surge that had overflowed the island. The seawall ran for over three miles along the beach, with a second section of nearly a mile completed two years later and still more sections built over the next six decades, for a total of ten full miles. The seawall was protected by a band of riprap some ten yards wide, built of giant granite boulders. To raise the city out of the reach of another de- structive storm surge, all of the new and surviving buildings, even the cathedral, were jacked up several feet and the space below filled with tons of sand dredged up from Galveston Bay and pumped onto the land. The original elevation of the city averaged about five or six feet above low tide, with the highest point at just above eight feet. Afterward, the elevation varied from eight feet along the bay to some twenty-two feet along the Gulf side. The work was paid for by taxpayers and property owners. Galveston's hopes would be rebuilt on this higher foundation: an entirely new commercial district, with forty blocks of new hotels, new banks, new city buildings, and even a grand new opera house to celebrate the city's rebirth.

People would rebuild their houses, too, and within just a few years, the city's residential neighborhoods would be full again, although it would take another decade before the streets would be lined with lush new gardens and trees, thriving in the new soil behind the security of the seawall. Eventually the reconstruction was done, and a good thing, too, for another hurricane tested the city in 1915, with a sixteen-foot storm surge and winds of 120 miles an hour. The seawall held firm, and only eleven citizens lost their lives. In that same year, however, the rival city of Houston completed the dredging of Buffalo Bayou and Galveston Bay, creating a navigable waterway and transforming it into the famous Houston Ship Channel, now infamously polluted with industrial poisons. Rebuild and fortified as it might, Galveston's advantage as a sheltering port was lost. The city could never again dream of becoming the New York of the Gulf.

Rachel Blackwood could not rebuild her home—not then, and not there. After the storm, she went to stay with her sister in Houston, where she remained for some time, virtually a recluse, overwhelmed by her grief and unable to confront life in the world without her husband and children. Early the next spring, despairing of her ability to recover on her own, her doctors sent her to an asylum in the mountains of Colorado, where she lived until 1905. Her treatment was paid for by the return on those highly speculative mineral rights that Augustus had purchased a few days before he died. The property was located near Beaumont, Texas, at a place called Spindletop, which blew its first gusher on January 1, 1901, just four months after the hurricane. The great Texas Oil Boom would change the world and reward everyone who had invested in it.

But all the money in the world could not heal Rachel or fill the empty place that had once been her heart. She had buried Augustus and knew where he lay, but the bodies of her children, and of Colleen and Patsy as well, were never found. Unburied, her grief remained with her, a constant and corrosive companion, enveloping her in a dark and bitter depression. Her doctors felt a sympathetic affection for this profoundly troubled woman who had lost everything precious to her in the world and could not find a way to go on without it, and they gave her a great deal of fatherly advice for the recovery of her spirits. One of them told her straightforwardly and with the deepest consideration that she would never be healed of her grief unless she busied herself with a worthy project, preferably one that would require her full attention for the rest of her life. She might, for instance, volunteer at Jane Addams' Hull House in Chicago, where she could devote both her time and her wealth to a good cause—a fitting memorial, he suggested, to the loved ones she had lost.

But Rachel, who mourned not only for her husband and children but for the house in which they had all lived so happily together, had a different idea for a memorial. She went to look at the land Augustus had bought the week before he died, fifteen hundred acres in Fayette County, some hundred miles inland from the coast and safely (she thought) out of the reach of hurricanes and tropical storms. It pleased her as well as any, although, to tell the truth, no place on earth could have pleased her unless her husband and children were with her. She built a house on the land, as nearly as possible like the house Augustus had built in Galveston. She lacked access to the plans and (at that time) even photographs, so she drew the house from the remembered images that were carved in her heart by grief. The builder did his best to correct her worst errors, but he could only go as far as Rachel would allow—and she would not allow him to go very far, because she had the courage of her convictions and was very sure that she had it right. The result, understandably, was not quite the house that

255

the original had been. It was, as Ruby Wilcox would later notice, a visibly *crooked* house.

But since Rachel did not often view her house from a distance (she mostly stayed indoors), it pleased her, and she went about furnishing it to resemble the house in Galveston—as it was on September 7, 1900, the day before the hurricane changed her life forever. She became obsessed with this effort, and as time went on, her imagination filled the house as it had been filled before that awful day, with the sounds of Colleen's kitchen, Matthew's flute and bouncing ball, the haunting melodies of Ida's harp, the twins' noisy play, and the comforting scent of Augustus' pipe tobacco. She lost herself in the pleasure of these haunted imaginings. She lost herself, too, in the accumulation of as many photographs, newspaper clippings, and accounts of the storm as she could find, thinking that she would make herself sit down and write about the experience that had robbed her of every happiness. But each time she tried, grief rose up and seized her pen, and finally she put it down and gave up the attempt.

Of course, there were other things that had to be done to attend to the practicalities of life in the country. Rachel built a small but comfortable cottage nearby and hired a young man and his wife—Will and Ellie Daily— to serve as caretaker and cook-housekeeper, positions they held for many years. When a young woman named Hazel Penland appeared on the scene, Rachel took her on as her personal companion, with the idea that Hazel, a bright if uneducated and exceptionally shy young lady, might be able to serve as her secretary and do the writing that she could not. She hired an attorney in La Grange, Wilberforce Bissonet Hoover, Sr., to oversee her financial and legal affairs. Mr. Hoover outlived her by several years, and his son, Wilberforce Bissonet Hoover, Jr., continued to act on behalf of the estate.

If Hazel, the Dailys, and the Hoovers (Senior and Junior) thought Rachel a little mad, they did not speak of it, for they, like her doctors, felt an affectionate compassion toward her. She was, after all, a very nice person who'd had the misfortune to survive an unspeakable tragedy and was condemned to live out the rest of her life with a loss that was larger than life itself. In the end, she gave up—almost—the idea of writing her story and settled for simply living in her grief, contained as it was in the house she had built to remind herself of her life before the hurricane destroyed everything.

When Rachel died, she left the house to Hazel, who was by that time no longer young. Hazel lived quite companionably with its ghosts until her death, when the house went to Ruth, and then to Claire. And that is when . . .

And that is when Rachel discovered that she might at last have found someone who could tell her story.

Chapter Nineteen

It is said that the cypress tree (*Cupressus* sp.) became the symbol of death because, if it is cut severely, it will not grow again. Cypress wood contains a natural chemical preservative that resists decay; hence, it was used by the Greeks and Romans to make coffins, and by the Egyptians for wooden mummy cases, to protect the dead. Cypress branches were carried by mourners to protect both the living and the dead, and the idea of protection was extended symbolically: cypress trees were planted near graves to protect the immortal souls of the dead from the power of evil. The bald cypress (*Taxodium distichum*) that is native to Texas and the southeastern United States is distantly related.

In the language of flowers, cypress represents death and protection from evil.

China Bayles
"Herbs and Flowers That Tell a Story"
Pecan Springs Enterprise

"*Fire!*"

Two urgencies drove me as Ruby's shrill scream sliced the dark. One was to put out that licking, hungry tongue of flame before the fuel-fed fire could kindle the wooden floor of a room that was crammed to the ceiling with old books, in a wood-frame house that was over a century old. The other was to stave off the attack of the hulking figure staggering toward us across the room, a sharp-pointed spear raised over his head, poised to strike at Ruby.

Not that I thought all this out logically, of course. I acted by instinct, stamping swiftly on the darting flicker of flame, shoving Ruby out of the assailant's way, and aiming a clumsy diving tackle at the creature's knees.

And missed, of course. It was dark and he—the *thing*—wasn't where he'd been when Claire dropped the lamp. I ended up cracking my head against the half-open door and seeing a burst of colorful stars cascading like a dying Roman candle through the blackness. Ruby ended up, from the sound of it, falling against the table that held our plates and cups. I heard her sharp "Ow!" and the noisy cascade of dishes to the floor. At least she was out of the way, although as I scrambled stupidly to my feet, I couldn't see where she was, or where Claire was.

Or where *he* was. The dark was absolute. Where was the lightning when we needed it?

But if I couldn't see our attacker, he couldn't see us, although I could hear him stumbling violently around the room, as he knocked things over, whacked the furniture with his wickedly pointed spear, and mumbled, moaned, groaned—terrifying nonhuman noises, the brutish sounds of an animal in agony. And then I heard him topple, full length, the heavy, floor-shaking thud of a falling body.

The thud was followed by a moment's silence, then another noise, the thump of a piece of furniture—one of the wingback chairs?—going over, and a half-muffled "Damn!"

The *damn* came from Claire, I thought, blundering panic-stricken around the room, trying to keep away from the guy's swinging spear as it slashed through the air. But if he was already down and out—

"Claire, Ruby stop," I said loudly. "Just *stop* where you are. Let's figure out what's going on."

Ruby was muttering something under her breath, almost like a prayer.

"Ssshh, Ruby," I said urgently. "Listen for him." I could hear a gurgling wheeze and the scrabbling of fingernails on the floor. Was he trying to get up? Where was he? Mentally, I mapped the room, trying to come up with a weapon I could use to bash the man's head and keep him down on the floor until—

Until *what*? Our cell phones weren't working, the cars were out of commission, and there was no hope of any reinforcements until Claire's caretaker and his wife got back the next day. We'd have to tie the guy up, which meant that we had to keep him flat on the floor until we could find some rope. But we couldn't go groping around this place in the dark. We needed *light*.

Ruby was still muttering. I couldn't make out what she was saying until I heard the whispered words, "*Please, Rachel.*" In the stillness, I heard an answering whisper. It sounded like a long, sibilant *yesssss*.

Then something entirely unexpected happened. I felt a faint hum in the floor beneath my feet and a distinct vibration in the air, as if molecules were bumping together. The table lamps in the room began to come on, first with an uncertain, flickering glimmer, and then with the kind of brief, dazzling, blue-white brilliance that comes when you get a power surge somewhere on the line. A bulb exploded with a loud *PING!* and then the lamps in the room settled down to a full, steady glow. The shadows ebbed into the darkened corners and died. Ah, light!

"Thank you," I heard Ruby say. I was too busy looking around for our assailant to ask her who she was thanking, but I could guess.

Blinking in the unaccustomed bright light, I saw the man halfway across the room, flat on his face on the floor, unmoving. His head was turned to one side, his face mostly hidden by his dark hood. His right arm was folded awkwardly under him. His left arm was stretched out to one side, his hand clasping the spear. But it wasn't a spear. It was the twisted rod of a wrought-iron fence, with a sharp-pointed finial on the business end. The mistake had been an easy one for me to make, given the surprise of his appearance in the doorway in the guttering light of Claire's oil lamp. And if he'd aimed to use it as a spear, what was the difference?

Ruby stumbled around the fallen chairs and stood beside the man on the floor. "What *is* it?" she asked fearfully, looking down at the sprawled form. A puddle of blood seeped from under one cheek. "Is it . . . is he *dead*?" The bloody fingers holding the spear twitched and splayed, and Ruby stepped back, eyes widening. "No, he's not!" she whispered. "He's alive!"

Claire was bending over the figure, putting out a trembling hand toward the unmoving shoulder, then drawing back. "I think . . ." Her voice quavered. "I think it's . . ." But she couldn't bring herself to touch the body.

I skirted the broken glass and spreading patch of lamp oil and went to kneel beside the man. A warning kindled inside me, but I steeled myself against it and, with difficulty, rolled him over onto his right side, then his back.

Then wished fervently that I hadn't. It wasn't a man. It was a woman, her dark hair rain-soaked and bloody from a cut across her forehead. Someone—or something—had sliced the skin from the left half of her face from cheekbone to the point of her jaw, opening a gaping, meat-cleaver slit down the left side of her neck, exposing her collarbone. The right side of her face was deeply abraded and raw, like freshly ground meat, and her right eye was . . .

I swallowed. The right eye was probably gone. Welling blood pooled in the socket. It looked as though her right arm might be broken, and her sweatshirt was sodden and bloody. Her jeans were soaked as well, as if she'd been swimming, and the denim of the right leg was ripped open from thigh to ankle. She wore only one sneaker, on her left foot. The right foot was shoeless and turned outward at an impossible angle. It occurred to me then that she might have picked up the iron fence piece to use it as a support, like a walking cane.

Beside me, Claire gasped when she saw the woman's face. "Kitty!" she cried. "It's . . . this is Kitty Rawlings!"

"Kitty?" Ruby whispered. "Kitty?"

"Who?" I asked. A neighbor, maybe? A friend?

"My caretaker's wife," Claire said. "She and Sam left this afternoon to drive to Houston. I guess the weather must have been so bad that they decided they'd better drive back home. But where . . . where's Sam?" She bent lower and raised her voice. "Kitty? Can you hear me? Where's Sam?"

At the question, the woman's left eyelid fluttered. "Sam . . ." she muttered thickly. "Truck. In the . . ." She tried again, whispering. "In the creek."

"In the *creek*?" Claire cried, aghast. "You mean, your truck went into the water?"

Ruby put a hand on my shoulder, squeezing hard with her fingers. I looked up. She was staring down at Kitty, her eyes wide and oddly blank. *"Crooked man,"* she whispered. *"Crooked cat."* She paused, then said it again. *"Crooked cat."*

I frowned at her. "What? What are you saying?" It sounded like the words she and Claire had seen written on the menu board in the kitchen.

"Crooked sixpence," she muttered. *"Crooked sixpence!"*

Kitty raised her one good hand and clamped bloody fingers on my wrist in a surprisingly tight grip. "Help . . . him," Kitty wheezed. She coughed. "Help . . . Sam." Her one good eye rolled up until only the white was visible, and her hand dropped. She was gone again, at least for the moment.

I thought of the steep hill, the road I had driven down—skidded down, more accurately. The road was slippery then, hours ago, and the low concrete bridge at the foot of the hill had already been covered by eight inches of fast-moving water. It could be eight feet deep at the bridge by this time—and still rising, depending on how much rain had fallen in the creek's watershed. It was entirely possible that the bridge itself was gone. Even concrete bridges don't always stand up to our Texas flash floods.

I got to my feet. I don't mind telling you that I was scared. My palms were suddenly clammy and my knees were shaking. I am by nature a cautious person (translation: I don't have an ounce of bravado in my makeup kit) and I understand all too well the dangers involved in swift-water rescue. We had no equipment and not even a prayer of getting any professional help, and it was utterly foolhardy for me to even think about attempting anything.

But this woman's husband was out there somewhere, maybe in the water and out of reach of anybody's help—but maybe on the bank or somewhere else reachable. Somebody had to make an effort to find out what the situation was. And now that the electricity was back on—courtesy of Ruby's ghost, perhaps?—I wondered about the flashlights. Were they working, too?

Kitty was back again. "The truck," she moaned. "The truck . . . washed off the bridge . . . downstream. Don't know how I got out. Crawled all the . . ." She began to cough, bloody spittle on her lips. Internal injuries, maybe. A punctured lung? Her face was pallid, her lips blue.

"Flashlights," I said tersely. "Now that Rachel's turned the power back on, maybe we've got operational batteries again." You'd better believe I felt dumb saying that, but what other explanation was there? "Where do you keep the flashlights? And maybe some rope? It's probably too late, but—"

Ruby's lapse into nursery rhymes seemed to have ended. "I'll stay with

Kitty," she offered. "Claire knows her way around this place better than
I do."

Claire was already halfway to the door. "Come on, China," she said
over her shoulder.

Ten minutes later, clad in ponchos and armed with working flashlights
and a coil of clothesline, we were out in the rain. I paused long enough to
check my cell phone and—hooray!—discover that it was operating again.
I had no idea whether the Fayette County's sheriff's office was set up to
receive 911 text messages, but I could try to get a message through to Mc-
Quaid, who had the address of Claire's place.

I was even more fumble-fingered than usual, but I managed to send a
text message that I hoped would prompt him to immediately call Star
Flight in Austin and try to get a helicopter medic team out here for Kitty.
Star Flight responds to emergency service requests in counties across Central Texas—I was hoping that Fayette County was one of them. But Mc-
Quaid would know what to do. He had worked with Star Flight when he
was acting police chief of Pecan Springs, before Sheila Dawson got the job,
and one of his buddies was a Star Flight crew member. The helicopter
wouldn't be able to fly in the storm, but we'd be on the list when the weather
cleared. And knowing McQuaid, I was sure he'd be in touch with the Fayette County emergency services, too.

We went out the back door, around the house, and down the slope,
Claire leading the way. The rain was still coming down in buckets. The
path was ankle deep in water and it was a struggle to keep my footing. My
sneakers were immediately soaked and the hood of my poncho kept blowing off. I finally gave up trying to keep my hair dry and concentrated on
the task in front of me: getting down to the creek safely. I could already
hear it roaring, out of its banks, and my heart sank. If this storm had
dumped as much rain across the region as it had here, we might have to

wait quite a while for Star Flight. On a night like this, their helicopter fleet and their emergency teams would likely be called out for several swift-water rescues. We might be at the bottom of a long list.

At the foot of the path, Claire turned and pointed. "The bridge is downstream about a hundred yards." She had to yell to make herself heard above the rush of the water. She turned the beam of her flashlight onto the raging creek. "I've never seen the water this high. Most of the time, it's only a couple of feet deep right here, and so clear that you can see the bottom. This . . . this is incredible."

It was. The creek was a churning torrent, a muddy maelstrom of rushing water that tumbled tree branches and rocks and chunks of debris in a foaming flood. Our flashlights weren't a lot of help, but I could see enough to convince me that if Kitty's husband was caught in that gushing, rushing water, he was a dead man.

We picked our way downstream, moving cautiously among the scrub willows, roughleaf dogwood, and buttonbush that grew along the bank. We had to stay well above the water, because stream banks are often deeply undercut by floods, and the last thing either of us wanted was to feel the ground under our feet give way and pitch us into that roaring water. Lightning played along the low ridge behind the house and thunder banged like a chorus of kettledrums. Ahead of us, a cottonwood tree had dropped a couple of thick limbs, and we had to clamber over and through the obstruction. A hundred yards to the bridge? It was beginning to seem like ten miles.

But at last we reached it—or reached the spot where the bridge was supposed to be. At that point, the creek was maybe thirty yards wide, and our flashlights could scarcely illuminate the other side. But dimly, through the sheeting rain, I could see where the road came down the hill. And on this side of the creek, I could see where it curved around behind the house.

The bridge itself was under six or seven feet of rushing water. I shone my light downstream, searching the muddy water for the truck. Where was it? If it had gone off the road here, at the bridge, it couldn't be far.

And then my moving flashlight beam picked up a gleam of something metallic, and I swung it back. It was the back bumper of a pickup truck, nose down, the cab roof flattened down as if it had been in a rollover. It was wedged beneath a fallen tree and almost fully submerged, the bed jacked up on a boulder, *FORD* clearly visible across the tailgate. It was thirty yards or so downstream of the bridge, about four or five yards from the bank, completely surrounded by rushing water, completely out of our reach.

"There, China!" Claire yelled, seeing it at the same time I did. "That's Sam's pickup." She started downstream toward it.

"Can you see if he's in there?" I called. A jagged streak of lightning crossed the sky, and in its blue-white light I saw that the hood of the truck was wedged under a huge bald cypress that had broken off ten feet above the ground and now lay across the creek. The truck's windshield was entirely underwater, and it looked like the cab was completely filled with water, right up to the flattened, crumpled roof.

As I scrambled through the rocks along the water's edge, I could see that the driver's-side window was broken and the door looked like it had been pretty well caved in, but that didn't mean a lot, either way. The driver could have gotten out before the water swept the truck off the bridge and rolled it over downstream. His passenger had not only managed to scramble out of the truck, but she'd gotten out of the water and made her way to the house, where she still had enough presence of mind to break a window and get in. Whether she would survive until help got here was another question, of course. I had no way of knowing what kind of internal injuries she might have.

"I can't see whether he's in there or not," Claire said, in answer to my question. "But if he is, he's a goner." She turned and began shining her light along the creek bank, upstream and downstream. "Sam!" she shouted. "Sam Rawlings! Can you hear me?"

I called, too, using my light to pick out possible places where somebody might have crawled out of the water, but it was a hopeless task. The water was still rising, and while the truck seemed to be pretty securely wedged under that tree, there was always the chance that a more powerful surge could come along and flip it over.

We stood there helplessly, flashing our lights around. Then my light happened to shine on the rear window of the cab, and I saw something that made my heart stop. It was a square, official-looking sticker, about six by eight inches. *Protected by AK-47*, it read, with a drawing of the assault rifle.

And a few inches from that sticker I could see a neat, round bullet hole.

I was looking at the getaway vehicle for the robbers of the Ranchers State Bank in Pecan Springs, and Bonnie Roth's killers.

THE rain had stopped and it was almost dawn by the time Star Flight was finally able to take off from the heliport atop University Medical Center Brackenridge in Austin. Less than half an hour later, we heard the unmistakable *whump-whump-whump* of the helicopter rotor. McQuaid and I had exchanged a dozen text messages by that time, so I wasn't surprised to see him jump out of the helicopter on the heels of the medevac crew, or to see a heavy-duty tow truck lumbering down the hill, followed by two Fayette County sheriff's cars.

It took the medevac team about ten minutes to strap Kitty Rawlings onto a gurney and load her into the helicopter. Then they headed back to Austin, where she would be met not only by doctors and nurses but by the police as well. McQuaid, having seen that the three of us—Ruby, Claire, and I—were perfectly okay and in no danger, had flown back to Austin. After all, he had to get the kids off to school in the morning and administer his final exam at the university in the afternoon. My car started easily when I tried it, but it would be a day or maybe two before the water went down far enough to cross the bridge and the road dried out enough for my Toyota to make it up the hill.

The water was going down quickly, but the creek was still flowing fast and deep. It took several tries for the deputies to get a chain on the rear end of Sam Rawlings' pickup truck. Once that was done, however, it took less than five minutes to winch the battered truck out of the creek and onto the far bank, where the deputies opened the passenger door and pulled out Rawlings' body. It looked as though he had drowned when the cab had filled up and he could not escape.

And if there was any doubt that this was the truck used in the robbery, it was laid to rest by the sodden, disintegrating paper bag the deputies found stuffed under the truck's seat, the bag of bills that Bonnie had handed over before she was shot. The ten-dollar bills were banded in bundles of twenty, ten of them, and the bands were stamped with *Ranchers State Bank*.

It was well after ten in the morning before Ruby, Claire, and I finally got some breakfast. And then, utterly exhausted from having been up all night dealing with ghosts, spear-wielding monsters, and submerged pickup trucks, we went to bed. Believe me, we slept the sleep of the dead. And if Rachel was out and about, haunting her house, we slept right through it.

Chapter Twenty

Sleep thou, and I will wind thee in my arms . . .
So doth the woodbine—the sweet honeysuckle
A Midsummer Night's Dream
William Shakespeare

Honeysuckle or woodbine (*Lonicera* sp.) was once used widely to soothe labor pains in women giving birth and to treat respiratory and urinary ailments. The ancient Roman writer Pliny suggested the use of honeysuckle for disorders of the spleen, and in the Chinese medical treatise, *Tang Bencao* (C.E. 659), it was recommended to eliminate heat and toxins from the human body.

In the language of flowers, honeysuckle represented generous, selfless, devoted love.

China Bayles
"Herbs and Flowers That Tell a Story"
Pecan Springs Enterprise

As it turned out, Rawlings hadn't drowned. The bank guard's bullet had struck him in the neck, and he had bled to death. That much we learned from the autopsy. The rest of the story we learned from Kitty Rawlings, who spilled the ugly details—and then some—to the Pecan Springs detectives who questioned her in Brackenridge Hospital before charging her as an accessory to capital murder in the shooting of Bonnie Roth. When she recovers enough to leave Brackenridge, she will be arraigned and jailed until the grand jury meets. Under Texas' law, some-one can be held criminally responsible for aiding and abetting a felony in the course of which a murder is committed. That is, the law doesn't distin-guish between the person who pulls the trigger and his (or her) accomplice. The accomplice is equally guilty.

The bond schedule in Adams County permits the judge to refuse bail for capital felonies, and since Kitty could face the death penalty, she'll likely be held without bail while awaiting trial. My guess is that, at trial, her attorney will attempt to argue that her husband forced her to commit robbery by threat of death or serious bodily harm: the "duress defense," described in Section 8.05 of the Texas Penal Code. The court is likely to reject that defense, however, because Kitty "intentionally, knowingly, or recklessly placed herself in a situation in which it was probable that she would be subjected to compulsion"—the penal code's way of saying that she could have chosen to walk out on her husband at any time. Or she could simply have got out of the truck, walked up to the bank guard, and given herself up.

In fact, she could have done this at any time in the last year, because the Ranchers robbery was just one in a string of a half dozen Bonnie-and-Clyde robberies the pair had committed, hitting small-town banks where the security was likely to be lax. Then they'd head back to the Blackwood place, where they'd hang out quietly, under everyone's radar, until they were ready to rob another bank. In some cases, Kitty drove the getaway vehicle while Sam committed the robbery; in other cases, Sam drove while Kitty went in for the money. But until the Pecan Springs robbery, they had never used their own vehicle—the Ford Ranger—as their getaway vehicle. Instead, they had always stolen a vehicle, one of them driving it, the other driving the Ford until they reached their target, parked the Ford and went on together in the stolen car. After the robbery, they abandoned the stolen vehicle and returned home in their truck.

For the Ranchers robbery, they had stolen a Mazda in San Antonio, but it broke down en route to the bank. It was near the bank's closing time, so they simply transferred the tags to their pickup and hoped for the best, which was not the way it turned out. One of the morals of this sad story: if you commit a robbery, don't use a truck that advertises the fact that you possess an AK-47. Even in Texas, people are likely to find that sort of thing memorable.

After all this unexpected excitement, it was good to get back to a normal life at the shop and at home, with the kids winding up their school year, McQuaid undertaking a new and interesting investigation, and the garden yielding its usual early crop of spring veggies and herbs. Ruby stayed with Claire for another ten days, while Dawn and Cass and I managed things at the shops and the tearoom. When she got back from her vacation, she brought more news with her. And after we had closed the shops that afternoon, we sat down together at a table in the tearoom. Our work was done for the day, the late afternoon was warm and quiet, and in the center of the table was a vase of sweet-smelling honeysuckle.

Over cups of hot tea and a couple of pieces of Cass' rose-geranium pound cake, Ruby told me what had happened after I'd left her and Claire at the Blackwood house the day after the storm.

As soon as the Fayette County sheriff figured out that the Rawlingses were the notorious bank robbers that everybody had been looking for, he sent a team of deputies to search their house and outbuildings. It didn't take them long to find the ill-gotten gains from their bank robberies. Most of the loot was stashed in the metal garbage can where Kitty stored the feed for her chickens, and the rest of it was tucked behind the nests in the chicken coop. It wasn't chicken feed, either. When the deputies were finished counting, it amounted to more than a quarter of a million dollars.

"There was a crooked man," Ruby said, leaning her elbows on the table. "Crooked sixpence." She looked slantwise at me. "Crooked cat."

I frowned. "Okay, Ruby. I get the crooked man. That's Sam Rawlings. I even get the crooked sixpence—the take from the bank robberies, although it's a good bit more than sixpence. But I don't get the crooked cat."

Ruby licked her fork. "Oh, come on, China. Crooked cat? That's an easy one."

"Easy for you. You're psychic. But I didn't see a single cat—straight *or* crooked—while I was at Claire's."

"Yes, you did."

"No, I didn't."

"Yes, you did. You saw Kitty. Kitty Rawlings."

I groaned. "Oh, come on. You're kidding."

"Nope." Ruby giggled. "Crooked man, crooked cat, crooked sixpence. A perfect description." She put her fork on her empty plate.

"You'd *have* to be psychic to figure that one out," I grumbled.

"Maybe so." Ruby picked up her teacup. "Anyway, as far as I'm concerned, that's the best thing that's come out of these past few days. Being psychic. And being okay with being psychic."

I opened my mouth to remark that I thought this was a very good thing, then closed it because Ruby had more to say—and she was saying it with an affectionate pride.

"It's a gift that came down from my great-grandmother, Colleen, to my grandmother, and now to me. It's who I *am*." She took something out of the pocket of her denim jumper and pushed it across the table. "You see?"

I leaned forward. I was looking at a photograph of two smiling women in turn-of-the-century clothes. One was dark-haired and elegant-looking, dressed in a ruffled white long-sleeve shirtwaist and dark skirt, her hair piled up in a Gibson-Girl style. In her arms, she held a pretty little girl with light-colored curls. The other—tall and slender, with a dusting of freckles and hair that frizzed around her face just like Ruby's—wore a plain white apron over a work dress with the sleeves rolled up. Against one hip she held a wicker basket of laundry. In the background was a large bush, heavy with white roses.

"Who?" I asked. But I could guess.

"This is Rachel Blackstone," Ruby said, pointing to the elegant woman holding the child. "With her daughter Angela. And this is Colleen O'Reilly. My great-grandmother." She turned the photo over. "See the date? September first, 1900."

"Oh my gosh," I said quietly. "The week before the hurricane." In another week, two of the three people pictured here would be dead, the third doomed to a long life drowned in grief.

Ruby nodded. "Claire and I found this in Rachel's stash of scrapbooks and letters, along with several pages that Rachel had written about Colleen. She said that Colleen had what she called 'second sight.' Colleen once saw a neighbor disappear right in front of her eyes. Two days later, the neighbor was struck down in the street by a runaway horse. She died on the very spot where Colleen had seen her vanish." Ruby paused, and her voice became softly sad. "Colleen left the house the morning of the hurricane, Rachel wrote, to take her mother and her little girl, Annie—who grew up to be my grandmother—to the Ursuline convent. But instead of staying with them in a place she knew was safe, she came back to be with the children, even though she knew that they were going to die—that *she* was going to die."

We were silent for a long moment. I turned the photo over and studied it. "Tall, with freckles and frizzy hair," I said quietly. "Colleen looks just like *you*."

"It's the other way around," Ruby said. "I look just like her, I'm proud to say." She glanced down at the photo again. "And the Rachel of this photograph looks just like the Rachel who showed herself to me and Claire. We think she chose that form because it was the way she looked just before the hurricane—the last happy time of her life."

"I see," I said as Ruby pocketed her precious photograph. I picked up my teacup. "Did Rachel leave you in peace for the rest of your visit with Claire? And has Claire resigned herself to the task of ghostwriting Rachel's story?"

"Claire is *more* than resigned," Ruby said. "The longer we looked at those scrapbooks, the more excited she got about the possibilities. She's thinking about writing a novel about the storm, with Rachel's story as the central focus. And as far as Rachel herself is concerned, she seems to be content to stay in the background, at least for now."

"No more encore appearances? No pan banging or bell ringing or harp playing?"

Ruby shook her head. "Not so far, anyway. Of course, she might be waiting to see if Claire keeps her part of the bargain. But I hope she'll be patient. Claire has a lot of work to do right now. For one thing, she's got to find a live-in caretaker to replace Sam Rawlings. And she's got to get phone and Internet service out to that house—although that might not be as hard as she thought. It turns out that the church camp has leased part of its land for fracking, and the oil company is building a communications tower about three miles away. That will likely make it possible to get cell phone coverage out there."

"Uh-oh," I said. "Fracking in the neighborhood. Is that going to be a problem?"

"Probably. But there's nothing she can do about it. And the oil company is promising to upgrade the road, so at least she'll get something out of the deal. She definitely needs a better road if she's going to get people to stay at her B and B. Of course, it's not perfect, but nothing is. I think she's resigned to that, too. Anyway, she's getting a satellite installation out there for television and the Internet. She especially needs the Internet to build her business."

"Sounds like a big job," I said. It was the opening I'd been waiting for, and I changed the subject. "How about you, Ruby? Any more second thoughts about our business? The partnership, I mean?"

"I talked to Ramona this morning," Ruby said. "I've told her that I appreciate her offer, but I can't take her up on it. She's not right for the Crystal Cave." She grinned ruefully. "And she's definitely not the right partner for you and Cass. I couldn't live with myself if I foisted my sister on my two best friends. I'll find a way to do more teaching. And I want to spend some time developing my gift—Colleen's gift. And not just with parlor games, either. But I want to keep on doing what we're doing, together." She paused and repeated the word. *"Together."*

"I'm glad you see it that way." I was more than glad, I was hugely relieved. "I'm not sure I'd want to stay in business without my best friend."

"Really?" Ruby asked, looking pleased.

"Really," I said emphatically. "But we've been letting ourselves get stuck in our work. We need to be able to get away every now and then. Let's give some thought to bringing in more people to help us out every now and then. I don't want any of us—you, me, Cass—to suffer from burnout."

Ruby nodded, but her gaze was distant, and I could tell that she was thinking of something else.

"What?" I asked.

"I was just thinking of what we found in the graveyard," Ruby said. "And something I read in Rachel's notes. Remember that Claire uncovered a couple of words on the pedestal of the statue in the graveyard? The stone angel?"

I nodded. "'My angels,' wasn't it?"

"Yes," Ruby said. "When we pulled the honeysuckle aside and cleaned off the lichen and the moss, we could see all of it. It read 'Sleep well, my angels. 'Twon't be long now.'"

"That's lovely," I said. "But I don't think I—"

"It was explained in Rachel's notes," Ruby said. "In the hurricane, Rachel and Colleen took the kids upstairs to the third floor, where they fell asleep on the bed. Rachel thought the storm was just about over and they would all be safe, but Colleen knew what was coming. Just before the house went over, Rachel said, Colleen kissed the children. Those were her last words to them. 'Sleep well, my angels. 'Twon't be long now.' I think," she added, "that as time went on, Rachel began to picture Colleen herself as an angel—for coming back to the house to help with the children, I mean."

"So she had the words carved on the angel in the cemetery," I said thoughtfully. "Keeping watch over all of the family graves."

"There's something else, too," Ruby said. She took the photograph out of her pocket again and looked at it. "All of the crosses in the graveyard bear just the name and no more. But on Colleen's cross, there's a Bible reference. It reads 'John 15:13. Greater love . . .'" She bit her lip. "Just those two words. 'Greater love . . .'"

I'm no Bible expert, but even I could complete that verse. "'Greater love has no one than this, that he lay down his life for his friends.'"

"That *she* lay down *her* life," Ruby murmured. Tenderly, she touched the old photo, and when she looked up, her eyes were bright with tears. "That gives me something to live up to, don't you think, China?"

Touched, I smiled. "Just don't go hunting up any hurricanes," I said. "We need you *here*." I put out my hand.

"Thank you," Ruby said quietly, and took my hand. "I'll remember that."

Resources

These are some of the books and other sources that I found helpful in writing *Widow's Tears*.

Flora's Dictionary: The Victorian Language of Herbs and Flowers, by Kathleen Gips, Chagrin Falls, OH: T.M. Publications, 1992. The most complete catalogue of Victorian-era plant symbolism, with an excellent introduction, several informative appendices, and a resource list.

"Galveston: A City Transformed." A significant archival collection of letters, photographs, oral histories, and other materials, from the pre-storm and post-storm periods. Rosenberg Library: Galveston and Texas History Center. http://www.gthcenter.org/exhibits/storms/index.html (accessed Feb. 27, 2012).

Isaac's Storm: A Man, A Time, and the Deadliest Hurricane in History, by Erik Larson. New York, NY: Vintage Books, 1999. A compelling account of the Galveston Hurricane, from the point of view of the weatherman who failed to predict it. Isaac Cline's detailed report of the hurricane is available online: http://www.history.noaa.gov/stories_tales/cline2.html (accessed Feb. 27, 2012).

Through a Night of Horrors: Voices from the 1900 Galveston Storm, edited by Casey Edward Greene and Shelly Henley Kelly. College Station, TX: Texas A&M University Press, 2000. A remarkable collection of oral and written histories (many previously unpublished) collected from the storm's survivors.

A Weekend in September, by John Edward Weems. College Station, TX: Texas A&M University Press, 1957, 1980. The first comprehensive, chronological account of the storm, gathered from interviews with storm survivors. Excellent photographs.

When the Heavens Frowned, by Joseph L. Cline. Dallas: Mathis, Van Nort & Co., 1946. The autobiography of Isaac Cline's brother, also a weatherman, who has his own hurricane story to tell.

Tomato Quiche with Basil and Green Onions

Quiche is a perfect dish for a light lunch or a quick supper. Served with soup, it's extra-special!

CRUST
Single piecrust (use your favorite recipe)
1 teaspoon finely minced rosemary

FILLING
3 green onions, tops and bottoms, finely chopped
¼ cup shredded mozzarella cheese
¼ cup oil
2 cups loosely packed fresh basil leaves
½ teaspoon ground black pepper
2 cloves garlic, cut in half
5 large eggs
½ cup evaporated milk or half-and-half
½ cup ricotta cheese
½ cup plus 1 tablespoon freshly grated Parmesan cheese, divided
6 to 8 thin slices tomato

TO MAKE THE CRUST:
Heat oven to 425°F. Prepare piecrust, adding minced rosemary to flour mixture. Roll out dough. Place in 9-inch pie plate or quiche dish and flute the edge. Bake 10 minutes. Set out to cool. Reduce oven temperature to 350°F.

TO MAKE THE FILLING:

Sprinkle chopped green onions over bottom of pie shell and top with mozzarella cheese. In a food processor or blender, combine oil, basil, pepper, and garlic. Blend at high speed until smooth; set aside. With an electric mixer, beat eggs in large bowl until foamy. Add evaporated milk or half-and-half, ricotta cheese, and ½ cup Parmesan cheese. Beat on low speed to blend well. Continuing to beat, gradually add oil-basil mixture. Pour over cheese and onions in pie shell. Bake 20 minutes. Remove from oven and top with tomato slices. Return to oven and bake an additional 25 minutes, or until center is firm (if serving hot). Immediately sprinkle with remaining 1 tablespoon Parmesan cheese. If serving warm or cold, remove from oven when center is barely firm: it will firm up as it cools.

Spring Green Bisque with Spinach and Basil

Luncheon soups have a special flair when they come straight from the garden to your table.

   3 tablespoons olive oil
   1 small onion, diced
   1 clove garlic, minced
   2 cups frozen peas
   2 cups fresh spinach leaves, washed, ribs/stems removed, chopped
   ¾ cup fresh basil leaves, coarsely chopped
   2 cups broth (chicken or vegetable), divided
   1 cup sour cream
   Salt and pepper to taste
   ¼ cup finely chopped red bell pepper
   ¼ cup grated Parmesan cheese

In a large pan over medium heat, sauté onion and garlic in the olive oil until the onion is soft and translucent, about 5 minutes.

(Be careful not to burn the garlic.) Add the peas, spinach, and basil. Cook, stirring, until the peas are thawed and the spinach and basil leaves are slightly wilted. Pour mixture into a blender or food processor. Add 1 cup of the broth and puree, adding more broth if necessary. Return the pureed mixture to the pot. Stir in the remaining broth and the sour cream. Add salt and pepper to taste. Return the pan to medium heat and cook until hot, but not boiling. Place soup in four bowls. Garnish with chopped red bell pepper and grated Parmesan.

Ruby's Romaine Salad

A treat to look at, as well as a taste treat!

> 1 roasted sweet red pepper
> Greens: spinach, romaine, red leaf lettuce, other greens
> Fresh mushrooms, sliced
> Sweet red onion, thinly sliced
> ¼ cup grated Parmesan cheese
> Orange-Ginger dressing

To roast the pepper, slice it in half, remove the seeds and stem, and place under the broiler, peel-side up. Broil until the skin chars. With tongs or a fork, quickly place in a dish and cover tightly; allow to steam for a few minutes. Then pull off the charred skin and chop. Tear greens into bite-size pieces and arrange in 4 serving bowls. Add chopped peppers, sliced mushrooms, sliced onion, and Parmesan cheese. Toss with Orange-Ginger dressing.

> ORANGE-GINGER DRESSING
> ½ cup canola oil
> ¼ cup white wine vinegar
> 4 tablespoons orange juice

2 tablespoons green onion tops, chopped
2 tablespoons minced fresh parsley
1 tablespoon grated fresh ginger
1 teaspoon sugar
Salt and pepper to taste

Place all ingredients in blender and mix until well blended. Cover and chill for several hours to blend flavors.

Two-Bean Soup with Herbs

A hearty bean soup is welcome for lunch or supper. This one is quick and easy with canned beans, or substitute your own home-cooked dry beans. Pair with hot cornbread for an extra treat.

3 tablespoons olive oil
3 cups chopped onions (about 2 medium)
4 garlic cloves, minced
1 tablespoon finely chopped fresh rosemary
1 teaspoon dried thyme
½ teaspoon ground bay
5 cups chicken or vegetable broth
2 cups cooked great northern or cannellini beans or 2 15- to
   16-ounce cans, drained
2 cups cooked garbanzo beans (chickpeas) or 2 15- to 16-ounce
   cans, drained
Salt and pepper to taste
¼ cup green onion tops, chopped
Sour cream

Heat 3 tablespoons olive oil in large pan over medium-high heat. Add onions and garlic and sauté until onions are soft, about 12–15 minutes. Add herbs and blend. Add broth and beans. Bring soup to boil; reduce to medium-low and simmer until flavors blend, about 10 minutes. In batches, transfer soup to blender and puree until smooth; return to pan. Season to taste with salt and pepper. Ladle hot soup into 4–6 bowls. Top with green onions and a dollop of sour cream.

Garden-Style Cornbread

Cornbread is a tasty partner with bean soup. This garden-style cornbread, chock-full of veggies, has a lot going for it!

> 2 tablespoons butter, for the baking pan
> 1⅓ cups yellow cornmeal
> 1 teaspoon baking powder
> 1 teaspoon garlic salt
> 1 teaspoon salt
> ¾ cup buttermilk
> 2 eggs, lightly beaten
> ¼ cup vegetable oil
> 1 green onion, top and bottom, chopped
> 1 cup unpeeled zucchini, grated
> ½ cup seeded, finely chopped sweet red bell pepper
> ½ cup tomatoes, seeded and chopped
> 2 tablespoons chopped green chiles or jalapeño peppers
> ¾ cup sweet corn, fresh or canned
> 1 cup grated cheddar cheese

Preheat the oven to 350°F. Grease a 9 x 12–inch baking pan or a large cast-iron skillet. In a mixing bowl, combine all dry ingredients. In a separate bowl, combine buttermilk, eggs, and oil, and mix well. Add the liquid ingredients to the dry ingredients and mix well. Fold in the vegetables and grated cheese. Pour the batter into the pan and bake for 35 minutes, until a tester comes out clean.

Rose-Geranium Pound Cake with White Chocolate Glaze

This traditional recipe has appeared on tea tables for several hundred years and is a special favorite with herb gardeners. If you don't have rose-geranium leaves, try peppermint, lemon, or lemon-rose.

> **6 pesticide-free rose-geranium leaves**
> **3½ cups sifted cake flour**
> **½ cup unsweetened cocoa powder**
> **½ teaspoon salt**
> **2 cups unsalted butter, softened**
> **1⅔ cups sugar**
> **8 egg yolks**
> **½ cup half-and-half**
> **2 teaspoons rosewater (use vanilla if you've substituted another geranium)**
> **8 egg whites**
> **1 cup sugar**

Preheat oven to 340°F. Butter and flour a 10-inch tube pan (angel food cake pan). Line bottom with 6 geranium leaves. Sift together flour, cocoa, and salt. Mix well and set aside. In large mixer bowl, beat butter at medium speed until creamy. Gradually add 1⅔ cups sugar, beating until light and fluffy. Set aside. In small mixer bowl, beat egg yolks at high speed until thick and lemon-colored, about 5 minutes. At medium speed, gradually beat egg yolks into butter-sugar mixture. Add sifted flour mixture alternately with half-and-half, beating until smooth after each addition. Beat in rosewater or vanilla. Set aside. In a large bowl, beat egg whites at high speed until soft peaks start to form. Gradually add 1 cup of sugar, beating until stiff, glossy peaks form. Fold this meringue into the batter. Pour into prepared pan, spreading evenly. Bake on bottom rack of oven for 1¼ to 1½ hours, until tester inserted near center comes out clean. Cool in pan set on rack 10 minutes. Remove from pan. Carefully remove leaves. Cool on rack.

WHITE CHOCOLATE GLAZE
4 ounces white chocolate
Pesticide free rose-geranium leaves and blossoms for garnish

Melt white chocolate in top of double boiler over hot water, stirring often until smooth. Place cake on serving plate. Drizzle glaze over top. Garnish with rose-geranium leaves and blossoms.

The Symbolic Meanings of the Plants in Widow's Tears

Most of the plants that appear in this book have also been used to convey meanings in the Victorian language of flowers. Here is a list of their traditional associations, selected from florigraphic dictionaries, to illustrate their use in the story.

Chaste tree (*Vitex* sp.): chastity, aloofness, separation
Cherry tree: a good education
Coreopsis: cheerfulness, gladness, love at first sight
Cypress: death, protection from evil
Dead leaves: melancholy, sadness
Feverfew: protection against fever, illness
Holly: "Am I forgotten?"
Hollyhock: ambition, abundance
Honeysuckle: Generous, devoted love
Iris: "I bring you a message"
Juniper: asylum, sanctuary, protection against evil spirits
Lantana: rigor, severity, sharpness
Larkspur: lightness, swiftness
Mistletoe: protection against storms
Mock orange: memory, but also disappointment and deceit
Morning glory: bound by love, sustained by bonds of affection
Mugwort: safe travels, insightful dreams
Oak: hospitality
Parsley: feast and abundance, joy, victory; "The woman rules the household"
Phlox: "We think alike"
Prickly pear: satire, sarcasm, irony
Rose, red: "May you ever be pure and lovely"
Rosemary: remembrance, loyalty, faithfulness until death

Santolina: protection against bad things
Sunflower: pride, haughtiness, lofty thoughts
Sweet Annie (*Artemisia annua*): absence
Sweet bay (bay laurel): consistency, constancy; "I change only in death"
Sweet pea: delicate pleasure
Tansy: life everlasting, immortality, hostile thoughts
Verbena: enchantment
Vinca: friendship, binding affection
Violet: love, faithfulness, loyalty
White poppy: forgetting, consolation, a sleep of the heart
Widow's tears: grief
Wisteria: "I cling to you"
Yarrow: foretelling the future, cure for heartache